The chaos made sense to Olivia now; Tinker was going to war. She was being a *domi*. Olivia felt like a pale shadow.

Tinker turned back to Olivia. "Look, I know you can't have any idea what you've gotten into because I'm still learning and I've been at this for months." Much to Olivia's relief, Tinker had slipped back into English. Her relief was short-lived as Tinker pointed hard at Olivia. "I don't know where you came from or how you got onto Elfhome or why you're here. It really doesn't matter. What matters is that every elf in Pittsburgh now sees you as a general in the middle of a very ugly war. For better or worse, I'm considered an elf, because once upon a time, my family were elves. If I screw up, it's on the Wind Clan's shoulders. If you screw up, it *could* be marked against all the humans because, strictly speaking, you're still human. You cannot think of just yourself. If you do anything that could be considered treason, you could accidently kill every human man, woman, and child in this city."

"I find that unlikely," Olivia said calmly, despite her morning sickness's causing a sudden urge to vomit.

"Have you been paying attention to what is going on in this city for the last few months?" Tinker pointed westward. "I found out today that I totally missed fish monsters attacking Downtown! Do you know how messed up things have to be that no one thought to tell me about fifty-foot-long, walking catfish throwing around lightning bolts? Why? Because I was busy falling off the planet, hijacking spaceships, fighting dragons, and all sorts of other crap! This is the life you just opted into!"

BAEN BOOKS by WEN SPENCER

THE ELFHOME SERIES
Tinker
Wolf Who Rules
Elfhome
Wood Sprites
Project Elfhome
Harbinger

ALSO BY WEN SPENCER
Endless Blue
Eight Million Gods
The Black Wolves of Boston

To purchase these and all Baen Book titles
in e-book format, please go to www.baen.com.

HARBINGER

WEN SPENCER

HARBINGER

Copyright © 2022 by Wen Spencer

A Baen Books Original

Baen Publishing Enterprises
P.O. Box 1403
Riverdale, NY 10471
www.baen.com

ISBN: 978-1-9821-9245-7

Cover art by Dominic Harman

First printing, April 2022
First mass market printing, February 2023

Library of Congress Control Number: 2021060301

Distributed by Simon & Schuster
1230 Avenue of the Americas
New York, NY 10020

Printed in the United States of America

10 9 8 7 6 5 4 3 2 1

This book is dedicated to my wonderful patrons.
It is through their support that I am
able to do what I do.

Special thanks to
Marti Garner
Roger A. Josephson
Andrew Riley Prest
Torsten Steinert

And
Andrew Hart
Richard Jamison
Anders Ljungquist
Kathy Brann
Michael Carter
Robert Williamson

And an Extra-Special Thank-You to
Ellen McMicking

1: BLACKBIRD SINGING
IN THE DEAD OF NIGHT

"What? Wait!" Tinker cried, cutting off the flow of Jin's explanation. She'd been wakened up in the middle of the night to be told that the tengu's spiritual leader needed to speak with her immediately. The household staff had set out a formal tea in the dining hall and made themselves scarce. They were probably lurking in the deep shadows nearby, just in case she would need more dainty sandwiches or little fruit tarts or another pot of strong tea.

Tinker suspected that the shadows also held Jin's bodyguards. She knew from experience the tengu could come and go like ghosts despite their massive wings. It would explain why her entire Hand was present for the meeting. The five holy *sekasha* warriors were fully dressed, heavily armed, and standing guard at her back as if they hadn't been asleep just minutes before.

Lightning flickered; it lit up the garden outside the dining hall's windows. The thunder made Tinker jump a little. Was Windwolf fighting for his life someplace? Most of the *domana* elves in Pittsburgh were gathered at the far eastern edge of the Rim; they planned on fighting the oni in the morning. She hadn't felt Windwolf call the Wind Clan Spell Stones to cast lightning. Nor could she sense anyone using Fire Clan or Stone Clan *esva*. None of the *domana* elves were fighting. The lightning was normal electrical discharge and nothing else. Rain started to drum on the dining hall's roof. It was an oddly comforting sound.

"I have what?" Tinker was sure this conversation would make sense if it weren't some ungodly hour in the middle of the night.

"Twin siblings." Jin looked exhausted. Since she'd seen him late in the evening, he must have flown to his village and back. "Six of them."

Tinker squinted at him. Maybe she was still asleep. This could be a weird dream. She had had a lot of those lately. "You're—you're kidding. Right?"

"No, I'm not." His great black wings rustled with his nervousness. "I know that technically that they belong to Esme Shanske, but Gracie Wong would love to adopt Leo's—"

"Back up. Back up," Tinker said. "I have what?"

Jin sighed. "Twin siblings. Six of them."

"How can I have six twin siblings? Wouldn't they be six-something—sextuplets?" No, that sounded like a porn video. "No, wait, if I have six siblings then we would be seven. Seven...seven...seven..."

The conversation was in English, so only Storm-song was following her muttering. The tall warrior leaned over Tinker's shoulder to pour her more tea. "Septuplets, *domi.*"

"Are you sure?" Tinker spooned several teaspoons of honey into the tea before gulping it. "September is the ninth month."

"It was the seventh month, but it changed to the ninth when the Gregorian calendar added . . ." Jin sighed again and rubbed at the bridge of his nose. "It's a naming convention. I believe it's because all of the eggs are fertilized at the same time. If all the resulting embryos were implanted immediately in one woman, the resulting children would be twins. The term 'twin' stays true to that concept even if the embryos are used at different times by different women."

He was talking about how Tinker had been conceived in vitro ten years after her father died. She vaguely knew the mechanics; Lain had explained it to her when she was very young. She'd alarmed Lain by talking about having a brother who lived far away. (Only after Lain went through all the biology had Tinker confessed that she confused "brother" with "cousin." She had meant Oilcan, who lived in Boston at the time.) Lain had kept referring to possible siblings as "theoretical" until Tinker thought that the word meant "imaginary" because Lain indicated that it was quite impossible for such siblings to exist.

But Jin wouldn't wake Tinker up in the middle of the night for imaginary siblings. Since Stormsong was quietly translating the conversation to the others of her Hand, Tinker switched to Elvish.

"Wasn't all that stuff—the genetic material—stored at some place in New York City?" She had found the paperwork recently while digging through her grandfather's belongings.

"It was," Jin said slowly and his wings rustled. "All

of the stored fertilized eggs have been used. To make children. Many children."

"Six of them?" Tinker said.

"As far as I know."

She wasn't sure what she was supposed to do with the information. "Two more and we would have had a baseball team."

"Domi," Pony murmured. "Since cousin could tap the Stone Clan Spell Stones even prior to being spell-worked, we need to know where these children are located."

Tinker wasn't sure if he meant "we" as in her Hand or the entire *sekasha*-caste whose job was to keep tabs on the *domana*-caste. It made suddenly clear why Jin was there, in the middle of the night, to report the news. She'd been thinking that this could have been handled by a phone call in the morning. To the elves, her siblings were potential walking weapons.

Jin was waiting for her to ask. His people were safe only because he promised to be her loyal servant. She was learning that everyone else understood that they had to wait for her to realize what the hell was going on and give the appropriate order.

"Where exactly are these..." Tinker paused as she realized that Jin was implying that her siblings weren't adults. "Did you say children?"

"Technically two are children, and the other four are about to be newborns. They are at Haven."

The tengu village was someplace deep in the virgin forest, in a location secret even to her. The adults kept travel from Pittsburgh to where their children were hidden to the minimum, going so far as staying at safe houses within the city instead of going home. Jin apparently returned to Haven to discover he'd been invaded by an army of little Dufaes.

"That is not all," Jin added.

"This gets worse?" Tinker cried.

"In a manner of speaking—possibly. There is a third dragon in Pittsburgh."

Okay, a dragon was not a phone call in the morning.

"Malice-size?" She spread her hands wide as possible to indicate the massive dragon that Jin helped her kill a few weeks earlier. The monster had been the size of a house. "Or Impatience?"

The second dragon was "small" only in scale to Malice. They were still talking large as a pickup truck.

Jin put his hands together so that they nearly touched. "Her name is Joy. She has claimed all your siblings as her Chosen. We cannot do anything with the children without her approval. She is very protective."

Tinker snorted. "How protective can a pocket-size dragon get?"

"Very. She can and will summon help. We would be facing Impatience and most likely Providence against any attempts to go against her wishes."

Dragon tag-team fighting. Okay, that was a very scary thought. Impatience nearly killed Tinker and her Hand when they first met. He had a mouth filled with razor-sharp teeth and impenetrable magical shields all backed with a genius that intimidated even her. Providence was dead and not-dead in a way that made her brain hurt. He was the guardian spirit of the tengu and they worshipped him as a god. It meant that in addition to fighting something that couldn't be "killed," it could push the tengu's loyalty to her to a breaking point. The elves considered the tengu a valuable ally because of

Jin's alliance with Tinker. Otherwise, the elves would have wiped out the tengu—adults and children alike.

What Joy wants, Joy gets. Check. That's assuming what Little Miss Pocket Dragon wanted was within reason.

Gracie Wong had been married to Tinker's father and loved him deeply. There was little wonder that she would want to adopt Leo's babies...

"Wait," Tinker said again as she stumbled over another weird turn of phrase. "*About* to be newborn?"

"Yes, in a few months." Jin's wings rustled loudly. "Forgiveness, *domi*." He murmured the command to dispel his wings and they vanished from his back. The dining room suddenly seemed a lot less crowded.

"So there's really two kids and a very pregnant woman about to pop? Or are we talking four women about to have babies? What the hell? Is someone on Earth giving out Dufae kids like lottery tickets?"

"It's—" Jin paused for a minute, obviously trying to find a safe, sane explanation. Considering Tinker's summer to date, there might not be one. Single-handedly, she'd managed to accidently change her species, rip a hole in the fabric of realty, kidnap a major USA city, fall off the planet, crash a spaceship into Turtle Creek, kill a dragon...

Tinker was sure there was more but she was losing track of the weirdness. Not a good sign.

"It's...it's complicated," Jin finally understated. "Maybe I should back up." He paused again for several moments, mouth open, eyes flicking back and forth as he tried to find a safe place to start. "There are two girls, Louise and Jillian Mayer. They are twins, and very much like you."

What did that mean? Short? Dark skin? Genius? Snarky? All of the above?

"Their father worked at the clinic where Leo's sperm was stored," Jin said. "Esme used Leo's sperm to fertilize a dozen or so of her eggs. Some number of the fertilized eggs were used to create you and the rest were put into storage. Nine years ago, Mr. Mayer took some of the frozen embryos and implanted them into his wife. They raised your sisters as their natural-born children and I gather they were very good parents."

"Were?" Tinker latched onto the word. Adoption usually happened after parents died. "Are they dead?"

"Yes. I'm not clear how they were killed but it was recent. After that, your grandmother gained custody of them."

"My grandmother? I don't have a grandmother. I had a grandfather. Two, if you count Forge, but he's more like a great-great-great-something." She'd made peace with her elf ancestor that afternoon, though he was still on probation with her for what he'd done to Oilcan. Forge was going to be ecstatic at the news that he had six more grandkids. If they were orphans, he'd probably want custody of them. She wasn't sure if this was a good thing or a bad thing. Certainly, it would make the *sekasha* happy if the babies were with a *domana*, but her siblings were still human. She would prefer that they stay that way. No more of this changing species without warning.

"Esme's mother," Jin stated. When she looked at him confused, he expanded the statement with, "Esme's mother is your grandmother. Anna Desmarais."

"Desmarais? Shouldn't it be Shanske?" Tinker tried to remember if Lain ever even talked about her family.

Lain talked about Esme in terms of "my sister, the astronaut" but never anything else. Wait, there been something recently about Empire of Evil and Flying Monkeys. That didn't sound good.

"Your grandmother remarried after Esme's father was killed. I didn't actually talk to the twins; they were asleep and apparently very emotionally fragile after everything they've been through. I thought you should be told immediately. I didn't want to blindside you with any of this."

"This didn't count as being blindsided?" Tinker asked.

"This is still just between us—and Joy—and the other dragons. I believe that the Stone Clan might want to claim the children. And there is Esme to be considered. I owe your mother a great deal; without her intervention none of this could be possible. You would not have been born. Everyone on my ship would have been lost. My people would still be enslaved. Biologically, your siblings are her offspring. She did, however, abandon her genetic material when she left Earth. The children were carried by other women. Nor is Esme in a situation where she could take on the responsibility of raising six children, four of which are newborn."

"Yyyeeeaaah." Tinker wasn't even sure where Esme was living since Tinker planted her mother's spaceship into Turtle Creek. She knew Esme had spent several days in the hospital. Tinker had last seen Esme when they'd dropped her at Lain's. No, wait, the sisters had come together to Poppymeadows—later—sometime. Tinker had totally lost track of time. It had been a super-condensed-weird summer and not yet officially over.

Esme and six kids in Lain's house? With all those deadly plants? Tinker had spent the first two years of her life on a literal leash to keep her from toddling into the reach of the various man-eating plants. And there was a good reason why she hadn't moved in with Lain when her grandfather died. Lain was the type of person who loved kids as long as she could send them home. Tinker had lived with Lain the month it took Tinker's grandfather to fetch Oilcan from Boston after his mother was killed. Her stay degraded into a battle of wills that only stopped before open warfare because her grandfather had returned.

Esme had been distraught when she thought her "son" had been killed. She'd been overjoyed when she found out that Tinker was her daughter.

"Esme is capable of committing to crazy, impossible plans," Tinker said. "She might want to try."

"*Domi*," Pony murmured. "By our laws, a child belongs foremost to its mother, but then to its clan. Who exactly qualifies as the children's mother might be debated, since what your mother has done has never been tried among our people. It means that Stone Clan has the strongest claim, lacking a birth mother. Sunder is currently head of Stone Clan in the Westernlands."

Tinker growled in frustration. "The Dufae stopped being Stone Clan generations ago. I have always considered myself as Wind Clan."

"It was your right as an adult to choose a clan, but children are not considered mature enough to decide this."

That was the same line of bullshit that Iron Mace used to justify what was done to Oilcan, despite the fact that her cousin was twenty-two and, as a human, adult. Tinker hadn't met Sunder yet; the three new Stone Clan *domana* had arrived while she was out playing hide-and-seek with Chloe Polanski. With a name like Sunder, though, he or she probably wasn't a pushover. Forge had promised never to betray any of his grandchildren again. He would be the lesser of evils—if he could be trusted.

"The children are only the tip of the iceberg," Jin said.

"Oh good gods!" Tinker shouted. "What else? You didn't even talk with the twins!"

Jin nodded that this was true. "They have been in Haven since you disappeared. I was focused on finding you and supporting Wolf Who Rules. It is our policy to maintain no communication between Haven and Pittsburgh, lest it would give away Haven's location. They arrived, however, with one of the *yamabushi*..."

"A what?"

"Forgiveness." Jin pinched the bridge of his nose. "I forgot you do not know the term. There is so much that we should share with you about ourselves, but there never seems to be time."

Tinker laughed tiredly. "Yes, I know. Story of my life lately." She needed a crash course on everything from proper etiquette of "formal" meetings between clans to elf reproduction cycles. (The talk of babies reminded her that she wasn't using birth control and earlier conversations on the subject boiled down to "don't worry about that now." She really should find out *why* she didn't have to.)

"The *yamabushi* are what we call the blood guard of the Chosen One. They are descendants of Wong Jin's loyal servants who—" He caught himself with a grimace. "It's a very long story and most of it is not important right now. Your siblings arrived at Haven with a young male tengu by the name of Haruka Sessai. He's been trained since birth to gather information. Haruka gave me a brief but concise report. I wanted to bring him with me so you could question him yourself. The girls, however, wake often from nightmares and find his presence comforting. They trust him and Joy tolerates him, so he is keeping guard over them."

Tinker made a motion for Jin to move on. "What important details?"

"Your ancestor—Forge's son, Unbounded Brilliance— died in France during the Revolution. Apparently when he fled Elfhome, he had with him a spell-locked box, which we believe he'd stolen from Iron Mace, hence the reason that the warlord came to Pittsburgh. Iron Mace wanted to know if your family knew what was in the box. When Unbounded Brilliance was beheaded in France, his infant son was taken to America, but the box was lost."

It felt painfully wrong for something that happened over two hundred years ago to still be important, but Iron Mace had tried to kill Oilcan because of this box. "The only thing my family knows about it is some song." Oilcan had sung it to her while telling her about his kidnapping. "Knock, knock, open the box..."

Jin nodded. "The box was recently found in France and flown to New York. It was at the American Museum of Natural History. It was part of a traveling exhibit that the humans put together using objects that the elves left on Earth before contact between the two worlds were lost."

Stormsong gasped.

"What?" Tinker asked.

"I've seen this box!" Stormsong said. "I was—oh—oh—oh sweet light—I've seen one of your sisters."

"And you didn't think to tell me?" Tinker shouted.

"You were still human and we had not yet met. Officially," Stormsong added the qualifier. Tinker wasn't sure what that was supposed to mean; she would remember meeting a blue-haired *sekasha*. Officially or unofficially. "I didn't recognize the girl as your sister at the time. She was just a little human child, one of millions in New York City."

"How do you know it was my sister?"

"She was at the museum after it was closed to the public, inside an invisible paper box."

Was this "confound *domi*" night? "A *what?*"

Stormsong spread her hands. "I'm not sure how she managed it, but she was using a spell to be invisible so she could move through the museum unseen."

That did sound like something Tinker would try to do. "But how? There's isn't magic on Earth!"

Stormsong spread her hands wider and clicked her tongue in an elvish version of a shrug.

"Esme is a powerful dreamer," Jin said. "She foresaw that your presence was needed to save Pittsburgh. She apparently also knew that her attempts to produce you might create multiple children. It seems that she set up fail-safes to protect your siblings on Earth before she left the planet. One of the things that she gave them was the Dufae Codex."

"How did Esme get a copy of that?" Tinker asked. "My grandfather never let anyone outside the family even see it."

Jin spread his hands to indicate helpless ignorance. "The girls had it when Haruki joined forces with them. From what he could gather, it was through the Codex that they learned of the box and the *nactka*."

Tinker stared at Jin while her mind raced. Her copy of the Codex had an entire section on spell-locked boxes. She'd studied it closely before designing a custom lockpick spell to unlock the box she found in the oni whelping pens. Did the Codex mention Iron Mace's box specifically? Far as she could remember, there hadn't been any warning written in it about Dufae's uncle. She was fairly sure that the Codex didn't say anything about invisible cardboard—she would have been all over that. How would you make something invisible? In New York City? "But-but-but Earth doesn't have magic!"

"The twins are very intelligent and resourceful," Jin said slowly, as if every word out of his mouth was carefully chosen. "I would guess they are your equals in that regard."

Why her siblings were running around invisible was fairly easy to guess. Tinker had seen enough movies to know that Earth's museums were filled with security cameras to protect their valuable artwork. The most confounding tidbit of information, though, was that Stormsong had been in New York City.

"What were you doing there, Stormsong?" Tinker didn't think the elves ever went to Earth.

"I was with Sparrow. It was a diplomatic mission. She had taken half of Wolf's First Hand because they had been to Earth long ago, before the war with the oni. Since I speak English, I was included—or at least, that was the reason Sparrow gave for taking me. It's obvious now that she took the people most likely able to counter the attack on Wolf. When we returned, Pony met us at the train station with news that Wolf was missing and Hawk Scream was dead. The bitch ran us in circles all day until you brought Wolf to the hospice."

Sparrow hadn't survived Pony finding out that she was a traitor. She had been killed little more than a month ago but it seemed like forever now.

"And the box?" Jin asked. "Where is it?"

Stormsong shook her head. "It didn't come with us."

"Sparrow claimed it," Jin said. "The twins hacked the museum's computer system and intercepted emails stating that it had been taken by her."

Invisibility aside, her siblings apparently hadn't gotten what they were after. "What was in the box—and what are *nactka*?"

"There were twelve magical devices inside." Jin took out what looked like a Fabergé egg done on a bowling-ball-size scale. "They are called a *nactka*. This is the one that your sisters took from the box. The twins could not take the other eleven that day and when they realized how important the contents were, it was too late. The box was gone."

"What is it?" Tinker pointed at the oddly decorated egg.

"The term is oni; it means 'trap.' They were developed on Onihida. These, however, seem as if they were crafted on Elfhome; their esthetics are very elvish. Joy was inside this one."

"Little Miss Pocket Dragon?" Tinker eyed the egg-like container. Yes, Joy would have to be quite small to fit inside it. "You think there's eleven more baby dragons inside the other traps?"

"We do not know for sure what are in the other eleven devices but we know that your ancestor referred to the *nactka* as 'fully loaded.' It seems likely that they hold dragons."

Yes, twelve baby dragons and six siblings warranted an immediate visit in the middle of the night. And perhaps more house insurance.

Tinker was positive, though, that the Dufae Codex said nothing about weird magical egg traps. "Are you sure that what the twins have is the same thing I'm calling the Dufae Codex?"

Jin frowned. "I hadn't considered . . . there wasn't time to verify that. We can determine it later."

"Okay. Assuming the spell-locked box at the museum was the one that Dufae stole from Iron Mace—where did Iron Mace get twelve baby dragons?"

"I don't know," Jin said. "I will try to get the information from Joy. She . . . She . . . I'm told that she is quite . . . difficult to work with. You should be aware that the spell the oni used to transform my people—all of my people in a single transformation—was done using Providence's body. It was a test run of an even greater spell they had developed that required his soul as well as his body. It is why he asked us to kill him."

"Oh." Tinker felt like someone had punched her. Eleven possible world-changing spells all locked into one deadly box. "Stormsong, are you sure the box that we took from the whelping pens wasn't it?"

"No, the box at the museum was smaller." She measured it out with her hands. "Such boxes are common in the Easternlands. We traded with humans on Earth for centuries. I thought a traveling merchant must have lost it."

"This is a picture of the actual box." Jin pulled a slickie from his bag and flipped the pages until he found the desired picture.

Everyone leaned over the digital magazine to eye the gleaming photo. The box was roughly the size of a footlocker with the locking spell along its top edge. On Earth, the lid would have been sealed at a molecular level. The twins shouldn't have been able to open it to take anything out—nor could anyone else.

"I believe," Cloudwalker said slowly, "that I've seen this box here in Pittsburgh. Or, at least, pieces of it."

Everyone stared at him in surprise.

"You have?" Pony asked the question that Tinker couldn't form.

"While you and *domi* were being held captive by the oni, a fight broke out in the house of history." Cloudwalker pointed toward the direction of the Carnegie Museum. Elves didn't have museums so they didn't have a word for them; it seemed to be a weird side effect of being immortal. "The humans that killed the river monsters in the . . . the . . . the . . . I don't remember the word for it. The big round place down by the river. The middle is flat. There are many seats. Thousands of seats."

"The stadium?" Stormsong prompted while Pony continued to look confused. "The thing that looks like an amphitheater but without a stage?"

"Yes. That. The humans with the big. . ." Cloudwalker struggled with another English word that didn't have a direct Elvish equivalent. "Ca—ca—cannon?"

"Cannon?" Tinker shouted. "What river monsters? What were river monsters doing in the stadium? Why didn't anyone tell me about this?"

Cloudwalker spread his hands helplessly. "Because the monsters were already long dead before we could talk with you again?"

"Because there were so many other things to tell you?" Stormsong said.

"Because this is the first that I've heard about it?" Pony said. "What river monsters?"

"Massive carp that could walk on land and throw lightning!" Little Egret threw his arms wide open in an attempt to demonstrate either the large size or the throwing of lightning. Tinker wasn't sure which.

"What? Carp? Like fish?" Tinker asked.

"Yes!" all the *sekasha* except Pony said.

"Very big fish," Stormsong added. "Malice-sized."

"That could throw lightning and walk on land," Little Egret repeated.

It was oddly comforting to know that she wasn't responsible for all the weirdness that hit Pittsburgh that summer. Tinker had lost track of how the river monsters related to her six siblings. "What does this have to do with..." What were they talking about? Her sisters being invisible on Earth? No. "The missing box with the baby dragons?"

"The people that killed the river monsters found the box at the house of history," Cloudwalker said.

"Hal Rogers," Stormsong supplied a name.

"Who? Wait! Hal Rogers as in *Pittsburgh Backyard and Garden*? That Hal Rogers? He's a dangerous maniac! The police all hate him. He sets people on fire!"

"He's got a new show," Stormsong said. "*Monsters in Our Midst*. He's been very aggressive at educating Pittsburghers about the dangers they're facing at the hands of the oni. The people who wear blue hats are his fans. Hal's Heroes."

Tinker wanted to ask about the hats but didn't want to derail the conversation even more. Now that Stormsong mentioned it, she realized that she'd been seeing a ton of people out on the streets wearing the same blue hat. "So *PB&G* was at the museum?"

The conversation screeched to a halt as all of the elves were confused by the initials.

"Yes," Cloudwalker said once it was clear that they were all discussing the same thing. "I had been delivering a message from the queen, so I arrived just after the fighting broke out."

Tinker locked down on a confused "What fighting?" because she didn't want to change the subject again. Obviously, there was much she missed during the summer while being kidnapped by oni and falling off the planet. "You saw this box?"

"Pieces of it. There is a wood shop in the basement of the house of history. We found parts of a spell-locked box that had been cut open. I thought it was odd but the entire building is filled with odd things. They have life-sized dolls that look like humans being attacked by lions. Why would they have that?"

"Stay on target! Stay on target!" Tinker pointed at the fancy egg-thing that Jin claimed to hold the baby dragons. "There was nothing that looked like that?"

"I did not see anything that looked like that," Cloudwalker said.

Which was a very careful way to say that the eggs could have been at the museum but Cloudwalker didn't see them. At least the location made sense; Sparrow must have had the New York museum ship the box to its Elfhome counterpart. It would have allowed Sparrow to keep the *sekasha* with her ignorant of the box's existence even as she orchestrated its shipment.

"Why would they need to cut the box open?" Tinker had taken days to carefully pick the lock on the box they found at the whelping pens because it was booby-trapped. Cutting that box open would have set off an explosion, destroying the contents and part of Poppymeadows' enclave. "If it was Iron Mace's box that Unbounded Brilliance stole, wouldn't the Skin Clan know the key word to open it?"

Pony shook his head. "According to his Hand, Iron Mace owned a medium-sized spell-locked box for centuries before Unbounded Brilliance was born. He alone knew the key word for it. His Hand did not realize the box had been stolen. Only after Iron Mace was killed did they realize that the last time that they could remember seeing the box was prior to his nephew's disappearance. Red Knife determined that while the song 'knock, knock, open the box' seems to indicate that the two events are linked, there is no concrete proof of treason on their part."

It sounded as if Iron Mace's entire household was questioned after Oilcan's kidnapping. Tinker hadn't been aware of it, so it probably had been done by the Wyverns. The Fire Clan's *sekasha* were considered the head of their caste. Red Knife, Prince True Flame's First, would have beheaded Iron Mace's people if he thought that they were in league with the Skin Clan. The idea was weirdly comforting and terrifying at the same time.

"After Iron Mace lost the box, the Skin Clan probably didn't trust him enough to tell him that they had found it again," Stormsong said. "Iron Mace came to Pittsburgh to find out what you and Oilcan knew about its contents. He wouldn't have done that if he knew that Dufae had lost it hundreds of years ago."

Tinker agreed with that logic. "If the box from the whelping pens hadn't been booby-trapped, I could have cut it open. Most Pittsburghers don't know how to work with ironwood, but the oni had dozens of carpenters disguised by magic to appear human. They made the wooden framework of the gate I built. Some of them might have worked at the museum." Tinker ticked off what they knew on her fingers. "Sparrow went to Earth during May Shutdown. She told the museum in New York that the box belonged to her. To make sure that the *sekasha* with her didn't find out about it, though, she asked the staff to ship it to Elfhome separately. The museum on Earth ships it to the Carnegie during the June Shutdown. Someone cut it open and took out the egg-thingies. After the July Shutdown, Cloudwalker finds the box in pieces. It's September now."

"Kajo has had the dragons for months," Jin whispered, his voice filled with horror.

"He hasn't done anything with them yet." Tinker stood up, her mind racing. So many problems that needed to be answered. Now. She snapped her fingers, calling to everyone that was hiding in the shadows: elves and tengu. "I need my datapad from my bedroom. Someone find me a printer, a whiteboard, some power strips, and every lamp you can bring me. There's a cardboard box in my closet; get that."

The box contained the original Codex. She needed to cross-reference her digital copy with it. She had noticed recently that her grandfather had deleted key information, presumably to protect her as a child. What exactly had he taken out? She needed to know what Dufae actually knew about the Skin Clan's plan. What else? She was still in her nightgown, bathrobe, and slippers. "Get me some clothes! Pants and a shirt, not a dress! I want my boots. A couple yards of string in five different colors. Send someone to get my cousin. Tell him to bring his digital copy of the Codex. And get me another pot of strong tea."

2: TEAM MISCHIEF

-+=⊙⊂=+-

"Oilcan." The tiny voice whispered in the ultrasonic range. "Oilcan!"

He opened his eyes and blinked. And blinked again. Four mice on tiny hoverbikes stood in the pool of light on his nightstand. They wore racing goggles perched on their heads and scarfs of various colors wrapped about their necks.

"We did it!" The pink-scarfed mouse fist-pumped its little paw. "Hooyah!"

This made the other three mice cheer and clap their hands.

"Hello?" Oilcan whispered. He might be dreaming—or his life just got a whole lot odder.

"Oilcan, we have an important mission for you!" Pink Mouse cried.

"Life and death!" the Green Mouse and Red Mouse squeaked in unison.

"Me?" He couldn't imagine what he could do for talking mice.

"You are Orville Wright, correct?" Blue Mouse asked. Unlike the other three, this one sounded male. Like Christopher Robin to be exact.

Oilcan glanced around, trying to determine if he was actually awake or still asleep. His new bedroom at Sacred Heart still disoriented him by the unfamiliar play of darkness and moonlight through the tall windows. The bed beside him was empty. Thorne Scratch had gotten up, turned on the lamp, and gotten dressed. Her sword and armor were missing.

He seemed awake . . .

"And you hate your name, correct?" Pink asked. "Orrrville."

Which was exactly how the kids in grade school used to mangle his name.

"Yeah," Oilcan said. "But what does that have to do with anything?"

"You have to find us wonderful names!" Red and Green cried. "Orville Oilcan, you're our only hope!"

"They don't want to call me Chuck Norris," Pink explained. "They want to call me Charlene! Chaaar-leeennnneee!"

"And they say we can't be Jawbreaker!" Red and Green cried.

"Jawbreaker?" Oilcan echoed.

A wordless squeal of delight and the rattle of hard sugar candy within a cardboard box announced a fifth visitor. A tiny dragon phased out of his nightstand with its discovery. Oilcan thought for a moment that Impatience had somehow been reduced to squirrel size. He realized that the colors were wrong. This tiny dragon was a delicate dusky pink color instead of bold red.

The dragon held up the box of Everlasting Gobstoppers that Oilcan had bought for Impatience. In a little girl voice, it said, "Candy! Yummy!"

She tore open the box. She stuck in her arm up to her armpit, fished about and pulled out a piece of candy the size of her fist. "Nom, nom, nom!"

"Jawbreakers are Joy's favorite candy!" Green and Red explained in unison.

"By the time we can do anything about our names, it's going to be too late," Chuck Norris said. "We'll be stuck with horrible names. Once those names get pinned on us, we won't be able to get everyone to use the ones we really want."

Their point wasn't completely off since Oilcan still had people who refused to call him anything but Orville. All the tax forms and legal documents too, required him to use his "real" name.

"We want cool names!" the Jawbreakers cried.

"I want to be Chuck Norris. If Alexander can be Alexander Graham Bell then I can be Chuck Norris Dufae."

Dufae? That was his mother's maiden name. Were these mice somehow related to him? Were they descendants of some long-lost great-great-uncle? His grandfather had handed out some stupid names to his grandchildren—Orville Wright and Alexander Graham Bell—but Oilcan never thought being bad at naming children was a genetic trait.

Two kids both called Jawbreaker was worse than anything his grandfather handed out. It should be easy to pick out something better.

"What names do you want?" Oilcan asked.

"Crimson Death!" Red cried.

"Cthulhu!" Green cried.

This wasn't going to be simple as it sounded. This was so surreal. It had to be a dream. He glanced down at the mice feet. His notepad lay open with his to-do list written on the top piece of paper.

Find more dishes for Barley. Thrift clothes for Cattail Reeds? Sheet music for Merry and Rustle. Dog food for Repeat. Find out where the piglet came from! Tell Baby Duck no more pets!

If he could read the list, was he really dreaming? If he wasn't dreaming, was there really a tiny dragon standing on his nightstand, inhaling gumballs? Whose "children" were these mice? Were they really related to him?

The door of his bedroom opened.

"Code red!" Chuck Norris cried. "Abort!"

She vanished, along with Crimson Death and Cthulhu. The tiny dragon bounded away, phasing through the wall.

The mouse in blue was the only one that remained. "Please, Oilcan, help them. I don't want to be the only one with a cool name."

"What's your name?" Oilcan asked.

"Nikola Tesla Dufae." Nikola looked past Oilcan toward the opening door. "Got-to-go-bye!"

"*Domou?*" Thorne Scratch stalked into the room, *ejae* drawn and pointed toward the nightstand. "Who are you talking to?"

That was a good question.

"I might have been talking in my sleep," Oilcan said.

Thorne Scratch looked troubled as she sheathed her *ejae*. "Most *domana* do not true dream but most are not wood sprites."

Tinker had told him about her odd Wizard of Oz dreams fueled by her mother desperately calling for help. What in the world could the mice symbolize? What was the importance of the weird names?

He realized that his nightstand was littered with pieces of cardboard. He picked up a jagged shard of brightly colored paper. It was the remains of the Everlasting Gobstopper box.

His future was going to be very odd if it involved a miniature dragon and talking mice.

"A runner from cousin is at the door." That explained why Thorne was awake and armed. "Beloved Tinker of the Wind wishes to talk to you immediately. She wants you to bring your copy of the Dufae Codex."

"The Codex?" Oilcan glanced at his bedside clock to confirm that it was indeed in the middle of the night. Tinker was still recovering from breaking her arm twice. She should be deep asleep, not in mad-scientist mode. "Oh, that can't be good."

He was right. Something was obviously very, very wrong. He'd seen Tinker that afternoon. She'd been surprisingly polished and all princess like, complete with an elegant tea with little tarts and finger sandwiches. She'd given him a fistful of cash with the promise of more later, they'd mapped out a plan for the future like old times, and he'd gone home to paint his door Wind Clan blue.

Someone had rattled her cage after he left. Hard.

Tinker was still in her nightgown but had pulled on steel-toed work boots. She was clumping around Poppymeadows' dining room as loudly as her hundred pounds allowed. She must have had a bath prior to going to sleep as she had serious bed head that made her look somewhat crazed. Pieces of paper were taped to the walls, and she was weaving colored thread from one point to another.

Her Hand looked slightly frightened.

Thorne Scratch gave Oilcan a questioning glance. She'd never really met the Godzilla of Pittsburgh in full rampage. He motioned to his First to be silent and still; Tinker rarely noticed anything that wasn't moving when she was in this mode. Thorne wordlessly took up guard one step back and to the left of him.

"How hard is to find a pair of pants, for gods' sake?" Tinker shouted. "Is this all the lamps we can get? It still looks like a cave in here!"

There were a dozen mismatched lamps scattered about, trying to fight back the dark "intimate dining" ambiance of the restaurant.

"We're still looking, *domi*," a tengu said from the shadows and disappeared without a sound.

"What's wrong, Tink?" Oilcan asked.

"I just got handed several ticking bombs! I'm trying to defuse them all at the same time." She held out her hand and twiddled her fingers through a "gimme" motion. "Let me see your Codex." She flipped through the pages of his digital copy at a furious speed. She would pause occasionally to swear loudly. "Damn! Damn! Damn! Yours is doctored too. Our paranoid grandfather cut us off at the knees by giving us both the same highly edited version of the Dufae Codex. There are pages and pages of stuff he left out on purpose. Look!" She snatched up the original version. She flipped to the last page and read it aloud. "*My beloved grandchildren, Leo was killed by his efforts to build a gateway to Elfhome. Dufae's enemies have been on Earth all this time. It is possible that they already have the contents of Dufae's lost box. Stay hidden. Trust only each other and no one else. Keep yourself safe.* Keep yourself safe!" She shouted the last sentence a second time after reading it aloud. "Why write this and then hide it from us? I wouldn't have applied to CMU if I had known this! I wouldn't have trusted Riki when he showed up. There's so many things I would have done differently this summer if I'd just had the original."

"You did have the original." Oilcan felt the need to point out. "He knew we'd find it after he died."

Tinker gave him a hurt look, like he'd thrust a knife into her. "It was buried in his files with all the other secrets he didn't want me to know!"

"I'm sorry." He felt guilty. She was rattled; he should have just sided with her. The truth could have waited until another day. "It was a shitty thing to do but you know how he was. He hid out on that island under a fake name. He'd help anyone but if they got too friendly, he would start hiding from them. It's what really killed him. He didn't trust anyone. When he got sick, he wouldn't go to the hospital. He didn't even want you to call Lain. If he'd just taken care of himself, he might have lived for a hundred more years. We are—were—part elf."

She rubbed either sleep or tears out of her eyes. "We're missing hundreds of pages. Grandpa copied only the stuff focused on certain spells. There's big sections that seem to be just raw data output of something. I don't know what. I'm going to have to figure out how to search through the original just for information on the box."

"What ticking bombs do you need to defuse? Literal bombs or figurative?" With Tinker one could never be sure. It was a good thing to find out quickly. "What can I do to help?"

She glanced about the chaos that she was brewing. Her gaze settled on the pictures connected with the multicolored string. "You were ten when your mother was killed. You know what it's like to lose your parents, live with people you don't know, and be dragged to a completely new world to live."

"Yes," Oilcan said slowly. They had a long-standing agreement that they'd never talk about his mother's murder. He didn't like talking to anyone about it, not even Tinker.

"So imagine me—two of me at the same time—at nine years old," Tinker continued. "The two mini-mes had a normal childhood on Earth in New York City. Regular house for a family of four—whatever that looks like. School. No monsters. Just like you when you grew up in Boston. These mini-mes had actual parents—like you did—that had been killed in some manner. I don't think in front of the mini-mes, but it's possible."

"Are we talking theoretical nine-year-old girls?" Oilcan asked carefully. "Or are there real children involved?"

"Real live orphans! Try to keep up!"

Oilcan sucked in his breath as the memory of warm blood seeping under bare toes flashed through his mind. Twelve years. One would think he would start to forget. Certainly he had no clear memory of the series of foster parents who followed until his grandfather arrived from another world; he only remembered the sense of being adrift in a sea of strangers. The night his mother died, however, was etched in stone. Along with it, a sense of guilt for not doing something to save his mother.

"Now," Tinker charged on, seemingly unaware of the emotional storm she'd just triggered in him. "We're talking mini-me—did I mention there are two? Well, actually, six but four aren't born yet, so we'll deal with them later. Two nine-year-old mini-mes. Crazy smart like me; they worked magic while on Earth. God knows what else they're capable of—including using the Spell Stones. I know that if someone tried to make me live somewhere against my will, there would be hell to pay. Because I'm me, 'hell to pay' could be mind-boggling. Two of me—mind-blowing. The choices are: living with Esme, who is their rightful mother." Tinker pointed at a photo of her mother taped to the wall. Tinker indicated Lain's picture beside Esme's. "Lain—although that's nearly the same since Esme is living with Lain right now. Me—but what do I know about raising kids? You—but you have a house full of kids already. Forge, who promises to be good but I don't really trust him completely. Gracie, who was married to my father and loved him desperately but I know almost nothing else about her." Tinker tapped a hand-drawn picture of a tengu woman that stood in for Gracie. "She's Jin's cousin, one of the Chosen bloodline, and the flock's 'dream crow,' which means she can see the future. We would be unleashing two of me on a woman who does not know what I'm capable of. I take that back—Gracie might suspect what I'm like since she was in space when I fell off the planet. No. No. I still think she'll be totally blindsided, but who wouldn't be—except for maybe Lain because she's lived through one of me already."

"Sunder," Stormsong murmured.

"I am not giving up my siblings to be political hostages," Tinker snapped.

Tinker's Hand flinched. If the Stone Clan viewed the children as their responsibility, fighting could break out among the elves while they were still at war with the oni.

Oilcan stared at the pictures on the wall, trying to grasp all the implications. "I think—I think I need coffee."

"There's tea." Tinker waved toward the pot. "Coffee tastes like shit now."

He kept expecting things to taste the same and being surprised when they weren't. The tea was an explosion of subtle flavors. It was a forceful reminder that he'd been changed from a human to an elf via powerful magic—against his will—by Forge.

Two cups of tea later, Oilcan said. "Start over. What do you mean, two of you?"

Tinker scrubbed at her hair, making it stand up like an annoyed hedgehog's quills. "Jin was just here. The tengu rescued six of my siblings while I was busy blowing up Neville Island. Jin had been here in town, overseeing the search for the both of us and something about a train wreck at Oktoberfest." She paused to pick up a pen and paper. "This is the first I've heard about the train. I need to find out if the trains can still run; we need that connection with the East Coast."

Tinker wrote herself a note. "Jin was exhausted; I told him to go get some sleep." She continued explaining where the mini-Tinkers had come from and how they came to be. When she got to the baby dragon and the four unborn siblings, Oilcan felt an odd dawning sense of horror and confusion.

"Four Dufae babies?" Oilcan repeated. "Three girls and a boy?"

"That's weirdly specific," Tinker said as Stormsong said, "Yes."

Oilcan pinched the bridge of his nose. How did he know? How in God's name did they manage to "talk" to him? They weren't born yet! Had being turned into an elf somehow reinforced his wood sprite heritage, unlocking new abilities? Or had he just imagined it all? No, he couldn't explain the shredded jawbreaker box. He had to accept the situation and then give the best advice he could. He pointed at the threads connecting the photographs on the wall. "What does the string represent?"

"Since you could tap the Stone Clan Spell Stones before you were even spell-worked into a true full elf, this is going to go political quickly," Tinker said. "Even if the mini-mes can't call the stones, the children are going to be considered *domana* caste. The different-colored string tracks who the Wyverns will allow to act as guardian, who has the needed security level to keep the children safe, and who the twins might accept as foster parents. The last one is the tricky one. You've been in their shoes. Who do you think the twins would want to be their foster parent?"

"Couldn't we just ask the twins?" Oilcan asked.

"We *can*," Tinker said "can" as if it was a horrible idea. "One of the bad things about being smarter than everyone else: I've always thought I knew everything. Like—like dating Nathan. I thought that was harmless.

You told me it was a bad idea. Tooloo told me it would end badly. I thought I was right and everyone else was being stupid. I was wrong and Nathan ended up dead."

Oilcan had to admit that she was right. Tinker plowed through people because she was always so sure she knew better. He shuddered at the thought of living through her tween years again—times two.

Tinker continued. "Grandpa rarely said no, but he always limited my choices. Like that time that I wanted to play with dynamite. He allowed me to design and build a delivery system for flinging it into the river, and then he never bought dynamite again."

"I'm always amazed you survived your childhood," Stormsong murmured in English.

Oilcan pointed to the string. "You want to figure out the best choices and then only present those as options to the mini-mes."

"Yes." Tinker pointed to the pictures of the Shanske sisters. "I don't know Esme well but I know Lain will not be okay with trying to raise six mini-mes at once. Lain will want to split the kids up. She will *probably* take the two older kids and farm out the babies to separate foster parents. Lain most likely thinks that no one can handle more than two Dufae at a time— and she might be right. When I was nine, though, I would have arm-wrestled a saurus to keep my family together. I don't know if Esme would want to deal with six kids at once. Lain is the older sister and it's her house. Not to say that Esme couldn't start up her own household, but she just did the impossible to make Lain happy. I think Esme would want Lain to share her . . . I don't know what to call it. Happiness? Insanity?"

That explained the single strand of thread connecting to Esme's and Lain's pictures.

Tinker pointed at the hand drawing of Gracie. It had a single thread running to it. "Gracie has an unlimited number of babysitters at Haven but the Wyverns aren't going to agree to that."

"No, they will not," Pony said firmly. By his tone, he might not allow it either.

Tinker indicated the newspaper clipping with the photo of Forge that had multiple strands connecting to it. "The Wyverns would allow Forge to foster the children. He has a large household, and has that whole grandpa thing going on, but we couldn't be sure that he wouldn't pick up the kids and move back to Easternlands. I wouldn't be happy there after living in Pittsburgh. Coming from someplace like New York City? The twins would hate it. If they're like me, that could lead to very bad things."

It left the heavily connected photos of Oilcan and Tinker.

They stood and eyed the pictures in long silence.

"Frankly, this scares the shit out of me," Tinker finally admitted. In eight simple words, it explained the insanity of the pictures, the thread, and the heavy stomping in the middle of the night. "Being a big sister would rock, but being 'Mom' frightens me. Baby songbirds. Kittens. Peeps. Every little and helpless thing that I've tried to raise, ended up dead. I'm not good at it. I half-expected to kill Windwolf when he landed in my lap."

"You will have all of us," Pony said quietly. "My mother helped raise Wolf Who Rules. We can help raise all of your siblings."

Pony's words did little to lessen the scared look on Tinker's face, probably because she knew that her little sisters could think rings around the *sekasha* warriors. Six of them at once? Oilcan thought of the little Dufae mice, already plotting when they weren't yet born.

Tinker was right to be scared.

He gazed at all the threads leading to his photo. In theory, he was well suited to take six more kids. He had spare bedrooms. Forge had stated he was going to stay in Pittsburgh with his ten *sekasha* warriors. At some point the rest of Forge's household should arrive, adding dozens of *laedin*-caste guards. Thorne Scratch had plans on how they could add to Oilcan's Hand.

Maybe if he hadn't talked to the mice, he would be more willing to gamble that his household could handle the added chaos of Tinker's siblings. The mice made him honestly consider the problem.

Their grandfather, Tim Dufae, had barely been able to ride herd on Tinker when it was just her. Oilcan had been only ten years old and newly orphaned when he came to Elfhome. He had been an emotional train wreck from watching his mother be murdered by his father. Yet he'd still found himself acting as a semi-parent to his six-year-old cousin. He supposed it just came with the territory of being in a household with a younger child. He'd been lucky that Tinker adored him from the first day. She never tried to make trouble for him; it just worked out that way.

The five Stone Clan children in his care had been betrayed by their clan, captured by the enemy, imprisoned without hope of rescue, raped and tortured, and had watched helplessly as other children were slaughtered and eaten. Rustle's arm was still shattered.

Baby Duck had amnesia with no idea what her real name was or how she ended up in Pittsburgh. Cattail Reeds and Barley were emotionally fragile. Merry was already acting as emotional support for the other four children since Oilcan kept her safe from being kidnapped. To make those kids be semi-parents to six Tinkers? No, that would be criminal.

"I think it needs to be you," Oilcan said.

"I—I—I—please?" Tinker said. "At least think about it?"

He didn't want to say yes but looking at her with bed head, steel-toed boots and nightgown on, he had doubts that Tinker's household could cope with another two magical girl geniuses terrorizing them, let alone six. It might also end up like Lain and Tinker's relationship—they often butted their heads together like big-horn sheep. Tinker might not get along with her little sisters.

Thorne Scratch shifted so she was in his side vision. Once she had his attention, she nodded to indicate that she was sure it would be fine for him to take the twins.

She was so naïve.

Oilcan looked down at his feet so he wouldn't have to meet their eyes. Could he actually say yes, considering the state of his kids? Yes, being semiparent to Tinker had been harrowing at times, but Tinker had always listened to him when he put his foot down. She could be reasoned with. She'd been insanely mature for her age, even at six years old. By thirteen, Tinker had set up her own business and, in most practical terms, conducted herself as an adult. Tinker had shown him nothing but compassion when he arrived on Elfhome. The twins would probably be considerate of his kids' emotional state. It might even be helpful to have someone else at Sacred Heart who understood human technology.

He looked back up at the strings connecting the various photos of possible guardians. "I'll take the kids. I can see if Esme wants to live with me for a while to give the twins options. Maybe even Gracie too. Not as part of my household but like co-mothers for the babies or something. I don't know. We can get inventive. This is Pittsburgh."

3: ROCK-A-BYE BABY, ON THE TREETOPS: REFRAIN

❖═◎═❖

Louise jolted out of sleep. She flailed with the light sheet covering her. Her quiet cries of dismay turned to ones of frustration. Her twin, Jillian, had her left hand pinned to the futon mattress that they shared.

For a moment Louise was completely disoriented. She expected her old bedroom, the one she had shared with Jillian most of her life. The streetlights would shine through the one window to fall across the foot of their beds. There was always the hum of traffic, the sirens of distant ambulances and police cars responding to some unknowable emergency, and occasionally the bark of a lonely dog.

The airy space wasn't their bedroom. It swayed ever so slightly in the wind. The smell of autumn leaves hung in the air. Elf shines floated like fireflies through the air, barely holding back the cave dark of moonless night.

"Oh," she whispered as she realized that she was in Gracie's small treehouse, far above the forest floor, on Elfhome. Their home in Queens was hundreds of miles and another universe away. The treehouse, while charming, was rustic in almost every sense of the word. Their playhouse on Earth had more bells and whistles before they blew it up. Electricity. Wi-Fi. Furniture. Direct access to the ground.

The twins were in the roughly eight-foot-square living room of the treehouse that looked like a Japanese teahouse. Tatami mats covered the floor. One wall was the trunk of the ironwood tree. The other three walls had sliding shoji doors. The east and west panels of translucent paper over wooden frames were closed against night drafts. The southern door stood open to the narrow patio that wrapped the treehouse. There was an overhead light fixture powered by small windmills but they weren't allowed to turn it on. The oni might spot it. The only piece of furniture was a *kotatsu* table currently leaning against the wall to make room for their futon mattress. The rest of the area was taken up by the nesting box.

Gracie Wong Dufae—their biological father's widow— was asleep in her tiny bedroom, another thirty feet up the massive tree. Proving that the tengu weren't just humans with wings, the poor female had spent the day laying four huge eggs, each larger than an ostrich egg. They were sky blue with black speckles; apparently it was the normal coloration for oni crows. The twins had strategically missed all the drama; they'd deliberately spent the day exploring the hidden tengu village, returning only to find another egg had been laid in the blanket-lined, temperature-controlled nest. Louise was glad they managed to save her unborn siblings but Gracie popping out eggs was a little weird and creepy.

"Oh, you little brats," Louise whispered as she remembered the dream that woke her. Crow Boy—the *yamabushi* Haruka Sessai—was missing from his normal sleeping spot of the treehouse's patio. It could mean that her dream had been true; he might have met or was meeting with Jin Wong even now to give the tengu spiritual leader a report on all that they knew.

"Hm?" Jillian woke. She tightened her hold on Louise's hand.

"I dreamed that—that—that . . ." Louise stuttered to a halt. Had she told Jillian that her dreams had been coming true since they first turned on their magic generator? At first Louise didn't know what was happening. She couldn't see magic like Jillian could; she never thought that it would affect her in any way. By the time she realized she had a special power, Jillian was lost in grief. Her sister was still fragile.

"I dreamed of Mommy and Daddy," Jillian raised their joined hands to wipe tears from her face. "Peter Pan had taken Mommy away to tell the lost boys stories. Daddy went too because he wanted to fly. We were tiny and helpless like Tinker Bell; just little gleams of light. We tried to find Mommy and Ming locked us in a birdcage like the one we saved Crow Boy from."

Louise didn't know what to say or do to make things right for her sister. Their grandmother hadn't let them go to the funeral. They hadn't gotten a chance to say goodbye or even confirm with their own eyes that their parents were dead. Louise hadn't truly believed it until she talked with their Aunt Kitty, who had no reason to lie. Considering Jillian's state, though, perhaps it had been for the best. Maybe Jillian couldn't have taken the brutal truth.

What could Louise do? Her own dream pressed close, frightening not because it was of things that could not be changed in the past, but loomed over them as things that might yet come. Was Jillian strong enough to deal with all the things that Louise had seen in her dream? Did they have the time for Louise to even delay the truth?

She decided to start small. "In my dreams, the babies rode little hoverbikes to visit Orville. They wanted him to help them pick out new names. They're not very happy with the ones we chose."

Jillian laughed, sounding more like her old self. "What? Don't you think Chuck will like Charlene?"

"No. She hates it," Louise said. "Orville wasn't any help. He doesn't like his name either. He likes to be called Oilcan."

"Oilcan?" Jillian let go of Louise's hand to stretch. "Oilcan? What a weird name. How do you think he got it?"

"I'm not sure." Louise frowned in the darkness at the innocent-looking incubator. While they were at the mansion, the babies said that Joy had taught them to dream walk, allowing them to explore. The babies had known about the caves under the house long before the twins. Were they really still restlessly exploring despite growing in eggs instead of suspended in frozen nitrogen? How did they interact with Oilcan? It didn't seem safe, them wandering around like that, even if they weren't really leaving their eggs. "I think we really need to pick other names for the babies."

"I liked Charlene." Jillian even looked more like herself, as her short "Peter Pan" haircut of June had grown out. Her hair had been a brash carrot orange after she'd bleached it in New York City in an attempt to disguise herself. The tengu had taken pity on her and produced a hairdresser to dye Jillian's hair back to her original brown color.

"Charleeene." Louise mimicked Chuck Norris.

Jillian laughed again. "Okay. Why don't we just call her Chuck Norris Dufae and be done with it? No one seems to go by their real name on Elfhome. At least, not in our family."

"I want to stay Louise Mayer." Louise lay back down beside her twin.

"I want to stay Jillian Eloise Mayer." Jillian shifted the blue-flannel pillowcase that housed the remains of her childhood huggy blanket Fritz to curl beside Louise. "Together, we're Lemon-Lime JEl-Lo. But what do we call the Jawbreakers?"

They'd picked out two girl names after considering hundreds. Louise couldn't even remember what they settled on. Obviously the babies didn't like the choices.

"Jawbreaker could be their middle names," Louise said. "It's not like we use our middle names. I bet no one outside our family knows what they are. We could use some other names that still mean Red and Green. Red. Rose. Ruby."

"What's wrong with Cherry? It's a flavor of candy."

Was that what they settled on? Louise couldn't remember but apparently the babies didn't like the name. It wasn't as dramatic as Crimson Death. She was blanking on the shades of red. "Maybe Vermilion?"

"Gag!" Jillian cried. "Cerise."

"That's just cherry in French."

"They won't know."

Louise wasn't too sure of that. "Magenta."

"Makes me think of *Rocky Horror*." Jillian threw her hands up in the air and sang, "Let's do the time warp again!"

"That might be a good thing." *Rocky Horror* was cool and that's what the babies wanted. Still it felt off. "Scarlet? Scarlet Witch. Scarlet Overkill."

"Oh she would love that!" Jillian said. "Or Skarlet from *Mortal Kombat*. Finish him!"

"Scarlet Dufae." Louise tried it with the last name that the babies had already claimed.

"I like it. It rolls. One down. Green. Moss. Olive."

"No and no." Louise vetoed both Moss and Olive.

"Why not?"

"I don't know. They just don't feel—right. Emerald. Lime."

"We're Lime," Jillian said. "Lemon-Lime JEl-Lo."

In other words, both Lemon and Lime were off the list.

Louise tried to think of another green name. All that was coming to mind was Avocado. The babies' names weren't their most pressing of problems. If her dream was true, then the box full of baby dragons—possibly Joy's brothers and sisters—had fallen into oni hands.

"Pickle," Jillian said.

"What?" Louise asked in confusion.

"I'm still trying to think of green names. It sucks that this place doesn't have Wi-Fi. We could look up shades of green. None of the ones I can think of sound like a little girl."

"I don't think they want to have names that sound like little girls."

"All the green words I can think of is food. Basil. Mint. Pistachio. I think I'm hungry. I want ice cream."

"Ice cream!" Joy cried from the shadows. The baby dragon bounded across the floor to their futon bed. She had a Gobstopper in either paw.

"Where you get that candy?" Jillian cried.

"Found them! Yummy! Nomnomnom!" Joy shoved both into her mouth to demonstrate.

Louise's heart sank at the proof that Joy had raided Oilcan's nightstand. It meant that her dream of Jin telling Tinker about the box was probably also true. Louise had noticed that the tengu leader had carefully given the impression that the babies would be born, not hatched. He'd dodged the question about how many women were pregnant with Dufae babies. He'd said nothing about eggs.

Crow Boy had told them that it normally took a great deal of ceremony to summon Providence's spirit to discuss important issues. Impatience had vanished after the dragons had implanted the babies into Gracie. Joy was uncommunicative to the tengu, whom she saw as Providence's property. She might tell the twins but her English mostly consisted of food-related words. It wasn't that she couldn't learn more, she merely refused to.

It meant that no one knew exactly what the dragons had done to the babies in order for them to survive.

When the twins had taken Crow Boy to the hospital, it became apparent that the tengu weren't human at a very basic level. It was possible that the dragons had changed the babies so that they could thrive within eggs. They might be genetically tengu in addition to elf, dragon, and human. No one would know until the eggs hatched.

Louise didn't care what kind of feet the babies had when they were born. Human. Crow. It didn't matter to her. Jin probably avoided the issue because it would matter greatly to the elves. Would it matter to their older sister, Alexander, who obviously liked to be called Tinker? To their "biological" mother, Esme? To Oilcan, who probably was going to end up as their guardian? It made Louise uneasy just thinking about it.

Even more worrisome was the matter of the box. If only she'd known while they were robbing the museum to take all of the eggs. If only they'd tried to intercept the shipment to Elfhome. She and Jillian had been so focused on the babies, they hadn't thought beyond their own needs.

There was a lot that Jin didn't tell Tinker *domi*. It was possible that in all the chaos, the information had gotten lost. Had she and Jillian told Crow Boy everything that they knew? It had been July when they rescued the tengu youth out of the cage. It had been a frantic scramble to escape from the fortress of evil, get safely to Monroeville, and then rescue the Nestlings. It was now September. Louise had lost most of August while recovering from being shot by Yves. Surely, sometime while Louise hadn't been fully conscious, Jillian had covered everything that they hadn't told Crow Boy.

Did Jillian *know* everything?

After their parents died, Louise kept more and more secrets from her twin. Jillian had been so fragile. Louise had been afraid that if Jillian knew how truly perilous their situation was that Jillian would break. Even now, with all the surviving members of their family safe, she wasn't sure if Jillian could handle more.

Louise had a terrible feeling that "more" was in store in the near future.

"I'm sorry, Lou." Jillian distracted Louise from

her quiet fears. "I lost it at the mansion. I was so scared for the babies. They'd become real to me—as real as Mom and Dad. They're our baby brother and sisters—and I couldn't see how we were going to save them. I'm angry at myself now. I should have known that the two of us can do anything when we put our minds together. We robbed the Museum of Natural History! We stole millions and millions of dollars from Ming the Merciless. We checked into the Waldorf Astoria and lived like queens. We rescued all those kids and...and...and...we're Lemon-Lime JEl-Lo! We've been internationally famous video producers since we were seven years old with millions of fans around the world. We can do anything!"

Louise wanted to believe that Jillian wasn't that broken after all. She might have grown stronger while Louise was sick. Or maybe Jillian was lying to herself. Maybe Jillian needed to believe she was stronger in order to be stronger. Louise didn't know.

"You were great," Louise said. "The fake elves didn't know how scared you were."

"It was just an act."

"You could have won an Oscar for your performance."

"It helped to be someone else," Jillian whispered. "Someone a lot braver than me. Next time, I'll pretend to be you. You were amazing."

Louise hoped that there would be no "next time."

"Oh!" Jillian made an odd hurt sound.

"What's wrong?" Louise stood, ready to fight because fleeing would be impossible.

"Crow Boy!" Jillian had noticed that the teenager was missing. "I told him that he'd roll off the patio if he slept out there!"

Louise followed Jillian out onto the patio. Night pressed in around them, full of the rustle of leaves.

"That idiot!" Jillian peered down at the ground, two hundred feet below. The forest floor was lost in the darkness; it was like looking down into a well. "How do you think we're going to get down to check on him? I don't think tying our sheets together would work. They'd only get us twenty feet at most. Maybe if we made parachutes."

"Shhh!" Louise pointed up to indicate the sleeping Gracie somewhere above them; it was too dark to see the tiny bedroom. "I don't think he fell. I think he went to talk to someone."

"In the middle of the night?" Jillian whispered.

"The warriors have returned." Crow Boy's voice came out of the darkness.

It was surprising how quietly he could fly. One moment the twins were alone on the balcony, and the next, the teenaged tengu was landing on the railing. With a soft rustle, he closed his large black wings. He'd abandoned all pretense of being human since arriving on Elfhome. He was bare chested and barefoot, wearing only a pair of blue jean shorts. Jillian must have gotten used to it while they were at the caves; she didn't seem to notice his bird toes curling down to grip the railing tightly. Louise was still trying to see it as normal. It took all her control not to stare at his feet.

"You just left without telling us?" Jillian crossed her arms and looked just like when their mother would go into warrior princess mode.

"I'm sorry." Crow Boy gave a slight bow. The tips of his black hair were still bleached blond from their

attempts to disguise him in New York City. For some
reason Louise found it comforting, as if they still had
some claim on his loyalty. "I thought I would return
before you woke up. The warriors, who had been out
searching for Tinker *domi*, have returned to Haven.
I saw Jin Wong! I never thought I would ever meet
him; he left Earth before I was born. He's been lost
to us my entire life. He has this—this—calmness. It's
like a deep mountain lake."

"You could have left a note," Jillian grumbled.
"'Dear Jillian and Louise, I didn't fall to my death.'"

Louise stuffed her knuckles into her mouth to keep
from crying out in dismay. Was Jin still flying to warn
their older sister or had that already happened too?
Joy had the candy. Tinker had sent for Oilcan after Jin
left. Yes, Jin had delivered Crow Boy's report in full.

"What did you tell Jin?" Louise tried to keep her
voice steady. "I know you—you—you probably told
him about the babies and Joy and the box—but did
you tell him about Ming? Crown Prince Kiss Butt?
Flying Monkey Four and Five? Tristan and..." What
had been Tristan's older brother's name? The elves at
Ming's mansion had talked about Esme's half brothers and the mysterious "Eyes" only once or twice.
Tristan had been scolded when he asked about his
younger sisters, raised in secret from their mother,
Anne. What was his brother's name? "Lucien. His
name was Lucien."

"Monkeys?" Crow Boy's confusion was clear on his
face. "Crown Prince Kiss Butt?"

"They're all back on Earth." Fear tinged Jillian's
voice. "Aren't they?"

Louise slowly shook her head. Crow Boy's confusion

she half expected, since she was using Esme's nicknames for her stepfather, stepbrother and half brothers. Louise was sure she'd told Jillian about the conversation that she overheard at the mansion. She'd been so angry at Ming for stopping Tristan from seeing his mother. Ming made Tristan live alone even though he was still technically a child. In her dreams, she'd seen how lonely Tristan's existence had been. Did she leave out that Tristan had been sent to help his older brother? "Lucien has been here on Elfhome the whole time. Tristan was sent to back him up in July. Ming came across too."

"Yves?" Jillian whispered.

Louise flinched as the memories from the cave flashed through her mind. Huddling in the absolute dark. A killer nearby. The pain of being shot. Her blood spilling warm down her arm. She thought that Jillian and Crow Boy would have seen Yves' body when they found her. There must have been a second cave-in.

I killed him. Louise opened her mouth but couldn't force the words out. She tried for an less than honest truth. "He's—he's still on Earth." Under a ton of rocks. Better him than her. He had a gun. She thought she was unarmed until she tried to do magic out of sheer desperation.

I did a force strike! Louise gasped as she realized that if she had done it once, she could do it again.

"What?" Jillian asked as Louise stared at her hand.

"We can call the Spell Stones," Louise whispered.

Jillian squealed with excitement. Jillian put her left hand to her mouth and called the Spell Stones to cast a shield. Louise felt a sudden tingling flush like static electricity and the air pressure around them changed. "Yes! Yes! Yes!"

The sense of power disappeared as Jillian bounced about the room in the dance of joy.

"We can do magic!" Louise whispered, full of happiness.

"We're elves!" Jillian whispered loudly. "We can do magic! We're *domana* elves!"

Oh, yes, that.

Crow Boy was looking slightly alarm. "I think I need to talk to Jin again."

"No, don't tell him!" The words were out of Louise's mouth before she even knew what she was going to say. "No one can know that we can cast spells."

"He's my leader. I've dedicated my life to him," Crow Boy said in a low, serious tone.

The words continued to pour out. "If you tell him, he'll need to tell Tinker *domi*. Tinker *domi* will need to tell Prince True Flame. He'll have to tell the current head of the Stone Clan, which is Sunder. If Sunder finds out, then everyone will die."

"The tengu can't lie to Tinker *domi*," Crow Boy said. "We cannot afford to lose faith."

"There's lying and then there's just not saying anything," Jillian said.

"Jin isn't even here in Haven," Louise said as Crow Boy frowned at Jillian's statement. "He's in Pittsburgh talking to Tinker *domi*. He won't fly back tonight. It's four in the morning. He'll sleep at one of the safe houses in the city. We need time."

"Time for what?" Crow Boy asked.

"To be ready," Louise said. She wasn't sure for what.

Jillian gave her an odd look, obviously unsure if Louise was lying or not.

Crow Boy frowned at the floor, thinking. His left

foot scratched at the railing as he considered Louise's request. "If you had not pulled me out of that cage, saved the Nestlings, and got us all safely to Haven, I would never allow this. You could have left me in the cage—at the hospital—at the hotel—and gone on without me or mine at any time. It would have been easier and safer for you. I have seen you move mountains for the good of my people. You are Joy's Chosen. While it goes against my training, I will keep my silence for now."

"Thank you," Louise said.

Jillian held up her finger. "What exactly are we getting ready for?"

Louise waited for the answer. Whatever truth had battered its way out of her, it was spent. Gone. "I don't know." She glanced around the room. The tengu gave them forest camo towels. She picked up a middle-sized one to use as a blindfold. "I might be able to find out."

"You want to dream walk?" Crow Boy pointed toward Gracie's bedroom. There were no lights on in it. Their talking hadn't woken the female. "I could get Wai Sze. She's the Flock's dream crow."

Louise shook her head as she tied the blindfold into place. She wanted to say yes. There was a little niggle in her chest that made it seem like a bad idea. As darkness closed in, the feeling grew. "She would tell Jin. She doesn't really know me. She doesn't trust us like you do. She sees us as her husband's children. Small. Helpless. She will feel like she needs to protect us. She will stop us from doing what needs to be done."

Jillian caught Louise's hand and squeezed it tight. "We'll kick butt and take names."

Brave words. Jillian, though, was shaking.

Louise took a deep breath. She had only done this

once before on purpose. It seemed as if she needed to enter search words to lock in on a vision. Last time it had been like being hit by lightning. What was coming? How did they prepare for it? Why shouldn't they tell Jin or Gracie? She said that if Sunder found out, everyone would die. Why?

Was this going to work? Could she actually control seeing the future? There was something she was missing. The other times she had focused on their older sister. If magic worked some weird quantum effect on time, then at some distant point, she and Tinker had been within their mother's body and then a test tube and bathed in their father's seed. It could have just as easily been Louise that ended up in the salvage yard when Windwolf came over the fence. Tinker could have been the one who became Jillian's twin…

"Hurry! Hurry! The time is at hand!" It was like plugging into an outlet. Power surged through her, sure and strong. "Clarity's Vision reaches across time and space! All that she has put in place must come together or perish! Youngest to the oldest, Brilliance must stand against the darkness. Heed the words written by the father. He was guided by Vision. He provides the protection against the danger that comes for them all. When the times come, the youngest will save them."

Then it was gone.

"Well," Jillian said after a moment, "that was helpful. Not! What the hell did that mean?"

The power was gone but a stain of the image remained. "Something horrible is about to happen. Everyone is in danger. We have to do something. If we don't, everyone will die."

"Do what?" Jillian asked.

"What's going to happen?" Crow Boy asked.

Louise shook her head. "I don't know. Something horrible. Something huge. We're the only ones that can save everyone."

They sat in silence for a minute, lost before the vision.

"Okay," Jillian broke the silence. "We're not going to save the day stuck way up here with no power or tools or anything. We're going to have to go down to the ground, get all our stuff, and get linked into whatever passes as internet here."

The drop-down out of the treehouse was scary. Crow Boy took them one at a time. Louise first. It was even more scary than the first big drop on a roller coaster; those were safety tested. She tried not to scream but a squeak slipped out.

"It's okay," Crow Boy said. "I've got you."

Louise nodded, not wanting to point out that what made it scary was no one had *him*. Somehow the trip had been less frightening when her transporter was a middle-aged tengu male instead of the fourteen-year-old. She *knew* that Crow Boy was stronger than an average human, and as a *yamabushi*, perhaps even an average tengu. Certainly all the adults treated Crow Boy with reverence. She had seen him, though, bound, hurt, and helpless. He was still a "boy" to her.

"They salvaged everything that we brought across," Crow Boy said as he alighted next to a well-hidden storage shed. "What we didn't get in the first trip, they went back for."

"Everything" included the tall, mottled brown birds that came trotting out of the undergrowth to investigate them. She had made the mistake of letting Chuck Norris and the others pick out the self-driving truck during their rescue of the nestlings. The babies decided to take one transporting a herd of ostriches just because they wanted to see the birds firsthand.

The tall birds gathered around Crow Boy and Louise, cocking their heads to get a better look at the children.

"I swear, they seem even bigger in the dark." Louise loved animals. It was hard, though, not to be a little afraid as the flock loomed over them.

"They *are* bigger," Crow Boy said. "Wai Sze believes that they're not fully grown; their mottled coloring is more like a chick's than an adult bird's. They've gained like a foot in height in the last month."

"A foot?" Louise whispered in surprise. "Ostriches only grow to be between five and seven feet tall. They were all at least six feet tall when we stole them."

"Wai Sze says that they're not ostriches; they lack even vestigial wings. She thinks they might be moa."

"Moa?" Louise repeated. "Moa were hunted into extinction over five hundred years ago."

"There were experiments being done of injecting moa DNA into ostrich eggs," Crow Boy said. "It's possible that these are the result."

"We stole the only living moas on Earth?" Louise whispered fiercely.

"I'm sure they can make more," Crow Boy said. "Wai Sze says that because they were so special, they were most likely hand raised. They were fairly tame even when we first found them. Since they made good guard dogs, we kept them close to the camp and they bonded with us."

He demonstrated by petting one on the neck. "I'll need to get Jillian."

In other words "I need to leave you alone with these birds."

"Okay." Louise reminded herself that she was supposed to be the brave one. She loved animals—even ones that towered over her and made deep rumbling dinosaur noises. She felt like they were very much alone deep in the virgin forest even though she knew thousands of tengu were asleep high overhead. The only light came from elf shines that drifted through the bracken, which was just enough to make out the barest details.

Crow Boy sprang up into the air, unfurling his wings with a loud rustle. He labored upward, the flapping growing quieter as he rose.

Something wrapped itself around Louise's neck. She jumped, reaching for her throat in alarm.

"Hungry," Joy complained from under her chin.

"Joy!" Louise whispered loudly. "You scared me!"

Joy blew a raspberry. "Mine!"

This seemed to be to the giant birds eyeing Louise closely. The moa rumbled and clacked their beaks and stomped their feet.

Crow Boy landed lightly beside her carrying Jillian.

"That's just like being Peter Pan again!" Jillian said. "I love flying! I wish I had wings."

"You would need more than just wings to fly," Crow Boy said.

"It would help," Jillian muttered.

It made Louise think of the babies who may or may not have bird bones and feet. Chuck Norris would want to be able to fly. Probably the Jawbreakers too.

Nikola would want to be like his sisters. What were they going to do with the babies if they turned out to be tengu? Perhaps Orville was right to worry. "Will the eggs be okay? Unattended?"

"The incubator has an alarm on it," Crow Boy said. "If the power fails or the eggs get too hot, several adults will be notified. We only have a short period of time before the nest mothers who turn the eggs show up and notice that you are gone."

Louise nodded in understanding. If they wanted to keep things secret from the tengu—and thus the elves—they needed to move quickly.

Crow Boy had called it "a storage shed" but the structure looked more like a concrete bunker tucked under a hill. Most of the building was covered with earth and what looked like undisturbed forest detritus. Large ferns grew in strategic pockets to disguise vents. The heavy steel door was painted to match the dead leaves. The entire structure seemed invisible in the faint light of the elf shines that danced in the area. Despite the camouflage, the door had a number-pad keylock. Crow Boy punched in the code, opened the door, and turned on the lights. The interior was larger than Louise expected, with a Quonset hut high-arched roofline.

The tengu had recovered all of the twins' supplies but had simply dropped them in one large pile in the center of the floor.

When she and Jillian planned the rescue of the nestlings, they'd loaded down the luggage mules with everything they thought they would need to escape to Elfhome. They hadn't given much thought on what would come afterwards.

It *was* "afterward." What did they need?

They'd brought a stunning amount of stuff. The food was long gone but everything else made a small mountain to sort through. Solar rechargers. Power strips. Survival blankets. Tools. Nonlethal weapons like Tasers and pepper spray. Signal repeaters. Spare tablets. Small 3D printers. Supplies for casting magic. A monster whistle. Hundreds upon hundreds of robotic mice. A fleet of luggage mules to haul it all.

The twins started to dig through the mound without a plan. They slowed down to a crawl, defaulting to dividing things into piles, hoping that organization would trigger inspiration.

Louise finally sat down in despair. Where did they even really start? What were they supposed to do? They were two nine-year-old orphans on a foreign planet against an army. They had broken toys and ancient magic that they didn't fully understand.

"Let's recharge everything that can hold a charge," Jillian said after standing still for several minutes, thinking. "That way if we find that we need something, it's ready to go."

"I can do that." Crow Boy picked up a power strip and plugged it into the building's only outlet.

"We can do this," Jillian said. "We're smarter—"

"Than the average bear," Louise said dryly.

"Bear. Oni. Human. We're smarter than everyone."

"With a brain the size of a planet," Louise quoted from *Hitchhiker's Guide to the Galaxy*.

"And you can see the future." Jillian gestured at Louise with one of the robotic mice. "You knew the moment that the hyperphase gate failed that Esme was saving Jin Wong. No one could have just guessed at that one. Jin Wong went through the gate the first time that the Chinese turned it on. Esme left years later. Both of them were thought to be five light-years away. You *knew*."

"I don't know now," Louise whispered.

"Yes, you do. 'Youngest to the oldest, Brilliance must stand against the darkness.' That's us! You and me and Alexander and maybe even Orville. We're the great-great-great-grandchildren of Unbounded Brilliance."

"'Heed the words written by the father.'" Louise repeated what seemed to be a key phrase in the prophecy. She remembered her dream of Alexander—Tinker *domi*—talking about her doctored version of the Codex. "It has to be something that Unbounded Brilliance wrote."

Louise found one of the spare tablets that didn't have a dead battery. Esme had left them a digital copy of the Dufae Codex. It had been on an ancient memory stick inside a Chinese puzzle box. The twins had copied the journal onto all their devices. Louise flipped through the spell book.

"Maybe," Jillian said with less certainty. "The word 'father' might have meant Leonardo Dufae. He made the gate that started this mess. Maybe he kept a diary too."

Louise shook her head. "No, Sparrow delivered Dufae's box to her partners in crime. They have the *nactka*. The oni plan to use them to do something horrible. Unbounded Brilliance knew what they planned; it's why he didn't just hand the box over to his parents after he stole it. He had a plan to counter the oni."

"Stupid plan," Jillian muttered. "He should have just opened up all the *nactka* and freed the baby dragons."

If Louise had known what was in the *nactka*, that's what she would have done. Twelve Joys would have been impossible to keep hidden but that was because Earth had no magic. Unbounded Brilliance had been on Elfhome when he stole the box. Why hadn't he just opened them? Three universes would have been vastly different if he had. "We wouldn't exist if Dufae hadn't been in France to meet our great-great-great-grandmother."

"Yay for us, but Unbounded Brilliance wouldn't have been killed in the Revolution. He would still be alive now. The baby dragons would be free. The oni wouldn't have the box to do whatever they're going to do with it. And this book is thousands of pages long! How are we going to find what we're looking before it's too late?" Jillian's voice quavered with fear.

Louise felt a flutter of it in her stomach. "We'll figure it out." They had to. "Okay. Let's back up and rethink this."

"You don't think 'father' means Unbounded Brilliance? You just said—"

"Wait! You're Unbounded Brilliance. You find out that the enemy has the *nactka* and plan to do something with them."

"It would help to know who he stole them off of."

According to Louise's dream about Tinker, the box originally belonged to Iron Mace, who tried to kill Oilcan just a few days ago. Iron Mace didn't know that the box had been recovered by Sparrow; he was just a tool, used and then abandoned. It was possible that Unbounded Brilliance realized that his uncle wasn't the real enemy.

"Maybe Unbounded didn't know." Louise felt her

way through what *might* have happened hundreds of years ago. "He sees his uncle's spell-locked box. A box that most people don't know how to open without the key word or phrase. Unbounded picked the lock because he's curious and clever. Inside, he found a dozen bombs. Think about it. You find *several* doomsday devices. You don't know who made it or how it works or, most importantly, if there are more of them somewhere else. The box belongs to your uncle so you don't know who you can even trust with this information. Instead of destroying the bombs, you—"

"Try and figure out how to disarm them," Jillian said. "Or at least get them far away from my family. I would want to keep them safe."

"Yes! He went to Earth and did experiments! Hundreds and hundreds of experiments. That's what the Codex is. It's his findings of-of-of . . ." Louise fumbled as she scanned over her memories of the work. "He's trying to figure out how certain spells work. Exactly—as in down to the decimal point—how effective they are."

"Okay." Jillian squinted at Louise. "Where are you going with this?"

"Unbounded had a plan," Louise felt sure of this. "*We* would have had a plan. Run away to someplace safe. Use our time in hiding to figure out how to get around the bad guys. Go back and blow them all to pieces. Right?"

Jillian threw up her hands. "We've both read the Codex cover to cover. Well—skimmed it at least. There's no storyboard or outline or even a project management flowchart."

Louise picked up her tablet and opened up the Codex. "The first thing he does is figure out a way to 'clean' magic. Earth and Elfhome are mirrors of each other, except Earth doesn't have magic. Unbounded Brilliance realizes if he goes to the same location on Earth where there is a powerful natural spring of magic on Elfhome, there will be some spillover onto Earth. It's the same reason that Desmarais had a mansion in New York."

Jillian sighed. She pulled up a notepad on her tablet and started to make notes. "Okay. You think if we work through the logic of what Dufae did, we can figure out what his ultimate plan was. He camps on top of a powerful source of magic, only to discover the magic is too incoherent to use. The crossing between worlds seems to affect the angular momentum of magic the same as throwing a disco ball into a beam of light. If you don't know about quantum mechanics, 'dirty' would be one way to describe it."

"The evil elves at the Desmarais' mansion said something along the same lines," Louise said. "The magic was too dirty to allow Desmarais to do major spells."

Jillian consulted her own copy of the Codex. "So the first spell we have in the Codex is the cleaning one, which basically funnels in power and gives it all one alignment and funnels it out to the storage system that he invented. Then he has the initiation spell the one that sets up a connection between a *domana* and the Spell Stones so they can do magic."

"He has some success with it. It needs to channel magic between worlds and the same diffusion process happens. He charts out the successes and fails."

"Yes, and then we have all these shield spells." Jillian flipped rapidly through the hundreds of pages that followed. "So many shield spells."

"Shields only." Louise noted as she slowly paged forward. "If the Spell Stones operate the way we think they do, then he's writing these out these from memory. I think that's why they're in the order that they're in—the easiest to remember to the hardest."

Jillian flipped backward. "Yeah, I think you're right. The first is the *sekasha* shield spell; even we can do that from memory. Hm, he has these weird pages of numbers and such after each shield. It appears that he was testing them to see how much damage they could absorb or something."

"Maybe he wanted a shield that could protect against the doomsday device." Louise's guess was based on the evidence.

"Ewww," Jillian said. "That's bad."

"What? Why?"

"If he found one then he would have stopped. The only reason to keep going and going was because none of them could shield against it. These are all the shields that the elves are going to use to protect themselves when the shit hits the fan."

"Oh," Louise said. "Oh, that is bad."

"But . . ." Jillian started and then stopped.

"But what?" Louise asked.

"The only way that he could know that each shield failed is if he knows what he needed to block," Jillian started to flip back and forth, looking for the clue.

"Oh! Yes! If we know what we're blocking, then we could use our knowledge of quantum mechanics—" Louise said.

"And magic," Jillian added.

"And magic to figure it out."

4: WILLIAM FREAKING PENN

◆◇◯◇◆

When Tommy Chang had left the half-oni warren to
find Jewel Tear, he'd told his cousin Bingo to shift
their family to someplace else. He hadn't been able
to give detailed instructions as they were whispering
to each other under the gaze of the elves. Tommy
thought he could trust his cousin to pick someplace
safe and reasonable.

He was wrong.

Tommy had meant someplace in a deserted part
of town, big enough to take them all, but easily
defended. It needed electricity, running water, sewage, and enough heat that they wouldn't freeze come
winter. Pittsburgh was filled with hundreds of empty
warehouses and industrial parks. Any one of them
would have worked.

Bingo had moved them into the William freaking
Penn Hotel.

Nor was it just their family in the twenty-story hotel.
Somehow while Tommy had been tracking down Jewel
Tear, saving Oilcan, and finding Tinker, Bingo had taken

in three other families made homeless by the fighting on the South Side. It doubled the size of their warren to over a hundred people, but most of them were under the age of twenty.

"We need to get out of this shithole." Tommy had been woken up by a phone call from Oilcan. He'd promised to drive out to Oakland as soon as he could get dressed. He would need to trust Bingo—again—to move their warren. This time, he was going to give detailed instructions.

"What? Don't you like your room?" Bingo gazed about Tommy's suite. It looked like something out of a movie. "It was a real circus getting everyone settled in, what with us having so many little ones. I let Mokoto figure it all out and then me and Babe made sure people went where they were supposed to go. I think Mokoto did a swell job. There are apartments upstairs with two bedrooms and a little mini kitchen. He put my mom, Aunt Amy and Aunt Flo in those so that all the babies could be with them. Some of the rooms have a door connecting it to the room beside it. Mokoto put four little ones on one side and then two teens on one other side to be built-in babysitters. He made sure that almost everyone doubled so we only take up two or three floors instead of scattering throughout the hotel. Just you, me, and Mokoto have our own place. Mokoto calls them 'sweets' like candy. I think it's a great room."

Sweets. Tommy shook his head. They were suites, as in having separate sitting rooms. All the colors in Tommy's—from the subtle gold-printed wallpaper to the ornate carpet in blends of mute reds to the fancy umber curtains—worked together to say "money." The bedroom had a massive bed with more pillows than any five people could use piled on it. The sitting room had two matching armchairs and a coffee table of gleaming perfection. Between the two areas was a bathroom that looked too nice to pee in.

"It's a hotel in the middle of Downtown!" Tommy's family had shifted all his belongs to his new room. Someone had washed, folded, and neatly put everything away, but Tommy couldn't figure out how they decided where to put what. He opened the top drawer of the dresser and found it filled with underwear. He had boxers on, so he closed it and tried the next drawer.

"Yeah—it's a hotel," Bingo said slowly, his brain obviously overheating as he tried to figure out why Tommy was upset. He became Tommy's lieutenant by default of birth order and size. He was the biggest and strongest member of their family. He wasn't, however, very smart. It came as no surprise that he let older and smarter Mokoto deal with the circus of assigning rooms. "This place was being renovated when the first Startup happened. The oni worked some deal Stateside and took it over. Aunt Flo says that the greater bloods lived here the first year or two—all quiet like—before they disappeared into the woodwork."

Tommy jerked to a stop. "You moved us to a greater blood camp? You said you found someplace safe!"

"It's safe." Bingo waved away Tommy's concern. "The greater bloods abandoned it years ago—not that anyone seemed to notice. We needed someplace big, what with the others losing their places in the train derail—"

Tommy smacked Bingo in the head. "Stupid! The greater bloods burn down the places that they don't plan to use again! They'll be back!"

"No, they won't!" Bingo cried. "They stripped out all the rooms that they were using instead of burning the whole place. The biggest apartment upstairs—the one with three bedrooms—has been gutted. They even took down the wallpaper and ripped out the carpet. Half of the sweet rooms like this one had all the beds and chairs and dressers taken out—which isn't all bad. The little ones are using them as playrooms. I thought about this hard! I talked to Mokoto and Trixie and even my mom and our aunties. We think that the greater bloods couldn't burn this place without the wrong people taking notice. It's a big, historic building in the middle of Downtown, not some house out in the boonies. Presidents of the United States have stayed at this hotel."

"Maybe." Tommy wasn't sure. His father had been the commander of the lesser bloods; he'd murdered Tommy's mother and didn't give a shit if Tommy lived or died. Tommy only knew about the greater bloods from a lifetime of chance remarks. "I don't have time for this."

"I figured if the oni could waltz in and out of this hotel without anyone knowing what they were doing, that we could use it too." Bingo continued to defend his choice.

"Things have changed." Tommy found the drawer holding his shirts. Were all his shirts black? He dug out his only blue one; if he was going out to Oakland, he wanted to be recognized as one of the good guys. "Downtown is full of royal marines, and what's left of the EIA knows that we exist."

"There's ways in and out so people can't see us coming and going." Bingo plowed on in the hotel's defense. "Besides, I thought we were with the elves now—all part of working with Oilcan."

"Oilcan isn't a god." Tommy went through the other drawers, looking for clean pants. The blue jeans that he'd taken off the night before were covered with dirt and blood. "Oilcan isn't going to be down here, making sure each new train full of marines knows that we're to be left alone. Even if he was down here, I don't know if he could stop them if they wanted to screw with us. Being made an elf hasn't changed him; he's still a little pacifist squirt."

"Then why team up with him?" Bingo asked.

"Because I said so!" Tommy didn't want to go into what Jin had told him about creating peace nor his own emotional journey to come to his decision. None of the drawers had jeans. Where were his jeans? "I need you to go out and find someplace else for us to live. Oilcan called and said they needed me at some kind of war conference."

"We're going to fight the oni?" Bingo's voice was filled with fearful doubt. "With Oilcan calling the shots?"

"When did Team Tinker ever start a fight?" Tommy opened the closet and found his blue jeans hanging up on wooden hangers. He took a pair out and pulled them on.

Bingo worked through being unhappy about being wrong to realizing what it meant for the half-oni. "Never, but Team Tinker always won any fight they got into."

"Exactly." Tommy pulled on socks and boots. "I think Tinker and Oilcan just want to pump me for information about my father's warriors. They've already called in the tengu, but my father never trusted them completely."

"Your father never trusted anyone completely," Bingo said.

Tommy grunted and opened the door to the hall. Bingo's eight-year-old little brother, Spot, sat on the floor opposite the door. Spot looked up with silent expectation.

"I'm going to Poppymeadows," Tommy said to crush any hope that Spot had about going back to Sacred Heart. The day before, Tommy had taken a carload of his younger cousins with him, saying that they needed to socialize more with people outside the half-oni. It had been an excuse to give Tommy the freedom to roam the building, looking for Jewel Tear.

Spot had found a soulmate at Sacred Heart; a cute little elf girl by the name of Baby Duck.

"Poppymeadows is on the other end of the street from Sacred Heart." Tommy headed down the hall. The hotel put him on edge. It was too nice. Even their old place above their Oakland restaurant hadn't been this nice. It made him feel like he'd fallen into a movie.

"I need you to find someplace else for us," Tommy told Bingo as they walked toward the stairwell. The building had elevators but they hadn't gotten them running yet. On the theory that no one could or would quietly climb seventeen flights to attack them, Mokoto set them up on the top three floors.

"This place is nice," Bingo whined. "Even at the restaurant we were always on top of each other. One newborn with colic could keep everyone up. All of us grown kids have our own room now so we don't have to deal with the little ones. No more sharp elbows in the middle of the night. No more waking up in someone else's pee. No more waiting to piss. There's a big industrial kitchen in the basement and the bar is still fully stocked."

"It's too nice," Tommy said. "There's no way we could defend the lobby. The doors are glass and there's two dozen twenty-foot-tall windows. If someone just set a big enough fire, they could burn us out. There would be no need for them to climb seventeen floors."

"I've set guards on all the entrances." Bingo said. "We've got more teens and adults now."

The stairwell obviously had only been meant to be used in an emergency. It was a bare echoing place. Tommy found it comforting after the richness of the hallway.

"We made nice with the elves," Bingo said as he followed Tommy down the steps. "Sooner or later, they will leave us alone—won't they? Why can't we have a nice place like this?"

"Because we can't afford it. I don't know where the power is coming from..."

"It was on when we got here."

"That doesn't mean anything. The greater bloods had some kind of system in place. Either it was on some kind of automated payment plan, or one of them was writing a check every month, or they have some kind of illegal tap. It doesn't matter which, we can't count on it continuing even another day. Tomorrow the power company might find the tap or the bank might stop the payments because we're cut off from Earth or the elves cut off the head of whoever was paying the bills. Sooner or later, we're going to have to pay for the power and we don't have that kind of money. More importantly, we certainly won't be able to heat a building this size come winter. At that point it becomes twenty floors of frozen pipes."

A herd of children between the ages of six and twelve burst through the door—all in their underwear—to charge down the steps ahead of him. They'd picked up more adults and teens with the addition of the other households but they'd also doubled the number of little kids. There were more than two dozen children heading downstairs, laughing and shouting.

"Where the hell are they going in their underwear?" Tommy asked.

"They're probably going swimming," Bingo said.

"There's a pool?"

"Yeah, brand new, never been used, in the base-ment. Like I said, they were in the middle of reno-vations when the first Startup hit. The sixth floor is totally gutted down to studs. It looks like it had been office space and they planned on converting back to hotel—ow!"

Tommy had smacked Bingo to shut him up. "You put water in the pool?"

"I didn't. Some of the teens did it. Filled it up. Got the chemicals into it—bleach—whatever—to make it safe to swim in."

Tommy growled. He was "head of the half-oni" because he was the oldest and meanest. He liked to think he was the absolute ruler—it was best that the elves thought so too—but he knew that his aunts could dig in their heels and make his life hell. It was going to be hard to lever his family out of this building if his aunts took a liking to it. "Find someplace else. Fast. It should be anyplace but Downtown: there's too many new elves moving through this area. It should be big enough for all of us but we need to be able to keep it heated through the winter even if the oni take out the electrical grid. Think wood stoves and fireplaces."

Bingo whimpered his disappointment.

"And do something about the elevators!" Tommy said. "The little ones aren't going to be able to do twenty floors of stairs and they'll crash wherever they run out of steam. We'll be losing kids all over the building."

"Okay, Tommy." Bingo detoured off to go check on the elevators.

The stairs had opened to the massive lobby, which had been cave dark the night before. Morning sunlight poured through the tall windows, reflecting on the crystals of the unlit chandeliers. Someone was sitting at a grand piano at the edge of the dust-filled shaft of light, playing a melody that Tommy didn't recognize. For a minute he thought a stranger had wandered in off the street. Then the musician lifted their head and Tommy saw it was Bingo's younger brother, Babe.

"Hey." Babe nodded and went back to playing.

"Hey, Tommy!" Mokoto sprawled on a couch behind Babe.

The two were the brawn and brains of the night crew.

Babe was six-foot-three of pure muscle with a baby face. It surprised Tommy that the big man knew how to play piano, but that was like Babe. Fierce on the outside, sensitive on the inside.

Short and slim, most people needed a second look to be sure that Mokoto was a male. His sultry makeup didn't help—the smoldering eye shadow and deep red lipstick read as female. He had on a pink midrift shirt and a black miniskirt so low on his hips it was surprising it didn't fall off. Tommy was never sure if Mokoto consciously posed sexily, or it was some weird uncontrollable habit. The man always managed to look like a female porn star, complete with a "come hither" look.

"Why are you two still up?" Tommy asked.

"We walked the Lee sisters back to their warren," Mokoto answered for the two of them. "Some of the regulars have stopped showing up. You know how it is; someone disappears and you don't know if they decided to find someplace safer or *something* decided that Liberty Avenue is a good hunting ground."

"Are we missing anyone?" Tommy had been out of touch for days chasing after missing elves and not-yet-elves and elves-that-used-to-be-humans.

"No, none of ours. All the heads and fingers and toes accounted for. It's all been the Undefended. You know how it is. They always show up in the early spring, like cherry blossoms. Beautiful. Smelling amazing. Oh so delicate. Then the summer winds come and they drift away. One by one."

Tommy nodded. The Undefended were all off-worlders. Some came to Elfhome on student visas to attend the University of Pittsburgh and then dropped out of school. The rest were illegals, slipping through the cracks that the oni made in the border to get their own people in and out.

The Undefended were easy to spot. They wore fashion trends that wouldn't hit Pittsburgh for another year or two. They did exotic things with their hair like dye it odd colors or shave their heads into patterns. They carried fancy smartphones that they had a habit of pulling out and staring at as if they were getting messages from God. They talked louder, with odd slang sprinkled into their conversation. Most of them walked faster than a normal Pittsburgher would. And as Mokoto pointed out, they smelled like flowers. It was as if they blasted all trace of humanity off their skin and replaced it with perfume.

While the Undefended ran in small herds, using their numbers as a defense, everyone in Pittsburgh knew that they had no real protection. They were without family and sometimes friends. They couldn't go to the police because they would be deported. They couldn't even use their real names: the list of expired visas was a matter of public record. It made them an easy target.

Any whore working Liberty Avenue, though, could be mistaken as Undefended. It sounded like Tommy might have to hurt someone hard.

Tommy didn't like being a pimp; it made him feel like his father. He made anyone who forced him into the role of protector regret it. "All of them recent?"

Mokoto looked oddly pained by the question. "They disappeared while we were moving the warren."

Babe stopped playing the piano to join the conversation. "I think the Lee family should move in with us. There's just the four sisters and the two baby brothers that can't pass as human."

Tommy sighed. What was six more people after a hundred? "Let them know I would like them in our warren." Wherever that ended up being. "We might want to put the night crew on hold until we find out why whores are disappearing."

"Sure thing," Babe said.

Mokoto glanced at the back of Babe's head, pouting that his opinion wasn't consulted. It was a measure of how uneasy he felt that he shrugged in the end and said, "Yeah, sure. It would be safer for the girls."

"We'll talk," Tommy said to soothe Mokoto's pride. Babe might be the muscle but Mokoto was the scary one of the two.

As Tommy headed toward the door, he realized that Spot was following him.

"I'm not going to Sacred Heart," Tommy repeated slower and louder. Since Spot rarely talked, he was never sure how much the boy understood.

Spot reached out, took his hand, and looked up at him. His father had been a brute doglike thing. Spot had inherited his father's looks but Aunt Vera's sweetness. He stared up at Tommy with sad puppy-dog eyes.

"No," Tommy said.

Spot considered and then quietly said, "Please."

Tommy growled softly. Normally he wouldn't give in to begging but Spot had walked alone into an oni camp for him. He owed the boy. "Fine. I'll drop you there. Oilcan is not going to be there, so find Baby Duck and stay with her. Don't let her out of your sight."

Tommy rode his hoverbike out to Oakland with Spot perched on behind him. The boy was beaming with joy, ears flapping in the wind. Tommy still wasn't sure, though, that dropping Spot at the enclave by himself was a good idea.

He was less sure when he reached Sacred Heart.

There were dozens of strange elves at the enclave all dressed in Stone Clan black. They were attempting to maneuver a gossamer into place over the three-story brick building. Tengu flitted about on massive black wings, catching mooring ropes that were being dropped from the gondola.

There was a small knot of humans gathered around a Roach Refuse dumpster hauler. Tommy recognized that most of them were part of Team Tinker, so he pulled into their midst. They weren't "friends" but at least they were known quantity: Tommy had watched most of the team grow up from kids to adult. Tinker invented the hoverbike. Roach invented hoverbike racing. Tommy created a place for the races to be held.

"Tommy." Roach lifted his hand in greeting. He had his little brother, Andy, and two of his massive elfhounds with him. The man paused, head cocked, as he looked past Tommy at Spot.

"This is Bingo's little brother," Tommy said to make clear how the boy was related to him. "Spot."

Roach blinked, obviously still thrown off-balance.

Roach's little brother, Andy was a simpler man. "We've got a puppy named Spot." He came to pet Spot's head as if the boy was a dog. "He's a good boy!"

Tommy curled his fist, controlling the urge to punch the teenager. It might be better for Andy to see Spot as a dog instead of a human being as Andy wouldn't hurt a dog.

Roach squinted. "So Bingo and him aren't . . . are?"

"Our mothers are human." Tommy didn't want to be having this conversation but it had to take place sooner or later if Spot and the others were going to be free to leave the warren. "Our mothers weren't given a choice in cooperating with the oni. We've thrown in with Oilcan—now that he's an elf. My family—all of it—are Oilcan's Beholden."

Tommy hated the word but it was a needed shield for Spot—especially if Tommy was going to be leaving the boy alone at the enclave. Maybe he shouldn't. Maybe he should just take Spot with him.

"This has been a weird summer." Roach indicated the tall stranger beside him. "We're helping out my cousin."

His cousin looked like an elf. Tall. Powerfully built. Long blond hair. Decked out in elf-made clothes. He had large bandage on his left temple and a vivid bruise on his cheek.

"Geoffrey Kryskill." Roach's cousin offered his name along with his hand. "I've heard how you went out and found Jewel Tear and then saved Oilcan's life. Good work."

It was a firm shake with a steady look that said, "I respect you." It was an odd, unfamiliar feeling, although not completely hateful. The question was: how the hell did Kryskill know when Roach was looking startled at the news? Tommy would have expected Team Tinker to be up to date on the latest news regarding their best riders.

"Geoffrey owns Gryffin Doors," Roach motioned to two big slabs of ironwood on the back of his truck. "Oilcan paid Geoff to do front and back gates for his enclave. Oilcan needed something out of wood because of..." Roach waved his hand toward the stone walls enclosing the enclave. The walls weren't there when lesser bloods disguised as humans squatted in the building. "...magic or whatever that his Grandpa Forge is doing."

"The enclaves have a defensive barrier much like the *sekasha* personal shields," Geoffrey said. "Forge is building the walls with the spells between the layers of stone. I'm going to hang out after we get the gates up and see what I can learn."

Ironwood needed spells and magically sharpened tools to work with. Some of the true-blood oni were carpenters who knew how to do it but Tommy hadn't realized that any of the humans had learned the trick. It meant that Geoffrey was trusted by the elves, which would explain the clothes and the long hair.

Blue Sky Montana came roaring up on a hoverbike. He slid to a stop beside Tommy's bike. Spot brightened and waved to the half-elf.

"Hey, Spot!" Blue Sky bounded off his bike. He picked the smaller boy up and swung him around, making Spot laugh.

Blue Sky might ride for Team Big Sky but Team Tinker welcomed him as if he was their rider. There was full minute as the various people greeted the half-elf.

There was a younger brother to Geoffrey by the name of Guy, who seemed to be around Blue Sky's and Andy's age. The three seemed to be fast friends. Thus it wasn't surprising that the boy knew Geoffrey too.

"What happened?" Blue Sky pointed to the bandage on Geoffrey's temple.

"Oh, some idiots showed up at my place. They'd heard that I knew some magic. For some insane reason, they thought if I just put my mind to it, I could make a gate for them."

"A gate?" Blue Sky pointed at the massive piece of wood on Roach's truck and then spread his arms to indicate something bigger. "Or a gate?"

Geoffrey waved toward the sky where the orbital hyperphase gate used to be. "A world gate, only on the ground. I told them that I only know a handful of spells related to working with wood. That didn't seem to register. They seemed like they weren't going to take no for an answer. One of them tried to coldcock me."

"Are you okay?" Blue Sky asked.

Geoffrey waved off the concern. "Yeah, I'm fine. He punched like a five-year-old. My sister hits harder. He had a ring on, though, and did a number on my face. My mom is pissed. We've got a wedding in two weeks and I'm still going to be healing."

"Who were they?" Tommy asked. "Disguised oni?"

"No. At least, I don't think so. They sounded like they were from Stateside. I pulled a gun, which they weren't expecting, scared them off. I was bleeding like a stuck pig, so Rebecca stayed with me instead of going after them."

"Rebecca?" Roach asked.

"That's me!" a young tengu girl chirped, waving her hand. "Rebecca Brotman."

Tommy eyed the girl, who looked all of eighteen. Her effortlessly fashionable-looking clothes, the cut of her hair, and the fact that her purple fingernail polish matched her lipstick shade indicated that she was a new arrival to Elfhome. He hadn't dealt much with the tengu but he knew enough to recognize what his father failed to: Rebecca was one of the special scary tengu warriors—the *yamabushi*—carefully disguised to be a normal American from Stateside where the most Asian thing about her was her eyes.

The money question was: Why was the *yamabushi* babysitting Geoffrey Kryskill?

Then Jewel Tear drifted into their midst and all questions vanished out of Tommy's brain.

Tinker had blasted Ginger Wine's enclave into smoldering bits. One of her flame strikes had taken out all of Jewel Tear's gowns made in the Easternlands. Her household fled Pittsburgh, apparently considering Jewel Tear "as good as dead." They took with them all that they had brought to Pittsburgh, apparently considering it jointly owned and theirs by being survivors of the oni attack.

Tommy had rescued Jewel Tear from the oni, but when he delivered her to Prince True Flame, she learned that she had nothing but virgin forest left to her name. The Wind Clan enclaves were overflowing with the incoming Harbingers. They directed her to Sacred Heart, which had been standing empty. She picked out a room on the top floor, settled in, and waited for Oilcan's return. Tommy wasn't sure what terms the two had agreed on. One of Oilcan's kids had made clothes for Jewel Tear to replace her lost wardrobe. Today, she wore a yellow sundress that made the most of her dark skin, long legs, and full breasts. The thin straps made Tommy want to slide them down off her shoulders.

The female was made of steel. She barely glanced at Tommy or Spot, focusing instead on Blue Sky. One would never know by looking at her that, in the privacy of her room, she was like a cat in heat. "Are these the gates that we are waiting on?"

While she talked, Jewel Tear petted Spot on the head in a seemingly absentminded manner. The boy leaned into the attention the way Tommy wished he could. One of the Stone Clan *sekasha*, though, was standing nearby with "on duty" attention on the *domana* female. Jewel Tear had made it clear that it would be dangerous to be anything but cold to each other in public.

Tommy struggled not to stare at her. He pretended to be looking at Spot who leaned into her softness. During her capture, the oni had caught hold of Jewel Tear's braid and trapped her even as they killed her people. After Tommy rescued her, in a fit of grief and rage she had hacked off her long dark-brown hair. The haphazard haircut, the countless small cuts, and the dark bruises that covered her body had given her a broken, manic look. Someone had neatened her butchered locks since Tommy had seen her last; she sported a cute pixie haircut that looked intentional. The bruises were fading to shades of yellow. She looked less broken and that made him happy.

"Are you going to be helping?" Blue Sky asked Jewel Tear.

"Yes, Forge has been gracious enough to accept my help," she told Blue Sky and the group at large. Tommy liked to think that the information, though, was for his ears. "I've studied defense building as I would need it for anything I built here in the Westernlands, but I've had no chance to put it into practice."

"I need to go," Tommy said to Jewel Tear and anyone else who might be within hearing range. He focused on Blue Sky. "Spot wants to stay and play with Baby Duck. Can you make sure that he finds her safely in all this confusion?"

"She's in the dining room, clearing tables," Jewel Tear said.

"Come on!" Blue Sky caught Spot by the wrist and dragged him off. "Barley was going to try out a recipe for crepes for breakfast! Let's see if any are left."

"Crepes?" Guy and Andy both echoed and followed the younger boys.

Jewel Tear drifted closer as she turned and watched the boys go. All around them, the moment for discussion had passed and people surged to new positions, focusing in the next step in their project. In that confusion, she brushed Tommy's hand with her fingertips. "We'll make sure that everyone here knows that Spot is not to be harmed."

And then she was gone, letting the chaos seemingly shift them apart.

5: OLIVE BRANCH
CASTING SHADE

Olivia's father—the man she considered her real dad, not her slime of a zealot stepfather—had always said when you didn't want to do something, do it immediately to get it over with before you could talk yourself out of it. He also said that after doing something difficult, to remind yourself that you were strong and succeeded despite the hardship. At the time, he'd been talking about cleaning her room and combing out the tangles in her thick red hair, but the advice had served her well over the years.

So, despite not wanting to talk to the famous Wind Clan *domi*, Olivia marched down the hill, over the bridge, and across Oakland to Poppymeadows enclave, where the Viceroy was currently living. Yes, it was insanely early in the morning to be calling on neighbors. The sun was still on the horizon like a baneful eye. She was discovering, though, that elves kept farmer hours. Chances were good that Tinker *domi* would be planning to leave the enclave on some unlikely and earthshattering adventure. Olivia wanted to be sure to catch the girl—woman—female.

Her Wyvern escort was off with Forest Moss. All the *domana* that were fit to fight had gone off someplace far east of the city, beyond the Rim. It left her with an escort made up of twenty royal marines.

The marines followed Olivia like a pack of puppies. Some trotted ahead. Some lagged behind. Some stopped to pee on bushes. In ones and twos, they would pause to investigate anything that struck them as odd. Being that all of them were new to human civilization, there was something every few feet.

Why were there manhole covers in the middle of the streets? What were under them? They insisted in prying one up and peering down into the dark storm drains beneath. What were the fire hydrants for? She was glad that she could tell them that it was illegal to open one up. Why were there lines painted on the road? What did the bus stop sign say? What did the graffiti mean? Then they hit the museum with all its odd statues and the questions came nonstop.

She was already vexed with the marines, as they had let someone or something get into her precious supply of keva beans that she planned to plant. There was a hole in the side, suggesting a rat had gotten into the bag. If she wasn't so versed on rodents chewing their way into feed sacks, she might have accepted the possibility at face value. But the fabric looked cut to her, not chewed.

The problem was she was on Elfhome, not Earth. There were sharks in the fresh water rivers. Giant electric catfishes that walked on land. Wolves that were the size of ponies and breathed cones of deadly cold. Trees that could stalk people down and eat them. Vines that would strangle you and then feast on your dead rotting body.

Maybe the rats carried switchblades. Who knew? She didn't. Unfortunately, neither did the royal marines. They were as out of their element as she was. They were from a section of Elfhome that corresponded to Northern Italy on Earth. They didn't know what kind of animals lived in the Westernlands.

Like puppies, they didn't see the problem of vanishing seeds. They had come to fight oni, not rats. There was plenty of food for them at their field mess. They held a profound belief in their *domana;* Prince True Flame would provide. The Wyverns guaranteed that.

Olivia didn't share that belief. The *domana* might be immortal but they weren't gods. An army functioned only when it was fed; supply lines would be the oni's first target. They had already derailed the train at Station Square in the middle of the Oktoberfest festival. She heard the massive thunder of destruction all the way in Oakland as the diesel engine and passengers cars crashed.

Food from the Easternlands was no longer a sure thing.

Yes, the Fire Clan Wyverns may be able to feed their marines but Forest Moss was Stone Clan. He was in Pittsburgh as a paid mercenary. He was also considered dangerously unbalanced. The Wyverns had considered executing him rather than trying to help him. Olivia's presence was the only reason Forest Moss was still alive.

No, she could not count on the elves for food.

What little was being locally produced would need

to be shared with all the humans in Pittsburgh, some sixty thousand people. The locals were already canning their harvest but there were college students, diplomats, and EIA employees, who had thought that they were only going to be on Elfhome for a few months. While they might not realize yet the danger they faced, they belonged to powerful organizations. The EIA. The University of Pittsburgh. Embassies of Earth's nations. Those powers were probably already stockpiling food for their people and their people alone. It was the human way of dealing with such emergencies.

Olivia had to prepare for a winter with no supplies from the humans or the elves.

She was two months pregnant; starvation could lead to birth defects in her baby. For her unborn child's entire future, she needed to be sure she had access to a healthy diet for the next seven months. She had picked the crystal palace of the Phipps Conservatory because its massive greenhouse could allow her to grow food through the winter. She had had the seeds that would allow her to do that. Thanks to the unknown vermin, she needed to replace what she had lost. Quickly.

While the war with the oni kept Forest Moss from her side, she had herded the royal marines all over the city, looking for seeds. Annoyingly every time she stopped to talk to any humans, the puppies would suddenly snap to attention and became fierce-looking warriors, scaring the fudge out of everyone. If she managed to beat the marines aside, everyone would then react with confusion. It was the beginning of September. Hard frost could come at any time, killing anything planted outdoors. Growing season was over.

She would nod. She wouldn't volunteer that she

was living in a massive greenhouse. She felt vulnerable enough with something quietly stealing her seed out from under the royal marines' noses. She didn't want the entire city to be reminded that the Phipps Conservatory stood abandoned until she squatted in it. She didn't want to anyone showing up with a stronger claim on the property.

She'd planned on talking to Forest Moss about the seeds, but he didn't come home. The marine who fetched the evening meal said that all the *domana* were gathering far to the east for an attack on the oni encampments deep in the forest. Only one Hand of Wyvern and a platoon of marines were still in Prince True Flame's camp at the edge of Oakland.

"The holy ones asked about you." The marine meant the Wyverns, as the caste members were thought to be divinely perfect. "I told them you were searching the city for seeds. They said that you should talk to the Viceroy's *domi.*"

Tinker *domi* was the last person in Pittsburgh she wanted to talk to.

Olivia's life was a series of deceptions stacked like a house of cards. She'd deliberately led the elves to believe she was older than her sixteen years. When she admitted to being old enough to be married, she left out that she been forced into a polygamous marriage at fifteen as the youngest of three wives to a man twice her age. She omitted the fact that she fled Kansas and illegally crossed into Pittsburgh during Shutdown so she would be an entire universe away from her husband and his religious cult family.

Her life wouldn't stand up to close inspection. She could normally evade most questions with half-truths but Tinker *domi* was famous for her brilliance. The older girl would probably see through any dodge. Since the vicereine was now an elf with *sekasha* bodyguards, Olivia wouldn't be able to lie.

If anyone in the city could get seeds, though, it would be Tinker.

There was also the possibility that "should talk to" was a command. Her Elvish wasn't very good.

The street in front of the enclaves was an unsettling place. On one side were human buildings that could come from any city on Earth. They were two and three stories tall with storefronts at ground level and offices on the upper stories. Sidewalks. Curbs. Gutters. Street signs. All utterly normal.

Then—as if sliced by God's sword—it ended.

There was a swatch of no-man's-land of fine rubble where the Rim divided Earth city from Elfhome forest. A dozen yards beyond that were the tall walls of granite stone that enclosed the elfin communes. A single wide gate allowed access into the enclosure, painted Wind Clan blue.

The puppies lined up behind her, transforming into seasoned war dogs, braced for attack.

Fear roiled in Olivia's stomach, or maybe that was morning sickness. She clamped down on the urge to vomit; throwing up on the doorstep would make a very bad impression. She knocked.

The spyhole opened and blue eyes narrowed at her. Annoyance turned to confusion. They shifted to the line of red-uniformed royal marines. Flicked back to her. Glanced again at the marines with more confusion in them.

"Yes?" the male owner of the eyes said in Elvish.

"I wish to see Tinker *domi*," Olivia replied in the same. "I need some seeds and the Wyverns said I should talk to her."

"F-F-F-Forgiveness." And the slot closed.

What did that mean? No? Tinker wasn't home? Olivia should leave?

Olivia was still debating its meaning when the slot opened again. A new pair of eyes gazed out at her.

"I wish to see Tinker *domi*," Olive repeated in Elvish. "I need some seeds and the Wyverns said I should talk to her."

"Your Elvish sucks," the female owner of the eyes said in a Pittsburgh accent. "Just speak English."

"Oh. Okay," Olivia said in English. "I-I-I was told by the Wyverns that I should get seeds off Tinker *domi*."

"The Wyverns told you to get what?" the female said in confusion. "Seeds?"

"Yes. Seeds. To plant. Keva beans. Rats or something got into mine. I've been combing the city for—"

"Who are you?"

"Olivia—" She caught herself before she used her real last name. "Prince True Flame calls me Olive Branch over Stone. I'm Forest Moss's *domi*."

"When it rains, it pours." The female sighed and undid the gate's lock with a loud clank. "Today is not a good day for a visit, but if the Wyverns sent you, we must receive you."

All the Wyverns that Olivia had met since becoming Forest Moss's *domi* had been tall, red-haired males so alike that they seemed like identical twins. She had only seen the Wind Clan's holy *sekasha*-caste warriors from a distance. Like the Wyverns, they seemed to be made with one mold—tall and dark-haired with deep blue eyes.

The female who opened the door was a *sekasha*, identified by the tattoos on her arms. Olivia wasn't sure if she was one of the Wind Clan warriors; she wasn't stamped out of the same mold as the others. She was fair in coloring with the nearly translucent white skin that pale blonds normally had. She'd dyed her hair the same dark blue as the door. Her eyebrows and eyelashes were darkened with makeup. She wore the same scale armor chest piece as the Wyverns, but hers was dyed blue to match the markings on her arms. Her blue jeans looked handmade.

"I give my word that she will not be harmed," the *sekasha* told the puppies. She pointed firmly at the ground. "Stay."

"Yes, holy one." The puppies bowed as one, completely believing what the female said as the God-spoken truth.

Olivia hoped she could trust the female. The perfect holy warriors were considered above the law. They could kill anyone that they thought needed killing.

Beyond the gate was a small, enclosed garden acting as a second defense against anyone who breeched the front door. There was a foyer into the main building with murder holes hidden in the ceiling and another stout door. No wonder the elves looked at her greenhouse crystal palace and shook their heads.

They stepped through the front door and into sheer chaos. The area seemed as if it normally was a restaurant dining room with a scattering of tables and chairs. For some reason there were dozens of lamps scattered randomly through the room, sometimes as many as three on one table. Food was being laid out on a nearby table, buffet-style, while dirty dishes were being cleared away. The smell of it made Olivia's stomach roil.

Oh, please God, not now. She pressed a hand to her mouth, wishing she had brought a pregnancy lollipop with her. She should have had a snack to hedge off morning sickness. She looked away from the food, trying to find something else to focus on.

In one corner, pictures were taped to a wall and multicolored string had been woven into a haphazard web. Several paper maps had been taped to a neighboring wall with its own collection of pins and string.

Elves of different ages and rank she expected, even the other blue-tattooed *sekasha*. Olivia had heard about the tengu but she hadn't seen any of them before. It surprised her that there were a dozen or so coming and going. Some were taking off in the courtyard beyond the windows, leaping upward while unfurling their massive black wings. Some were arriving with more lamps in hand. Some were foraging for breakfast from the buffet, their wings blocking the rest of the room from her view.

Then the screen of black feathers shifted and she forgot all about her morning sickness.

On the other side of the buffet, there was a knot of people gathered around a large Oriental dragon. She'd heard about it on the radio. The deejays of WESA were telling people not to be alarmed if they spotted the creature; it was considered friendly but could be deadly if provoked. The radio hadn't mentioned that the dragon could talk. It spoke with a deep, breathy voice that rumbled, hummed, and scraped like a cello.

It had a mane that flowed in the air as if the dragon was standing in a high wind. Olivia couldn't tell if it was saying one long word or just never inserted pauses between words. It was a constant stream of syllables interrupted only when it would snatch a tart off the buffet to swallow whole.

"What's is he saying, Riki?" a woman hidden within the knot of tall males asked.

"I'm not sure," one of the tengu men answered, presumably Riki. He wore a black tank top and blue jeans. If it weren't for his wings, he'd look like a normal Japanese man. "I think he's telling me his family tree. Dragon names are really long. It takes about five minutes to say all of Providence's proper name."

"Most my life, the oni were split between two camps," another man said, drawing Olivia's attention. "My father, Lord Tomtom, led the oni assault troops. He oversaw the grunt work of preparing for the upcoming invasion: training the troops, feeding them, housing them, and keeping them hidden. His men were considered fodder; the greater bloods expected them to be slaughtered by the elves during the initial attacks. Lord Tomtom was expected to win by sheer numbers. The other camp was controlled by Lord Yutakajodo, also known as Kajo, which means 'snake.' Something like this box would have gone to him."

Olivia recognized Tommy Chang from her nights working as a whore on Liberty Avenue. He was king of the underworld in Pittsburgh, supposedly running everything from music raves to hoverbike races. She originally heard about him at the bakery, where he sounded harmless enough. She'd been surprised to discover that he also had a stable of prostitutes who worked the streets downtown. The girls that Olivia hung out with had nasty things to say about Tommy Chang, but they had nasty things to say about everyone, especially one another. It was hard not to believe the rumors because he radiated aloof menace, from the tank tops that showed off his muscular arms to the way he stalked down the street.

Olivia stopped believing all the rumors after the third time she'd been told to run to Tommy or his enforcer Babe if she seriously thought a man was going to hurt her. Tommy couldn't be as evil as the street-walkers painted him if he'd protect a total stranger.

Tommy Chang wasn't wearing his normal bandana. It revealed the fact that he had catlike ears instead of human ones. They were covered with black fur, short and sleek on the outside but with tufts of hair on the inside, just like the one black barn cat at the Ranch. The ears rotated to catch different sounds in the room.

One of the most common complaints about Tommy that the Liberty Avenue whores had was that he was cold and aloof. Was Tommy unapproachable because he was half cat? Was Tommy always a cat or had someone made him a cat the way Tinker had been made an elf? Like Forest Moss wanted to make Olivia an elf?

Olivia realized that she was staring and looked away. Now was not the time for an existential crisis. This did explain why Tommy and his people had suddenly disappeared off Liberty Avenue when the Wyverns started to comb the city for hidden oni.

"The tengu were considered part of the assault troops under Lord Tomtom," Riki said while the dragon inhaled several more pastries. "There was a handful of our people that Lord Kajo used as spies but he killed them all a few days prior to Jin Wong's return. We don't know why. They hadn't reported anything about the box. It's possible Kajo knew that they would have rebelled against him once they learned what was within it."

"Kajo is always one step ahead of everyone." Tommy's cat ears laid back in anger. "My father would have otherwise killed him years ago. Lord Tomtom wanted to be sole commander of the Pittsburgh forces and thought he could achieve that by assassination. Kajo danced rings around him. I never knew if I should cheer or be embarrassed."

The hidden woman spoke again. The room seemed to quiet as if everyone paused to hear what she had to say. "Chloe Polanski danced rings around me until I figured out what she was doing and how to get one step ahead of her. She was like Esme and Stormsong. She could see the future. Could Chloe be Kajo?"

Chloe Polanski? The television field reporter?

When Olivia had first arrived on Elfhome, she found work at a bakery. It didn't ask for immigration papers; it couldn't afford to since Pittsburgh had a severe labor shortage. Most of her coworkers had been women living on Elfhome illegally.

It was common knowledge at the bakery that Chloe Polanski was pure evil. Duff Kryskill had a score of horror stories about how badly Polanski had treated his family when his baby sister disappeared. All the bakers knew to avoid talking to her. The reporter would gleefully see them all deported.

It came as no surprise to Olivia that Polanski was part of the oni war force, but clearly she wasn't the leader. She had to be part of the oni intelligence network, gathering information on the elves and humans, spreading misinformation to create tension.

"I don't think so," Tommy said. "Polanski was too young. Kajo was here from the start. I remember her showing up on the news when I was about ten. She aged well but she has gotten noticeably older. It means she's not immortal and would have been born about a decade before the first Shutdown."

"*Domi!*" Olivia's female *sekasha* escort called out. "You have a visitor."

The tall wall of men parted even as the center of the chaos turned its attention on Olivia.

"This is Olive Branch over Stone," her escort introduced Olivia. "Forest Moss has taken her as his *domi*."

"Wolf's child bride," Forest Moss had called Tinker many times and now Olivia understood why. Surrounded by tall elves and the large dragon, Tinker was stunningly tiny. For the minute of stunned silence that followed the introduction, Tinker seemed younger than Olivia.

And then Tinker started to move, and the impression was lost. "Oh fucking hell, no!"

"What is wrong, *domi*?" The *sekasha* started to move between Olivia and Tinker.

The girl smacked them out of her way and bore down on Olivia. The impression of "tiny" vanished.

"How old are you?" Tinker snapped in English.

"Nearly as old as you," Olivia said.

"The hell you are!" Tinker cried. "I'm an adult."

"You're eighteen," Olivia said as calmly as she could.

"This isn't about me," Tinker said. "That crazy old loon—"

"He is not a loon!" Olivia clenched her fist tight. "If you're not going to be civil, I'll talk with your husband."

"I *am* being civil!" Tinker snorted. "'Civil'? Who talks like that?"

"Obviously, I do."

"And you're what? Fourteen?"

"I'm not here to discuss my age," Olivia stated firmly. If Tinker guessed the truth, Olivia wouldn't be able to lie. She needed to put the brakes on the question. "You have no say in what I do with my life, so—" Telling Tinker to shut up would probably be a bad idea.

"Shut the hell up?" Tinker guessed what Olivia hadn't said aloud.

"Something like that," Olivia whispered.

"Did he force you?" Tinker asked.

"I tracked him down and asked him to take me as his *domi*," Olivia said.

"Do you even know what you've signed up for?" Tinker said.

"I was turning tricks on Liberty Avenue," Olivia said. "Trust me, I know exactly what I was proposing."

Tinker turned to glare at Tommy Chang.

"She's not one of mine." He backed away, hands up, ears flattened to his head like a scared cat. "I only do that for my people. Most of them are my cousins."

It was amazing to see the most feared underworld figure in Pittsburgh backing up in panic. Then again, there were six *sekasha* in the room. One female, Olivia noticed, had black tattoos and chest armor instead of blue. Why was she in different colors?

"Why are you here?" Tinker switched back to Elvish.

Olivia wished they could continue in English. It was taxing to verbally spar with the *domi* while translating. It was probable, though, that none of the elves in the room knew English well enough to follow the conversation. Tinker wanted her people to know the reason for Olivia's visit.

"The Wyverns said that I should talk to the Viceroy's *domi*." Olivia swung the phrase around like a sledgehammer. It was her only weapon; it had already gotten her in the door. "I've scoured the city for seeds. I haven't been able to find any."

"Seeds?" Tinker echoed in confusion.

"So I can grow food," Olivia said.

"We're in September already. We'll get a hard frost . . ." Tinker *domi* started to repeat the lines that Olivia already heard over and over.

"I've taken over the Phipps Conservatory!" Olivia was surprised that Tinker *domi* didn't know but then again, the girl had disappeared while Olivia was finding a place to live. Considering all the people coming and going from the enclave, it was only a matter of time before Tinker was up to speed. "It has a huge greenhouse that's fully operational."

"That glass palace?" Tinker said.

It frustrated Olivia that no one had been willing to help her find a place to live but everyone seemed quite willing to criticize her choice. She defended her pick. "There's a fortifiable stone building that will function as our main living area. I have plans on building walls." She needed materials and bricklayers but she could only tackle one thing at a time. Starting the plants growing seemed to be the most pressing need.

"The oni might attack at any time," Tinker plowed

on. "The Phipps is way over on the other side of Oakland. Maybe you can move to Sacred—"

"No," the female *sekasha* in black stated coldly. "I will not allow it."

Tinker squinted at a short male elf who looked much like her. He must be her cousin with the improbable name. What was it again? Oilslick? No. Oilstain? Oilpan? Oilcan? Wait—was he an elf now too?

"I took the kids in," Tinker's cousin whispered in English, "because Thorne didn't want them to be in the same household as Forest Moss."

Olivia glared at the female in black. What a bitch! Forest Moss had lost his eye and everyone he loved when he'd been captured by the oni. After he escaped, he couldn't find anyone who would take him in. He'd spent centuries isolated. The sheer loneliness of it had driven him mad.

Tinker glanced to the shortest, darkest male *sekasha* to her immediate left for advice. "Pony?"

"If the Wyverns sent her here," the male said, "then the Wyverns have seen her set up and approved of it. They would not allow Forest Moss to be exposed to danger."

Olivia winced as that cut close to the bone. She had learned that the Wyverns had debated killing Forest Moss as he ran amok after Ginger Wine's enclave had been leveled. The slaughter of Jewel Tear's *sekasha* had been too close to his own horrific loss. The only value the Wyverns saw in Olivia was her ability to keep Forest Moss calm and rational. That was why she only had royal marines as guards instead of Wyverns. Not that she minded; she didn't want any guards at all. In her own mind, they made her more of a target.

"Who might have some seeds?" Tinker bounced in place as if hopping up and down would jar loose ideas. "The stores only stock them at the end of spring because most people order online from places on Earth. Pittsburghers like the Burpee brand because they're based in Pennsylvania, which is as close as you're going to get to Pittsburgh's growing season. People order seeds in January. They're delivered during the February Shutdown. Most of the greenhouses are unheated, cobbled together from windows torn out of abandoned houses. Not a lot of people have the money to do a sophisticated automated system like what the Phipps has. Doing it all by hand takes a lot of time and knowledge and some way to keep the greenhouse warm all winter."

"You know what kind of system the Phipps has?" Olivia asked in surprise. She had gotten the impression that the place had been abandoned for decades. It certainly looked it. Most of the plants were still alive, though, thanks to an automatic watering system.

"Lain took me there a couple of times to fix some of its automated systems. She's been in Pittsburgh since the first Startup. She had wanted to set up her operation at the Phipps, but at the time the city wouldn't allow her to take it over. By the time they closed down, she had her own greenhouses designed to deal with Elfhome's ecosystem. She's been trying to work through the EIA to set up an Earth-based trust to take over the building. It hasn't been going well, probably because of all the oni moles within the EIA. Lain didn't want the plants to die off, so she's been keeping an eye on the buildings since they closed the Conservatory. It's solar powered but I think she covers the water bills. She has it set up so the university heats it in the winter via the Oakland steam tunnel system."

The Conservatory didn't sound as abandoned as Olivia had been led to believe. It explained how so many of the plants were still alive. Olivia hoped that this "Lain" wouldn't fight her for possession of the Phipps if the woman had her own greenhouses elsewhere.

"Does this Lain have seeds?" Olivia asked.

Tinker winced. "She planted all her keva beans and is guarding them with a big gun. A very big gun. She is a xenobiologist; she studies the 'alien' life of Elfhome. She collects things like strangle vines and black willows, not your run-of-the-mill garden plants. Her florae are the 'it eats you' type, not the 'you eat it' kind. She planted her beans earlier this summer." Tinker cocked her head as if something new occurred to her. "Huh. It probably does not bode well that Lain thinks that she will need the crop to get through winter. We should probably do something about getting more food shipped in from the Easternlands."

"Yes, *domi*." Pony took the comment as a command. He lifted a hand to summon a female *laedin* warrior to him.

Tinker continued, seemingly unaware that she had triggered action. "The shelf life for most seeds is between two to five years, if they're stored in a cool, dry place. It's possible that people have seeds leftover from the spring planting. If anyone has seeds, though, they're probably not going to give them up, especially after the train derailment. I had the keva shipment passed out early for free so that anyone with a greenhouse could start growing food immediately. Yes, we'll have a hard frost in a month or so, but with an unheated greenhouse cobbled together from recycled windows, the plants should be safe into December. I thought it would go far to calm people."

It had been the keva bean handout that had made Olivia realize Tinker *domi* had catapulted from hover-bike racer to something more than just a trophy wife. Tinker's position as Windwolf's "consort" carried a great deal of influence. Olivia hadn't realized all the implications when she tracked Forest Moss down in a bid for similar power. Obviously, she still had much to learn.

Tinker had paused to think. "Did I remember to do anything with those DIY greenhouse plans I drew up?"

The vicereine asked the room at large. All of the tengu in the room nodded and looked to Riki to be their voice.

"I had our people set up a website," Riki said. Forest Moss had told Olivia that the entire tengu Flock was now beholden to Tinker. It hadn't dawned on Olivia until this moment that it gave Tinker a work force of twenty thousand individuals. "Anyone that needs the information can download your plans. We also added some information on soil preparation, planting, watering, and the like. KDKA, WQED and WESA have been broadcasting public service announcements that give the URL. The website has had several thousand hits since the PSAs started."

Tinker waved a hand to indicate that "yes" would have been enough. "Sorry, Riki. The last week or so has been sketchy. Spells healed my broken arm in a matter of days but I kept falling asleep mid-thought and then having the weirdest dreams."

Riki gave a slight bow. "Understood."

Olivia's blue-haired escort shifted forward. "*Domi*, we can use the distant voices to order seeds from the Clan leader, Longwind. It could be counted as part of Forest Moss's 'room and board' since he isn't being housed in one of our enclaves."

Tinker nodded. "Please, Stormsong, can you make that happen?"

The female bowed and left.

Tinker waved off an incoming tengu bearing another lamp. "Enough with the lamps, we're going to start blowing fuses. Riki, can you keep pumping Impatience; see what he can tell you about Little Miss Pocket. I want everything about that box that he might know. It was plain stupid luck that the oni haven't used it yet. We can't count on them delaying even a day longer. The game of hide-and-seek that they've been playing is over now that the Harbingers are here. They need to strike soon or they're going to lose their big advantage against us."

The chaos made sense to Olivia now; Tinker was going to war. This was her command room. She was gathering information to decide on her next action. She was being a *domi*. Olivia felt like a pale shadow.

Tinker turned back to Olivia. "Look, I know you can't have any idea what you've gotten into because I'm still learning and I've been at this for months." Much to Olivia's relief, Tinker had slipped back into English. Her relief was short-lived as Tinker pointed hard at Olivia. "I don't know where you came from or how you got onto Elfhome or why you're here. It really doesn't matter. What matters is that every elf in Pittsburgh now sees you as a general in the middle of a very ugly war. For better or worse, I'm considered an elf, because once upon a time, my family were elves. If I screw up, it's on the Wind Clan's shoulders. If you screw up, it *could* be marked against all the humans because, strictly speaking, you're still human. You cannot think of just yourself. If you do anything that could be considered treason, you could accidently kill every human man, woman, and child in this city."

"I find that unlikely," Olivia said calmly despite the sudden urge to vomit. She sidled over to the breakfast bar to see if there was any toast to quell her stomach.

"Have you been paying attention to what is going on in this city for the last few months?" Tinker pointed westward. "I found out today that I totally missed fish monsters attacking Downtown! Do you know how messed up things have to be that no one thought to tell me about fifty-foot-long, walking catfish throwing around lightning bolts? I apparently also missed an attack on Oktoberfest and a train derailment. Why? Because I was busy falling off the planet, hijacking spaceships, fighting dragons, and all sorts of other bullshit! This is the life you just opted into! The bad guys grabbed elf kids younger than you off the streets, tortured them, raped them, beat them to death, and then cooked and ate their bodies. We don't even know how many were killed because there's nothing left of them but roasted cracked bones."

Olivia was going to hurl. She grabbed a pastry that looked like a biscotti and shoved it into her mouth. It was fire berry. The unexpected spicy cinnamon sweetness helped distract Olivia from her roiling stomach.

Luckily Tinker had sidetracked herself. "Someone contact Brotherly Love. See if there are any more

Stone Clan kids that got stuck there when the train derailed. We want to make sure those kids stay safe. Once all this has ended—if it ends well—they can continue here and we'll figure something out."

"Yes, *domi*." A male elf bowed and left to carry out her orders.

"There are some whores missing too," Tommy Chang added quietly. "The ones that work downtown on Liberty Avenue."

Tinker turned her attention to king of the underworld. "Do the police know?"

"I doubt it," Tommy admitted uneasily. "The missing kids are all off-worlders. They don't have family to keep tabs on them."

Like Olivia had been. No one would notice them falling through the cracks. Certainly no one probably had noticed that she had stopped showing up, except the few hookers she walked Liberty Avenue with.

"We can't let anyone fall between the cracks just because they're here alone," Tinker said. "Human. Elf. Tengu. Half-oni. It doesn't matter. We need to watch out for everyone. We need to stick together. Things are going to get ugly fast."

Everyone nodded as if they'd been issued marching orders.

Tinker pointed at Olivia. "Look, there's lots of ins and outs of elf society I know that you don't have a clue about. The important one is that you gave your word to Forest Moss to be his *domi*. It's like getting married but more so. You've agreed to be part of all the craziness. You've made yourself part of the elf society. You've given your word. You need to keep it."

❖   ❖   ❖

The royal marines played games when they were idle. The similarity to the games that Olivia played on the Ranch surprised her. They had lengths of string to play cat's cradle, pieces of chalk for a game like hopscotch, knucklebone dice, and small bean-filled bags to kick around like a hacky sack. They'd gotten bored waiting for Olivia; all their toys were out. They had posted lookouts at the cardinal points, thus Ox spotted Olivia first as she came out of the enclave.

"Chi-chi-chi!" Ox called, trying to untie his hands from a cat's cradle. It was a noise that the marines made when they were surprised. "Dagger!"

"She's back!" Dagger kicked the hacky sack high in the air and caught it. The tall female acted as the group leader even though, as far as Olivia could tell, she had no higher rank than the others. "Fall in!"

Ox shoved his string into his pocket. Rage snatched up her dice. Dart found his cap that had fallen to the ground. Coal picked up the chalk that had marked out the hopscotch board. With a good deal of breathless laughing and shoving, the twenty marines fell into line.

The marines were all *laedin*-caste, a term Olivia hadn't learned until she came to Pittsburgh. Her online homeschool Elvish class never mentioned the caste system that was so important to the elves. *Laedin* were the warhorses of the race, bred to be big and strong and enjoy competitive games. Olivia was tall for a human girl, the tallest girl on the Ranch, but the marines all towered over her another foot. They were from the Fire Clan, so they were uniformly red-haired and green-eyed. They tended to be more strawberry blond to copper red than her auburn color.

She had just spent the last few days trying to ignore

them and failing as they had constantly asked her questions about everything new and strange to them. Against her will, she'd learned all twenty of their names and the personalities of the most outspoken ones. At first she thought they asked her questions because she was there—helpless to escape their demands. After meeting with Tinker *domi*, though, she realized that it was much more like them seeking answers from a commanding officer.

From offhand comments that Forest Moss and the Wyverns who guarded him said, Olivia had pieced together that the royal marines that made up her guard were all very young in elf terms. The average age of the elves guarding her was ninety-six years old; they were approximately teenagers. She hadn't put any weight on this information because it seemed that no matter how you looked at it, they were still older than her human age of sixteen. They had decades of combat training, and seemed to have casual sex with one another right and left.

The marines might be older than her in every possible way but there was something oddly innocent about them. They dealt with her and all the humans in the city with open curiosity, without a shred of suspicion. They trusted that their leaders would provide. Would make the correct choices. Lead with wisdom.

Olivia had had all her innocence systematically ground out of her since she was eleven. Her mother had dragged her away from everyone she knew and loved in Boston and taken her to an isolated Kansas ranch run by selfish misogynists who twisted the word of God to suit their own bigoted views of the world. When Olivia ran away and called her father, she found out her "parents" weren't who she thought they were. Her "god-fearing" mother had gotten pregnant by a passing stranger and then refused to marry the man that she moved in with. Her dad was her father only in Olivia's eyes. He wasn't willing to face both the heavily armed religious bigots and the United States legal system to rescue her. Nor was his family—Pap-pap, Grammy, and Aunty June. When the police caught Olivia shoplifting food, they returned her to the Ranch without even checking on her claims that underaged girls were being forced into polygamous marriages to older men.

The second time she ran away, she put an entire universe between her and the man that she'd been forced to marry at fifteen. Getting to Elfhome had been only slightly harder than escaping the Ranch with enough money to reach Pennsylvania safely.

"Where to now?" Dagger asked.

Where indeed?

Since arriving in Pittsburgh, she had focused on her baby. It was the only reason she had sought out Forest Moss. She was worried about his well-being but even the mission to find seeds had been about her baby's future.

Before she used her position to take over the Phipps, she had forced her way into the Cathedral of Learning to squat in one of its opulent Nationality Rooms. The Dean had come and tried to talk her into leaving. The woman had warned Olivia that being Forest Moss's *domi* didn't make her the equal of Tinker. Windwolf was the Viceroy and head of the Wind Clan in Pittsburgh.

Olivia heeded the warning, perhaps too well. She

fled the Cathedral, taking refuge at the Phipps only because it seemed abandoned.

"The bad guys grabbed elf kids younger than you off the streets," Tinker had said. *"We don't even know how many were killed because there's nothing left of them but roasted cracked bones."*

Since becoming Forest Moss's *domi*, Olivia hadn't given a thought to any of the women that she'd called "friends." Not her young and naïve Irish anthropology student neighbor, Aiofe, who helped her move into the empty house on Mt. Washington. Aiofe had been stranded on Elfhome after the gate fell, cut off from her family. Not the prostitute Peanut Butter Pie, who had helped Olivia learn how to turn tricks on Liberty Avenue. Peanut could be one of the missing whores. Not the other illegal immigrant women who worked at the bakery and treated Olivia like a little sister. They probably had been let go the same time that Olivia was.

It was one thing to be selfishly focused on her own needs when it was just her, alone on a new world with only the clothes on her back. It was another when she had a hidden fortune of elf gold and a platoon of royal marines at her beck and call. She had been aware that being Forest Moss's *domi* changed her status. Hadn't she squatted in the Cathedral? Faced down the Dean of the University? Marched up to the enclave and demanded to see the Wind Clan *domi* as an equal?

She had sought out Forest Moss for the power that being *domi* would give her. Tinker was using her power to protect everyone in the city, even the prostitutes. Olivia had a responsibility to do the same.

6: MONSTERS IN OUR MIDST

❖⇒◉⇐❖

Jane Kryskill stared at her phone, willing it to be silent.

She was in the middle of a rare production meeting at WQED for her team's new television show: *Monsters in Our Midst*. In June, they had put *Pittsburgh Backyard and Garden* on hiatus to focus on the new show. Outwardly, the two shows were nearly identical: Hal Rogers discussed how to safely deal with Pittsburgh's dangerous monsters. The emphasis had been shifted from "natural" monsters like strangle weed to bioengineered weapons of war like the wargs. It was such a small change that most people didn't pick up on it. The new format also helped to secretly organize their viewers into a trained militia willing to protect their city against the oni invasion. Every episode, Hal would sing the praises of some resident who came forward to help him eliminate the oni-borne threat, calling them "Hal's Heroes." He would gift them with a blue boonie hat. Jane's family sold Hal's Heroes merchandise as a way to scout for potential militia members, who were then set up in spy cells so that despite their loose recruiting method, a strike against the militia wouldn't uncover all the members.

No one at WQED had been told about the show's real agenda. Her coworkers might guess, but if asked they could honestly say that they knew nothing about the militia's activities.

The deception had made Jane uneasy; she didn't like lying to friends and coworkers. But then she found out that reporter Chloe Polanski had been working as an oni spy. She knew that Polanski had the morals of a snake but Jane hadn't known how low the woman had sunk. Nor could she be sure that Chloe worked alone. Pittsburgh's three television stations were logical targets of any convert activity. There was no way Jane could be sure that WQED didn't have its own infestation of oni spies.

Jane's phone had just vibrated with a call from her little brother, Duff, that she couldn't answer. Duff ran the communication hub for their covert militia. He could be calling with anything as trivial as yet another glitch to her impending wedding or as important as a warning that heavily armed oni forces were spilling into the city.

If it was about her wedding, he wouldn't call a second time. He would wait for her to return his call. If her phone rang a second time, it was a life-or-death emergency. Duff knew that nothing short of an oni offensive—not even her seemingly cursed wedding—was more vital than keeping the show on the air and running smoothly. The fate of Pittsburgh might balance on the militia that they were building behind the façade of *Monsters in Our Midst*. Her boss, Dmitri Vassiliev, was hands-off since *MiOM* had proved as successful as *PB&G* but he had a strict "no cell phones at meetings" policy. Even Jane could not break the rule; she was broadly skirting it just having her phone out.

Not that the "production meeting" was being very productive. Somebody had put "Jane's wedding" on the conference room schedule board. Nor did it help that someone else—most likely multiple people—had decorated it. She suspected the entire art department had been involved—partly because of the quality of the work, but mostly because of the massive quantity of the art. The pictures had been printed onto paper and tacked beside the board with sticky putty until they covered the entire wall. There were wedding bells, churches, hearts, ribbons, roses, cupids, and an odd assortment of "romantic pairings." There was a very swoon-worthy drawing of her fiancé, Keaweaheulu Ka'ihikapu Taggart, as a bare-chested Tarzan and a "Jane" with a yellow Victorian gown and a sniper rifle. Another had a scruffy "Aragorn" Taggart and Jane as a blond Arwen. There were a handful of other pairings that Jane didn't recognize but they were obviously from some popular fantasy work. (The art department folks were all romantic-minded geeks.)

Hal was being Hal because the schedule board was there, reminding him in the most romantic of ways that Jane wasn't marrying him. At the moment, Hal was standing on the conference room table, demonstrating his new toy: a bullwhip.

"I had one of these in grad school," Hal was saying, making it crack loudly. "I went full-on Indiana Jones: bullwhip, safari shirt, brown fedora. UC-Davis took the whip away from me; the students were complaining. I don't know why. The archeologists shouldn't be the only ones to get to have fun!" Hal pretended to be

addressing an undergraduate student. "Cytosine! Gua-
nine! Adenine! Thymine!" Hal cracked the whip at his
imaginary student with each scientific term. "If you want
to call yourself a biologist, you need to know the basics!"

Dmitri was holding up a chair like a lion tamer.
"Sit!" he commanded. "Sit!"

There was a reason that their production meetings
were rare. (Jane was letting Hal keep the bullwhip
in favor of the box of dynamite she had confiscated
and stashed with her cousin, Roach. Where was Hal
getting his endless supply of explosives?) Hal's chaos,
at least, was keeping anyone from noticing that Jane
had checked her phone.

Could Jane get up and walk out of the meeting to
find some place more private to call Duff? Everyone
from station manager down to head of accounting was
crowded into the conference room with her but nothing was getting done, not with Hal trying to prove . . .
something . . . with the bullwhip.

Jane looked at the meeting's agenda memo. They
had already covered all preproduction issues for their
next six episodes including budget concerns. All they
really needed to do was make delivery of rough-cut
video for the upcoming episode and discuss a handful
of postproduction details. It shouldn't be too harm-
ful if Jane slipped away. Hal ignored mundane work
issues, using his position of "star" to skip anything
that could be boring. Could she trust Taggart and
Nigel to cover for her?

Taggart was working on his laptop, ignoring Hal's
insanity. His ability to generate a pocket of calm in
the middle of chaos was one of the many things that
she loved about him. They were running behind on

the rough cut as every frame needed to be checked to make sure they hadn't included anything that gave away their many secrets. Taggart had a video editor open in one window but in the other he was answering an email. Jane's mother had discovered Taggart paid more attention to the fine details of their wedding than Jane did. Her mother called it "getting the groom's input" but mostly it gave her plausible deniability if she forgot to ask Jane about something truly important. Jane hated to dump yet more of her responsibilities onto Taggart but she supposed that was part and parcel of getting married. (Every day she discovered new joys of marriage—the only downside so far was the actual event.)

Nigel was patting his pockets and glancing at the floor in an out-of-character air of alarm.

"What's wrong?" Jane asked.

"I've seemed to have lost my snake." Nigel looked under the table, making everyone sitting at the table push back from it as an Elfhome-honed defensive mechanism kicked into overdrive.

"Snake?" asked the head of Accounting, Joe McGreevy. He was a big man with a Neanderthal-like response to snakes: grab the nearest item and use it to club any snakelike object to death. The clubbing usually only stopped once both snake and club were reduced to pulp. Everyone in the room edged away from Joe, taking their belongings with them.

"What snake?" Dmitri said in a tone of voice that seemed like he was afraid that he'd heard correctly but was hoping otherwise.

"I found the most beautiful snake out in the car park. I was afraid he'd get run over, so I put him in my pocket. Just a little thing."

Hal paused, whip cocked. "Banded with red and black and yellow?"

"The very one!" Nigel cried, sounding like a British schoolboy. "Yes, I know it was most likely venomous with those colors, but it was such a wee thing!"

That triggered a sudden exodus from the room with the exception of her team and Dmitri. Taggart didn't look up from his laptop but changed to sitting cross-legged on the table.

Dmitri put down the chair and stood on it. "This changes nothing. We still need your rough footage for next week's show so that we can start producing promotional material and music score." Dmitri worked his way across the room, going from chair seat to chair seat in a version of "the floor is lava." He paused at the door once he was safely in the hallway. "You are not to leave this room until that snake is found and contained. And keep it away from Accounting."

Snake wrangling was not one of Jane's skills. Pittsburgh had a few poisonous snakes, most of them rattlesnakes and their Elfhome cousins. She'd never encountered any brightly colored ones but she wasn't a naturalist. She joined Taggart on the table while Hal and Nigel looked for the snake. "Is it deadly, Hal?"

"Possibly." Hal lapsed in to host mode. "There are sixty-five recognized species of coral snake on Earth. Those in North America have the most dangerous venom found on the continent. Their bite contains a powerful neurotoxin that paralyzes the breathing muscles—so they can be deadly. There are also multiple nonpoisonous species that mimic the coral snake's coloration as protection from predators, such as the red milk snake. Coral snakes are quite reclusive and non-aggressive, so there are very few recorded bites on Earth. It tends to be a warmer clime breed but I've been hoping for one to show in Pittsburgh so we could compare the Elfhome species to Earth ones."

"Whatever." Jane shook her head. Naturalists! She was glad that she'd left Chesty at the motor pool, guarding her SUV. Her big elfhound would have insisted on joining the hunt. "Find the snake."

She called Duff. "I'm clear. What's up?"

"Yumiko tracked Alton down this morning to rake him over the coals: Hal's name came up in an emergency meeting between Jin Wong and Tinker *domi*. Yumiko wanted to know about finding a box in pieces after a gunfight at the Carnegie." Duff raised the pitch of his voice slightly to mimic Yumiko. "*Why hadn't yinz told the tengu about it*?"

Jane doubted that Yumiko used the Pittsburgh slang of "yinz" for "you guys," but the sentiment was probably correct.

Duff dropped his voice back to normal. "Alton called me since he didn't know. What shoot-out at the museum? Does she mean Nigel's baby-dragon box? Did you find that?"

Did Jane not tell her family about the shoot-out? It happened a week after July's shutdown—back when Sparrow was still alive and second-in-command of the elves. It seemed like a lifetime ago. Two little girls— known to Nigel only as Lemon-Lime JEl-Lo—had somehow crashed a ritzy party in New York City to give Nigel a magical whistle. The girls weren't alone; they had a baby dragon with them. Lemon-Lime told Nigel about a box filled with other baby dragons and then warned him that Sparrow was an oni double agent.

Jane hadn't wanted to believe the information but Lemon-Lime had made a cartoon of Jane's fight with a saurus—months before it happened. There was no denying that the whistle worked; Jane's team used it on the *namazu*. Somehow these little girls on Earth were magical geniuses who *knew* the future.

What's more, Jane had had an odd conversation with Tooloo. The elf talked about playing poker with children. Tooloo's coded message seemed to be that Nigel and Taggart were "cards" being played by Lemon-Lime in a dangerous game against other people who could "see" the future. To seal the deal, "an anonymous female" called the EIA with wildly specific details of what was about to happen at the museum, and then, from halfway around the world, Queen Soulful Ember had gotten a message to the Wind Clan to intercede on behalf of Jane's team. While it seemed to indicate that the queen's oracle, Pure Radiance, and Tooloo were two "poker players" helping Jane's team, the question became who else was playing? Normally you needed five to seven people to play the game correctly. Did Lemon-Lime count as one player or two? Did the oni have people who could see the future?

To protect Lemon-Lime, Nigel hadn't told Yumiko about the box, only Jane and her family. He had already done some legwork on tracking the box: the official report on Earth was that the curator accompanying the museum pieces had vanished on Elfhome during the June Shutdown. Jane and her team had gone to the Carnegie just to double-check that the box hadn't arrived after Startup. What they found was a horde of oni disguised as humans.

Jane thought that her family knew about the shootout at the museum. Hal had blown up part of the Hall of Architecture during the fight. It had been on the news—hadn't it? Actually, now that she thought about, no reporters had shown up at the museum as Maynard had personally debriefed them. Windwolf had done something newsworthy while searching for his bride; all the local reporters had been in the South Hills covering the Viceroy. Maynard might have put a lid on the information because of the queen's rare and odd intercession.

Jane glanced at Hal; he and Nigel were carefully peering under the credenza across the room. She lowered her voice and explained why the shoot-out slipped her mind. "That was the day that Hal found out about the wedding."

"Ahhh." Duff made sounds of understanding the problem. "You got distracted by Hal going ballistic."

"Yup." Jane explained to Duff in quiet tones how her team ended up in a fight at the museum. They were rescued from the oni via the arrival of the Elfhome Interdimensional Agency. They were then saved from being arrested for blowing up parts of the museum by a message from Queen Soul Ember. The short note—arriving via one of the holy *sekasha* warriors—reminded Director Derek Maynard that the treaty had made the museum property of the crown. "The queen gave us free run of the place. We found parts of the box in the woodshop but nothing of the baby dragons or the eggs that they were in. I didn't consider it as 'finding' anything. All we managed to do was verify what we already suspected: Sparrow had gotten the box to her oni masters. We just put more dots on the line. I would have thought that the tengu spy network would have connected those dots before now."

Duff laughed. "I got the impression that Yumiko knew about the shoot-out but bought whatever official statement you gave the EIA. Something about filming that scary-ass wyvern they got strung up?"

"Something like that." Jane had lied so much that week that she'd lost track of everything she said. She would have stuck as close to the truth as possible. She probably did blame their presence on the wyvern. Nigel had been struck speechless by it.

"Yumiko let something slip," Duff said. "Although I don't think she's connected all the dots. Lemon-Lime is in town."

"What?" Jane snapped in surprise.

Duff explained that the emergency meeting with Tinker *domi* had been focused on the baby dragons inside the missing box. The female *yamabushi* had let slip that the tengu had learned of the box when some Nestlings and "other children" suddenly arrived from Earth with a tiny dragon named Joy. "Given how Yumiko talked about dragons in the past, the chances of being more than one tiny dragon teamed up with a bunch of kids seems unlikely."

Tooloo had made it sound like the new player at the dangerous poker game had just arrived.

"Okay," Jane said slowly. "That doesn't change much. Yeah, we found the box but it was empty. The egg thingies inside were what was important. The trail went cold at the museum. We searched the whole place, top to bottom."

"Maybe," Duff said. Jane could hear him typing on a keyboard. "The Carnegie runs on human tech, not oni magic. I'm going try to get people in to see if there's any computers still have any stray usable information on them."

Jane doubted it. They'd gone through the director's office and the woman—oni—whatever—had been a sticky-note kind of person. There was a rainbow of little squares littering every surface, all with cryptic comments. They'd taken pictures of everything and pored over the notes later. They hadn't found anything that suggested where the box's contents had been moved to. "Give it a whirl."

"Will do," Duff said.

"Is that it?" Jane prepared to hang up.

"You're going to want to call Mom," Duff said. "She's on the warpath about something. Bye!"

Taggart must have overheard that part as he nodded and murmured, "We lost the band."

"Oh no! Why?" Jane cried. Carl Moser had been best friends with her younger brother Geoffrey all through elementary and high school. He'd started an elf fusion-rock band with a mix of human and elf artists and set up an enclave-styled commune in the Strip District. Unbeknownst to her mother and other brothers, Geoffrey had been dating the band's male elf drummer, but that was a whole other kettle of fish. Jane had picked Moser's band to play at her wedding because she could trust him and his band mates to keep their mouths shut if any of the family's dangerous secrets—tengu involvement, resistance leadership, rescued baby sister, yadayadayada—slipped out during the wedding. Replacing Moser's band would be a matter more complicated than just finding a group of people who could play instruments together.

"We locked them in months ago!" Jane cried. "Oh, Moser is dead meat if he pulls out on my mom."

Taggart shrugged in ignorance or acceptance of Moser's fate.

Jane growled with frustration. She hated being the center of attention as it usually meant that she had lost control of a life-or-death situation.

If Jane had had her way, she would have married Taggart in July. Pittsburgh kept the Pennsylvanian law that required a three-day waiting period. They could have gone to the Frick Building on Grant Street and gotten married at the weirdly named Orphans' Court. She and Taggart had to go there to apply for the marriage license anyhow.

But her mother had spent twenty-six years dreaming of a huge blowout wedding for her daughter. Her mother wanted all the bells and whistles. The fancy wedding invitations on linen paper, engraved with charcoal ink, with a square of tissue to protect the type. The calligraphy addresses printed by hand on the outer envelopes. The white dress with the full train (ordered for her mother's wedding but never used and carefully kept in tissue paper for the day that Jane could wear it.) A full church service. An elaborate reception with tons of flowers and cookies and booze and a live band. Jane hated the whole thing because she would be center stage from the moment she walked down the aisle to the first dance.

She needed to live with her mother, though, so she had compromised on a small wedding held on the last weekend before Taggart's visa expired. The fact that they had little more than two months to plan the wedding made it seem as if they could skip many of the embarrassing bells and whistles.

Life had other plans.

Things started to go wrong immediately. Another couple had already claimed the Kryskill family's church for that date. Jane suggested that they just have the ceremony at Hyeholde, seamlessly going from wedding to reception, but her mother insisted on a church. After days of frantic searching, her mother begged her way into a Russian Orthodox church. The onion-domed cathedral sat in an abandoned section of Homestead, ironically not far from Sandcastle Water Park.

The ceremony location finally secured, they could have the invitations printed. The printing company that her family normally used had had a car dropped on it during the Veterans Bridge shoot-out in June. Their fallback printer seemed to have a death wish, dragging out the normal hour-long decision process into a week of back-and-forth phone calls. It didn't have cardstock for Jane's first three choices—but it took an entire day to verify that for each selection. After Jane had picked out a fourth choice, the printer kept putting holds on the print run as they checked and rechecked that they were spelling everyone's name correctly. (Any company with the name of Kolodziejski Kwikie Print shouldn't complain about Aheahe, Elikapeka, and Keaweaheulu Ka'ihikapu Taggart.) Jane had been seriously worried her mother would firebomb the company and start over with a new printer.

Then Tinker *domi* dropped an orbital gate on Jane's wedding plans. The entire visa problem for both Taggart and Nigel had been instantly rendered moot. At that point it seemed saner to just push back the date of the wedding to when the Kryskill family church was free.

Jane had regretted the choice since the moment she agreed to it. It had given her mother more time to get more extravagant and more time for things to go wrong.

"There! See? In that crack?" Hal lay on the floor, shining his phone's flashlight under the credenza.

"Oh, yes, there's my beauty." Nigel was in a slightly more cautious pose but right there beside Hal in terms of danger.

Much as Jane didn't want to talk to her mother, she couldn't in good conscience leave the conference room until the snake was caught. "Do not get bit!" she ordered the two naturalists as she dialed her mother's phone number.

"Jane!" Her mother answered the phone with the joy generated by the planning one of her children's massive flashy wedding.

"I just got off the phone with Duff. He said you wanted to talk to me . . . ?"

"Elliot is trying not to let it show, but Elliot is really feeling blue about being left out of the wedding. I had a thought, if we double up the wedding party size, no one will notice one or two stray people."

Jane had been braced for a rant against Carl Moser. "What? Who is Elli . . . Oh!"

The oni warlord, Kajo, had kidnapped Jane's baby sister, Carla Marie—generally called Boo by everyone— and transformed her into a tengu of the Chosen bloodline. He planned to use her as a tool to control the tengu Flock. It was only by luck and daring that Jane managed to finally find and rescue Boo in July. They'd kept Boo secret from everyone—even extended family—in fear that Kajo might try to steal Boo back.

Duff created daily code words for the family to use when discussing Boo, just in case the oni were monitoring their cell phones. "Elliot" was today's codeword for Boo.

In July and most of August, it had been unthinkable that Boo could be involved in the wedding as the tengu had been still enslaved by the oni. Tinker *domi*, however, had performed miracles and now it *might* be safe for Boo to attend the wedding. The place was going to be crawling with good-looking blond people once you counted all Jane's aunts, cousins, and kids. Could Boo be part of the wedding party? Center stage of the entire long ceremony? Jane had serious doubts.

Her mother obviously hoped that if Jane's wedding party was larger, they could slip Boo into the mix without anyone noticing. "You have your uncle standing in for your father, but it's not right to leave your siblings out of the most important day of your life. You have five brothers. They should be part of the wedding party. And what about Hal? His nose is already out of joint over you picking Taggart over him."

If they added Hal and her five brothers on top of Taggart and Nigel as his best man, the male side of the wedding party would jump to eight. Sixteen people. Good God, what a circus.

Jane wanted to say no but she didn't want to hurt Boo's feelings. "Mom, the wedding is in two weeks!"

Her mom plowed on. "We're already renting tuxedoes for your brothers. I've got enough of that dusty rose fabric to make six more dresses. I've lined up a team of dressmakers. I've talked to Julia, Cora, and Ina already and they've said yes. That will give us six counting you and Brandy. We just need two more

women—preferably ones that your cousins don't know.
As soon as possible."

"What about Rachel?" Jane asked since her mom
had only named three of her four first cousins.

"Rachel is in Mercy Hospital with preeclampsia."
Her mother used the tone of voice that indicated that
her mom believed she had told Jane this more than
once. She might have or she might have emailed Taggart and he hadn't passed the information on yet. Jane
had been tuning out the wedding stuff. "She might be
having the baby on the day of the wedding. I really
hope not, I want all of my sisters to be there. I'm
going to need them for damage control."

"Okay. Rachel is a no-go. Wait." The numbers didn't
add up. They would need six women to balance her
five brothers and Hal. Her mother had only recruited
three of her cousins. "Don't I need three more?"

"Elliot and two others."

"Oh, yes. Okay." Boo would be one of the three
girls. Two would still be impossible. Jane's father had
died when she was twelve, just days after Boo was
born. It left Jane as a semi-parent to her five younger
brothers. It had also made her impatient with typical
high school drama. She knew what real-life problems
looked like. It wasn't getting a date to the dance but
trying to cope with a two-year-old who was grieving
for his dead father at three a.m.

Her attitude hadn't made her popular in high school.
Her friends were mostly girls like Brandy Lyn Pomeroy-
Brooks-Abernethy who had their own life problems that
gave them similar outlooks. Others like Cesia Cwik-
linski . . . Jane was never sure why she was friends with
Cesia beyond the rule of opposites attract.

"Mom! I already asked Brandy to be my maid of honor. CC is pissed off that I didn't ask her. She says we made some weird vow back in junior high school to be each other's maid of honor. I don't remember it. Frankly, I think she's confusing me with someone else. I'm fairly sure I never thought about wedding parties until July. Whatever—Cesia isn't talking to me. Brandy will not give up the spot either, not to CC. You know how competitive they are with each other."

"What about what's-her-name? You and Brandy and CC went to the prom together with her? I still can't believe that all the boys in your class were too afraid of the four of you to ask any of you out."

"Mel? She moved Stateside! Most of the girls in my class went off to college and didn't come back. I don't know any other women! I've been too busy since high school doing *Pittsburgh Backyard and Garden* to make new friends. The wedding is in two weeks! Who wants to go to a stranger's wedding with that short a notice?"

"Oh, Jane, don't be so dramatic. We're talking about half of the population of the city. Surely you know someone who will bite the bullet for you. Just find two more women that your cousins won't know and we can trust. Ask them to be your bridesmaids. We can slip Elliot in opposite to Guy and no one will question it."

Like hell people wouldn't! They hadn't told anyone in their extended family that Jane had found Boo. The minute her cousins saw Boo, though, they would recognize her. Boo was a young woman instead of a child, but she had the same halo of curly white-blond hair. Jane was going to have to tell her cousin

Roach since he'd spent most of the summer putting his neck on the line for her. Roach had loaned her use of his boat, volunteered to run the merchandise end of Hal's Heroes, and was currently babysitting a crate of dynamite.

"Open up, let me see what you have in your mouth," Hal murmured quietly. He was kneeling beside the credenza with a small striped snake in hand. The "wee thing" looked only slightly bigger than a ballpoint pen. "Winner, winner, chicken dinner!"

In Hal-talk, it meant that the snake was venomous.

"Hal!" Jane snapped. "Get that into some kind of cage!"

The naturalists set off in search of a secure container, snake in hand.

"What does he have?" her mother asked.

"A cute deadly snake that Nigel carried into the building in his pants pocket." Jane snapped her fingers and indicated that Taggart should follow. The collective common sense of the naturalists was about on par with a five-year-old.

Her mother sighed. "Boys and their trouser snakes."

"Mom!" What was she saying to her mother? "I don't have a lot of friends. I've really focused on my job for the last eight years."

"Which was not entirely a good thing," her mother said. "I'm sure, though, you have more friends than you realize. Just ask some of the girls at WQED. You'll need to hurry, though, we only have a few days to get their dresses made. Call me with their dress sizes."

Her mother said goodbye and hung up while Jane was trying to figure out some sane answer.

There were certain things that Jane knew was fact.

Her mother had spent twenty-six years dreaming of Jane's wedding. Having been married shortly before her own husband was shipped off to war, her mother didn't see the oni menace as an excuse not to celebrate the day. She would move hell and high water to make sure it was perfect. She would not be stopped. Anyone who got in her way would pay dearly.

To keep peace in the family, Jane needed to call her cousins and let them know the truth. But first, she needed to find two women she could trust not to betray her family's secrets.

There were plenty of women at WQED. In theory, Jane knew everyone who worked for the station. She'd started as a production assistant eight years ago. She could walk through the building and name all her female coworkers. Courtney. Stephanie. Chelsea. Jasmine. Virginia. A score more.

She really didn't *know* them, though. Most of her time was out in the field, with Hal and a camera. She came to the building to have their truck serviced by the motor pool, drop paperwork with Accounting, update legal (when Hal set something or someone on fire—which happened much more often than one imagined), and monitor postproduction work.

Hal got dangerous when he was bored and anything that didn't put him in a spotlight bored him, which was why Jane and Hal rarely worked in the offices. They didn't even have permanent desks. Jane did her paperwork at home or in the production truck or at any flat surface not currently being used at the station—hence the reason that her team camped out in the old Mr. Rogers studio from time to time.

She had always been a bit of an outsider at the station. She was a local. She was younger than most of the women—taller—louder—more prone to violence— heavily armed...

Frankly, she scared all of her coworkers.

Most of the women at the station had come to Elfhome from Earth. They were highly educated, idealistic, and inexperienced in violence. Jane would roll in from the field—often covered in blood—and usually angry enough to beat something or someone to death. A monster. Hal. A local government official. All of the above.

And then there was how she got her job...

Her family had three passions: cooking, guns, and cameras. It wasn't a family outing without all three. She got her first camera when she was ten at a cookout at the family's shooting range. Her grandfather patiently explained framing a picture and composition.

"It's just like a gun," he said since she been shooting rifles since she was six. "You want whatever you target in the crosshairs so it stays in focus. Keep the camera steady. Don't jerk about but smoothly follow the target as it moves."

Her grandfather had been to Africa to take pictures of animals she had only seen in *The Lion King*.

"You kill only to live," he told her. "Be it an animal or another human being. Life is a sacred thing. Recording life is a way to honor it."

Up to Boo's disappearance, Jane had been torn between callings. She liked to cook but she wasn't sure she wanted to make it a career. She loved the camera, but it didn't seem possible to make a living with it in Pittsburgh. She'd taken enough pictures of her family to know that she didn't have the patience for a lifetime of baby photos, high school senior pictures, or weddings. Sooner or later she would snap. The Pittsburgh television stations all required their camera operators to have a four-year degree in broadcasting, something that the University of Pittsburgh no longer offered.

Her family didn't have the money to pay for an off-world school. Her grades were good but not good enough for a full scholarship to a college on Earth. With her skill in martial arts and with a rifle, she could have gone into the military. She couldn't imagine the military ignoring her sharpshooting skills to let her pursue a career in photography. She had been afraid that she would get pressured to become a sniper like her father. It was a career that was useful only on the front line and had gotten her father killed.

Everything had changed when Boo vanished. Jane couldn't leave Elfhome without feeling like she'd abandoned all hope for her baby sister. She couldn't walk away from her little brothers, who had lost yet another family member. She couldn't turn her back on her widowed mother, who had lost her baby.

The days following Boo's disappearance in the Strip District during Shutdown, the Kryskills had become the big news story. The crews from all three television networks became intertwined with the Kryskills' daily lives as the search for Boo dragged on and on. Because her brothers were minors, no one was allowed to interview them. Chloe Polanski turned public opinion against Jane's mother, so the other networks focused on Jane.

It was probably the source of Jane's uneasiness about being the center of attention. Certainly, it was the first time in her life that someone had turned a video camera on her. All the interviews, though, only made Jane aware of how badly she had failed at protecting her baby sister. She was only in the spotlight because she had screwed up. No one would be paying attention to Jane if she hadn't lost her sister first.

Mark Webster had been WQED's reporter; he'd been the one who suggested that Jane try for a job with his station. Later, Jane realized that he'd been flirting with her. He'd meant a temporary job at the front desk since the receptionist was going on maternity leave shortly, but by then Jane had filled out an application citing any camera experience that she could claim, including one Christmas working a Santa photo op booth. Nor was she completely sure what position WQED intended to interview her for—they gave her only a date and time.

She was sitting in the building's lobby, waiting to be called back for her interview, when a drunk stumbled through the front door with a gun. Without thinking, she disarmed the gunman and pinned him to the floor. It wasn't hard. He was a little man, reeking of whiskey and smelling like he'd slept in his rumbled clothes for at least two days in a row.

"Do you know who I am?" the drunk had cried as he squirmed helplessly.

"No," Jane glanced at the very pregnant receptionist who was standing, staring openmouthed at her. "Call the police."

"He—he works here," the receptionist said as if she wasn't sure which of them scared her more.

"I am Hal Rogers!" the drunk roared. "I'm the star of the Emmy-winning program *Backyard Rehab*! I—I—I think I'm going to be sick."

Jane got Hal up and to the men's bathroom before he could vomit on the carpet. By then she realized that she could get arrested for assault and possibly exiled from Elfhome, never mind not getting hired. She considered drowning Hal in the toilet. She probably would have if he hadn't started to cry.

"I thought I could do something important here," he sobbed. "Be someone more than some glorified gardener. A whole world to explore and I'm talking about growing flowers. Marigolds! Pansies! God, anyone can grow pansies! You could throw the seeds on the ground and they would grow. That's how it works in nature. Seeds are meant to survive haphazard treatment."

Jane didn't know what to do. She paced the bathroom as Hal sat on the floor of the stall and wept.

Jane had no idea who Dmitri was when he swept into the bathroom but he had that "I am the king, this is my castle, you're trespassing" kind of air about him.

"He had a pistol that he was waving around," Jane said before Hal could accuse her of assault. She was fairly sure that the receptionist had ratted her out to the king and perhaps the police. Jane took out Hal's pistol and sat it on the ledge under the bathroom's mirror. "I didn't recognize him." She put the magazine beside the gun to show it wasn't loaded anymore and then added, "There's no bullet in the chamber. I checked."

At the time, she was amazed that her explanation had been enough to turn Dmitri's attention to Hal. Once she got to know the two men better, it wasn't surprising at all.

"Why do you have a gun, Hal?" Dmitri asked in

the quiet, intimidating manner that Jane would get to know well.

"Because every freaking thing on this planet wants to eat me!" Hal flailed his hand. "It's not just the animals. I could deal with it if it was just the animals! But the plants and the trees! The trees! The trees!"

Dmitri sighed and focused on Jane. "You're my ten o'clock interview. You're the older sister of the little lost girl."

Was that a question? Jane wasn't sure. She decided to treat it as such. "Yes."

Dmitri's eyes narrowed. "Family is military. Father is deceased. You've got five younger brothers."

"Yes," Jane said.

"Fine," Dmitri said. "You're hired. Get him sober, cleaned up, and back to filming."

"What?" both Jane and Hal said.

"You're the new PA for his show," Dmitri said.

"New what?" Jane had no idea what a PA was.

"Production assistant," Dmitri said. "It means you do whatever is needed to be done to make sure the show is filmed on time for its timeslot, which is in four days."

"Wait!" Hal cried. "What about—what's his name? John? Jack? J-J-Jarrold?"

"Jarrold was the PA you ran over," Dmitri said. "John is the one you set on fire yesterday."

"Oh, well, he shouldn't have been standing so close to me when I had a flamethrower."

"John was twenty feet from you; he'd been warned."

"I'm sure he'll be up and about in no time," Hal said. "I had a fire extinguisher ready..."

"John quit. Jarrold quit and left the planet." Dmitri pointed at Jane. "Stop at HR and get insurance forms."

Hired or not, Jane was still angry, although she wasn't sure at whom. Hal for being drunk and waving around a gun? Dmitri for hiring her for a position that seemed like a glorified babysitting job? She wasn't sure she wanted that job. She wanted to be a camera operator.

She took being hired as permission to do what she wanted to Hal Rogers. If they fired her, so be it. After getting the paperwork signed in Human Resources, she bullied Hal into taking her to his place.

He lived a few blocks away at one of the few hi-rise luxury condos in Oakland. It should have been a nice place to live as he had a sprawling penthouse apartment with big windows that showed off the city gloriously. Said windows had no drapes or blinds, just some cheap curtain rods left by the previous tenant. A small mountain of moving boxes filled most of the living room. There was a mattress thrown on the floor of the master bedroom. A second mountain of boxes filled the tiny spare bedroom. The only things unpacked were his clothes, some biology books, and his doctorate degree. He'd obviously arrived on Elfhome with high hopes and gotten lost somewhere along the way. The parts of the apartment not filled with moving boxes were littered with bachelor trash: empty food containers, dirty dishes, and empty whiskey bottles.

At that point, Jane became angry at her new coworkers. Hal was one of them—for better or worse. Why hadn't they helped him settle into his new home? Get some curtains up, unpacked the boxes, and found him a real bed? How could you turn your back on someone who was totally and utterly alone on a new world? Who obviously was struggling?

Hal needed help but Jane didn't have time to get his life in order while making sure the show hit its deadline. She called her older cousin, Rachel, who ran a service company for people new to Pittsburgh. It was a combination of native guide and maid service and personal chef.

"I'll leave the place unlocked," Jane told her cousin. She picked up Hal's wallet and took out all his cash. "Give the apartment the works. Laundry. Trash removal. A good scrub. And he needs furniture too. Talk to your guy at Once Upon A Mattress; see if you can get him to deliver a starter set."

"One bed, nightstand, love seat, dinette table, and a chair?"

"He has a mattress, so just the bedframe."

Rachel gave her a price for the works. Jane counted out the necessary bills and put them in the freezer as she gave directions to the apartment. "I put the money under the ice tray. Lock up when you're done."

It wouldn't solve all of Hal's problems but it would be a step in the right direction. Jane made a list of things that the man obviously needed. A coffeemaker. Dishes. Glasses. Silverware. Some real food. How did someone end up with so many condiments in his refrigerator and nothing to use them on?

Hal came out of his bedroom in cleaner clothes and a great deal more sober. "What was your name?"

"Jane," she said. She offered her hand like her father had taught her. "Jane Kryskill."

"Hal Rogers." He shook her hand, still peering at her as if through a fog. "How old are you? Sixteen?"

"Eighteen. Come on, let's go."

"Go? Where?"

"We have a show to film," she said.

"I'm not sure you understand how this works," Hal said. "I'm the show's star. You are the show's PA. You follow my orders. I do not follow yours."

She stepped close to take advantage of her height and used the cold, serious voice that her mother used so well to control her brothers. "I am responsible for making sure that the show is delivered on time. You will do what I say or I will hogtie you and carry you back to the station on my shoulder. Do I make myself clear?"

He worked his mouth for a moment (later she would realize how rare it would be for him to be shocked speechless) and then meekly said, "Yes, madam."

It turned out that setting the last PA on fire effectively had stopped all filming on the show. The show's producer was a nervous man from Stateside with an odd accent and odder expectations. Somehow, he thought that he didn't have to walk three steps to get a coffee but instead expected Jane to drop everything to get it for him. She disabused him of that notion within an hour. This triggered the director calling Dmitri, which resulted in the phone being handed to Jane.

"Kryskill, be nice to the man," Dmitri said over the phone. "Your producer is on the verge of a nervous breakdown. If he wants to pull stupid power plays, go along with it as far as it doesn't infringe on you keeping Rogers in check. You understand?"

"So, I'm to play 'Simon says' with this idiot?"

"Think of him as a prissy drill sergeant. He doesn't want coffee, he wants obedience. You're his soldier. Do what he tells you."

"Yes, sir."

She fetched coffee, scripts, light reflectors, and various other odd little bits while keeping an eye on Hal. After babysitting six younger siblings all her life, it was actually an easy thing to do. When Hal produced the flamethrower to finish out the segment, she quietly fetched the fire extinguisher. Thus, Hal and said producer's script only burned for a minute before being put out. (The petty little man was wise enough to dodge when the flamethrower swept the column of flame at him.)

While the producer went off to complain to Dmitri, Jane took Hal to the hospital for treatment. Afterward, she took him home.

"That wasn't necessary," Hal said as she made sure he got to his apartment. "I can deal with burns. I have a doctorate in biology. I can bandage my own wounds."

Jane was at the end of her patience. She considered ripping off the bandages and letting him reapply them like he wanted.

Hal unlocked his apartment door, swung it open. "Shit! I've been robbed. No. No. Not robbed. Cleaned! I've been cleaned! What the hell? Where did this love seat come from? I have a bed! A real bed with clean sheets! Oh! Oh! You're an angel!"

"The station manager..."

"Dmitri."

She realized that she had never gotten her boss's name. "Yes, Dmitri, the station manager, he told me to take care of you. You seem to really need someone on your side. I mean, you're all alone here, aren't you?"

His eyes widened and then some pure emotion filled his face. Sorrow. Regret. She didn't know the man enough to read it but she could tell it was raw and powerful. Then he banished it away with, "Yes, I wanted a fresh new start on a new world. It's—it's been harder than I thought it would be. God, I need a drink."

"I think you've had enough to drink." She blocked his move toward the bottles of alcohol that Rachel had collected together on a side counter as if it were some kind of minibar. "Look, as far as I can tell, Dmitri has given you a lot of rope. All you've done is hang yourself with it. Why don't you actually do something useful with all that freedom?"

"Like what?"

"People don't use flamethrowers on weeds here. They use them on steel spinners. You can't get a clear shot at the spiders because of their webbing, so you've got to burn your way through the nests. People like you—the people who are new to Elfhome—don't know that. A lot of them just ignore the nests, thinking that the spiders never leave them. They don't realize one spinner egg sack contains a thousand babies that scatter on the wind. If more people burned out nests when they found them, there'd be fewer spiders all over the city. We could get ahead of the problem if everyone was focused on it."

He was nodding. "Yes! Yes! That's what I wanted to do when I came here!" He surprised her and flung his arms around her in a tight hug. Unfortunately, it landed his face in her chest. "Oh, sorry."

He drifted away from her, embarrassed and uncertain. "So, you're eighteen, huh? You seem a lot older. I guess part of it is that you're tall and...umm...not starry-eyed. But yes, I want to do something important. Something that changes lives. Not distributing horticultural morsels to the unwashed masses."

Jane nodded as she parsed the last bit. She'd never actually heard anyone use those words aloud. "I figure that we wrap up this week's show, get it on the air, and then do the next show on steel spinners."

"Yes!" Hal rubbed his hands together. "We have the flamethrower. We just need a nest and a script."

"We can write the script." Jane figured that it couldn't be too hard. She had gotten an A-minus in AP English. "We just need to walk people through the basics. How to recognize nests before you walk into them. How to clean them out. Yadayadayada."

She sifted through the boxes until she found a box marked *Kitchen*. She took out her knife and cut it open. There was a large, mysterious, paper-wrapped bundle in the box that smelled horrible. She unwrapped it to find a trash can still holding rotting garage. "What the hell?"

Hal shook his head and began to tear packing tape off the other boxes. "I had the movers pack up my place in Los Angeles. Faster. Less painful. At least in theory. The station footed the bill. The movers were weirdly inefficient; I suspect because they were paid by the box."

"Okay." She put down the trash can and filled the empty box with bottles of alcohol.

"What are you doing?" Hal asked.

"Today is the first day of your new life," she said. "I have nothing against drinking. My family were moonshiners during the Prohibition. But when you show up at work, drunk and waving a gun, it's time to go cold turkey."

"No, no, no, no." He started to reach for the bottles. She stopped him with a cold look. "You will listen to me or I will hurt you."

He flinched back. "Do you know how expensive a good bottle of scotch is?"

She eyed the bottle that he tried to take out of the box. "Old Crow?"

"That's a whiskey and it's not expensive, but some of my scotches are a hundred dollars a bottle."

"I might be eighteen but there's very little about alcohol that I don't know. It's part of my family business to know. If you had anything worth that much, you'd have drunk it all. You can have this." She pulled out what she judged the best of the scotch that he owned. It was also the bottle with the least amount of liquid still left in it. "I'll give it back a bottle at a time."

"You are not in charge of me."

"Yes, I am."

"That's not how all this works."

"It is now."

They stared at each other in silence. She wasn't sure what his life was like up to this moment, but she had had staring contests like this with her brothers since she was four. You drew the line in the sand and stood your ground until the other person caved.

His anger slowly gave way to bewilderment and then something like hope. "You're really going to take care of me?"

"Yes. I'll see you tomorrow at the station. I've made a key to your apartment. If you don't show up, I'll come get you. I will not be gentle. If I were you, I'd be at the station at eight-thirty."

"Right," he said slowly and then smiled.

"Good night, Hal."

"Good night, Jane."

❖   ❖   ❖

It had taken a year to dry Hal out, as any little setback had him crawling back into any bottle he managed to hide from Jane. It had taken another year of chewing through Earth-trained producers until Jane learned how to do their job. It was a crazy two years total. Between her first day and the following seven hundred days of fighting with Hal, producers, and Dmitri, she hadn't left the best impression on her coworkers.

The next six years after that rocky start had repaired her image a little. *Pittsburgh Backyard and Garden* became the station's top show. Hal had gone from unknown to local icon. Jane learned the names of all the other coworkers and was friendly with them, but none of them were, strictly speaking, friends.

Nor was Jane particularly close to any of them. For example, she had totally missed the fact that Ginnilee Berger, who normally handled housing for new hires and interns, had gotten pregnant and returned to Earth in June due to the pregnancy being high-risk. As far as Jane was concerned, the woman had suddenly vanished without explanation—at least, until someone explained her disappearance to Jane in July. Jane couldn't say that she knew any employee any better than she had known Ginnilee.

Her coworkers were aware, however, that Jane was getting married, the rush nature of the wedding, and the possibility that Hal would be Hal. If Jane found two women she could trust, at least she wouldn't have to explain the basics to them. She could also—in theory—raid their personnel files prior to asking them.

Jane started in Legal, as it was the smallest department and both employees were female.

The station's lawyer, Virginia Jijon-Caamano, could be considered her friend; certainly they had fought battles together to clean up Hal's messes. They shared "tall blonde" fist bumps when Virginia got Hal out of trouble—again. Jane was fairly sure that Virginia had been the one who told Dmitri about Jane getting married. Someone in Legal had because they were worried that Taggart was taking advantage of her. It fit into Virginia's MO of seeing her coworkers as extended family. Although, Dmitri had added that Jane scared Legal. Jane was fairly sure that the only thing that scared Virginia was her kids getting bad grades.

"Jane!" Virginia greeted her with a warm smile. She was immaculately dressed as always in a freshly ironed white button-down blouse, a short black skirt that showed off her long legs, and a set of heels that closed her two-inch height difference with Jane. "What did Hal do now?"

"Hopefully, nothing, but it's been a few minutes since I last saw him." Jane paused and listened. No screaming. That was a good sign that the snake had been safely contained.

Virginia laughed, focusing back on what she had been doing, which was swapping out photographs of her children. They jumped forward in age by at least three or four years even as Jane looked on. The elementary school little kids became tall high school students. The last photograph was a group shot where Virginia's two girls were as tall as their mother and her son towered over her by a full head.

"Wow, your kids grew up fast," Jane said as she mentally adjusted Virginia's age. She thought of the woman as "only slightly older than me" but obviously

Virginia was closer to Jane's mother's age. "They were just little things when I started."

Virginia laughed. "Yes, my husband and I had started the 'where do we want to retire' discussion. It's all moot now."

"You weren't staying on Elfhome?" Jane asked with surprise.

"We couldn't stay. We're both on work visas. Once we retired, we would lose our visas. None of our children were born here. Once we retired, like it or not, the entire family would need to leave."

Jane wanted to say that it was terrible to be forced to leave the only home that the children probably remembered. If Virginia's kids were like Jane's classmates, though, having both a home and a good job usually wasn't possible in Pittsburgh. Jobs that required advanced degrees went to the best qualified, which were the people who went to Earth's finest schools. Those were colleges that kids from Pittsburgh rarely could attend for various reasons, starting with money, but it boiled down to the fact that Pittsburgh simply didn't have the resources to maintain a world-class high school.

"How can I help you today?" Virginia asked.

Jane's mother might say "any woman" but Jane knew that her mother wouldn't want a stranger as old as herself as part of the wedding party. The unspoken criteria included young, tall, and photogenic. Her mother might dream of possible daughter-in-law candidates as part of the mix but Jane wasn't about to go down that road.

"I wanted to double-check," Jane lied only slightly. "After the wedding, Taggart doesn't need anything beyond his visa and the wedding license to finalize his citizenship with the EIA?"

"Yes. I've triple-checked for you, even though that's all moot for now. If Taggart has any problems at all, he's to call me. I'll come down and mow through the red tape. They weeded out all the oni moles that made that department hell to work with, but the people left are all kind of clueless."

Jane glanced into the cubbyhole office that belonged to Virginia's paralegal assistant, Makayla Friedman. The girl was in her early twenties, reasonably tall, photogenic, and a fashion horse; Jane had never seen the girl in the same outfit twice. Makayla would be able to hold her own, surrounded by Jane and her statuesque family. Jane considered the girl annoyingly perky but she was good at keeping secrets. Her office, however, was empty. "Where is Makayla?"

Virginia sighed. "She's probably in the restroom, fixing her makeup again."

"Again?" Jane echoed. She had never seen the girl fiddle with her makeup while they were grinding through one of Hal's messes; Makayla always looked so flawless that she seemed unreal.

Virginia pursed her lips, considering what to tell Jane before admitting, "Makayla's not taking things well since the gate failed and stranded her in Pittsburgh. She had ambitions that this office was just a stepping-stone for her. It's difficult to pour your life into one direction and suddenly—through events that you couldn't possibly control—lose all of it. She's spending her breaks in the restroom, crying as quietly as she can. Poor girl. She ends up looking like a raccoon. I suggested that she stop wearing so much eye makeup but she says putting it on calms her."

What came out of the restroom was a far cry from

perky. Makayla was holding a tissue to her nose as if it was still dripping. She hadn't gotten all of the ruined mascara cleaned off; there was a faint dark mask around her eyes, which were red and moist with tears.

"Damn cheap drugstore makeup," Makayla growled in greeting. "I was supposed to get an order of Urban Decay in August."

Jane was fairly sure that the paralegal was talking about makeup, not the parts of Pittsburgh that were in disrepair. Urban Decay seemed an odd name for cosmetics. Jane wasn't sure what to say in response—which was the normal problem she had with women that worked at WQED. They might be her gender but they came from another world. They'd been to college, flown in airplanes, seen mountains, oceans, and the great lakes. Most of them had never fired a gun, killed an animal, or seen a walking tree. The lack of common ground kept most conversations focused on work.

Makayla wore what was cutting fashion for Earth: a bold, pink paisley sleeveless blouse, a white pencil-skirt that could nearly classify as a miniskirt, and clunky, thick-soled platform shoes. It was stylish and good looking (except for the shoes, in Jane's opinion) but anyone could identify Makayla at a glance as someone who hadn't been born in Pittsburgh. It always made Jane feel slightly underdressed when she was at the office, even when she tried dressing up for a production meeting, like she was now.

Makayla clunked past Jane, heading for her desk. "I'm running out of everything! I used up my Kona coffee, my boba tea supplies, and my Dr. Jart cryo rubber face masks. I'm down to my last six-pack of San Pellegrino. My parents were supposed to mail me a care package last Shutdown for my—my—my birthday!" She covered her face with her carefully manicured hands. "My mother wanted me to come home for the summer! Now I'm never going to see my family ever again!"

"I doubt that very much," Virginia said calmly. "WTAE reported that Princess Tinker had the EIA clear the Squirrel Hill Tunnel for her so she could build a land-based gate inside of them."

"Chloe Polanski made that up!" Makayla wailed. "Polanski was an oni mole! Hannah called me in hysterics from WTAE's legal department. She wanted to know if we had any job openings; she's desperate to jump ship. Polanski lied about everything: she gave their HR a fake home address and emergency contact information. All the photos of 'her family' are off of Shutterstock. The EIA searched her desk and found it booby-trapped with enough C4 to take out the entire floor. HR is pointing fingers at Hannah's department, saying that they thought Legal did a background check when they did Polanski's visa paperwork. Hannah wasn't even out of high school when that happened. When you go back and review Polanski's news stories from this summer, you can see she planted misinformation all over the place. Who was behind Windwolf's disappearance. What killed his bodyguard. How the shootout on Veterans Bridge started. Where the oni might be holding Princess Tinker. The Squirrel Hill Tunnel was just more of the same: the vicereine never talked about why she was at the tunnel during the interview; Polanski tacked that on afterward in her summation. No one questions a field reporter making educated guess; it's assumed that time will tell if they're right or wrong."

Jane snorted. Chloe Polanski had made "educated guesses" about Jane's mother on the air, making it seem Boo had run away from an abusive home. The woman would have known that Kajo had taken Boo. Polanski's smear of Jane's mother was simply a way to keep people from thinking about possible kidnappers.

"Everyone at WTAE is afraid that the elves are going to show up and behead everyone at the station." Makayla reached for her box of tissues.

"They let her walk all over people right and left," Jane said. "They had to know that sooner or later, she'd piss off the elves."

"You're one to talk, missy," Virginia murmured as Makayla loudly blew her nose. "Hal was plowing through people even before the conflict started. You've only gotten worse since nature boy number two showed up."

Virginia meant Nigel, who most of WQED saw as being the same make and model as Hal. Nigel might be as heedless of his own danger but he was much more cautious of other people's safety. It had been the discovery that the oni had been behind Boo's disappearance that made Jane's team's behavioral pattern "worse," not Nigel.

Just like Chloe Polanski, if things went south with Jane's team, everyone at WQED would bear the weight of suspicion.

"I'm sorry," Jane whispered.

"We've got your back," Virginia answered. "But please, be careful."

Jane nodded.

Virginia focused her attention back to her bawling paralegal. "Polanski might have lied about why Princess Tinker was at the Squirrel Hill tunnels, but the vicereine *did* make a gate that opened to Onihida. If she can make one, she can make another."

Jane knew for a fact that the EIA had cleared the tunnels in expectation that Tinker would use them to reconnect Pittsburgh to Earth. After the museum shoot-out, Director Maynard seemed to see Jane's team as a trustworthy pest-removal unit. He'd called them several times that summer to deal with Elfhome's deadlier flora and fauna. Jane had helped clear the tunnels of steel spinner nests while Taggart worked cameras. They hadn't used the footage yet because the powers that be—Tinker, Maynard, and Jin Wong—weren't sure that Tinker should attempt to build a gate. At least, not until the elves won the war against the oni. If Tinker accidently linked her gate to Onihida instead of Earth, the army that the oni had amassed could push through her gate before she could shut it down. The general consensus was that Tinker *domi* should wait until the elves could spare the firepower to deal with an incoming army.

It was possible that Polanski had reported Tinker's plan to create pressure on the girl genius. The entire off-world population of Pittsburgh wanted the city to be reconnected to Earth. Hopefully no one tried to act on the information. Jane wasn't about to explain what she knew to the emotionally distraught Makayla.

"I want to go home!" Makayla wailed. "I miss my mom and dad! I miss New York! The people here don't even understand how small this world is. I keep dreaming that it gets smaller and smaller and then just disappears totally."

Jane didn't want to trust Makayla with her family secrets. The woman was emotionally unstable and desperate. "Things will work out," Jane said, preparing her escape. "Just give it time."

"I turned twenty-four last month!" Makayla sobbed. "I had a schedule all worked out. Graduate college by twenty-one. Work off-world three years to get money for law school, work experience that would make me stand out, and glowing recommendations from a wide range of people. Since I'd be a whole different world from my friends and family and the Internet, I'd devote all my time to studying for my LSAT. Leave Elfhome in November *of this year* and take my LSAT and apply to Yale."

"You'll be the only applicant that lived through an interdimensional war between three universes," Virginia said.

"'Lived' is the key word here," Makayla complained darkly.

The lights flickered.

All three of the women looked up at the overhead lamps.

"Is Hal experimenting with an electric fence again?" Virginia asked.

"I don't think so," Jane said slowly. She didn't want to explain that Hal was preoccupied with a deadly snake loose in the offices. "I'll go check on him."

She headed back through the building as the lights flickered again. "Hal?"

"That's not me!" Hal called back, somewhere near the break room.

Jane was in the big windowless room of the news bullpen when the lights went off, dropping her into darkness.

"Still not me!" Hal shouted, definitely in the break room itself.

Jane swore softly. She was still in her dress clothes for the meeting. She didn't have her flashlight on her. Around her various uninterruptable power units signaled their distress with loud chirps. In the sea of darkness, lights started to appear as people turned on their phones and tablets to see. She didn't want to run down her phone battery. She fumbled her way toward the break room. Despite Hal's assurance that he had nothing to do with the blackout, she had a sinking feeling that things had just taken a turn for the worse.

"Can I have some light in the restroom?" a woman's voice called out, muffled by a door.

There was a thud and a soft curse as someone walked into something.

"Come on! Can we have power?" a woman called.

"Where's the snake?" Joe McGreevy called out with an edge of fear in his voice. He sounded close to Hal in the breakroom.

"Someone kick the generator!" Dmitri shouted from the direction of his office. "Get us back on the air!"

There was a deep, nearly inaudible rumble as the big diesel generator in the parking lot kicked on. The lights snapped back on.

"Where's the snake?" Joe repeated in a slightly more stressed voice.

Jane headed for the break room, hoping said snake was in an opaque container as she recognized Joe McGreevy on a verge of a meltdown. Jane was fairly sure that the broken wrist had taught Hal not to tease Joe, but Nigel and Taggart didn't know of the man's phobia. The British naturalist might try to "educate" Joe.

The WQED breakroom was a large windowless room designed to be a kitchen for the incoming staff to use as a place to cook real meals until they got settled. It had a range, a dishwasher, pots and pans, dishes, and any number of storage containers. Some were small clear Rubbermaid. The others, like the Disney souvenir cookie bucket that Nigel was holding, were recycled larger containers.

"I had nothing to do with the blackout," Hal said calmly, ignoring the fact that Joe stood trapped in the corner farthest from the door, looking like he wanted to phase through the wall.

"Jane, we need to talk," Taggart said and glanced toward Joe. "Privately."

"Where is the snake?" Joe shouted.

"It's safely contained," Taggart focused back on his laptop.

"You really don't want to know," Hal said calmly, pouring himself a cup of coffee. "If you were really concerned, you wouldn't be in the same room as us."

"I was here first!" Joe shouted.

"Oh, the snake?" Nigel lifted the lid on the bucket and held it out to Joe.

"No!" Jane shouted.

Joe smacked the bucket away from him with a scream. The bucket and snake parted company in midair, the snake landing on the table in front of Taggart.

"Taggart, move!" Jane caught the bucket as it came sailing past her. Taggart sprang back from the table, abandoning his laptop after slapping the screen down. "Calm down, Joe!"

Hal leaned back against the kitchen counter, obviously having learned from the last time not to get close to Joe. "Really? Can you not grow a pair? It's not going to hurt you. Look how small it is! It's like an earthworm—an earthworm on steroids—with deadly poison. Whoa, whoa, whoa!"

Joe had snatched up the chair that Taggart had been sitting on.

"Joe!" Jane didn't really want to punch the man who filled out their paychecks. "Put down the chair, Joe!"

With a roar, Joe smashed the tabletop with the chair. It missed the snake but hit Taggart's laptop.

Jane swore and leapt forward to save the laptop from further damage.

"We were in the break room, not Accounting," Hal explained patiently to Dmitri as to why the head of Accounting was being taken out on an ambulance gurney. "It's practically on the opposite side of the building! We needed a plastic bin to put the snake in. We didn't know that someone had brought in fresh donuts and Joe was there, binge-eating them. You know how he just stands there and grazes when he's stressed out."

Jane was letting Hal talk because it was Hal's magical power to charm people in and out of things. Also she had missed how it started and they hadn't had time for her to verify the important details, like why Joe had been in the kitchen. She would have gone with Nigel, since there was a certain "familiarity breeds contempt" vibe that diminished Hal's ability on Dmitri, but Nigel was part of the reason they needed an ambulance. Who would have thought that quiet, gentle Nigel could be so fierce when it came to protecting small animals?

Said snake was unharmed, recaptured, and currently back in the Disney cookie bucket.

Taggart was back at the table, checking the damage to his laptop, looking all kinds of concerned.

Dmitri turned to Jane. "Did you have to hit him with a chair?"

"I'm afraid that was me," Nigel said. "It was Joe's weapon of choice. Duel of honor and all."

"What?" Dmitri sounded as confused as Jane felt.

"I was honor bound to protect the wee thing. I brought it into this building; I had to care for it until I released it into the wild. Mr. McGreevy chose to wield a chair; I simply returned his volley."

"Right," Dmitri said after a long, calculating stare. He turned his attention to Taggart frowning at his laptop. "Is it broken? We still need the video for next week's show."

Taggart looked to Nigel and did an odd side glance to Dmitri. Taggart was horrible at lying. He also knew the limits of his ability.

"Unfortunately"—Nigel picked up whatever silent message that Taggart was trying to beam to him,— "prior to the blackout, Taggart had his laptop plugged in and there was a power surge that seems to have corrupted some of our data."

Jane remembered that Taggart had needed to talk to her privately. He must have found something in the video.

"Surely you have a backup," Dmitri said.

"The *Chased by Monsters* equipment isn't fully compatible with the ancient stuff in the *PB&G* truck." Jane kept to the truth. The gear that Nigel and Taggart brought with them from Earth far outstripped anything on Elfhome. "We're really having to juggle. We can upload video from *PB&G*'s equipment to *CBM*, but not vice versa. The software won't run on the old operating system. We port everything through *CBM* because it gives us more control over the video editing."

Her team was nodding along with her statements. She wished they would stop as that would probably tip off Dmitri the moment she needed to start lying.

"We have such a limited memory capacity on the *PB&G* equipment that we normally scrub the cards after we upload the video." Again, true. Head nods all around. She and Hal had been using the oldest cameras that WQED owned because Hal routinely broke everything. Since Dmitri was focused on her, Jane couldn't frown at her team. "We've been shooting with both cameras and then consolidating the footage on Taggart's laptop." They also had backups but she didn't want to discuss whether Taggart wanted the footage "lost" for some reason. "He has a state-of-the-art machine that handles the editing easily. Even the machines here at the office struggle with the new editing software."

Still true.

She paused, hating the need to lie to Dmitri. The man had trusted her since the day they first met. He'd given her everything: a career that she loved, responsibilities beyond what her education would normally obtain, a legal shield when Hal had gotten out of her control, the man of her dreams, and even her little sister's safe return. The man was responsible for the safety of the entire station, though, not just her team. Because he wouldn't be able to lie to the elves, she had to keep the truth from him to keep him safe.

Dmitri stopped her with a look. "So you're saying that you need to film more footage?"

Jane breathed out with relief that Dmitri had skipped ahead, probably guessing that he wasn't going to get the full truth if he pushed. She glanced to Taggart, who nodded. "Yes."

Dmitri pointed at Nigel. "Don't bring any more creatures into this station."

"Yes, sir." Nigel said.

"There was a reflection that I hadn't noticed." Taggart pointed to the screen of his laptop.

They had centered next week's show on the growing menace of wargs. They had been camped out at the top of the South Hills fire tower at edge of the Rim. Because of the remote location, Boo had been with them. Boo had helped out by holding the light reflector as they filmed. Her little sister had just gotten the magical tattoo that gave her the massive tengu wings. Unlike the other tengu, Boo's wings were angelic white. Occasionally she lost control of them as she was still learning the complex muscle memory for flight.

Somehow they hadn't noticed that every time Boo opened her wings, there was a perfect reflection of them in the fire tower's windows.

"If they were black like the other tengu, I would say just run with it. The tengu are trusted allies now, no one would be surprised that we had at least one helping out on the hunt. But they're white." Taggart didn't finish the statement.

"Can't you edit them out?" Hal said. "Industrial Light and Magic it?"

Taggart shook his head. "It would take me days to erase her out of every frame. If she hadn't been opening and closing them, it wouldn't have been as difficult. There's other factors that make it tricky—but it boils down to time. I can grind it out for the following week but not this week."

"But this means we need to film and edit an entire show in less than twenty-four hours," Hal said. "We don't have a script. We don't have a monster. We have nothing."

"We have a city at war and a secret militia," Jane whispered. "I'm sure we can come up with something."

7: WHISKEY TANGO FOXTROT

"Up you go!"

Wolf Who Rules Wind hadn't hit his growth spurt yet, so it was simple for his eldest brother, Whiskey Smoked With Peat Fire, to hoist him out of bed and toss him up into the air.

"Whiskey!" Wolf cried in surprise.

"Come on, it's your big day!" Whiskey caught him and tossed him again.

This time he stayed up in the air, supported by the wind. Whiskey was Fire Clan, having inherited their mother's red hair and ability to tap the Fire Spell Stones. It meant someone else was manipulating the wind.

Wolf guessed the culprit. "Jay Bird!"

With a snicker, Jay Bird Screaming in Wind swaggered out of his hiding place. He was dressed up to go to court in his namesake's colors of creamy tan with brilliant blue highlights. "What? A great warrior such as you should be able to escape that hold."

Whiskey smacked Jay Bird lightly. "Put our baby

brother down. No magic in the living quarters. Besides it would not do for him to be presented to the queen with a broken nose."

"Aunty Ember has seen him thousands of times! I don't know why he needs to be presented," Jay Bird sulked. He nevertheless lowered Wolf gently down to the floor. Whiskey was remarkably easy tempered for being Fire Clan, but he was fierce when riled.

Whiskey gave Jay Bird a worried look. "Are you seriously asking that question? You should know it's all about protocol."

"I know!" Jay Bird shouted. He turned and stomped out of the room in a huff.

"Looks like Father, acts like Mother," Whiskey murmured of their brother.

"He's jealous," Wolf said sadly. "He wants to live at Court too."

"Only because he doesn't know what it's really like." Whiskey pushed Wolf toward the hallway. "Yes, our cousins are good and gracious to us, but everyone else looks down their nose because we're mixed blood. If someone is kind to you, remember that they most likely have an ulterior motive."

Wolf wanted to say "I know" but it would echo Jay Bird. Besides, he didn't know. Not really. This day was decreed the day he was born. He'd spent his life knowing it would come. The future, though, was filled with uncertainty.

"I will only be able to be with you through Winter Court," Whiskey said. "Once thaw starts, I will need to go to my new holding."

Wolf nodded. He and his many siblings were spaced close together, yet another thing that set their family apart from the norm. There were only two hundred years between him and his eldest brother. It meant that most of his elder brothers and sisters had been busy gathering Hands of *sekasha* to them, recruiting young clan members to set up households, and building a house guard of *laedin* warriors. With the exception of Jay Bird and Cricket Chirping by the Hearth Fire, who were in their doubles, all his siblings planned to finish their tasks and set off to claim what they could as their own. Pickings were lean, as their parents had many children and very little could be passed on in the way of land. Whiskey had been given an island to the far north filled with volcanos. It sounded like icy hell to Wolf—and to most others, which was why it was free to claim—but Whiskey was fascinated by volcanos.

"Kiln, Charcoal, and Echo will go as soon as land can be found for them," Whiskey said.

"Ibis and Dove too," Wolf said.

Whiskey laughed, "Yes, but they won't be at Court with us."

Kiln Fired Vase, Charcoal Banked for the Night, and Sunrise Echo could only tap the Fire Clan Spell Stones. They'd been sent to Court to be trained by the teachers of the royal household. Ibis and Dove both were Wind Clan and had stayed at home.

They were nearly to the bathhouse when Starlight Singing in the Wind came sweeping down the hall.

"*Wolf turns fifty today, let us see him off and away,*" his sister sang. "*Searching in the moldering heaps, I found something for Wolf to keep.*"

Starlight had their father's hair and eyes but their mother's height. She was dressed for the day in her best gown, a shimmering black dress of fairy silk studded with hundreds of crystals that glimmered like stars in the night sky. She held out a map case to Wolf.

"A star map?" Wolf guessed since Starlight was as fascinated by stars as Whiskey was by volcanos.

Starlight laughed. "If it was a star map, I wouldn't be giving it away, silly! I was wandering through the Stone Clan market, digging through the stall of an old quad who used to trade with Earth. He only had the most outlandish things left. Humans must be frivolous beings, judging by his stock. Without magic, all they have to guide them are the sun and moon and stars, so their maps of the night sky far exceed ours."

If not a star map, then what did she have in the map case? Wolf opened it and found a map of unfamiliar coastline. The landmass seemed quite large but Wolf couldn't match it to any place he'd seen before. The lettering wasn't in Elvish; Wolf couldn't recognize any of the symbols. The map looked new, still smelling of ink. "What is this? I don't recognize any of this."

"The merchant couldn't remember how he came by it," Starlight said. "I got it for a smile and a nod. He saw no value in a map of Earth since all the pathways are closed."

"Earth?" Wolf eyed the alien symbols that must be human writing. "This isn't old enough to be from before the war with the oni."

"I had it copied for father's collection," Starlight said. "The land is not a secret, just little known. The merchant said that the 'French' and the 'British' had a war over it just before we closed the gates. The humans were just beginning to map it in earnest when we lost contact with Earth. The idiot merchant failed to understand the implications."

Implications? Wolf gasped as he realized what the map revealed. "There will be a mirror continent here on Elfhome. We could parcel it up for holdings for those who have none."

Starlight grinned. "Very good, Wolf. You see it immediately."

"Why give it to me? Why not Ibis or Dove? They're already in their triples." While their mother was Fire Clan, many would criticize Starlight if she gave the valuable maps to any of her non-Wind-Clan siblings. Even Wolf was a dangerous choice since he hadn't decided his clan yet.

"I knew you would ask." She took out another map case and pulled from it a map of the Summer Court and the waters around it. She pointed to an island in the northeast corner. "This is Whiskey's volcanic island. See this wedge of land, here, beyond it? That is the large island here on your map."

Whiskey had wanted to claim the larger island but it was more than a *mei* from the Fire Stones of Summer Court. It would require Whiskey to build a set of Spell Stones. He hadn't been able to gather enough Fire Clan households to warrant the Crown's backing. His failure had been a combination of the lack of prestige in his name and the perceived quality of his *sekasha*. Like their father, Whiskey had taken a female he loved as his First. Whiskey had to settle for the closer, smaller island that was at the very edge of the stones' range. If the scale was correct, Starlight's map showed a full continent two or three *mei* from the nearest Spell Stones, Fire Clan or Wind Clan.

Wolf cocked his head. "If no one has been there,

then there's no Spell Stones. A *domana* would be powerless. They couldn't protect their people."

"Yes, it would take someone with bold ambition to venture into uncharted land and set up a holding," Starlight said. "To gain the support that they will need, they would have to build an impressive personal household and a large number of Beholden. Ibis and Dove are living up to their names as peaceful, loyal followers. Ibis plans to settle in high country and breed gossamers. Dove is lost to silkworms. I don't understand the fascination. Neither has the desire nor the ambition needed to take on such a task. I plan to head to the mountains, to be closer to the stars. I'm not even sure I want to have a traditional household. If I can talk my way into a monastery, I might go that direction."

"A monastery?" He had never heard of anyone but *sekasha* living at the remote mountain temples.

"The *sekasha* will not allow me to wander the landscape alone. A female *domana* waltzing about, sleeping with who knows what? Everyone will be happier if I'm under their protective wing while I gaze at my stars."

Wolf loved his sister's clarity of vision. She knew what she wanted and went for it with all her passion. He had so many choices open to him. He knew that he could be anything—perhaps even the next king if he chose to be Fire Clan and something happened to his cousin, Queen Soulful Ember. When Halo Dust died, the Wyverns chose the late king's youngest child, not his oldest.

Wolf was named for greatness. He was bewildered, though: what was he supposed to do? He was the first *domana* born that could tap two *esva*. There was no blueprint for him to follow. Everyone was standing back and letting him figure it out. A new land would have no limits or expectations. Perhaps it needed someone like him to settle it.

Starlight leaned close. "Know this: No matter what clan you choose, you will always be our beloved baby brother. Be bold and brave as your name, Wolf Who Rules Wind. If you need us, you will only need to call and we will answer."

Whiskey nodded in agreement. "Wind or Fire. Blood binds us."

The deep rumble of the locomotive's diesel engine pulled Wolf out of his thoughts. The train squealed and hissed to a stop at their makeshift camp. They were twenty miles outside the Rim at an old railroad construction camp alongside the Youghiogheny River. It was nothing more than a large flat clearing, edged with towering ironwood trees, currently overflowing with Fire Clan red and Stone Clan black. It put them an uncomfortable forty miles from the enclaves in Oakland. The train's arrival meant that the last of the royal marines had arrived and that they would be moving out soon. All around Wolf was orderly chaos as his people pulled down their tents and packed up to move.

In a matter of a few minutes, he would march his people away from this last bastion of civilization with no idea when he might be able to easily communicate with the enclaves again. Any message would either have to pass through human hands via the EIA or some of his *laedin* soldiers would need to fight their way back to Oakland, forty miles or more, on foot. Wolf wanted to ponder long on this question but he didn't have time. Wolf looked down at the scrap of paper in his hand.

"*What?*" the distant-voices message read. "*Am I not good enough for you? Jay Bird Screaming in Wind.*"

Wolf had called on six of his nine siblings when Tinker vanished. Starlight and Charcoal were at Aum Renau. Whiskey and Ibis held down the eastern end of the railroad, putting his brothers at his seaport of Brotherly Love. Dove and Cricket were at New Haven. It gave each of his settlements one *domana* of Fire and another of Wind to protect it. As of yet, none had been attacked, which was good because his siblings were young and untried. Only through sheer desperation had he turned to them. Legally they could lay claim to anything they protected for a long period of time. His siblings were the only *domana* he could trust not to loot his Beholden.

He hadn't contacted Kiln, Echo, and Jay. The first two were artists with a bare minimum of combat training, with only Vanity Hands to protect their artwork and vulnerable city holdings.

He hadn't been sure if he could trust Jay Bird. His older brother had been the baby of the family until Wolf's birth. If Wolf hadn't been born able to tap the *esva* of both Wind Clan and Fire Clan, things might have been different between them. His older brother, though, could not stand being lost in the shadow of the new baby. The day that Wolf had left for Court had been the last time he'd seen Jay.

When the oni had taken Tinker, Wolf hadn't reached out to Jay because of how they'd been as children.

When he was little, he'd had to guard his favorite toys, lest Jay break them out of spite. Wolf had had childish spats with most of his older siblings. The difference was that his other brothers and sisters had occasionally shown him warm regards. They had also reached out to him, from time to time, since he had reached his majority to lend advice and aid. Starlight had even been to Pittsburgh, drawn by the human observatory. Every time Wolf traveled to visit his parents, Jay Bird would be traveling elsewhere. At first, Wolf had thought it was mere coincidence, but in later years, he wasn't sure.

He knew that Jay was the best combat trained of his siblings by default of insisting that he got the same training as Wolf. He knew that Jay had taken two Hands of *sekasha*. He knew that of all his brothers and sisters, Jay was the one who could easily shift base since he had yet to set up a permanent home outside of the Wind Clan quarters of Court. Yet, with all the broken toys in mind, he hadn't sent for Jay.

Now, with Forest Moss running mad, two Harbingers dismissing everything Wolf said as the rantings of a spoiled child, and Cana Lily ready to kill anything non-elvish—enemy or ally or innocent bystander—Wolf was fairly sure he'd chosen badly.

Perhaps.

Perhaps not.

Earth Son and half of Jewel Tear's household, one of Wolf's *sekasha*, an unknown number of Stone Clan children, and an entire battalion of royal marines were dead. More than a thousand elves gone and they had not yet faced the enemy in open battle.

Did he want his brother here and risk losing him?

Now that all sixty thousand of the humans and twenty thousand tengu in Pittsburgh were Wolf's responsibility to protect, how could he not?

Rainlily stood waiting, trying to hide her impatience. She was one of the *sekasha* "babies"—she and the other of Tinker's Hand were all just out of their doubles. Tinker's influence on her showed in subtle ways. Rainlily wore a pair of Discord's handmade blue jeans and was chewing gum. She had hand-delivered the distant-voices message from Blue Jay but obviously that wasn't her main mission.

Wraith Arrow stood at Wolf's side, listening quietly. His First, Second, and Third Hand stood guard, keeping away anyone who might overhear the conversation. Tinker had been kidnapped, held prisoner, escaped, fought Impatience, fell off the planet, killed Malice, and took on a Skin Clan mole. She had never sent Wolf a message through all that; considering the summer, though, Rainlily most likely did not carry a tender love note. It was almost guaranteed to be life changing.

The rest of his household was breaking down the camp, getting ready to move. Tents, cots, and field kitchens and rations were being loaded on his pack mules. Marines were spilling off the newly arrived train in a flood of red. Overhead, a Stone Clan gossamer waited for the signal to cast off.

"There is more?" Wolf asked.

"The tengu leader, Jin Wong, visited *domi* late last night," Rainlily said quietly so only Wolf and Wraith Arrow could hear. "He had important news. *Domi* would like Wolf Who Rules Wind to return to the enclave to discuss it personally but if that is not possible, she instructed me to explain recent developments." Then quietly she added, "If I can. I'm not sure I followed everything."

What could be so horribly wrong now?

Wolf glanced about the encampment. The tengu scouts had confirmed four fortified oni camps an hour apart at a warg's running pace, roughly in a diamond pattern. Each fort had three to four thousand oni warriors armed with human weapons and hundreds of wargs. Even with a full brigade of royal marines, the elves were outnumbered.

Much as Wolf doubted the wisdom of taking on the oni head on as the Harbingers planned, he didn't want the fight to reach Pittsburgh. As soon as the last of the Fire Clan troops unloaded from the train, the assembled elf forces were to move east toward the nearest oni camp.

Even if he flew, could he get to Oakland and back without delaying the attack?

"You cannot leave," Wraith Arrow whispered. "We could be stripped of everything if the Wind Clan pulls its only *domana* out of this."

Tinker might not know that but her Hand would. Little Horse and Discord were wise in the ways of political maneuvering between clans. They would have counseled her. That one of them was not here to explain suggested the weight of whatever Tinker was wrestling with now.

Still, Wraith Arrow was correct. Wolf would keep hold of the eastern coast if he left but Pittsburgh—all the humans—would fall to the Stone Clan. After the last month of insanity, he wouldn't trust a feral pig to the Stone Clan's care.

"What is the problem?" Wolf temporized. "Why did she send for me?"

Rainlily's eyes went wide at the prospect of explaining. She held up her hand to tick off points as her eyes tracked up and to the left in the effort to recall all that she been told. "Esme Shanske made many babies when she made *domi*. I do not understand this part but this is what I've been told. Two are females younger—biologically—than Baby Duck, which makes them very small considering how little *domi* and cousin are. The tengu say that they are like *domi*, only younger, which we take to mean that they are very much wood sprites and all that implies. The other four are infants. How or why they are so much younger, I do not understand either, but they do not seem like they are normal infants. Jin Wong was very nervous whenever *domi*'s questioning turned toward them; we're not sure why. Domi did not push for answers. It could be just the idea of having to keep six baby wood sprites *contained* until guardianship is decided. First assured *domi* that we could stand as blade parents. Personally, I'm doubtful since we are not doing well at keeping up with *domi*."

Wolf laughed as he thought of the trail of destruction that his beloved left behind her. Yes, the tengu had reason to be nervous.

Rainlily continued her briefing, shifting to the next finger. "The six baby wood sprites were captured on Earth by oni forces that they escaped from—after rescuing a goodly number of tengu children. I'm sure it's a very long story but we were told very little of it. All the children fled Earth after the gate crashed, meaning that there is or was a pathway from Earth to Elfhome open. Huh. Saying all that does really make the little females sound just like *domi*."

Rainlily shifted to her third finger. "The tengu

believe that the pathway is blocked but are not sure if it can be reopened or not. Jin Wong gave us a map to the cave's location. He says it's thirty miles southwest of here."

She paused to rummage through her bulky messenger pack. She had used the human word of "miles." Wolf nodded as he translated the distance in his head.

"Here." She found said map and handed it to him. It was one of the human-made topographical maps of the area. The tengu leader had circled "Laurel Caverns" to mark the pathway.

Rainlily considered her fingers to remember where she had left off. She squinted in effort to recall all the confusing details as she moved to her fourth finger. "The children are the ones that summoned the gossamer away from the airfield. It's been safely returned by the tengu. *Domi*'s little sisters have a command whistle on them that they made themselves, which kind of confirms our suspicions that the wood sprite traits breed true. All of the children are at the tengu village. The tengu want to cooperate in any way but they are not sure if they can shift the children out of the village."

"Why not?" Wraith Arrow grumbled. "The tengu are *domi*'s Beholden; they must obey her."

Rainlily fluttered a hand at Wraith Arrow, indicating that she was getting to that. "*Domi*'s sisters may be able to tap the Stone Clan Spell Stone just as cousin could even before he was transformed; Tinker *domi* felt two calls on the stones from the direction of Haven shortly before dawn. We believe that the children would be as formable as *domi* or cousin in battle as neither of them have had formal instruction either."

Wolf wondered if the "we" was solely Tinker's Hand discussing things among themselves as their *domi* focused on other matters. The last part sounded a little too tactical to be from Tinker.

"It also means that the other Stone Clan *domana* might realize that there are new members of their clan nearby." Rainlily paused, changed hands, and shifted her eyes to the right as if reading down a second list. "The children have a dragon—a new one—with them that has claimed all of them as 'hers' in the manner that Providence protects the tengu. Both Providence and Impatience are allied with Joy—which is the name of the baby dragon with the babies..."

"Good gods," Wraith whispered. "What madness now?"

"It gets worse." Wolf knew his beloved. She would not summon him for anything listed yet. A polite warning of incoming children and allied dragon, yes, but not a summons.

"Much worse," Rainlily said and then paused, staring at her fingers. She had lost track of her points. She tapped the tip of her left thumb. "Ah, yes, Joy might not allow the children to be moved from Haven, especially if the children do not want to leave."

Rainlily pulled a large egg covered with complex spell tracings out of her messenger bag. She explained how Joy had been trapped inside it, that all evidence pointed to there being eleven more objects containing baby dragons somewhere in Pittsburgh, and that the oni greater bloods had used Providence to transform the tengu from humans to part-crow. "We think that the oni greater blood, Kajo, *might* have the traps at one of the four encampments that you are heading for."

Rainlily stressed the word "might" in a manner that indicated that Tinker's Hand could not come to an agreement. It was possible that Discord had a strong feeling that ran counter to the evidence gathered. "First sent the empty trap with me so that you could scry it. He believes it's imperative that if you spot the traps, you can target all of our power toward destroying them. They should be considered possible genocide devices with a range of one *mei*."

Wolf's East Coast holdings with all his brothers and sisters were in range, then.

"I understand," Wolf said. Evacuation of the continent was not an option; it was his sworn duty to protect his world from invaders. Queen Soulful Ember had met him at the Wind Clan airfield thirty years ago. Pure Radiance foresaw Pittsburgh's first appearance on Elfhome. The queen charged Wolf with meeting the new arrivals—whoever they were—and holding the line against them.

Wolf had been trained as a warrior. He was given this land to protect because of his name.

It was his duty to stand and use whatever he could to keep the world safe.

"Send word to my brother, Jay Bird Screaming in the Wind," Wolf told Rainlily. "Tell him that I have need of him."

Rainlily left the egglike trap with Wolf. She had come on Discord's hoverbike. She fumbled with starting it up but roared away as confidently as Discord. More proof that Wolf's *domi* had chosen *sekasha* that fit her well.

Jay Bird should get Wolf's message at Summer

Court as soon as Rainlily returned to Pittsburgh. The distant voices allowed for instantaneous communication between devices. His older brother didn't have Wolf's level of wealth to pull from; he would need to borrow a gossamer. He would then need to cross four *mei* to reach Pittsburgh. It would take days for the beast to fly across the ocean, fighting a headwind the entire way. Wolf normally took the northern route, stopping at Whiskey's volcanic island as a way station. Depending on the weather and the beast, it could take up to a week to make the trip, although it could be made faster.

"What is your older brother like?" Wraith Arrow asked.

Wolf had recruited most of Howling's household after he turned a hundred. The *sekasha* had all withdrawn from society after his grandfather had been assassinated—centuries before he or Jay Bird had been born. Wolf had to trek to High Meadow Temple to lay out his plans and ask for their backing. By the time Wolf brought the *sekasha* back to Summer Court, Jay Bird was half a century into avoiding Wolf. His people knew his older brother by name alone. Considering his name was Jay Bird Screaming in Wind—that was probably not a good thing.

The jays of the Easternlands were smaller and drab compared to the brightly colored blue jays of the Westernland but they had the same annoyingly harsh call. A flock of blue jays had made themselves pests at Aum Renau. The birds nested in areas made safe from predators by Wolf's household—in fruit orchards, under the eaves of outbuildings, and even on laundry poles. Their numbers grew because of the elves' protection. The birds, though, would scream at anything that came too close to their badly placed nests: elves, hounds, cats, and even *indi*. The birds liked no one and nothing.

Jay Bird might be unfairly judged by his name.

"I'm not sure," Wolf admitted. "We were both young children when I last saw him. At the time, I thought him better than me in all things. After Little Horse was born, I saw what a difference two decades could make in a child. Jay Bird always had the advantage of me."

"Competition is good for growth," Wraith Arrow said.

Wolf nodded at the truth of this wisdom. "I pushed myself to be his equal. It makes it difficult, though, to judge him as the age difference made him larger than life. Nor can I be sure that he is now as he was then. I know I was just a seedling of what I am now. I have grown much since I left the Easternlands. Jay Bird most likely has changed since I've last seen him."

Wolf certainly hoped that Jay was wiser and less prone to temper flares.

"I know that he has two Hands," Wraith Arrow said. "You could not call them Vanity Hands but his *sekasha* are all just out of their doubles, like him. What of the rest of his people? How many *laedin* does he hold? Does he have Beholden?"

Most young *domana* had no clue how to build a successful household. Elfhome had been vastly changed from the world that their parents were born into, either by the Rebellion or the Clan Wars. They came to Court at their majority with ambitions but no useful guidance. Whatever plans they had made in their youth were drowned as they floundered in the unfamiliar waters of Court. Normally what ended up happening was that they would meet equally young and ambitious *sekasha* who had been raised in private households instead of temples.

Such warriors often had subpar training. The smaller the household, the more their parents were distracted by their day-to-day duties. There were no other *sekasha* children to team-build with or compete against. Interacting only with *laedin*-caste children, even those older than themselves, often gave young warriors a false sense of superiority. *Sekasha* born during the Rebellion had learned their skills in combat and knew nothing by rote to pass on. Parents born during the Clan War sometimes forgot how they were taught certain skills. If there had been only one Hand in the household, then there was no way for the young warriors to learn how multiple Hands should work together.

The biggest drawback of a young *sekasha* raised in a small household was that the warriors had no desire to be anything but First Hand. It's why they left their homes. Some refused to be anything but First.

When a *domana* attracted young, inexperienced *sekasha* to their First Hand, it normally started a cascade of failures. They rarely could gather a Second Hand or a following of *laedin*. Without the large number of warriors, the *domana* couldn't offer protection to the Beholden households necessary to feed, house, and maintain the warriors. Keeping everyone fed and housed became a difficult juggling act that many, like Jewel Tear, failed. His father's court as head of the Wind Clan had been an education on how important revenue streams were to protecting a household.

Wolf had gotten around the problem by recruiting his grandfather Howling's orphaned household. It gave him experienced, respected *sekasha* that attracted people who didn't want to risk everything on "a child's" unproven judgement. It had been a tactic open to any of his elder Wind Clan siblings like Ibis and Dove and Jay Bird but not one they pursued (though some would say that Wolf's ambition made him a good fit with his grandfather's household).

Jay attacked the problem in typical Jay-style: he'd traveled to the four Wind Clan temples and dueled with the warrior monks, using his sword skills to impress them. It was not as dangerous as it sounded as duels were carefully designed to avoid death. He risked only embarrassing himself, and even that was minimal as he and Wolf were both trained by Otter Dance, daughter of Perfection and Tempered Steel. She had spent her childhood bouncing between the two temples that her parents had founded, learning both of their polar-opposite fighting styles. The young warrior monks most likely had no idea how to counter the combination of the two.

"I don't know if he built the rest of his household." Wolf felt sad admitting this. When they were small, he and Jay shared a room and spent all of their time together. They had been friends, had they not? "He only started to gather his two Hands after I was made Viceroy. I'm not sure why he waited nearly a century."

"Perhaps the one he wanted as his First had not won their sword yet," Wraith Arrow said. "Your father waited for Otter Dance."

Wolf considered. He had wanted Discord as his First, but she insisted that if their dreams would come true, he needed to take Wraith Arrow and the others as his First Hand and Second Hand. Knowing that she had her parents' ruthless determination, he'd bowed to her wishes. He found comfort in the knowledge that it gave her time to consider what Pittsburgh could offer her personally. It also meant that she had been able to freely offer to Tinker.

Had Jay Bird found someone worth waiting for?

The rattle of drums reminded Wolf that he had a war to focus on. The royal marines had debarked from the train. With a deep rumble, the locomotive headed out, pushing its carriages back toward Pittsburgh. In a matter of minutes, everyone would start out for the nearest oni encampment.

"The others do not need to know of the children yet," Wolf said. "It would only distract us from the upcoming fight."

Wraith Arrow nodded in agreement. "The oni are our priority."

Wolf casted a fire scry. The spell tracings on the egglike trap reflected back with the same intensity as the inactive shields traced on the *sekasha*'s arms and a handful of magic items scattered through the camp. The potential of some sort of magical field was there but not active. It was going to be difficult to detect the traps with the fire *esva*, especially in the heat of battle.

He dropped the fire scry and cast a wind scry. As he expected, the trap was invisible as it was neither moving through the air nor blocking the natural flow of the wind. He only sensed Darkness's gossamer moored above the work camp, waiting for the rest of their force to move out.

"The Stone Clan might have an easier time spotting these." Wolf held out the trap to Wraith Arrow. "The others should be warned."

A wave of tension went through Wolf's guard. They shifted to face an incoming threat, their posture going from camp idle to possible combat. In this sea of heavily armed elves, the only possible conflict was with Stone Clan *domana*.

The Wyverns had been clear that they would brook no aggression between the clans during the war with the oni, but there were no guarantees that the Stone Clan would honor that decree.

A moment later, Forest Moss with his borrowed Wyverns came plowing through the royal marines. Because of the Wyverns' presence alone, his people allowed the incoming *domana* to close. Everyone knew that the Stone Clan should have already marched out as they had the greatest distance to travel. They knew Forest Moss shouldn't be bearing down on Wolf; they were afraid of a fight. It did not help that the male's unnaturally white hair hung in disarray and his ruined eye was clearly visible.

"Should you not be with Sunder?" Wolf asked cautiously. Forest Moss had fought bravely enough since arriving in Pittsburgh, but he'd been unhinged by the destruction of Ginger Wine's enclave. Wolf was uncertain how stable the male was. He'd seemed fine at Station Square, but they had only interacted for a few minutes.

"He just suddenly hared off this direction," one of the Wyverns reported to Wolf while tapping his temple, indicating that he thought that the *domana* was hopelessly mad.

"Is there a problem?" Wolf asked Forest Moss. "Do you not understand the plan?"

The Harbingers had sketched out a simple—but in Wolf's opinion dangerous—plan. They wanted to attack the enemy forts, one at a time, from all directions. They hoped to pin down the oni within each fortification and wipe them out before moving on to the next fort. Wolf had pointed out that reinforcements coming from the other encampments could surround anyone between the forts. Cana Lily took it as cowardice on Wolf's part. Sunder acknowledged the danger but brushed it off, saying that the bulk of the oni force were young creatures out of the whelping pens. They wouldn't have the intelligence or experience to counter the Harbingers.

In the end, it was decided that Darkness and Cana Lily would take the eastern flank. Sunder and Forest Moss would attack from the south. It meant only the Stone Clan risked being surrounded. They paired up so that the Harbingers would handle offense while the younger Stone Clan *domana* provided defense.

Forest Moss should be someplace else, protecting Sunder.

The male seemed much less sane than he was at Station Square. He rocked in place, his hands fluttering as if he didn't know what to do them. The Wyverns with him watched their charge closely, as if Forest Moss was more dangerous than an army of hidden oni. To be fair to the Wyverns, he was.

"How do you stand it?" Forest Moss asked Wolf. "Knowing that she is so small and helpless? That the city could be overrun in your absence?"

For a moment Wolf thought this was a jibe at

him, that the female in question was Tinker. Then he remembered that Forest Moss had taken a human female as his *domi*. The Wyverns allowed it because the woman was heavy with another male's child and her presence seemed to calm the mad *domana*.

Wolf could understand the fear. "You need to trust her. You love her for her strength. Let her be her own person. If she needs your help, she will tell you."

"How would she tell me?" Forest Moss's voice quavered with fear. "We are deep within the forest; Pittsburgh could be overrun and we would never know."

Tinker wouldn't have survived the summer thus far without being *domana*. She had been kidnapped, shot, bitten, and nearly killed multiple times. Elves had magic-based regeneration abilities that far exceeded a human's natural healing. Being *domana* allowed Tinker to take on *sekasha* Beholden and tap the power of the Spell Stones. It gave her instant access to powerful shields, multiple scrying spells, and an array of attacks. What's more, Wolf had the comfort that he could tell if Tinker tapped the Wind or Fire Clan's Spell Stones.

Forest Moss had linked his *domi* to the Stone Clan's Spell Stones via a *dau* mark. While it made it simple for Forest Moss to find the woman within the sea of humans, she wouldn't be able to pull power from the Spell Stones until after she was transformed into a *domana*-caste elf. She lacked the genetic key that allowed the initiation spell to set up a resonance between the *domana* and the Spell Stones. Nor could she be remade as an elf until after her child was born.

"Your *domi* has royal marines with her," Wolf said. "They would know how to get word to you."

This only made Forest Moss flail his hands more.

"They are but children themselves! All of them are young! Some are still in their doubles! The old guard thinks that watching over her is the safest assignment for their plebes."

"Oh, be quiet, mad one." Sunder came drifting through the royal marines. There was something oddly ethereal about this warlord who was neither female nor male. Hir wore white face paint with a narrow strip of black across hir eyes. Wraith Arrow said it was an ancient custom of Sunder's tribe, which had been wiped out hundreds of years before even Wraith Arrow had been born. A spell orb orbited hir; Wolf wasn't sure of its function but unlike the ones that Jewel Tear used, it did not seem to do anything as mundane as cool or perfume the air around its owner. Hir wore a cloak over hir wyvern-scale vest; it was woven out of something lighter than fairy silk. It floated in the faintest of breeze like it was a living entity separate from the elf.

Death had been the greatest Stone Clan warlord of the Rebellion. The Harbingers had been his five subcommanders that he sent ahead of him; heralds of the upcoming destruction. Together they would lay waste to entire regions, killing anyone they deemed loyal to the Skin Clan until the streets ran with blood. When they were done, they would burn the city to the ground and salt the fields beyond it.

Wolf did not want the Harbingers in Pittsburgh. He was glad that the battle had taken them far away from the city limits.

Sundar waved languidly at Forest Moss's fears. "As your *domi* is now, she's no different from all the other human females in Pittsburgh. The oni will have no special interest in her. The one you should fear is Darkness; given a chance, he will tear out your heart in recompense for what you did to his beloved Blossom Spring. Bad enough he lost his niece, but to learn that Blossom Spring was endlessly raped before being drowned in a piss pot—time has not dulled his hate of you."

Forest Moss nodded his head. "I would deserve any pain that he chose to rain down on me but that. My *domi* is innocent of any crime. Her great-grandmother had yet to be born when I blindly led Blossom Spring to Onihida."

"Which Darkness knows," Sunder said. "So far in this present mess, you are blameless. If you stray one step off that narrow path, though, he will crucify your entire household, however pitiful it may be."

Forest Moss nodded. "I will be worthy of my *domi*."

The male seemed calmer despite the implied threat. Perhaps he thought that Sunder was promising to shield Forest Moss if he stayed close and obedient.

"I have news," Wolf said without adding that it was from Tinker. He had learned young that the first rule in political discourse was to admit to as little as possible. "The oni have eleven more devices like this one."

Wraith Arrow held out the trap that he was holding.

Wolf gave a carefully edited explanation of the trap. "It's paramount that we find them before—"

Sunder interrupted to wave away Wolf's concern. "One must always assume that the enemy has a great and powerful weapon that it holds in reserve. It is why you must grind out every last one of them. Time and time again, someone would be merciful to our masters only to have them unleash a flood of horrors or a hideous plague upon their vanquisher."

"It looks like a wine cooler," Forest Moss said.

"The smallest packages are often the most dangerous." Sunder cocked hir fingers and brought hir hand to the mouth to cast a Stone Clan scry. It would search the land instead of the sky.

Wolf felt the gathering of power as Sunder made a connection between hir and the Stone Clan Spell Stones. The scry washed over Wolf as it scanned the entire clearing. Sunder had used a spell that allowed *domana* from other clans to perceive the signature readings, so everything laid clear to Wolf, from the Wyverns organizing the royal marines to the trap in Wraith Arrow's hands. It was a small, dense knot of potential nearly lost against the confusion of the work camp.

"It's not much to look at," Sunder said. "It will be difficult to spot in the middle of battle."

"If it is in one of their camps, I will find it," Forest Moss said.

Sunder dropped hir scry and cast another spell. Wolf could tell that the spell focused tightly on the trap and flashed oddly, but it wasn't until there was a flare of power from the gossamer overhead that he realized Sunder was using battle code. Hir was identifying the trap as an object of interest. Darkness had signaled his understanding.

"Good hunting." Sunder turned and drifted away. "Come along, clanmate."

Forest Moss followed Sunder like a lost child.

"See that all preparations to move out are finished," Wolf ordered, trusting that his Hand would delegate as he scanned the area for Prince True Flame.

His cousin had changed out of his white ceremonial

uniform to his combat gear. With five thousand royal
marines milling about, all in Fire Clan Red, the prince
was difficult to spot by design. Windwolf could feel,
though, the steady low thrum of a fire shield that
only a *domana* could cast.

Wolf spotted his cousin among the flood of crimson uniforms, the one golden head among the sea of
redheads.

"True!" Wolf called out in greeting.

"Wolf, my young pup," True Flame said fondly
as he cancelled his shield. He stepped forward and
recast it so that it now protected Wolf too. "All is
ready. I'm moving out. Keep yourself safe. You were
well trained for this."

"I need a word with you first." Wolf explained as
quickly as he could of the new weapons.

"This Kajo had them for three months?" True
Flame asked. "I wonder why he's not used at least
one. I suppose he hoped that Malice would be our
undoing. I suppose they might still be betting on the
supposed horrors that Jewel Tear reported."

"You doubt her report?" Wolf said.

True grunted, sounding unimpressed. "She's young
and inexperienced. She could be wrong about what
she scryed in those camps. To keep something like a
horror hidden for long enough for it to reach its full
growth . . ." True finished with a shake of his head to
indicate that he didn't think it was possible.

Wolf was less sure. The oni had had nearly thirty
years to raise any type of creature that they wanted
in the cover of the dense virgin forest. "My pilots
always use the train line as a landmark; it's nearly
impossible to miss. We came from the north or the

east, fighting the headwind. We never had cause to venture south of the tracks once we spotted them."

True waved aside the comment. "We're talking something the size of a wyvern or larger. Some horrors were nearly the size of dragons. How do you keep something like that caged and fed?"

"If the electric catfish are any indication, they could lose them in the wild and we would be none the wiser."

"The catfish were not true horrors, no matter how large and scary as they might seem to the humans. They are on scale with the wargs and the black willows. Malice comes close in size but, more importantly, in power. Horrors were deadly even to *domana*."

In Wolf's peripheral vision, Wraith Arrow was nodding. His First was a veteran of the Rebellion. He'd fought alongside Windwolf's grandfather, Howling. He would have dealt with horrors.

Malice had nearly killed Wolf.

"If you're ambushed, put up your wind shield and do a fire scry. I'll support you from my position," True Flame said.

Wolf nodded. The two spells used different hands so that they could be cast jointly.

The narrow railway was a blessing and a curse in that it provided a level straight road in the direction they needed to travel but it was also a perfect site for an ambush. They had decided to split up and travel in smaller groups. True Flame would lead the way and turn off where Jewel Tear had left a trail marker.

Wolf would follow True Flame at a distance, turn off before the trail marker, and travel in a parallel path to a point just west of the first oni camp. Sunder and

Forest Moss would head straight east, arriving south of the first camp. Darkness was to attack from the east. Both Harbingers would have a second camp at their back. Cana Lily would provide air support from Darkness's gossamer, allowing him to move quickly to where he was needed.

All things considered, it was the best attack plan for Wolf and his people. Wolf didn't have the *sekasha* or the *laedin* to lead the charge into a dense knot of oni backed by horrors. Sunder would deal with Forest Moss, who had had a mental breakdown after the attack on Ginger Wine. The Wyverns with him believed that he was stable enough to take part, but if they needed to put him down during the battle, his death could not be placed at Wolf's feet. Cana Lily, who clung to old resentments spawned during the Clan Wars, was as far away as the battle allowed. In the war council, Sunder seemed focused on the oni and equally irritated by Cana Lily's outbursts.

It was worrisome, though, that Wolf's first concerns were over his "allies" and not the enemy.

Darkness planned to fly his gossamer troop carrier over the oni camp. The gondola would be hidden from casual view by a spell that bent light rays. Once over the target, he and his people would leap from the gossamer, protected by the Stone Clan's most powerful shield. It was an attack that Darkness invented and he had warriors who trusted him enough to leap off a gossamer in. midair.

It was an insanely dangerous maneuver that only someone with centuries of war experience would attempt . . .

Or Wolf's *domi*.

Wolf had to be sure that Tinker didn't learn of this attack.

True Flame laughed. "Ah, you must be thinking of your *domi*. I've learned the look. One part fondness. One part terror."

Wolf smiled and nodded. "Keep yourself safe, cousin."

True Flame gave him a rough hug and headed off with his troops falling in behind him.

"If the oni truly have multiple horrors hidden away," Wraith Arrow murmured quietly as the Fire Clan surged ahead, "we will need all that we can muster to kill them. Hopefully, Blue Jay can come quickly."

8: HOPPING DOWN
THE BUNNY TRAIL

"Let me get this straight," Usagi Sensei, the head of the Bunny household, said. "You're all spies?"

This was not a conversation that Lawrie Munroe wanted to have. She'd been actively avoiding it since the June Shutdown. She sat as pushed-back from the Bunnies' long dining table as she could get, long legs kicked out to distance herself from the conversation. While Usagi was looking at her fellow Bunny, Widget, there was a stuffed rabbit under the table glaring accusingly at Law.

Law should have left after making sure that all the Bunnies were safe. She had taken, however, one too many lumps while trying to keep the oni from attacking Oktoberfest. She'd also left her Power Wagon parked at the train depot in Charleroi. There was a derailed train, a platoon of oni warriors, and an army of pissed-off elves between the Bunny enclave and the depot. At the time, it seemed wiser to hunker down, let Babs Bunny stitch up all her cuts, and make sure she didn't have any hairline fractures. The last day—or two—had been incredibly hazy as she recovered with the help of antibiotics, painkillers, and lots of bedrest.

"What are spies?" Bare Snow asked over the rim of her chocolate milk. Three months of living with Law had made Bare Snow somewhat fluent in English but there were still lots of words that she didn't know. The "teenage" elf female was wearing only an oversized nightshirt and one of the kids' bunny hats, her long blue-black hair done in little-girl braids. It was utterly an adorable outfit, but Law knew from experience that Bare Snow also had half a dozen weapons hidden on her at all times. (It was a fact that often boggled Law considering how little Bare Snow wore.)

The Bunny household was having an emergency family meeting before their half-elf children woke up. All five Bunnies were in attendance: Usagi, Babs, Clover, Hazel, and Widget. (Clover, though, had her head down on the table and seemed to be asleep. She'd been up half the night with her colicky newborn son.)

Law wasn't sure how she and Bare Snow had gotten roped into the meeting, as they weren't officially part of the household.

The Bunny children all called Bare Snow "big sister." After a lifetime of being an outcast in her own family, Bare Snow embraced the role with her whole being. The young elf wouldn't want to miss a "family meeting."

Usagi was in full mini-Martha-Stewart mode, complete with starched bandana. "A spy is someone who secretly collects information about an enemy."

Yes, Law could totally be what someone could

consider a spy. A freelance spy. Or an assassin. Or an avenging angel. Whatever. She had been one since the June Shutdown. She didn't want the Bunnies to know, because there were all sorts of dangerous secrets attached to what she'd learned in the last three months. While Usagi and Widget had gotten a massive information download in June—the evils of the Skin Clan Empire and how Windwolf's grandfather had been assassinated—they were missing key pieces of the story.

It wasn't that Law didn't trust Usagi. The problem was Usagi came with six sets of big ears and little mouths that endlessly repeated the most unlikely of things. (There were seven half-elf children but one couldn't talk yet.)

Law had been hoping that Usagi would never ask about Law's activities because she couldn't lie to the woman—not in front of Bare Snow. Elves viewed lying as the worst sin that you could do. Bare Snow wouldn't lie to save her soul. She would turn against Law if she heard Law lie, especially to someone like Usagi.

"No, we're not spies!" Widget was the youngest Bunny, a cute teenage African American girl. She was stunningly intelligent yet lacked common sense. She'd actually swum the shark-infested Ohio River during winter, thinking that river sharks hibernated. "We're Hal's Heroes! We're like the Sons of Liberty during the Revolutionary War, only less sexist."

Law controlled a grimace. Widget's other loyalties also made Law worried about telling the Bunnies the truth.

"Who exactly are these Hal's Heroes?" Usagi asked. "How did you get involved with them?"

"It's like Fight Club," Widget said. "The first rule of being in the Resistance is not to talk about the Resistance. Besides, you know how hard it is to keep a secret in this house with all the little kids hearing everything and repeating it over and over and over?"

"In the name of the moon, I'll punish you!" Bare Snow struck a Sailor Moon pose. Law wasn't sure if Bare Snow was actually following the conversation. The discussion slipped in and out of the two languages on the fly. Her quip, though, illustrated Widget's point, since it was one of the first things Bare Snow learned in English.

"The Resistance?" Babs was the oldest of the Bunnies. She had a skunk stripe of premature gray that she liked to dye various colors. Currently it was purple. Her lap was full of squirming ferrets, as part of her being the family doctor extended to the pets. Each ferret had a medical record in a binder that Babs was making notes in. "What exactly are you resisting?"

"We haven't completely settled on a name," Widget said. "Some people wanted us to be the Rebel Alliance but it was decided that's too hokey. We're using 'the Resistance' as in 'the French Resistance.' I think the name is to impress on people to be hush-hush and don't go blabbing stuff to anyone, not even people they trust, because those people might tell other people who would tell the wrong person."

"We need to know what you're involved in," Usagi said. "This time it saved all of our lives, but it could also endanger all of our lives. The elves believe that the head of household is responsible for all the actions of the individuals in their enclave. Who are these people? Why did you join them without talking to us first?"

Law squirmed but kept quiet; technically, she and Bare Snow weren't part of Usagi's household. Their activities *shouldn't* bring the elves down on the Bunnies.

"Well, I didn't seek them out and join them," Widget said. "I was crushing on this boy that works at the bakery. I met him when I went in to help them with their computers. He is so fine, with the bluest of eyes."

"Duff?" Usagi consulted with many of Pittsburgh-based companies, trading her Earth business savvy for things like dining tables. It was through her contacts that Widget ended up doing computer work for the bakery.

Duff was Alton Kryskill's younger brother; number five in the Kryskill clan. The siblings were all ruggedly handsome as Norse gods. Their stunningly beautiful mother had a coffee shop downtown but their dad had been a sniper for the US Marines. The family's sniper genetics meant all the siblings tended to keep to the shadows despite being incredibly good looking.

"Yeah, right?" Widget said. "Out of the blue, two months ago, Duff suddenly calls me and asks me to hack the city's security camera system. ASAP. Matter of life and death. If I hadn't done all the footwork while trying to find Windwolf the month before, I wouldn't have been able to do it. I'm not sure how he knew that I could." She glanced pointedly at Hazel, who worked at the bakery.

"I didn't tell him anything." Hazel had a silicon sheet down on the table, flour up to her elbows, and was kneading bread dough. "Duff seems to think you walk on water when it comes to computers, he probably just assumed you could do it."

"Me? Walk on water? Is that what Duff thinks?"

Widget smiled dreamingly at the news. After a minute, she realized that they were staring at her. She shook off the distraction. "Well, I am damn good at what I do, but not that good. I used the backdoor that I made in June. Anyhoo, I didn't know why he was so frantic and then boom, I'm looking at the pugugliest fishes walking around the city, trying eat the police. Duff is all code words and hush hush. We did it. Well...the guys in the Hummer did it but only with my help. We saved the policeman and killed the monsters. Duff was all 'Thank you, I love you, thank you' and 'Don't breathe a word to anyone about any of this.' Like I would talk to anyone about hacking the City of Pittsburgh's computer system! That was before Princess Tinker pulled the orbital gate out of the sky; Duff's family was worried about repercussions."

The Kryskills had produced an honest to God cannon, killed the giant walking electric catfish terrorizing the city, and then vanished without fanfare. There were a handful of people who knew it was them—the cop that they rescued for example—but no one offered up the family's name to the media. Not even the EIA named them in their press releases. It'd taken days for Law to connect the dots and figure it out who had saved the city.

"Duff is part of this Resistance?" Usagi asked.

Widget cringed. "You can't tell anyone."

"You know we won't tell anyone." Usagi glanced to Law.

"I swear on my honor, I'll tell no one." Law was fairly sure no one would ever think to ask her. People saw her as an antisocial backwoods man-hater. (She didn't hate men. It was simply a case that few seemed worthwhile and many needed a firm beating—administered by her—immediately.)

Bare Snow rarely talked to anyone outside of the Bunnies, so it was easy for her to nod in agreement.

"He's my cell leader," Widget whispered. "It's all been hush-hush from the very start. We don't really know who-all is working for the oni. We don't know what level of technology that they're operating at. We have to assume that anything we say might be overheard. I told Duff about the French guy—Mr. Fancypants—Brous-whatever."

"Andre Brousseau?" Law named the first person whose death she was responsible for, although technically he shot himself.

"Yeah, him. I told Duff how Andre looked human and worked for the EIA but was kidnapping girls like me off of Earth for the oni. I couldn't tell Duff what Andre's name was or I'd have to explain about everything that happened in June. It turns out that the tengu had told Duff that 'the people that look human' were oni greater bloods. When Tinker *domi* returned Jin Wong to the tengu, Jin ordered them to quietly wipe out the greater bloods. The problem is that 'the oni' never trusted the tengu completely. Jin's people only knew a few greater bloods. The tengu knew that there were more. I'm not sure if anyone knows about the Skin Clan angle—but I couldn't explain it without telling them about Bare Snow."

Widget had been hopping around certain information landmines from the very beginning.

"You've kept the right hand from knowing what the left hand was doing?" Law said.

"If the tengu knew about Bare Snow, I think they

would feel honor bound to tell Tinker *domi*," Widget whispered. "I know that Bare Snow was set up to be a scapegoat for the attack on Windwolf. I don't know if the *sekasha* would believe that she had nothing to do with it. I don't think they would hurt her, but what do I know? I thought river sharks hibernated. I couldn't risk it."

Law hugged Widget. "Good girl."

"I'm the only one without a baby," Widget whispered. "I felt like I was the only one able to fight to make sure they all stay safe."

"You could have told us," Usagi said. "Quietly. When the kids were sleeping. We can keep secrets."

Widget cringed. "I was afraid that if I started to talk I wouldn't stop. I needed to keep it all compartmentalized or I was going to start babbling it all out to the wrong people. And it seemed unfair to put that kind of pressure on you. You literally can't tell anyone about Duff and the Resistance. You wouldn't believe how stupid some humans are! There are people that are saying we should just step back and let the elves lose! Pull the police and the EIA off the streets and let the oni take control of the city! These idiots would be perfectly okay if the oni killed every single elf in the city 'because the humans would still be alive to make deals.' They don't realize that the greater bloods have always treated the true bloods and lesser bloods as disposable tools. It's why even the half-oni have turned against them. Once the oni wipe out the elves, there's no reason that they'll leave the humans unharmed. Or at least, most Pittsburghers used to be stupid. Maybe after what happened at Oktoberfest, they'll start to realize that the oni will kill everyone—empty the city—if that's what it takes."

That was a chilling bomb to drop but probably completely correct.

"I think Oktoberfest was a wake-up call," Usagi said. "It was for me. We've been cautious but I think we haven't been careful enough. A lot of people know that the Bunnies exist. That we have half-elf children. If the oni are bent on genocide, then we have to assume that they'll come after our babies."

"Yes, they will," Bare Snow said. "They'll see the children as dangerous mutts and will want to eliminate them before they can breed."

"But they're just little kids!" Widget shouted.

All the mothers hushed her. The meeting would have to end once the children woke up.

Widget whispered fiercely. "They're not dangerous. They're little and they're going to stay little for years and years."

Bare Snow leaned across the table to take Widget's hands. "I know that a hundred years would seem forever for you. It is all of my life plus few more turns around the sun. To the Skin Clan, it would be a blink of an eye. They are an ancient evil, easily ten thousand years old. They might not come for the children this week or this month or even this year, but they will come. They will want to wipe clean anything that could be immortal and remember what they've done here."

"What are we going to do?" Hazel whispered.

"Make sure they don't win!" Widget said loudly.

"Those of us without babies should focus on that," Law said, meaning her and Bare Snow.

Clover stirred for the first time. She opened her exhausted eyes and reached out to take Law's hand.

She proved that she hadn't been asleep the whole time by saying, "Thank you, Law. Bare Snow. Widget."

Clover had a toddler and a newborn who would be orphaned if she was killed fighting. Their fathers didn't know that the children existed, if Clover even knew which male impregnated her. Clover lived up to the "sex drive of a rabbit" myth.

"We'll do what we can without drawing the line of fire on everyone." Babs most likely would be a backline medic once fighting broke out. Her son was only a few months younger than Moon Rabbit.

"We need to double-up on our hoarding." Hazel started to shift her bread dough into the kitchen to rise. "What we got during the keva bean handout won't last long."

"We can gather food for you!" Bare Snow turned hopeful eyes to Law. "We can, can't we?"

"We'll make sure you have fresh fish and such." Law couldn't promise more as it was already September. In the last two months, more and more people were out foraging the old abandoned fruit trees, and hunting small game like turkeys, squirrels, and rabbits. It was pushing the bigger game animals deeper into the forest, making them harder to find.

"I think we should move." Usagi shifted into planning mode now that information gathering was over. "I only picked this restaurant so we had access to a kitchen that we could get FDA-approved. That's useless until Tinker links Pittsburgh back to Earth—assuming she stops getting hurt."

"She can do that?" Widget asked.

"She can only juggle so many grenades but yes, probably she can from what I've heard," Usagi said, making Law wonder where Usagi was getting her information. Law had heard that Tinker *domi* had been out at Squirrel Hill tunnels, looking them over, but there had been no confirmation that Tinker could actually link them to Earth. "We should find someplace farther from the front line. Someplace smaller that's easier to heat and easier to defend. We should get some weapons. We should learn how to use them."

"We can teach you!" Bare Snow said.

Hazel came back for another round of bread dough. "We need to come up with protocols on how we're going to deal with emergencies so we all know what the plan is. I had no idea what to do when fighting broke out at Station Square. If Widget hadn't been able to tell me that everyone was safe, I would have gone there."

There was a sudden stampede of little feet in the room over their heads.

"Oh, the children are awake," Hazel said.

The kids were good and didn't scream or shout as they came thundering down the stairs, but the damage was done. Clover's baby woke up crying.

"Once more into the breach, my friends." Clover stood up.

Counting Clover's infant, the commune had seven children. The six who could walk swarmed the table. The Bunnies were all shades of hair color, skin tones, and sizes. Their children, though, all looked like full siblings with straight black hair, blue almond-shaped eyes, and pointed ears. Moon Rabbit, the oldest, led the charge. She was fourteen but looked and acted six, which was why she only occasionally seemed able to dress herself. This morning she only had on her

Wonder Woman underwear and was dragging her rabbit onesie behind her. Her right pigtail braid had unraveled, so her black hair hung to her waist. The other children were equally in various stages of dress. Her little brother, Shield of a Thousand Leaves, still looked like a toddler at five years old. He was crying because he had tried to put on a pair of costume butterfly wings and gotten them stuck on his head. Blade climbed into Bare Snow's lap since his mother, Clover, had headed upstairs to deal with her colicky baby. Thunder went to lean against his mother, Babs, but her lap was still full of ferrets. All the kids were talking and crying and screaming.

Law loved the children and enjoyed the chaos in small doses, but she had hit her limit. She was already standing up when her phone rang. The screen showed that it was Alton Kryskill.

"I need to take this." She used the call as an excuse to flee the house completely. The sidewalk outside the house was strewn with toys. She had to pick her way carefully to a clear spot. "Hi, Alton! How did it go?"

She'd asked Alton to check her fish traps and deliver anything he found in them. Luckily she had only promised "water produce" to Caraway's enclave as she had expected Oktoberfest to chew up more of her time.

"I found your traps without any problem," Alton reported. "They were full. I got everything to Caraway's and Chili Pepper was happy."

"Great!"

"Are you free? There's something I want to talk to you about."

Law frowned at her phone. What would Alton want

to talk about? It boggled her mind. About how she found out about the train? She *had* left dead bodies behind her. How she derailed the train alone? She doubted Hazel or Widget would have mentioned Bare Snow to Duff.

"Now?" Law said when she realized that she'd been silent too long.

"Yeah, if you're free. I'm on Mount Washington at the moment."

Which was an alarming coincidence.

"What are you doing there?" Law glanced around.

"My little brother Marc has a place on Grandview, the old Greely place."

Law turned to look toward the distant WESA radio tower. She had only been to the house once during an epic high school party that went south when one of the football players didn't listen to the warning "she's drunk, leave her alone." He *did* listen to the autographed hockey stick to the side of the head, though. There was a reason she wasn't offered the place when the Greely family moved Stateside last year. "Okay, meet me at the Duquesne Incline."

Looking at Alton Kryskill, it was easy to see why Widget was crushing on his little brother Duff. The Kryskills all had piercing blue eyes, beautiful honey gold hair that poets would write sonnets for, and a build that made them seem godlike. Alton added a neatly trimmed beard, slightly darker in hue than his golden locks, that accented his strong chin.

The "Asian woman" who accompanied Alton had all the little tells of a tengu warrior: lean, muscular body, strong nose, ink-black hair. The female identified herself as Yumiko Sessai. A few months ago the name "Sessai" wouldn't have meant shit to Law. After a summer of covertly fighting the Skin Clan, Law knew it indicated that the woman was one of the near-mythical *yamabushi*, who were said to have magical powers. All her intel said that they were stalwart protectors of Jin Wong and the other members of the Chosen bloodline. The Kryskills had gotten very deep into the tengu camp somehow if Alton was running with a *yamabushi*.

Alton didn't want to talk about it—which was fine with Law, since she had her own secrets to keep.

Yumiko was willing to believe that Law was badass enough to take on an entire train full of oni warriors single-handedly and yet knew no more than the average Pittsburgher about oni history. It would seem naïve of Yumiko, except for the fact that the Kryskill family had pulled a cannon out of thin air and taken on six giant walking catfish. Yumiko might consider "foragers" on par with Paul Bunyan and Daniel Boone. It was also possible that Yumiko expected Alton to later educate his family.

Whatever the reason, Yumiko patiently covered oni history as it pertained to current events.

At one point, three worlds—Elfhome, Earth, and the oni homeworld of Onihida—had natural gateways connecting them at countless points. It was through these gates the first "greater bloods" appeared on Onihida. The invaders had a strange new magic unknown to the inhabitants: powerful bioengineering spells that allowed them to create horrific war monsters. They quickly conquered Onihida.

What the tengu only recently realized was that

these "greater bloods" were actually Skin Clan elves who had already conquered Elfhome in the same manner. Originally their entire race had rounded ears like humans, but the Skin Clan gifted their slaves with pointed ears, so that slaves could be identified instantly. It meant that the ancient members of the master race could pass as humans, and had been doing so in Pittsburgh since the first Startup.

This matched up with what Law had discovered on her own at the beginning of summer. She and Bare Snow had covertly fought and killed several EIA employees who looked human but were actually Skin Clan elves.

Yumiko connected many dots that Law was missing. The Skin Clan had set their sights on the powers held by the godlike dragons that were from a fourth world. Neither the tengu nor the elves were sure how many dragons the Skin Clan had managed to trap. They did have a list of known victims: Clarity, Brilliance, Honor, Impatience, Joy, Nirvana, and Providence.

According to Providence, the dragons had decided that the captured individuals had trespassed on the elves' homeworld and thus were responsible for their own sad fate. Because they thought waging a war with the Skin Clan would be unjust, the dragons simply put Elfhome and Earth under interdict. They attempted to protect Onihida by destroying the gates that linked it to the other worlds, not realizing that the elves had already pushed their way onto that planet.

The Skin Clan started out small in their experiments, using the genetic material from the slain dragons. They wanted various magical abilities like seeing the future, teleporting between worlds, and phasing through walls. They made the mistake of using their slaves as test subjects, accidentally gifting some of them with godlike abilities. The following rebellion was both ironic and inevitable. After that, the Skin Clan discovered a new application for the captured dragons: powerful spell bombs.

"With just one of these bombs, they could turn all the elves in the Westernlands into monsters," Yumiko explained. "We believe that the reach of the spell is limited to the wavelength of magic or one *mei*. When our people were transformed from humans into tengu, it took all of us, even the ones in hiding, far, far away. Our only advantage is that if the oni wanted the spell to transform all the elves in the West Coast Wind Clan holdings and the southern-most Stone Clan ones, they would need to stay near Pittsburgh. Otherwise they could cast the spell anywhere in the Westernlands."

"Just the elves? Not the humans and tengu too?" Law asked.

"The transformation spells—we think—need to be keyed to one genetic pattern. When we were transformed into tengu, there were oni guards surrounding us that weren't affected by the spell."

Yumiko showed Law a photo on her phone of a large, elaborately decorated egg. It looked like something made if Fabergé had been on acid. "The Skin Clan on Onihida only had access to Providence's body. Their people hidden among the elves manipulated Forest Moss into finding the sole remaining pathway between Earth and Onihida. In the brief time between its discovery and the elves destroying it, those moles created eleven of these genetic bombs. We believe Kajo has them but we don't know where Kajo is hiding.

Shortly before Jin Wong returned to us, Kajo killed all the tengu under his direct control and moved his camp. Tinker *domi* believes that he's using dream crows to stay one step in front of the elves. She says that she could only outwit Chloe's ability by doing things that Chloe couldn't understand, even if she saw what it was that Tinker *domi* was doing. We need to be unexpected to get ahead of Kajo."

"And I'm unexpected," Law said.

"You stopped the train," Yumiko said.

"Okay." That was not a comforting logic because Law knew how she sketchy her entire plan had been. "How do I pick out this Kajo from thousands of other oni? What does he look like?"

"We're not sure," Yumiko admitted reluctantly.

Everytime Pittsburgh traveled to Elfhome, a tiny uninhabited island in the middle of the China Sea traveled to Onihida. The Skin Clan were freed from their prison but needed to get across several of Earth's international borders to reach Pennsylvania. They also needed legal identification, visas, and the ability to pass as human on a planet that had no magic.

The original inhabitants of Onihida, known as "true bloods," could jump through all the legal hoops and security checks to make the trip. They were, though, now a small minority on their home world. The immortal Skin Clan had been experimenting on the native population for thousands of years. The bulk of the oni were "lesser bloods" that often had animal genetics mixed into their bloodlines. No amount of paperwork could get them across international borders.

It meant that the Skin Clan could smuggle very few of their warriors into Pittsburgh. They needed a standing army to take on the elves and humans. What they could get in large numbers were poor Chinese women and a wide range of Elfhome animals. These they could interbreed to create a fast-growing warrior stock. Most of the "half-oni" that Law knew, like Trixie Chang, were children of true bloods and humans. The ones hidden away were fathered by lesser bloods. Those ranged from humanlike beings to things so monstrous that they couldn't be called sentient.

The problem was that some of the lesser bloods would only obey orders from beings that appeared as fierce as themselves. To appear more menacing, the true bloods painted their faces and the greater bloods wore ferocious-looking masks.

Yumiko said that Kajo would be fairly easy to spot among the oni—he was short, slight of build, and wore a distinctive crimson demon mask with horns. She provided a drawing of the mask as the tengu never managed to get a photo of it.

"I'll keep my eyes open," Law promised. "But I'm not going to wade into that mess out east of Monroeville, not after what happened at Station Square. Cana Lily tried to kill me."

Windwolf had protected her but she couldn't count on his protection for Bare Snow.

"We're not asking for you to join that fray. It would be very like Kajo to allocate the fighting to an underling. Lord Tomtom would have led their forces on the battlefield if *domi* had not killed him. Kajo would have not trusted the spell bombs to Lord Tomtom or his replacement. The lesser bloods are cannon fodder, no more, to Kajo."

Law nodded her understanding even as she wondered if the tengu were giving her too much credit. She had been able to stop the oni before by sheer luck of being onetime lovers with Trixie Chang and having a grandfather who worked on the railroad. The two aspects combined to allow her to apply insider knowledge of how the trains worked to an offhand remark about what Tommy Chang had discovered about the oni movements.

This time she had two photographs, one of an egg and the other of a mask. What was she supposed to do with these?

9: BRACE FOR IMPACT

Two Tinkers.

Two.

Oilcan barely survived a childhood riding herd on one little mad scientist. He couldn't even count the number of times they'd narrowly escaped death and/or dismemberment. It started when he was ten and Tinker had been an insanely brilliant six-year-old. When most kids were learning how to read, she'd been making go-karts out of old lawn mowers. Making the go-karts led to racing them on a small island in the middle of a shark-infested river. Then there had been the "let's see if it explodes" phase that led to the rocket sled experiment. The larger and larger trebuchets until they accidentally leveled one of the Roach Refuse outbuildings with a three-hundred-pound cracked engine block. The homemade fireworks. The magical wiffleball shooter. The hoverbikes. The hoverbike racing on the prototype racecourse. The hovertank experiments put on hold merely because she couldn't gain legal access to a large enough printer.

What were two of Tinker going to be like?

Being older—and not fearless like her—Oilcan had been the voice of reason, reining in anything that was sure to be deadly, but that left a lot of wiggle room for Tinker to exploit. He had often wondered why he was so boringly sane compared to her. He and Tinker were both Dufaes. He thought it might be a case of nature vs. nurture, where his mother's quiet control won out over his grandfather's lax parenting. Having met Forge and Esme, Oilcan was having second thoughts on the whole subject. Forge, so far, had been quietly sane. Esme had been the one who crash-landed a spaceship and flew an attack helicopter against a dragon. Maybe it wasn't the Dufae bloodline that made Tinker so dangerous. Unfortunately, the twins were also Esme's daughters and all that implied.

"*Auejae*," Pony called from behind Oilcan.

Oilcan had started the summer thinking that he was highly fluent in Elvish. Since Tinker's transformation, though, he'd stumbled over one unfamiliar phrase after another. He wasn't sure what *auejae* meant but Thorne Scratch turned with pleased surprise on her face.

"What is it, Little Horse?" Thorne Scratch used Pony's nickname with the elves.

"This is for you, *auejae*." Pony held out a square package the size of a backpack, elegantly wrapped in cloth.

She undid the cloth wrapping to reveal a wyvern-scale vest dyed to Wind Clan blue. "I . . . I did not expect you to have one for me. Not so soon."

The tone of her wonderfully rough, scratchy voice said that she was very pleased with the gift.

"Rainlily had a late growth spurt after she came to

the Westernlands." Pony patted his hands to his chest to indicate Rainlily's ample breasts were the result. "She outgrew her armor. We brought both of her old sets with us from Aum Renau to alter for *domi*. I'm afraid we already cut the other one down to fit *domi*'s smaller frame. This is all we have at the moment. Forgiveness. You are one of us, now. We should provide—"

"It is fine." Thorne Scratch tugged off her black-dyed armor. "We are in a war zone."

It did odd things to Oilcan's heart to see that she was wearing his Team Tinker T-shirt underneath. His kids had done his laundry and left it stacked on his bedroom chair for him to put away. The shirt had been on the top of the clean clothes pile. Had she borrowed it to keep him close or as a secret show of solidarity or just simply grabbed the first thing at hand when Tinker's messenger showed up at Sacred Heart in the middle of the night?

Thorne Scratch shimmied into the new chest piece. She wasn't as endowed as Rainlily but judging by the minute adjustments that she made, the younger female had started out smaller than Thorne Scratch in the chest. "It is tight but does not bind. It will work for now."

"Darkness provided transportation for three Hands from Cold Mountain Temple." Pony handed Thorne Scratch a piece of paper. "I recognize most of the names from visiting my grandfather when I was young. I do not know their true temperament."

Thorne's hastily tied braid had come undone while she had pulled the different-colored armor pieces off and on. Her dark brown hair spilled over her shoulders, making her growl in frustration.

"Let me." Oilcan held out his hand for the blue ribbon. He hadn't known how to braid hair at the start of summer. Elves, though, had a thing about long hair. It seemed to be a quiet status symbol to them. The oni had shorn Barley of his hair to humiliate him and it worked. The poor male wore a headscarf in a vain attempt to hide the fact he'd been shaved. The others hadn't suffered that particular torture at the hands of their oni captors. Their scars were less visible.

Merry felt guilty asking for help from her battered housemates when she had been spared the abuse. Rustle with his shattered left hand needed help to tend to his waist-long hair. Cattail Reeds wanted the comfort of Oilcan's protection. Baby Duck liked to try different styles as if she was trying to find her lost identity. What did the "true her" really love beyond baby animals? Thorne Scratch was hungry for intimate contact after the rest of her Hand had shunned her.

Thorne studied the list as Oilcan braided the Wind Clan color back into her hair. "I recognize all these names. I think I know them well enough to know their intent. Most are true warrior monks; they have no desire to be Beholden. There will be no moral gray in this war; the Skin Clan are cut off from their resources on Earth. They will do whatever it takes to seize and hold the Westernlands, no matter how barbaric it may be. It is how they have always been. The warrior monks from Cold Mountain Temple will see it as the chance of a lifetime for glorious battle without any stain on their honor. There are only one or two of the younger ones who might be considering leaving the narrow path of moral combat."

"Warrior monks," Oilcan repeated the phrase. He'd

heard the term all his life but he thought it was just a fancy way of referring to the *sekasha*-caste. "How are they different from you?"

"Warrior monks are *sekasha* who have taken certain vows to limit when and where they enter into combat," Thorne Scratch said. "They are considered the holiest of the holy."

Pony nodded but added nothing. Oilcan was learning that now that he was *domana*, the rules of engagement had changed. Tinker's Hand had taken a step back, letting Thorne Scratch stay center stage in conversations with him. It was an invisible filtering device that the *sekasha* employed, one Oilcan never noticed until it was applied to him. Had Tinker noticed yet? She usually ignored social constructs, maybe because she was so isolated while growing up.

Another odd change was that Thorne Scratch stopped wearing the cold, unemotional warrior mask while dealing with Tinker's Hand.

She let uncertainty show as she considered the list. "I think the younger ones will vie to be Jewel Tear's First Hand. They will reason that the attack came while she was asleep. It had been up to Tiger Eyes to see her Hand safe; it was not her failing that led to their deaths."

Oh, they were having *that* conversation: Oilcan's First Hand. Here, he was thinking Tinker oblivious.

"There are warrior monks coming from High Meadow Temple," Pony said. "They are not familiar to me. I do not know their hearts' desire but I suspect some hoped to be Beholden to Wolf. They might be tempted by the promise of First Hand."

Oilcan cringed. He really didn't want more entanglements than he already had. He'd been a loner most of his adult life. His tangled knots of responsibility—with six babies looming on the horizon—felt suddenly claustrophobic. He didn't want to add to his household but Thorne Scratch had already changed her clan alliance for him. He didn't have the right to deny her support—strategically or emotionally—from other *sekasha*. Yes, they were ears deep in the holy warriors at Sacred Heart but none would put his desires above others. The fact Oilcan was now an elf was proof that he couldn't depend on Forge's Hand to protect him.

Thorne Scratch made a rude noise. "They will not want to serve under a First that abandoned her clan."

"If they are so blinded by clan loyalty from the obvious truth that we're all one people, then they are not for you," Pony said. "There were those that thought that Otter Dance should seek out her father's clan since she was short and dark. They were not the ones that make up Longwind's First Hand."

"What a mongrel group are we at Sacred Heart." Thorne Scratch tucked away the list. "Elf. Human. Stone Clan. Wind Clan. But verily, is that not what the *sekasha* are at their core? A mongrel of elf and dragon genetics."

Pony nodded. "Proceed with caution. Those who will decide the fate of *domi*'s siblings will be swayed by the presence of a strong Hand—but a Hand can only be strong if they fit."

There was a heavy transport gossamer delivering stones when Oilcan returned to his enclave. It was a stunning sight. The huge living airship shimmered in the sky over Sacred Heart, nearly transparent, its fins fanning the air has it hovered. The hull slung under its belly was painted black with accents of gold—Forge's color. A cargo elevator loaded with large rectangular foundation stones was slowly descending.

Tinker's experiments with trebuchets had been a lesson in what heavy stones could do if dropped from a great height. Oilcan slowed, torn between rushing forward to stop what was happening and the healthy desire to stay out from under any possible falling rock. He came to a halt as he realized that this wasn't the first delivery; the walls around Sacred Heart were nearly done.

Had life been so insane that he never questioned the appearance of a hundred tons of rock?

So far this summer, he'd become the "pet" of a hyperactive dragon, adopted five elf kids by accident, was transformed into a different race against his will, killed his great-great-great-great-granduncle with magic, taken on the entire half-oni tribe as his Beholden, and—for all intents and purposes—gotten married to Thorne Scratch. (Their relationship came with sex, children, and a "till death do us part" clause that included the fact that she might kill him if he screwed up as badly as Earth Son.) Just this morning, he'd had a conversation with talking mice that might be unborn cousins.

Yup, totally insane. The question was: What else had slipped his attention?

All the races of Pittsburgh were represented in the workers. Black-winged tengu worked mooring ropes to help the gossamer stay in place. Team Tinker was installing a stout ironwood gate made by Gryffin Doors. Mixed in with the others were the half-humans; Blue Sky was a half-elf and Spot was a half-oni. The construction crew was made up of elves.

Up to yesterday, all of the elves had been Wind Clan from the nearby enclaves. Sprinkled among them now were unfamiliar Stone Clan elves, marked by their shorter stature, dusky skin, and black duck-cloth overalls.

Had the strangers arrived on the gossamer with the stones? Were they going to stay? Did Sacred Heart have room for so many more and still have a separate space for the twins? And how did the stones and elves get to Pittsburgh? There hadn't been time for Forge's gossamer to get to the Easternlands and send a loaded ship back. Had the elves been in the Westernlands already?

The massive cargo elevator touched down. Workers swarmed forward to shift the load. They slapped paper inked with spells onto the stones, said the trigger words, and the blocks floated upward to be guided away. In less than a minute, they'd cleared the elevator. Elves didn't work fast; they were merely extremely efficient. Everyone knew exactly what they needed to do, as they had done similar work for hundreds of years.

Forge stood like a sun at the heart of the organized chaos; everything revolved around his center of gravity. He looked far too young to be a great-great-great-great-grandfather. His hair was still dark brown and the creases at the corners of his eyes were from smiling, not age. He'd changed his doeskin pants in favor of the same black overalls as the newcomers wore but with a crisp white cotton shirt.

"Where exactly are these coming from?" Oilcan called to Forge as he worked his way through the herd of floating stones. There was a silent squaring off between Thorne Scratch and Forge's First that seemed to be a standard *sekasha* thing.

"Grandson!" Forge smiled in greeting, clapping a hand to Oilcan's shoulder. "The stones came from my quarry near Aum Goutanat."

"Aum Goutanat?" Oilcan echoed. He'd never heard of it before.

Forge motioned to the south. "After it became obvious that the Wind Clan was growing fat on its monopoly of Pittsburgh, the Stone Clan demanded a land grant of unexplored Westernlands equal to what Wolf Who Rules Wind had been given. They hoped to establish a presence in the city. Queen Soulful Ember gave our clan—my clan—an area known as Alabamageorgia."

Forge smashed the names of the two states together like they were one word.

"I know of the area." Oilcan had studied American geography in elementary school. "But I thought you lived in the Easternlands."

Forge laugh. "Yes, I do. Queen Soulful Ember tasked me with building a set of dams on the Tennessee River. I think I'm saying that right. We kept the human names since all our maps are from them. I am to provide knowledge of dam building, skilled workers, and all construction materials. As part of my payment, the queen gave me a stone quarry and virgin forest within the land grant from which I could gather the needed materials for the dams. I had just started the preliminary work when I received the news that my son's children had been found: orphaned and in danger."

It explained how and why Forge appeared so quickly in Pittsburgh after the Wyverns discovered who Oilcan and Tinker were descended from. It also explained how Forge could quickly shift building materials and work crews to Oilcan's enclave.

"Won't the queen be angry that you . . ." Oilcan didn't want to imply that his grandfather stole construction material for the royal dams. ". . . abandoned the project?"

Forge laughed. "I haven't abandoned it. Water is a tricky element to work with; you can't just put a stone in place and hope it stays until you get around to setting another block. Everything needs to be poised, ready to go, before you lay that first stone. We have worked all summer setting up an airfield, starting a limestone quarry, building a camp with a deep well and high walls, and cutting a road linking them all together. You can't go at a large project slapdash. Patience is an engineer's greatest tool. With it, you can do anything that you can imagine."

Forge sounded like a true Dufae grandfather. Tim "Bell" Dufae had drilled project management into his grandchildren as the most important skill they could have.

"I have Beholden working the quarry." Forge pointed to one of the sandstone blocks roughly a yard long, two feet wide, and eighteen inches high. The chisel lines looked too clean to be cut by hand; the elves must have used some kind of magic to carve out the stones. "These were quarried for a mill pond once I found a suitable perennial stream, but that project can't begin until next summer. They'll have plenty of time to quarry other stones."

Oilcan nodded automatically, his mind racing. Should he tell Forge about the twins? The four babies? The talking mice? Tinker and he needed allies to keep control of the twins' future, but Forge might decide that he knew best. He had the means to whisk the twins off to the Easternlands hovering overhead.

It was only a matter of time, though, before Forge learned of the children. Tinker had dispatched Rainlily to update Windwolf; if he told his cousin True Flame, the prince might decide to inform the Harbingers.

"We might be—getting more—kids." Oilcan picked out his words carefully. "They came to Pittsburgh so that they can freely choose their future. Some, however, are quite young and might still fall within the Stone Clan's purview."

Thorne Scratch raised an eyebrow, which made Oilcan wonder if she objected to his walking the fine line between truth and fiction or if that last word didn't mean "purview" like he'd been taught.

He decided to jump to the point. "Sunder is head of the Stone Clan here in Pittsburgh. Do you know Sunder? Will he object to the children being kept by me?"

"Hir," Sunder said in the very same gentle but firm grandfatherly tone that Tim Bell used while teaching everything from physics to personal hygiene. "Sunder has no gender. The proper pronoun to use for Sunder is hir."

"Okay," Oilcan said slowly. He'd learned the pronoun as a child but never understood why it existed. All the elves in Pittsburgh seemed to be either male or female. Being that Skin Clan created everything from walking trees to giant electric catfish, what exactly did "no gender" entail? Oilcan shook his head, trying not to get derailed. "Do you know...hir?"

"Yes and no." Forge made a seesaw motion with his

hands. "The Harbingers have a long and sordid past with the wood sprites. They are why we are Stone Clan. When my mother and the rest of our kind were still children—dangerously clever children—they managed to stage a fiery escape. It was not a trick that they thought they would be able to do twice. Certainly not the thing with the methane again as the Skin Clan became much more careful of their sewage treatment after losing half of their largest city in the southeast."

The more Oilcan heard about wood sprites, the more he had to consider that Tinker was typical of the breed. It did not bode well for him raising the twins. "How do the Harbingers work into this?"

"The wood sprites were smart enough to know that they needed a protector; they were still quite small and only had been able to take what they could carry. They decided to negotiate an alliance with the Stone Clan warlord, Death. Their choice was fueled by the fact that Death was the most successful warlord that they could easily reach out to. Howling of the Wind Clan was half a continent away and Ashfall of the Fire Clan was farther still and Scourge of the Water Clan could have been anywhere on the Western Ocean. They still write songs about the forming of the pact between the wood sprites and Death; it was a battle of wits that changed the fate of elfkind. Death demanded unquestioning loyalty of those he kept within his protection."

Oilcan understood wanting loyalty but the word "unquestioning" made him uneasy. "The wood sprites wanted a choice?"

Forge laughed. "Exactly. It's the nature of wood sprites to question everything. My mother and Death came to a settlement where Death hid us in the jungle and kept us a secret. Even our name—wood sprites—was to make it seem as if Death had some mystical connection with supernatural forces. Only his five lieutenants, the Harbingers, knew the truth, since they often had to act as his liaison as we developed weapons to use against the Skin Clan."

The "we" seemed to be more personal than just the historical sense. "You fought in the Rebellion?"

"Yes. I was barely out of my doubles when we started the construction of the Spell Stones. I may have been the youngest but I was also the loudest when we debated who should be given access to the Spell Stones. Death wanted to carefully parcel them out, giving access to warlords only after they'd pledged loyalty to him. Not the Stone Clan but to him personally. It was a distinction that alarmed me. It seemed that he was using us to make himself the next emperor. We would have fought and died only to replace one absolute master with another."

"Do the Harbingers know that you championed the cause?"

Forge laughed. "Oh, they know. While it was a group decision, I was the one who traveled the world in secret, setting up stones for the other clans. My wealth and standing as Queen's Architect are a direct result of that work. It would be impossible for them not to know."

"Verily," Forge's First said. "Death could not have forced allegiance out of the other warlords, especially from Scourge. We would not have won the Rebellion if all four clans had not been able to bring the power of their Spell Stones to bear against the Skin Clan. The

Rebellion would have died when Death was captured on the Blood Plains."

"How do the Harbingers feel about the wood sprites sharing the Spell Stones?" Oilcan said.

"One would have to ask them," Forge said. "Something I've managed to avoid doing for *nae hae*. If you pore over the events that led up to Death's capture, our decision played no part in his downfall. Emperor Heaven's Blessing, though, had Death flayed alive, then stuffed and mounted as a footstool. Rational discourse cannot follow such a fate."

"I suppose not," Oilcan said.

"The salt in the wounds was the fact that the wood sprites also collectively decided to be neutral during the Clan Wars," Forge said. "We retreated to our jungle sanctuary, pulled up the bridges, set out defenses, and told all comers to leave us alone. All who persisted learned that wood sprites are not to be cornered."

Far to the east, there was a flare of power at the edge of Oilcan's awareness. It flashed off and on in a weird pattern that reminded him of Morse code.

Forge had gone still as if listening intently. "Speaking of Sunder, that is hir communicating to Darkness via battle code. Not a very private way to communicate but still it's better than trying to shout across a battlefield. I will have to teach it to you and your cousin. It is a handy tool."

The stones unloaded, Iron Mace's Hand shifted armor crates onto the cargo elevator. Traveling bags of clothing and equipment followed. There was something oddly final about their preparations.

"Are they leaving?" Oilcan asked.

"Aye," Forge said. "The distant voices brought word that they've been recalled for questioning at Summer Court. Sword Strike wants a full account from their own mouths, most likely with the queen and Pure Radiance on hand. I suspect that the crown is attempting to find who else might have been involved in Iron Mace's activities. I was sending my gossamer to my holdings at Summer Court, so I offered them passage."

"*Sama!*" someone called.

Oilcan glanced around. *Sama* was another elf word that Oilcan wasn't sure of its full meaning. He'd known that it meant "head of household" but he wasn't sure why Tinker's people called her *domi* instead. His kids hadn't stopped using it for him despite the fact he was now an elf.

"*Sama!*" The voice seemed to be coming from above.

An elf in Stone Clan black waved from the gondola. Oilcan didn't recognize the person.

"Hoi! Digger!" Forge raised his hand in acknowledgment. "I'm needed. I left my personal household in disarray when I came here. I need to give my *husepavua* some instructions before he heads to the Easternlands."

"What does *sama* mean? Exactly?"

Forge looked surprised and then pleased for being asked. "Ah, old habits die hard. Digger became my *husepavua* before I was given lands by the crown. Until a *domana* is given lands, normally they retain the title of *sama* as head of their households. I'm sure that Beloved Tinker will gift you lands and your household will need to learn a new title for you."

Forge stepped onto the lift and rode it up, looking more like an action hero than a great-great-great-great-grandfather.

Oilcan watched him go, mulling over what he'd learned. The bad news was that the Harbingers most likely hated all wood sprites and Forge in particular. The good news was that Sunder was also well versed on what a bad idea it would be to try and force the twins into something that they didn't want. The fact that they were children—historically—meant nothing in terms of their ability to act decisively.

It was possible that Sunder would decide to let the twins choose their own guardian, since that was the path of least resistance in the middle of a war. It would be the Wyverns that insisted on someone like Oilcan, who had *sekasha* in abundance at his enclave.

That led back to how would the twins feel about being given a guardian.

The twins had a plan. Oilcan was sure of that. Tinker would. The fact that the twins were on Elfhome, not Earth, was testament that they had planned *something*.

It was unlikely that the girls had planned on living with Oilcan in an old Catholic high school with a horde of elves. The twins left Earth before Oilcan had adopted a bunch of kids or moved out of his condo. Nor could the twins have known that Esme had returned from space or that Forge was in Pittsburgh, so their plan wouldn't have included the other two possible guardians. That left Lain or Tinker but those two were currently off the table. If the twins were truly like Tinker, they might even have some crazy plan of trying to live alone.

Tinker would be reluctant to abandon her plan. On the other hand, Tinker could be reasoned with. She could be persuaded to change her plan if something better was suggested.

What did Oilcan have to offer?

Sacred Heart's ground floor was mostly big public-space rooms. The gym. The dining room. The massive kitchen with walk-in coolers. There were a handful of offices and large closets but those were already in use. There were ten big classrooms converted into bedrooms on the second floor that he had dedicated for "guests" of the enclave. With Iron Mace's Hand leaving and taking his belongings with them, it would free up two of the ten rooms, but it seemed as if Forge had just tripled his number of people. Oilcan wasn't sure if there would be space to move Jewel Tear out of her room on the third floor. He never meant for anyone but family to be living in the space.

Tommy Chang, however, had returned Jewel Tear to Oakland during the latest round of chaos. Jewel Tear discovered that her people had abandoned her to her fate, taking all that she owned with them except for a few pieces of large furniture. The other Wind Clan enclaves were full, either with incoming Harbingers or displaced Wind Clan elves. Jewel Tear had ended up at Sacred Heart while no one was home. She had picked out an empty room on the third floor and had moved her furniture in.

Windwolf was paying for Jewel Tear's room and board. Oilcan's kids were ecstatic that they had an additional paying guest. Oilcan was glad the female had been rescued, he just wasn't happy that she had picked out a bedroom on the family level. It wasn't like he needed the space—until today. It left only three empty bedrooms on the third floor. Two if he gave one to Thorne Scratch. She had been sleeping in Oilcan's room since Ginger Wine had been attacked and the rest of her Hand killed. He wanted her to have a space to call her own now that she had accepted to be his First.

It left two big bedrooms on the third floor. The twins could share one and the other could be prepped to be a nursery. It didn't leave room for Esme or Gracie or any odd "other" that the twins might have in tow. They could get creative with room dividers, splitting the nursery into two spaces, but that wasn't a good long-term answer.

There were five mystery rooms that had either been huge closets with windows or small offices with nice views. While they were much smaller than the classrooms, they could still be respectable-sized bedrooms. They could hold a double-sized bed and still have space for a dresser and a desk. They needed to be deep cleaned, the many bullet holes in the plaster patched, and then painted. Oilcan started a list of supplies to get the rooms ready just in case they needed to house Esme or some other not-yet-identified twin ally.

The big classrooms were painted in a cheerful buttery yellow called "Pure Joy" but were completely empty. Merry was the only one of his kids with a real bed; the others only had the mattresses that the hospice donated. His old condo had a big walk-in closet, so he only had one small dresser left over from his childhood. His clothes were overflowing onto all flat surfaces.

If he was going to win over the twins, he would need to do better than empty rooms. If the twins were like Tinker then they would want desks, computers, tools, and all the bells and whistles of modern technology. If he was buying them furniture, he should also get some for his kids.

He needed to go shopping.

10: ARE YOU MY MOTHER?

✦◦═◦◦═◦✦

A certain irrefutable logic led Tinker to Lain's house. The only way that the twins could have unlocked Dufae's box was with the proper key word. The only way they could have learned it was if they had a copy of the Dufae Codex. Tinker could have asked the twins where they got it, but they scared her.

Her grandfather had given highly edited digital copies to Tinker and Oilcan, but he couldn't have known about the twins. He would have fought for legal custody of them if he'd known that they existed.

Esme saw bits and pieces of the future. She had created Tinker to protect Pittsburgh. She could have foreseen the twins' existence but she had left Earth shortly after Tinker's birth, eighteen years ago. She wouldn't have been able to interact with the twins directly. She could have, though, placed a copy of the Codex where they would be sure to find it.

Tinker wanted to see Esme's face when she explained how Esme's little experiment with frozen treats had unintended side effects. Tinker was still a little miffed

that Lain had lied about their relationship for eighteen
years just because Esme asked Lain to. It was some
nonsense about evil empires or something.

It reminded Tinker to ask Lain about her mother's
involvement in all this. Tinker's grandmother. The
one she never even knew that she had. The one she
would probably never get to meet. Grandmothers were
supposed to be like fairy godmothers of love; at least
everyone she knew acted like it. She'd never actually
met a real grandmother in the flesh. Blue Sky didn't
have one. Nathan's grandmother lived in Florida. Roach
had never introduced Tinker to his grandparents.

Forge's appearance made Tinker hyperaware that
grandparents were a mixed bag of gifts. It still pissed
her off, though, that Lain hadn't trusted her to be
smart enough to keep her mouth shut. Tinker could
keep secrets if she understood the reasons. Even now
she wasn't sure why Lain felt constrained to keep it
a secret. What did it matter if people knew?

Tinker mulled over the question all the way to
Lain's place. Jin had said that the twins' parents
had been killed and they ended up in the custody
of Lain's mother. How did that happen? Did it have
something to do with the reason that Lain had kept
Tinker hidden?

Tinker stomped up the front steps and rang the
ancient hand-cranked doorbell. Lain usually dead-
bolted her front door; she didn't trust her neighbors.
Tinker expected Lain to answer the door.

Esme calling "I'll get it!" was the only warning Tinker
got before the door was opened by her mother. Esme
kept surprising Tinker by popping up in odd places—like
in her dreams or the city morgue. Part of the surprise

was the fact that she looked nothing like what Tinker imagined her mother to look like: tall, thin, and white-blond hair with a purple dye job. Today she had added mysterious streaks of red, pink, blue, and green on her cheeks like war paint. Esme was in her early thirties but something about the way she moved suggested that she was only a few years older than Tinker's eighteen. It made her seem more like an older sister who would compete with Tinker for Lain's affection. It did not help that Esme wore a set of khaki shirt and pants that Tinker recognized as Lain's favorite outfit.

"Scarecrow!" Esme smiled brightly, although not looking surprised that it was Tinker at the door. "And your guard dogs."

"Don't call them that," Tinker said. "And don't call me Scarecrow."

"Okay, Princess!" Esme grinned widely.

"Don't call me that either!" Tinker brushed past Esme. She could smell sugar cookies; it might explain the war paint on Esme's face. Was getting frosting on your face a genetic trait? "Where is Lain?"

"Come. Sit. Talk," Lain called from the kitchen. "We have news."

"News?" Tinker headed for the kitchen.

"Alexander?" Esme called after Tinker, still searching for an acceptable name.

"Tinker!" Tinker shouted back.

"Tinker *domi*," Stormsong said as she drifted in Tinker's wake. The *sekasha* hadn't totally forgiven Esme for invading Tinker's dreams; it had nearly driven Tinker mad.

The rest of Tinker's Hand was quietly moving through the house, upstairs and down, checking for monsters. They would make themselves scarce after being sure that the house was safe. Stormsong was the only *sekasha* fluent in English; she would report to the others what was covered in the conversation.

Lain's house was a big Victorian mansion on Observatory Hill that served as her home and her workspace. It had been built in the late 1800s when the neighborhood was all homes of wealthy and influential families. A small forest had been used to decorate it with wood paneling, wainscoting, and carved molding, all stained to a rich cherry hue. A sage green damask wallpaper with woodland animals hidden within its elaborate design covered the few walls that weren't paneled. It had always been a warm and welcoming place of refuge for Tinker while she grew up.

Lain sat at the kitchen table with a plate of sugar cookies decorated with frosting. Tinker's favorite. Was it because the sisters had foreseen her arrival? There were two cups of tea for the sisters and a tall glass of cold milk for Tinker. Yes, they had.

Tinker thumped down into the chair in front of the glass of milk.

Lain refused to decorate her cookies; she made her guests go through the extra effort. Esme must have been the one who used the Mickey Mouse cutter to shape the cookies. Esme had painted the mice ears red, green, pink and blue.

"Have you been dreaming of mice?" Tinker asked. Oilcan had told her of his odd dream about the Dufae babies visiting him as mice wearing different colored scarfs. The colors matched up to the ones that Esme used.

"You too?" Esme answered with a question. "My

dreams have gotten really weird since I've hit Pittsburgh."

"That's a yes, then?" Lain asked.

"Oh, God, yes," Esme said. "Lots of mice. I'm not sure if the mice are literal or figurative. I don't think we're going to be besieged by talking mice—but odder things have happened lately. I do think something satisfyingly horrible happened to Yves, but I'm not sure. It seemed very real. Maybe it's going to happen."

"Who the hell is Yves?" Tinker asked.

"Our older stepbrother," Lain said. "Yves Desmarais."

"Satisfyingly horrible" was not a phrase you usually used when talking about family members.

"What exactly is so horrible about our family?" Tinker said. "Why couldn't you tell me, Lain, that you were my aunt?"

"Maybe we should start with our news," Lain said. "It is profoundly disturbing but it should give you a good idea what our family is like."

"Okay," Tinker said cautiously. The summer had served up so much disturbing information that Lain's statement kind of scared her.

Esme sat down directly opposite of Tinker. "A few nights ago, when we were at the morgue, I met that reporter, Chloe Polanski."

"She's dead." Tinker didn't add, "I killed her." She wasn't happy about the blood on her hands.

"Yes, her picture is on the front page of the newspaper." Lain believed that televised news was more of a popularity contest than real information. She only periodically watched WQED, mostly for Hal Roger's gardening show. She did get the *Pittsburgh Post-Gazette* daily and read it front to back.

"At the morgue, I thought I had met Chloe before," Esme continued. "She seemed very familiar. It wasn't until her picture was in the paper that it hit me why."

Lain took an old-fashioned photograph out of her breast pocket and pushed it across the table to Tinker.

For a moment, Tinker thought it was a picture of Chloe. It was more than that the woman had the same pale blue eyes and white-blond hair. She also wore the same bobbed haircut, flawless makeup, and chunky amber necklace. It was as if someone had tried to cosplayer the reporter. The picture appeared to be taken in New York; the Statue of Liberty stood far in the background. The vehicles in the foreground had the sharp-angled styling of the '70s or '80s.

Chloe was in her late thirties; she wouldn't have even been born at the time of the picture.

"Who is this?" Tinker asked.

"That's our mother," Esme said. "Anna Shanske Desmarais."

"What the hell?" Tinker said. "Why would Chloe be cosplaying as your mom?"

"It's a lot more than that." Lain fished a necklace out of her pants pocket and put it on the table beside the photo. "Chloe was wearing our mother's jewelry. Our father, Neil Shanske, had this made for her. See their wedding date was etched on the back of the pendant?"

"Mother loved amber." Esme tapped the necklace. "She never wore this particular piece after she remarried. Our stepfather showered her with amber jewelry that she would wear instead. She tried to keep this hidden from me. When we were little, I used to tear the mansion apart until I found it. I would march up to her, thrust it at her like a knife, and tell her to put it on. She never would. Shortly after I left for college, she called and asked if I took the necklace with me. She couldn't find it."

"She called me during Shutdown to ask about it," Lain said. "She was sure one of us had taken it but I hated the damn thing."

"I don't get it," Tinker said. "How did Chloe get the necklace and why was she trying to look like your mother?"

"I pulled some strings," Lain said. "Maynard was surprisingly cooperative when I used your name. I got a DNA sample from Chloe's body. Based on her mitochondria, Chloe was our sister."

"She was what?" Tinker said.

"Our sister," Esme repeated. "The three of us have the same mother."

Tinker frowned at the piece of jewelry. "Chloe was younger than Lain—but—not that much younger. She would have been born before Lain came to Pittsburgh."

Lain nodded. "Yes, that's right. And if she had this necklace, then she had to know who our mother was."

Stormsong breathed out a laugh.

"What's so funny?" Tinker asked, since her Hand normally did everything in their power to stay silent and invisible during a discussion.

"Chloe came dressed in black to the morgue," Stormsong said. "She had planned on taking the bodies of the Stone Clan children so no one could learn the truth about why the oni had kidnapped them. The moment you told Esme that you were her daughter, Chloe nearly tripped over herself trying to flee."

Tinker had noticed that Chloe seemed very unsettled

by the news. It had puzzled her. "What's so important about Esme being my mother?"

Stormsong shifted closer to the table. "If Chloe knew that Esme was a strong *intanyai seyosa*, she would have had to believe that you were too. Such abilities are passed by the mother's bloodline. It would instantly explain how you've managed to do so many impossible things. What's more, Chloe's blood tie to you through Esme's mother would mean it would have been easy for her *nuenae* to overlap with yours."

"My what?" Tinker knew that Stormsong had used the term before but she wasn't totally sure she understood the word.

"*Nuenae.*" Stormsong repeated and then paused, thinking. "I don't know the English word for it—if there is one. It is basically the world that you are trying to grow. *Intanyai seyosa* literally means 'someone who sows or farms the future.' When your *nuenae* overlaps with another *intanyai seyosa*, you share visions of things that might affect your shared future. It's why you and your mother were both having *Wizard of Oz* dreams. It was also why the tengu dream crow, Gracie Wong, was part of those visions—she was trapped on the damaged spaceship with your mother. She would share any future that Esme created. The more you interact with someone related to you, the more the *nuenae* transpose. Chloe had already interacted with you once. At the morgue, when she learned that you shared her bloodline, she realized any prolonged interactions with you would make it probable that you would dream of what she had planned."

Chloe Polanski had been Tinker's aunt and she had killed her. That totally sucked. It was also totally weird: Chloe knew that she was Esme's sister but Esme hadn't?

"How did you not know about her?" Tinker asked the sisters. "Why wouldn't your mother tell you that you had a younger sister? Or is it some weird compulsion that the women of our family have—to have secret babies that we scatter about the landscape like breadcrumbs?"

"We don't think our mother knows about Chloe," Lain said.

"But—but—but—Chloe knew who she was!" Tinker thumped the table beside the jewelry. "If she had this necklace, then she'd been to your mother's house. Right?"

Esme gave a bitter laugh. "Not necessarily. Yves or one of the boys could have taken it."

"Boys?" Tinker asked.

Esme and Lain exchanged looks.

"You really told her zilch about the family?" Esme said.

Lain shook her head. "I was afraid that if anything happened to me, she would feel the need to share the news with the boys. They would have wondered why I kept a child close to me, and the ball would start rolling."

Esme sighed. "Our father—as you might know—was Neil Shanske. He was an astronaut. Our mother is Anna; she was from a family of well-to-do bankers. When I was six, our mother met an evil snake of a man called Edmund Desmarais. Within a few weeks, our father was dead. Desmarais had him killed."

"There's no proof of that," Lain said quietly.

"Our stepfather is evil." Esme glared at Lain defiantly. "He killed our father."

Lain scoffed. "Your daughter has made me completely impervious to that look. I won't argue that he's evil, but we've never been able to prove he was behind the shooting."

"The man is a billionaire," Esme said. "He had enough money to make all proof disappear."

Lain didn't argue the point. Instead she turned to Tinker and asked, "Do you know how our father died?"

"He was killed in a random shooting." Tinker knew that small part of Lain's family history. Their family history. "He was doing a charity appearance in a bad neighborhood—in California? Someone opened fire on the crowd."

"Esme was six and I was twelve," Lain said. "Our father was training at the Marshall Space Flight Center, which is in Huntsville, Alabama. Our mother was an investment banker; she had relocated to Huntsville so we could be together as a family. That's how she met Desmarais. He had an isolated estate outside of Huntsville—a huge plantation house that had been in his family for generations. Our father was on a business trip to the Jet Propulsion Lab when he was killed."

"On Earth." Esme stood up to pace the kitchen. "Without magic, you never get that gut punch of 'this will be bad' and your dreams seem like they're just nightmares. But I know what I know: Edmund Desmarais killed our father."

"And I've always believed you," Lain said. "But to everyone else, you were just a child having nightmares after her father was murdered."

"Desmarais turned our life into hell to make our mother marry him. Oh, we could never prove it," Esme said as Lain lifted her hand to protest. "But we knew. He had our mother mugged. The robbers took her wallet, emptied her bank account, and maxed out her credit cards. Our house was burned down. Our car was stolen. It just went on and on. Anyone that she might have turned to was lured away with a job offer on the other side of the country, or had some crisis of their own spring up, or was simply killed."

"He loved her that bad?" Tinker wondered if it could even be called "love" if it moved a man to be so cruel.

Lain and Esme exchanged looks and shook their heads.

"We don't know why he wanted to marry her," Lain said. "We never did, but it wasn't because he loved her. It couldn't have been for her banking savvy; he could have had that without marrying her. She was already handling his money."

"It was his money, not hers," Stormsong said. "*Nuenae* extends from yourself. You must always be at the center. It does not include the wealth of other people. If you try to focus on others that way, it becomes like trying to walk two paths at once. Only the most powerful *intanyai seyosa* can keep track of multiple goals. My mother is part of the queen's personal household merely so their *nuenae* would align."

Lain shook her head. "He couldn't have known that. They're both humans living on Earth without magic. This was long before Pittsburgh traveled to Elfhome—at least, in human terms. I was twelve when they married; I was in my thirties when I came to Elfhome that first Startup." She frowned slightly. "But—you know—Yves was there that first day. He didn't seem as puzzled as everyone else by the ironwood forest."

"Yves never looked a day older the entire time we knew him," Esme whispered.

"Desmarais never seemed to age..." Lain paused. "Oh, God, it makes sense now. Desmarais is an elf trapped on Earth, just like the Dufaes. How did I not see that?"

"An elf would have recognized an *intanyai seyosa*," Stormsong said. "They would have known that they had to tie the oracle to them for their abilities to work."

Tinker gaze fell on the necklace. "But where does Chloe fit into this?"

"I have a theory," Lain said slowly, gaze distant as if she looked at far-off objects. "Desmarais tried to win our affection."

Esme made a rude noise. "Buy us off. I wasn't having it. I knew what he did."

Lain motioned to Esme not to derail the subject. "If he is an elf, then he's been on Earth for centuries. He married mother to bind her to his *nuenae* but that was a short-term fix for him. If he wanted her abilities over the centuries, then he would need to control her bloodline."

"Operation: Baby Machine," Esme snarled.

"What?" Tinker said.

"Desmarais talked our mother into quitting her job to devote herself to having children," Lain said.

"Mother loves babies," Esme said. "It wasn't that hard to do."

"Yes, there is that," Lain said. "The problem was that she was forty when they married and he had a really low sperm count, so they had to go through in vitro fertilization. It was such a big production that they couldn't keep it from us. We knew everything.

How many times it failed. How many times she miscarried. It took them two years for Lucien and she spent all nine months in bed. But Desmarais wanted more—she wanted more—so the medical circus continued. If a doctor said it was too risky, they would find another doctor. It always made me wonder: If she was the golden goose, why was he risking her? If he was an elf, though, he knew that she would die long before he did."

"She almost died giving birth to Tristan," Esme said. "She was forty-six. Some women are grandmothers at forty-six."

Tinker struggled to control the hurt welling up. "You have two younger half brothers that you never told me about? Lucien and Tristan?"

Lain sighed. "Yes, ladybug, Lucien and Tristan are our younger half brothers. Desmarais had a son by his first wife. Yves was ten years older than—well—if Desmarais was an elf there's no telling how old Yves is. Oh! Oh! If Desmarais was an elf, it means Lucien and Tristan are half elves."

"Oh crap!" Esme said. "That bastard! Autosomal dominant genetic disorder, my ass!"

"What?" Tinker said.

"Oh, I feel so stupid!" Lain was shaking her head. "Desmarais made out that the boys had some odd disease that made them look like children even when they were full grown. How could I not see that they were half-elf?"

Esme reached out to cover Lain's hand. "All that happened before the first Startup; we didn't know anything about elves and their immortality!"

Lain waved away the excuse. "Even afterward, I

never questioned it. It's so obvious now; the boys were like Blue Sky. When they were eighteen, they only looked like they were six or seven. They were still babies, but Desmarais treated them like they were grown men. He sent them away so they wouldn't distract Mother from her work."

"I never laid eyes on them again," Esme murmured. "Have you?"

Lain shook her head.

Oilcan's kids ranged from seventy to ninety years old but were still obviously "children." Even Windwolf was considered a "teenager" at 214. The Desmarais boys would be in their forties, which meant they were closer to tweens in age than teenagers.

Tinker had been thirteen when her grandfather died. She couldn't imagine being cut off from everyone she loved after losing him. "Did you abandon them because of me?"

"Oh, no, ladybug," Lain said. "We drifted apart long before you came into the picture. I—I don't know why. We were close when the boys were little but afterward things started to change."

"They're the ones that started it," Esme said. "Refusing to return phone calls or emails. I drove halfway across the country once to see Tristan before I left Earth. I wanted to say goodbye to him properly. He locked himself in the bathroom and cried until I left. I couldn't even get within spitting distance of Lucien; I'm not sure he was even living at the address that Mother gave me."

Tinker shook her head. "I'm still not seeing how Chloe fits into this."

"Our mother and Desmarais were trying to have

another child when the boys were both diagnosed with a genetic disorder," Lain said. "The plan was to use a surrogate to carry the baby to term instead of Mother. They'd already collected and fertilized the egg. Desmarais had paid a woman to act as the surrogate. Everything was set to go when Mother found out why the boys weren't thriving. She assumed all her children with Desmarais would be afflicted with the same genetic disorder. He seemed to agree. Chloe was the right age, though, to be a result of that experiment. We think that Desmarais implanted the egg into a surrogate and never told our mother."

"That's . . . that's horrible!" Tinker said.

"Desmarais is a monster. He's why I've never told you that I was your aunt. Why I never told you about our family. He sees people—his own children—as tools to be used. He'll kill to obtain what he wants. There's no way I could protect you from him if the wrong person found out the truth."

Jin had said that the twins had ended up in the custody of Esme's mother after their parents had been killed. Had Desmarais arranged another murder? Was that where the four other babies came from? Did Desmarais search out the frozen embryos after stumbling across the twins and had them implanted into a surrogate mother?

"How many frozen embryos did you leave in New York?" Tinker said.

"Me?" Esme said. "We're talking about Desmarais."

"More than six?" Tinker pointed at the mouse cookies. "Because there are six of your children at Haven. The tengu found them wandering out in the woods while I was out playing hide-and-seek with Chloe."

Esme stood up, hands over her mouth, eyes full of horror.

"Esme?" Lain said.

Esme muffled cries of dismay.

"Esme, what did you do?" Lain said.

Esme whimpered. "There was only supposed to be one! There was only supposed to be you! The one old enough to be able to save Pittsburgh. I've been dreaming of them. They're so little. So helpless. Just little mice of children."

"Six?" Lain had backtracked through the conversation to lock onto the most important detail. "Six?"

"Six," Tinker said. "Two nine-year-olds and four newborns—or something like that." She must have been very mentally off-balance not to get clarification on that. Was there one woman or four women pregnant with Dufae babies? Had Jin Wong been as rattled as she or was there a reason he didn't clarify? The summer had been so full of weirdness that it boggled her as to why Jin might have dodged the question. It was a fairly innocuous question—wasn't it? It might be something simple like two pregnant women carrying one to three babies each and thus it was just easier to skip to the punch line and say four babies. It was unsettling, though, that Jin hadn't given a fully accurate body count.

"My mother claimed that seeing across universes was nearly impossible," Stormsong said. "She likened each world to resting in a separate ocean with only tiny streams connecting them. To know how events were unfolding in a world, one must be in that ocean. Not even she could foresee these children until they traveled here."

"But she's aware of them now?" Lain asked.

"Most likely. The *intanyai seyosa* caste has their differences. Battles between them are like poker games where the cards are people. When I saw your little sister at the museum, I felt the resonance of another dreamer who shared my *nuenae*. If she was strong enough for me to sense her on Earth, my mother knows that she's here in Pittsburgh."

Her little sisters just got more terrifying. They had precognition on top of everything else? Tinker could remember being that age—she was always so sure that she was right about everything. If Tinker had been aware of her limited precognitive abilities, she would have been worse. Much worse.

Chloe had been after Oilcan's kids because they had special powers. Tinker's little sisters had power in spades. The only real advantage the twins had was that the oni didn't know that they existed. Or did they? Chloe was working for the oni.

"The twins reached Haven while I was playing hide-and-seek with Chloe. It means they got to Elfhome while Chloe was alive. Do you think that Chloe knew about the twins?"

Stormsong shook her head. "Chloe could dodge my sword but she was not at my mother's level. If she was, she would have known you were Esme's daughter long before that conversation at the morgue."

That was comforting. Tinker turned back to Esme. "Did you store more than six embryos?"

Esme shook her head. "I-I-I don't think so. The doctors retrieved a little more than a dozen eggs. One or two failed to be fertilized. We implanted three into your surrogate mother, just to be sure at least one took. I had dreams about twins, so I thought two of them would take. I'm fairly sure that they told me there were six embryos left over and all were of high enough quality to freeze. I left them in case the ones implanted in your surrogate mother failed to produce a genius."

Tinker shivered. Six babies all like her sitting in cold storage for years, quietly forgotten.

Well—not completely forgotten—or they wouldn't be up to their ears in Dufae babies.

"I think the twins have a copy of the Dufae Codex," Tinker said. "How would they have gotten it? Did Grandpa give you a digital copy? Was it a complete copy or doctored, like the one I have?"

"He didn't give me anything," Esme said. "Tooloo gave me a memory stick with some old photos of the Dufae family, a family tree, and a large text file. I barely looked at it; I didn't have time. I think I put some pictures in with the stick; I got blazing drunk that night. I gave it to your surrogate mother to pass on—I think. That last part is fairly hazy."

"Tooloo?" Tinker said. "How the hell did Tooloo get old Dufae family pictures?"

Esme shrugged. "I got the impression that she had always been your family's nanny. At least, that's what she made it sound like. She said something about taking a baby from France to Boston back during the French Revolution."

"What?" Tinker shouted. "Are you sure?"

"This was only a few months ago for me," Esme reminded Tinker.

"How—how—how?" Tinker sputtered with too many questions to pick just one. Tooloo always called

Tinker and Oilcan "her" wood sprites. Was it because the old crazy half-elf had something more to do with their existence than being an occasional babysitter?

"I've always had dreams that came true," Esme said. "On Earth, without magic, they were like getting one peek into a box. One quick flash of what was to come and then the image is gone. The summer I came to visit Lain here on Elfhome, I suddenly could take the lid off the box and stare at everything inside. But what was inside were horrible, terrible things. I didn't know how to stop it from happening—what I needed to do to make things right. I didn't even know if I could change the future. There's this old technique that some famous scientist used: right before he went to bed, he thought about his problem and then he dreamed the answer."

Tinker supplied the name of the scientist. "August Kekulé and his discovery of the molecular structure of benzene."

"It's one of the first things you learn when you're born to the *intanyai seyosa* caste," Stormsong said. "You focus your mind on what you want to see."

Esme nodded. "I wanted someone that could teach me how to use my powers. That night I dreamed that there was a red thread wrapped around my fingers, leading out of Lain's guest bedroom and down her stairs and out her door. I followed the thread into the dark streets and found on the other side of the river a beautiful elf female sitting in a grove of flowering lemon trees with a golden dragon the size of a mountain behind her. She had a red ribbon tied around her eyes and it trailed down and became the thread around my fingers."

Stormsong breathed in sharply. "Vision?"

"Who?" Tinker asked. "What?"

"Clarity was not the first dragon that the Skin Clan captured, but she was the last," Stormsong explained. "It is said that she allowed herself to be captured, knowing that her genetic material would create the caste that would lead the uprising. Like the *sekasha* before them, the *intanyai seyosa* were created in mass numbers, ruthlessly culled and refined while they were still helpless infants. There was an exception—one attempt to distill a perfect copy of Clarity in elf form. The resulting female child took the name Vision as she was the product of Clarity's prophecy. She was the most powerful *intanyai seyosa* ever born. Pure Radiance was her only child. None of the others could ever equal my mother because the blood of Clarity runs pure in her. I have just a pale, hollow reflection of her power. It is to be expected, though, as my father is of a dragon-born caste. When two dragon bloodlines are present in one child, they are often at odds with each other. It is very rare for them reinforce each other."

"When I woke up, I went looking for the female in my dreams," Esme said. "I found her in McKees Rocks. She was expecting me but there was no time for her to teach me more than a few things. If I was going to stop everything I could see in my dreams, countermeasures had to be set in motion immediately."

It was the first time Tinker had ever seen Stormsong completely flummoxed.

"Wh-wh-what?" Stormsong said. "You found her? Here?"

Esme pointed across the river. "Yes, she's been here since—well—I'm not sure. I think before the first Startup. Before that I think she was in Boston."

"She's in Pittsburgh?" Stormsong wasn't processing the news well.

"Wait? Who exactly are we talking about?" Tinker was confused. "If Pure Radiance was Vision's daughter, then we're talking about Stormsong's grandmother? Your grandmother is in Pittsburgh?"

Esme had said previously that Tooloo had taught her how to control her dreams. They had been in the middle of illegally obtaining elf DNA and bullying a local funeral home into cremating the dead Stone Clan kids, so Tinker had forgotten to follow up. Shortly after that, the oni blew up Tinker's limo, rebreaking her newly healed arm.

It had been a bad, bad night.

Stormsong looked uncertain as she shook her head. "I've never met my grandmother. Vision vanished before the Rebellion ended. The Skin Clan had bound her hand and foot. She was guarded by Vigilance. Like Malice, Vigilance could be considered a dragon but in truth was a spell-worked beast, pieced together from shattered pieces of other creatures. He wasn't as clever or powerful as the Ryu dragon that the Skin Clan had shattered down to make him, but he was massive in size with golden scales. Despite the shackles and the magical guardian, Vision managed to slip away. The Skin Clan sent Vigilance after her to bring her back. Neither one was ever seen again. It was assumed that Vigilance had killed her and gone wild. She couldn't possibly be in Pittsburgh."

"Tooloo has a bed made of dragon bones," Tinker said.

Stormsong shook her head. "I can't believe it is her. I know you would not lie about it but she went missing when our people needed her the most. We would have not won the war against the Skin Clan without Pure Radiance and the others to tip the scale."

"Oh, that reminds me," Esme said. "I went over to Tooloo's store earlier for milk and eggs. She gave me your mail."

"My mail?" Tinker thought the tengu had been collecting that for her.

Esme went to the kitchen counter and hunted through dirty baking pans. "Yeah, it looks like a greeting card. It's dated back in April. It's postmarked New York City."

"New York City?" Tinker took envelope that Esme handed her. "How long did Tooloo have it? Nothing has come from Earth since July!"

Esme shrugged. "She didn't say."

Tinker ripped open the envelope. Inside was a birthday card. It had a girl in a dress decorated with pink flowers. It read: *To a special sister on your eighteenth birthday.* "Oh shit, the twins sent me a birthday card!"

Tinker looked at the envelope again. It had been addressed to the Neville Island hotel but the Pittsburgh post office had forwarded it to her salvage yard. Ink stamps marked its passage from New York City in April to Elfhome days before her eighteenth birthday.

"Wait. Oh, that bitch! I remember Tooloo raiding my mail after the April Startup! She and her stupid chicken. She managed to slip this out from under my nose!"

Tinker headed for the door.

"*Domi*?" Stormsong followed. "Where are we going?"

"I'm going to get some answers out of Tooloo, one way or another."

11: BE OUR GUEST

⟡═◉═⟡

Tommy had forgotten his phone in his new fancy bedroom, so he had to swing past the William Penn Hotel to pick it up. It felt weird walking into the lobby, knowing that he'd slept in the building the night before and would probably do it again until Bingo found them a new place to live. The lobby was a huge room with marble floors, massive crystal chandeliers, and lush seating. Weirder yet, everything was lit up and gleaming as if dozens of half-oni just completed an intensive deep clean to the space.

Trixie had always been one of Tommy's favorite cousins. She cleaned up decently enough. Like most of the half-oni, she was painfully skinny after years of near starvation. She was, though, also painfully "sharp," in all ways that the word could be applied to a female.

She was standing behind the counter in the hotel lobby, fiddling with the machine that coded the room keys. Instead of the tank top, capris, and ballerina flats that she normally wore, she had on a dark blazer jacket over a white button-down shirt and black slacks.

"What the hell is going on?" Tommy asked. "Did you guys clean the lobby? Why are the lights all on? Why are you dressed like that?"

Trixie smiled tightly. "Welcome to the William Penn Hotel. How can I help you?"

"We are not running a hotel," Tommy growled.

Trixie shrugged. "We already have three guests."

"What?"

"It turns out that Tinker's fight with Malice took out half of the Wyndham Grand. Since all the hotels in the area were booked solid since the July Startup, the poor souls who had been staying at the Wyndham have been sleeping at their offices. When the ones in the Alcoa building noticed people coming and going from here, they strolled over to see if they could get a room."

"You gave them rooms?" Tommy could guess the answer but hoped that he was wrong. Surely Trixie was smarter than that.

"I explained we're not able to accept credit cards at this point in time, that they would need to pay cash up front. They went down to the bank and came back with oodles of cash."

"You gave them rooms?" he repeated in a growl.

"We need a cash flow," Trixie said. "I was hoping to make a nest egg at Oktoberfest but the oni crashed that party. I only made forty bucks before all the yelling and screaming started. We got lucky. We would have been in the middle of that mess if the tengu hadn't suddenly swooped in, yelled for everyone to get out, and grabbed the bunnies."

"They grabbed what?" Tommy missed something. "Rabbits?"

Trixie laughed. "You look like shit. How much sleep have you gotten lately?"

"Not enough." Tommy scrubbed at his face, annoyed that the lack of sleep was showing. He'd planned on sleeping the entire day after being up two nights in row. Oilcan's emergency planning session, however, had awakened him at the crack of dawn.

"Here." Trixie produced a Red Bull from under the counter and tossed it to him. "I've been hoarding that but you need it if you don't know who Babs Bunny is."

Tommy groaned as he realized who she was talking about. Babs was part of a commune of women who all had half-elf kids, collectively known as the Bunnies. All the women were illegal immigrants who hoped that their children created a legal loophole for them staying on the planet. No one was sure that they were right, not even the Bunnies. Just in case they were wrong, the women all used the names of famous rabbit cartoon characters instead of their real names. Because Babs couldn't go to the EIA or the elves without endangering herself, she was the only midwife in town that the half-oni had been able to trust with difficult births.

"Alita knows someone that works as a housekeeper at the Wyndham," Trixie said. "The story checked out."

Tommy nodded after he realized that Trixie had circled back to the men who asked for hotel rooms. Alita was one of Trixie's younger sisters. She was a smart, tough cookie, but then most of Aunt Amy's kids were. Tommy cracked the Red Bull open—he needed the caffeine.

Trixie continued, passing on her little sister's information. "Someone was bright enough to evacuate all the guests into the basement before the attack helicopter and dragon sideswiped the Wyndham. All the guests are alive but the rooms are toast. Alita also got some 'how to run a normal hotel' tips off of her friend. We found where the housekeeper carts were stored. The teens gave the lobby a quick scrub and went up to the eighth floor to deep-clean the rooms. Alita says that the linens on the beds need to be top notch, so we tracked down the laundry room and where the clean linens are stored. We even found an entire closet of itty-bitty soaps and shampoos. The men wanted to know if we offered room service. That was an interesting conversation. Turns out 'room service' is what you call take-out food in a hotel and has nothing to do with sex. I gave some of the cash that the men forked over to Alita and Zippo so they could buy groceries."

Tommy nodded at the wisdom of the pair going shopping. Zippo was one of Bingo's little brothers. He was only sixteen but nearly the size of Babe. Plus Zippo was chill enough to listen to the smaller but smarter girl. Alita and Zippo made a good brain-and-brawn team. It was wise to send them out with enough money to buy in bulk while the stores still had food to buy.

It was the whole cleaning thing that bothered Tommy. "Did Bingo not tell you about moving?"

"Look, I know how hard you've worked to keep us all safe, but I think you're making a mistake. We've had shitty lives and, for once, we've got something nice. We can make this work."

"We're at war."

"Yeah, every day of our freaking lives. What else is new?"

Tommy couldn't deny the truth of that.

Trixie scanned the lobby. "Where's Spot?"

"Spot?"

Trixie put her hand down to hip level to measure off how tall Spot was to her. "Bingo said you left with Spot."

"Oh shit!" He'd forgotten he'd dropped Spot at Oilcan's. He had planned to see Jewel Tear when he picked the boy back up. "He should be okay. Blue Sky was there and he promised to keep Spot safe. I need to grab my phone."

Trixie put her cupped hands to her head and wiggled them. "Your ears are showing too."

Swearing, he felt his head. "Oh, yeah. I didn't want the elves to think I was pretending to be human. I took off my bandana when I got to Poppymeadows."

"What did Tinker want?"

"She's worried about people falling between the cracks like Oilcan's kids did. I made the mistake of telling her about the girls on Liberty Avenue disappearing. I need to put together a list of missing whores to give to the police."

"Exactly how the hell did this end up as your responsibility?" Trixie asked.

"Do you really think Oilcan would know where to even look for a whore?"

Trixie burst out laughing. "No. All the girls he's ever brought to the track were cute but nerdy smart. He's into smart, strong females."

Tommy had never noticed who Oilcan dated. Trixie ran the concession booths at the racetrack; she saw who came and went with whom. She also had a thing for smart, strong women. Maybe she was crushing on Oilcan's girlfriends.

"I need to talk to Mokoto," Tommy said. "What room is he in?"

"My family is on the seventeenth floor. We put him away from the kids since he sleeps during the day. He's not going to be happy being woke up after two hours of sleep."

"At the moment, I don't care. Are those running yet?" Tommy pointed toward the elevators.

"The closest one is working but only up to the eighth floor. Alita programmed it so our customers can only get to the floor that their rooms are on. Alita said she'll work on the others later so we can use our room keys to access our floors."

Tommy sighed. It was better than he expected but it still meant he needed to climb nine floors.

The elevator stopped on the eighth floor as promised. What Tommy hadn't expected was a half dozen carts in the hallway, each parked beside an open doorway. As Tommy stepped off the elevator, a head cautiously poked out of the nearest room. It was Kiki, the bravest of the teen girls.

"It's just Tommy!" Kiki called out.

"Hi Tommy!" came a chorus of voices all up and down the hallway.

Kiki skipped out into the hall to show off the fact that she was wearing a gray dress. Kiki was Trixie's little sister; she was a year younger than Alita. Unlike her older sisters, Kiki couldn't pass as human. Her father had been a lesser blood; she had his wild mane of flame-red hair, short horns, and vivid red-brown eyes. Despite that, she was cute in a scary kind of way. "Look! We found housekeeping uniforms! Aren't they cute?"

"Yeah, I see," Tommy said.

It wasn't particularly cute, just a gray tailored button-down dress with a white apron. Kiki was also one of the tallest girls, so it was more like a long shirt on her. The girls, however, rarely got anything new. Everything was handed down and usually stained and heavily patched. Kiki probably cared more that it was a new piece of clothing than how it fashionable it was.

Down the hall someone started to sing, *"Be our guest! Be our guest! Our command is your request!"*

Kiki twirled the skirt of her housekeeping uniform, showing off that she was wearing shorts under it, and danced off singing. *"It's been years since we've had anybody here and we're obsessed!"*

Tommy shook his head. How could they all be so happy scrubbing toilets? But he knew that it was a safer, saner way than how they used to live, where his father's troops might idly beat, maim, rape, murder and even eat any one of them.

Tommy walked up the remaining flights, stewing over his growing problem.

He was the oldest of the half-oni. A few of the others, like Trixie, looked human enough to flee their home and find someplace safe in the city. Those who could, had. (Like Trixie, they'd trickled back after Lord Tomtom had been killed.) Tommy had been able to work outside the warren because he could cloud the minds of anyone looking too closely at him. With his bandana, he could pass as human if he was careful. Kiki—and many of the other kids whose fathers had been lesser bloods—hadn't been able to leave the warren. Anyone who saw them would know that they weren't human. The elves would have killed them on sight.

It left the children at the mercy of Lord Tomtom's warriors. Not all survived the experience. Over the years, Tommy had quietly disposed of dozens of small bodies.

The restaurant had been a means to an end. Neither Lord Tomtom nor Lord Kajo had contributed money to keep the half-oni fed and clothed. His mother and her three younger sisters worked the front of the house as waiters. The kids could do prep work, cook, clean— anything that contributed but kept them out of sight of customers. The restaurant barely made enough to keep the family fed. Every nine or ten months, another mouth would be added. That was just his family. All across the city were other pockets of abused women and half-oni children slowly starving to death.

The oni didn't trust human technology; they refused to use phones. Once Tommy got old enough to travel the city, his father used him as a messenger to network together all the hidden households. His mother would give Tommy food and money for those less fortunate. After Lord Tomtom killed her, Tommy did whatever he had to do to keep up her charity. Most of it was illegal. Shoplifting. Pickpocketing. His ability made it simple. If he had been caught, though, he could have brought the entire house of cards down.

He'd had several children adopted into his warren because they had no place else to go. Their mothers had been killed. They were too small to live alone. They couldn't hide what they were. They didn't know enough of the outside world to survive in it.

Tommy had started the racetrack as a way for the older kids who could pass as human to legally make money without fear. It did nothing for the children like Kiki. Nor was the racetrack a good, stable source of income. He needed teams to race. He needed an audience that had free time and the willingness to drive out into the countryside. He needed the weather to be fair. Winter ended the racing season; he'd learned the hard way that Pittsburghers wouldn't come out to the open stadium past November.

His family needed some other way to make a living.

Damn Bingo for finding such a seductive trap. The big building offered everyone privacy that they never had before. Nice beds. Hot showers. No waiting to use the toilet. The kids who could pass as human could do the jobs like the front desk while the others like Kiki could stay hidden doing housekeeping.

Even if they were safe from attack, the unknowns were massive. How much did it cost to operate? How soon would they have to start forking over money or have the power shut off? If they lost power, they would have to drain all the water pipes to keep them from freezing and breaking. Without water, the toilets would fill with shit. Unlike their old warehouse warren, there was no way to jury-rig a wood stove. Living in the hotel required keeping the power on at a time when he wasn't sure they could even buy food enough to keep from starving.

How many rooms would they need to fill to make a profit? How long would the off-worlders continue to pay for a room when they could simply go squat in one of Pittsburgh's many abandoned houses? One answer was simple math but the other was impossible to know.

That was all assuming that the war with the oni went well and the oni mystery box didn't unleash a killing blow to the elves. Judging by how nervous the tengu seemed at Poppymeadows, the box was a game changer. All his instincts were to run and hide while they had a chance.

It still felt unreal to open the door to a luxury suite and know by the scent that it was his. He had slept there. He had used the toilet. This was where all his things were.

It didn't feel like home. It felt like a trap. One his people wanted to stay in. One that he might not be able to get them out of.

He found a blue bandana and used it to hide his cat ears. The effect was far from perfect; it only worked because he could create the illusion in the mind of anyone he was talking to. He meant that he had to avoid crowds.

Still, it didn't seem like it was him looking back in the mirror. Maybe because he had never before seen himself in such a massive mirror. It was four feet wide and three feet high. Behind him was a gleaming marble-lined shower. The male he was used to seeing wasn't Beholden to any elf, wouldn't walk around in front of elves without a bandana on, and wouldn't care if a bunch of shit-for-brains human females had disappeared from Liberty Avenue. The male he usually saw in the mirror couldn't care about anyone but his own family.

"What the hell are you doing?" Tommy whispered to his reflection.

Neither one of them knew for sure.

His phone rang, dragging him away from the mirror. He didn't recognize the number on the screen.

He answered it with a cautious "What?"

"Hey, Tommy, it's Blue. Blue Sky Montana. Yeah, I thought I should call and tell you that we're going out for ice cream, so Spot isn't going to be at Sacred Heart for a while. He's coming with us."

"What? You're taking him out? Who is going?"

Blue Sky was spunky but he was still just a little kid. If they ran into someone who wanted to hurt Spot, he probably wouldn't be able to protect him.

"A bunch of us," Blue Sky said. "Oilcan. Thorne. All of Oilcan's kids. Guy, Andy, and Rebecca are coming too."

It sounded like they were taking half the neighborhood with them. Spot would be safe in that crowd since half of them tended to be heavily armed.

"Okay," Tommy said. "I'll swing by later and pick him up."

One less worry for the time being.

Mokoto hadn't been in bed yet. He answered his door wearing a silk kimono tied loosely at his hips, threating to slide off his narrow shoulders. A cloth headband held back his hair from his face and all his sultry makeup was scrubbed off. It had been months since Tommy last saw Mokoto without his whore mask. He looked years younger and a little lost.

"What's wrong?" Mokoto asked in a tone that indicated he was bracing for the worst.

"Nothing." Tommy explained about Tinker taking interest in finding everyone who had fallen through the cracks throughout the entire city.

As he talked, Mokoto relaxed into a sexy lean against the doorframe. The kimono slid off one shoulder. He looked up Tommy with a wistful face. "Tommy, Tommy,

Tommy, what are we going to do with you?" Mokoto took hold of Tommy's T-shirt. "Don't let them use you to take on the world. I'll tell you who I think is missing, but you got to promise me to be careful. I'm not going to trade you for anyone else in this universe. You're more important to us than any of them. You're a good man. A knight in shining armor! But you're our knight, not theirs. We're the ones that love you, not them. We'll be the ones crying ourselves to sleep years after you get yourself killed, not them."

"I'm not going to get myself killed."

"Promise?" Mokoto let go of Tommy's shirt to offer up his little finger with its gem-crusted black nail polish. "Pinkie swear?"

Tommy, Bingo, and Mokoto were the oldest of the half-oni. Bingo would always do whatever Tommy told him to do. Mokoto needed promises made and religiously kept. He was a little thing, but fearless and cunning in his anger. If you made him mad, he wouldn't hit you. He'd wait until you were asleep, tie you up, and then piss in your face. Tommy learned the hard way not to include "stick a needle in my eye" in any promise to Mokoto.

"I swear to be careful." Tommy linked pinkies.

Mokoto tightened his grip on Tommy's pinkie after the shake and used it to pull him into the room. "Come, come, come. This is going to take a while."

"How many kids are missing?" Surely it wouldn't take long to get a short list. Any more than a dozen and the police would have noticed.

"You know how it is. Some of the off-worlders start with one name and then realize how stupid it sounds, so they change to another. Plus they'll lie to your face if they think you're some scary-ass tranny that will go psycho on them or something."

If Tommy could erase his presence from the mind of someone looking at him, Mokoto's secret power seemed to be making strangers very aware of how dangerous he could be despite his small size.

Mokoto was in a big two-room suite like Tommy. He'd pulled the curtains shut on all the windows to block out the daylight. In the big dark space, he'd put up strands of white Christmas lights. In a corner of the sitting room, he had a big plastic bottle filled with elf shines that drifted about, gleaming. A candle flickered on one of the nightstands, filling the space with a musk scent. Some piece of small electronics was playing piano music softly but Tommy couldn't spot it among the clutter. Mokoto's huggy blanket—the newer one, not the one that been worn to tatters—was on the big bed along with all his cat plushies. His beloved books were scattered everywhere, including the bed.

As Tommy suspected, Mokoto dragged him past the two armchairs to the big bed. Mokoto liked to cuddle as much as possible, hence the huggy blanket and all the stuffed cats. He'd been that way since they were little. Tommy had made the mistake of vaguely promising Mokoto that they'd talk without specifying where and how much. He should have known better.

"If I fall asleep," Tommy said, "You need to wake me up."

"Pft." Mokoto made it clear that he wasn't promising anything.

When they were very little, their mothers had converted the restaurant's attic space into a small bedroom with ridiculously low ceilings. Even tiny Aunt Flo needed to stoop. Only later in life had Tommy realized it had been to protect them from the oni, who couldn't fit through the trapdoor. Tommy and Mokoto and Bingo and Babe shared a futon mattress that had been wedged up through the hole in the floor. They slept together like a litter of puppies until Bingo got stuck in the trapdoor.

By then they were old enough to find separate quarters in the buildings surrounding the restaurant. They'd knocked holes into the walls to create a proper warren. Tommy liked sleeping alone; it released him from the responsibility of being the oldest. Mokoto hated it. He tended to read until he drifted off.

Mokoto grabbed his books off the bed. One was a paperback romance featuring a half-naked man. The other was a hardcover titled *Hotel Administration on Hospitality*. Between the Christmas lights and the business guide filled with bookmarks, Mokoto was clearly in the "stay at the William Penn Hotel" camp.

Tommy flopped onto the bed, landing on one of Mokoto's many homemade stuffed cats. It released a cloud of lavender scent that threatened to make Tommy sneeze. He pulled the toy out from under him. Like its many brothers, the stuffed cat was crudely made of scraps of bright colored cloth, decorated with derpy eyes and a crude heart stitched onto its flank.

"Why only cats?" Tommy tossed the cats one by one at the bedside chair. "Why no dogs?"

Bingo's father had been a lesser blood with a little dog in him. Bingo could pass as a human as long as he had clothes on.

"Cats are braver than dogs." Mokoto curled up beside him, head on Tommy's chest. Mokoto liked to listen to his heartbeat.

Tommy was currently twenty-eight to Mokoto's twenty-seven and Bingo's twenty-six. When they were little, twenty-four months didn't seem like much. He knew now there was a world of difference between a four-year-old and a toddler. "Doesn't seem fair to Bingo."

"Fear and love are not logical constructs."

Tommy thought of his stupid, illogical love of Jewel Tear. He couldn't argue with that. "Tell me about these missing kids."

"Seven girls, three boys," Mokoto said. "I know the boys better than the girls, for obvious reasons. They went by the names..." He sighed deeply. His voice cracked a little as he continued. "Bad me. Counting them as dead already. They use the names Knickknack, Toad, and Joyboy."

Ah, this was true reason they were in bed; Mokoto was hurting over the disappearances. It put the entire family in danger if someone developed feelings for an outsider. They'd all gone through it when they were young and stupid. They'd all had to deal with walking away from someone because it was impossible to keep secrets from them. It made Tommy feel guilty that he'd been sneaking around with Jewel Tear.

"Knickknack?" Tommy guessed which one meant the most to Mokoto. He'd mentioned Knickknack first.

Mokoto nodded. "Knickknack hates his real name. He thinks it's boring. He went by Knickknack even before he started working Liberty Avenue. He goes to Pitt. He's going to be a senior this fall. Every other summer, he's gone home. This time he decided to stay the summer. He'd asked his parents for money to make it through to fall, but they didn't want him to stay, so they didn't send him any. He suspects it's because they think he'll try to get a job on Elfhome and stay forever. They were against him going off-world to start with."

This was a lot more detail than Tommy expected. "How long have you known him?"

"Three years," Mokoto whispered and laughed brokenly. "We met at the library, of all places. He thought I was hot and asked me out for pizza. We ended up fucking in his dorm room. It was great sex. He's very attentive and likes to cuddle. But afterward, everything he had in his room, all his little tech toys and the places he'd been and the things he'd seen and the stuff he bitched about missing while on Elfhome... We were both there, in his room, but it was like we were in two different universes."

Tommy understood. It been one thing to have sex with Jewel Tear out in the woods, but then to see her at the enclave, cleaned up and surrounded by other elves, he'd felt to his core how much they lived in different worlds.

"I shouldn't have seen him again," Mokoto said. "But I did. It wasn't just the sex. It was talking about books, and seeing movies that didn't have guns in them, and cool music." He waved a hand toward whatever he had softly playing music. "We would have these discussions that seemed so deep and meaningful. It was like I could be someone that wasn't pulling tricks on Liberty to keep his family alive."

The pain was knowing that this kid, who meant so much to Mokoto, was probably dead. The other kids might be in hiding, but Knickknack probably wouldn't have disappeared without getting word to Mokoto. If the oni grabbed all the whores, they would keep only the girls alive. The boys they would have killed and maybe eaten.

"I knew I was being greedy," Mokoto said. "I should have just cut him off—but I always felt so thin when he wasn't around. Like I was just a shadow of what I could be. I liked myself more when he was around."

Mokoto was too tough to cry. Bingo would be bawling his head off at this point.

"I never told Knickknack anything," Mokoto said. "Not about the family. Not about the restaurant. Not about what I did in the evenings. He figured out that I lived in Oakland from things I let slip, like how I planned to walk home from his dorm room. When he decided to stay the summer, he asked if he could stay with me. He thought it would be romantic. I told him I didn't have space; my room was too small. That made him want to see where I lived. So I told him that my pimp wouldn't let me bring home tricks."

That went south fast. The kid must have backed off quick because Mokoto would have probably knifed him otherwise.

"What does this Knickknack look like?" Tommy had been down to Liberty Avenue a couple of times this summer but he'd left most of the night crew management to Mokoto and Babe. They usually only called him in when they couldn't kick the shit out of whoever was bothering their people. During those times, Tommy's focus wasn't on the other whores working the street.

"I've got pictures of them all." Mokoto reached over to the nightstand to grab his phone. "I'm not sure why. I just had this feeling that one day I would need something to help identify them."

Mokoto secretly took pictures of almost everyone

he knew, which wasn't hard since most of his family didn't realize some phones had cameras. The first few were of Babe, alternating being his dorky lovable self with the family and full-on angry enforcer mode at some stranger.

Mokoto growled with irritation and swiped at the phone's surface and got a grid of photos. He leafed through the pages and pages of thumbnails. Apparently Mokoto liked to take pictures of Tommy when he wasn't paying attention too.

"This is Knickknack." Mokoto held out his phone for inspection. The picture was the two of them together. The boy was taller than Tommy expected. He seemed unexpectedly sunny, but that impression might be based on his yellow hair, blue eyes, and huge smile of white straight teeth. Nothing said off-worlder more than perfect teeth.

"This is Toad." The boy seemed surprisingly ugly to be a whore. He had the teeth of an off-worlder but nothing else appealing about him. "He's actually been on Elfhome for a couple of years and works Liberty Avenue only when he hits a rocky period. He's very bold and funny. He can usually talk himself into and out of any sort of trouble. I didn't think I had to worry about him."

Another boy, much cuter than Toad, followed. "Joyboy—but he's full of himself, so not much of a joy to be around. I've figured that he would be the first to die; he's such a drama queen. There's been times I've been tempted to stab him just to shut him up."

The girls were named Bambi, Candy, Chardonnay, Nevaeh, Peanut Butter Pie, Red, and Tawny. They all looked about twenty, except Red.

Tommy pointed at Red's photo. "I just saw her. She cut some deal with Forest Moss. She's got an entire troop of royal marines following her around like puppy dogs. The elves are acting like she's equal to Tinker."

"Really?" Mokoto said surprise and amazement. "Wow! Okay. I can see that. Red's not like the other girls. She showed up about a month ago, at least two weeks after the last Shutdown. She didn't come to Pittsburgh because of elves and magic and fairy tales. Something nasty happened to her on Earth. Other girls would talk about where they were from and why they were in Pittsburgh, but not Red. She kept walls up around her. Massive stone fortress walls. Nobody got in. She would walk with Peanut Butter Pie and Candy but at the end of the night, she'd head in the direction of Station Square. I think she had a squat on Mount Washington."

"Where did Knickknack squat? Oakland?"

Mokoto flinched at the question. "They closed his dorms and he couldn't find any place to squat in Oakland. Toad has a big place somewhere on the North Side that he calls Toad Hall. From what they've told me, it's like a warren, taking up part of a block. Joyboy moved in first, and then Knickknack, and then when everything started to go south, most of the girls. The girls started to jokingly call Toad their pimp, but I know that he didn't carry any weapons."

"They all disappeared at once?"

Mokoto shrugged. "A couple of girls had been killed on Liberty Avenue. One died when Tinker's fight with Malice went through Downtown and dropped an entire building's worth of broken glass on the girl. Another whore was killed across from the train station. Red disappeared. None of that seemed related. Then one night all the rest of the Undefended stopped coming to work."

"Did you go to the squat?"

Mokoto curled tight and shook his head. "The elves hit our warren, you took off, and we had to find someplace safe to move everyone to. I couldn't take off to go find this Toad Hall—not with all the shit going down. It's not like the Undefended are children; they're all adults. They're human. They decided to work without protection. They signed up for all this shit. Our little ones who don't pass for human are the ones that need me. I was hoping that the Undefended got smart and just decided it was too dangerous to go out. I was hoping that they would be out on Liberty last night. None of them showed up. Whatever happened to them, happened days ago. There was no point of leaving Babe alone to protect our people."

"Do you know the address?" Tommy asked.

"No," Mokoto whispered. "I didn't want to fight with Knickknack. If I didn't ask him where he lived, then he couldn't ask me where I lived. Things weren't going well between us. He was starting to realize that he didn't know me at all. He did share these pictures with me. I think he was trying to get me to ask him where it was."

Tommy studied the photo of Knickknack standing in an open doorway of a brick town house. "This looks like the Mexican War Streets district. It shouldn't be too hard to find it."

"Really?" Mokoto's voice was full of doubt.

Tommy realized that his work as his father's messenger meant that he'd learned the city better than his other cousins. Mokoto only left Oakland to work Downtown on Liberty Avenue. The North Side had been heavily infested with true-blood oni until the royal marines stacked their dead bodies on the sidewalks. Mokoto would have avoided the area.

"I'll find out what happened to Knickknack and the others," Tommy promised.

Mokoto rolled suddenly to pin Tommy down. "Remember that you promised to be careful. We all need you, Tommy, so don't even think of going off and getting killed." And his voice broke again as he added, "I don't want to be the oldest. I can't do that. I can't."

"Hey, hey, I promised."

There were two men in business suits sitting and chatting in the lobby. Tommy could smell bourbon in the lowball glasses on the cocktail table between them. A small mountain of luggage surrounded them. He counted ten pieces of wheeled suitcases—all different sizes.

Tommy could easily control what one person saw, but with each additional person it became more difficult. Luckily the two were sitting so that only one of them could see the counter where Trixie and Quinn were standing.

Tommy focused on the man facing Trixie. The man was in good spirits, thinking of nothing but good food, a hot shower, and a big, clean, soft bed. Tommy blurred himself out as he walked to the counter.

Quinn was one of the teenage boys who could pass as human. He sported the same black blazer over a white button-down shirt combination as Trixie. Instead of black slacks, though, Quinn wore a pair of worn but clean blue jeans. Several room service menus lay on the counter in front of Quinn—apparently "borrowed" from other hotels in the area—along with a supermarket receipt showing the purchase of rice, a long list of fruits and vegetables, and fresh fish.

"They all feature 'a special selection of international cheeses with crackers' called All Hands On Deck," Quinn whispered to Trixie as Tommy walked up. "What's this fascination with cheese and why haven't I heard of it before?"

Quinn sounded like his mother, Aunt Flo.

"We're Chinese; we don't believe in cheese," Trixie answered while counting out hundred-dollar bills. "If the other hotels are all offering it, then we should get some too. We'll send Alita and Zippo back out since they probably didn't look in the dairy section. You can make up a new menu if they find any. For now, figure out what we can make with what they already bought and what the price point should be."

"What the hell?" Tommy whispered, waving toward the businessmen. "Why are they just sitting there?"

"The first three guys had to go back and get their things," Trixie murmured. "Those guys called these two. They work for different companies but they all know each other. Since these two were told that we had rooms, they just brought their luggage with them. I told them that the teens—housekeeping—weren't finished cleaning and offered them free drinks if they sat and waited."

Trixie wrote down a total for the hundred-dollar bills. She had six thousand dollars in her hand.

"How much are you charging them?" Tommie said.

"I told the first guys that it was two hundred a night, one week minimum, paid up front. I thought that would discourage them. All five paid for a week. I gave Alita and Zippo a thousand to buy all the groceries that they could find; food is only going to get scarcer. These two made noises that if they liked what they get for the money, they'd want to stay for at least a month. A month would be six grand each. Who the hell has six grand to fork over like it's nothing?"

"Apparently these guys," Tommy said.

"We should get into whatever business these guys do," Quinn whispered.

Tommy silenced him with a hard look. They were already in way over their heads with this hotel idea. He didn't need his people larking off on other crazy ideas.

"These guys also called other people that had been at the Wyndham." Trixie seemed torn between being annoyed and pleased. Her initial response had been to discourage them but the seven thousand in cash obviously shifted her thinking. "I told housekeeping to move up to the ninth floor after they finish with the eighth. Right now they're waiting on the laundry room to finish drying the bed linen."

She tucked the hundred-dollar bills into a cash box.

"This is frustrating," Quinn said. "The other hotels have what I think is 'American comfort food' of pizza, hamburgers, macaroni and cheese, and chicken nuggets. There's no other way to explain why they all have this really basic food. The problem is, we either don't know how to make them—like pizza—or can't get the ingredients in bulk—like hamburger patties. One thing that we have a lot of and can do well is hot dogs with a choice of onion and relish or sauerkraut."

"Yeah, we do those for the racetrack," Trixie said. "People love them."

"Why are we doing food at all?" Tommy asked.

"Because it's part of being a four-star hotel," Quinn said while Trixie gave Tommy a "how stupid can you get" look that only she dared to do. "For appetizers we can do spring rolls, hot and sour soup, or wonton soup for twelve dollars."

"Twelve?" Tommy said. "We only charged six at the restaurant."

"That's what the others are charging for soup." Quinn tapped the menus before him. "They seem to double all the prices because it gets delivered to the rooms."

Tommy turned to Trixie. "I thought you said it's take-out?"

"Take-out we deliver to the room as if we were taking it to a table." Trixie mimed carrying a loaded tray. "Room service: as in service to the room. We take them the food on a plate with silverware instead of inside a box."

It was like trying to stop a train. Tommy shook his head. "Whatever. I'll be back later."

12: THE REDCOATS

"Whoa, whoa, whoa!" the driver of the Oakland-to-Downtown bus cried as the royal marines bounded up the steps behind Olivia. The puppies were all excited about the bus trip; the only other mechanical transport they'd experienced in their entire lives was the train ride from the East Coast. They bounced around the large interior, testing all the seats and examining every overhead advertisement.

"Are the redcoats with you, miss?" The bus driver watched the antics in his rearview mirror. "Are you one of those poor interns that the EIA hired to translate for the summer?"

Redcoats? Olivia hadn't heard the nickname before but it was easy to tell why it sprung up. The royal marines were Fire Clan, whose "official color" was scarlet red. The marines' uniforms looked like those of the British soldiers during the Revolutionary War; they wore the same kind of red wool tunics with big brass buttons down the center.

During the last few days, Olivia had been forced

into close quarters with the marines and had seen them in every mode of undress possible, including buck naked. (They were very comfortable in their own skin and unabashed in their nakedness.) What was blazed across her brain was the white linen of their underclothes. She only saw them in their coats when they were away from wherever she'd set up camp. Their felt tricorne hats were black, as were their low boots. They also wore white cotton slacks and leather button-up gaiters that went up over their knees. She supposed that to any normal person, the other colors of the marines' uniforms were lost against the brilliance of their coats.

"I am Forest Moss's *domi*." Olivia fed her fare into the box and took the transfer slip that it spit out. Did the driver know what a *domi* was? She hadn't until a few days earlier. Olivia added, "I'm like Princess Tinker. I'm married to Forest Moss." Sort of. At least the general impression in the city was that Tinker had gotten married to Windwolf. "These royal marines are my guard."

"You're going to pay for them?" It was a question but the driver said it more like a statement.

Last time she had taken a bus, she'd been shadowed by Wyverns. The *sekasha* had gotten on without paying. Not surprisingly, no one had tried to make the holy warriors cough up their fare—not with them lopping the heads off people right and left.

Olivia didn't want to have to pay for the marines. It would be nearly thirty dollars for all of them and then she would need to juggle twenty-one transfer papers to get them back to Oakland. "I'm sure that the Wind Clan made arrangements through the EIA for the royal marines to have use of the public transit system."

The bus driver blinked in surprise. "I—I—I don't know."

"It would stand to reason that the newly arrived elves from the Easternlands would ride for free," she said. "There's no other way for them to get around the city easily; they haven't had time to ship in hundreds of horses and carriages. They don't have human money, nor could the EIA pass out bus passes to all the incoming marines—not quickly."

"I-I-I should call in..." the bus driver started but then stopped as his dashboard dinged repeatedly as the marines discovered the button that signaled a desired stop. He sighed and glanced up at his mirror. "Forgiveness!" the bus driver called in fluent Elvish. "Don't push that, please—not unless you want off."

"Chi-chi-chi!" Coal cried. "You speak Elvish so well."

"I was born in Pittsburgh," the bus driver said.

"He sounds like Wind Clan," Ox stated bluntly.

"Ya! Fire Clan would be: Stop it, you kids!" Coal did a gesture that was possibly obscene. It was hard to tell, considering how often the marines used it with one another. He added a dozen more words that Olivia didn't know.

The driver knew. He snickered, shaking his head. He closed the door and the bus trundled forward.

Olivia took it as a victory, the second for the day, maybe the third.

She'd forgotten to follow her father's advice to see each success as proof of her own strength. It didn't seem like much. She had no seeds in hand and no idea how she was going to find the missing prostitutes.

Certainly what she had accomplished, however, had been more difficult than cleaning her room. She'd gotten in to see Tinker. She'd talked Tinker into using her great powers to help. She'd bullied a bus driver into giving the marines free rides. *Yay, me.*

Olivia squashed down hard on the negative thought as she herded the marines toward the back of the bus. Her dad always said that big victories were made of countless little wins. The bigger problems of life would seem impossible to overcome if you ignored all the little wins.

I was strong, Olivia reminded herself. *I can do this. I've done the impossible to get this far.*

It was still insanely early for a social call when Olivia hit Mount Washington with the royal marines in tow. She had dragged them through the light-rail subway stations under Downtown, gotten off at Station Square—which was still in chaos from the derailment—and then up the Monongahela Incline. Every leg of the trip was greeted with exclamations of surprise and excitement. It felt very much like taking a group of kindergarteners to Disneyland. All that was missing was Mickey Mouse.

Olivia wasn't sure where Aiofe worked as an intern at the EIA. She entertained thoughts of marching up and demanding to see Director Maynard and asking him. That's what Tinker *domi* probably would have done. Olivia doubted, though, that the man would know where one of his lowest-level employees was. The last time she'd seen Aiofe, she'd been working in the field with the troops setting up the keva bean handout. Olivia was hoping that if she arrived early enough, she would catch Aiofe before she went off to work.

She used the travel time to explain to the marines who she was going to see. It was an interesting exchange of information. Explaining Aiofe required explaining the university to the marines, which led to high school, which led to the subject of education in general. The elves didn't do schools like humans. Apparently there were too few children to even fill a one-room schoolhouse. They were taught their letters and numbers by traveling scholars. After they'd learned the fundamentals, it depended on their caste if they received any further education.

It sounded suspiciously like the type of education that girls received at the Ranch. If it weren't for state mandates, Olivia's schooling would have stopped the day her mother packed up their car and drove cross-country to the Ranch. As it was, Olivia never saw the inside of a school again. Her mother claimed it was because of the low quality of the schools in rural areas, but the truth was that the church elders didn't want their young people exposed to the basic freedoms that others their age normally enjoyed. Brainwashing someone into accepting a narrow vision of the world only worked if you kept the blinders firmly in place.

As *laedin*-caste, all the marines had been carefully guided to go into combat training. Once they reached maturity, they had limited directions to go in terms of career. They could be a private guard for a household like Poppymeadows or join the general pool of royal marines. They claimed that they were happy, but then they didn't know anything else but fighting and playing at their childlike games.

Olivia was furious for their sake but they didn't understand her anger, which only made her angrier. When they finally reached her leveled house, she marched past it, up onto Aiofe's front porch, and banged on her door, which was painted Wind Clan blue.

"Who's that pounding on me door?" Aiofe called fearfully.

"Aiofe!" Olivia called out to reassure the girl. "It's me."

There was the sound of bare feet running toward the door. It jerked open to reveal Aiofe in pink and green plaid flannel pajamas, her long dark hair up in a messy bun.

"Red!" Aoife cried and flung herself onto Olivia to hug her hard. "Oh, I was that worried! What in the world?"

Aiofe had noticed the royal marines lined up behind Olivia.

"They're with me." Olivia pushed up her bangs to show off the mark that Forest Moss had put on her forehead. "I'm Forest Moss's *domi* now."

She said it quick and fast to get it over with, bracing for the same sort of outrage that Tinker *domi* had leveled at her.

"*Domi*?" Aiofe's eyes went wide. She pointed at the marines. "So—they're yours?"

"Yes, for now," she said.

"Smashing!" Aiofe pulled Olivia into the house. "Come on in. I'll wet the tea. I've got biscuits that I've been saving for a special occasion. Some Digestives and some Fig Rolls. We can sit in the garden and have a proper talk."

Olivia hadn't gotten the door shut behind her as

Aiofe pulled her through the house. The marines followed her in, excited at the chance to see the inside of a "normal" human house. Aiofe had squatted in a lovely big Victorian and over the years, sparsely decorated it with a style that TV shows called shabby chic.

"Shouldn't you put some clothes on?" Olivia asked since Aiofe was still in her flannel pajamas.

Aiofe laughed. "This is perfectly decent!" Aiofe grabbed her teapot and started to fill it. "Just let me put the kettle on and grab me tablet."

"Tablet?"

"I need to document all this! The anthropology department hasn't been able to get a single straight answer on elf courtship customs. Tinker *domi* just suddenly popped up 'married' to Windwolf. The subject has been totally off-limits since some idiots from the tabloids asked some seriously intrusive questions. And no one really has had the time to sit and talk to the royal marines. This is absolutely fabulous!"

Normally Olivia thought of Aiofe's kitchen as bright and cheerful and large. With the addition of the royal marines, it suddenly seemed quite small. Olivia sat down at the table in an attempt to make it seem less crowded. Aiofe had tidied up since she last visited— her laptop, textbooks, and research materials were all neatly stacked.

Aiofe put the teapot onto the stove and gave the dial a savage twist. The flame shot up. Dagger and Ox crowded in close, murmuring with surprise, and played with the dial to change the level of the flame.

"Don't touch," Olivia whispered at them, making shooing motions.

"They're fine! They're fine!" Aiofe opened and

closed cabinets as she got the makings of tea ready. "Smashing, in fact! I tried to weasel my way onto the EIA support team that is backing up the Viceroy on the front line, but those plonkers weren't having it. They told me to take the day off and then emptied the city of elves! I bawled me eyes out."

"I'm sorry," Olivia said. "But I really didn't mean to stay. I just wanted to make sure you were okay. I kind of left in the middle of the night. I was hoping you were okay—and that maybe you could help me—a little."

"Me?" Aiofe said.

"I went out to talk to Tinker *domi*..."

"You talked to her?" Aiofe sat down across from Olivia and leaned in close. "What's she like? They say she's like a tiny lioness. So little. So fierce. Did she say anything about how she got married to Windwolf? Wait! Your *dau* mark is different! Oh, I need to take a picture of it! Can I?"

This was not going how Olivia imagined this conversation to go.

In the name of science, she let Aiofe photograph her *dau* mark and measure it. It put the girl intimately close. It made it harder to talk about what had happened over the last few days. She wanted to make it sound romantic but she didn't want to lie. An ugly mess was an ugly mess no matter how many layers of white silk and red roses you layered over it.

In little embarrassing fits and starts, she skipped over the uglier points of her discovery that Forest Moss was looking for someone like Tinker *domi*.

"I got scared by everything that was going on. I could see that being a *domi* was more than just a bed warmer. I decided to track Forest Moss down and make him an offer."

"Which was . . . ?" Aiofe pressed a small plastic ruler to the *dau* mark.

"To be with him."

"Forever?" Aiofe asked. "Is he going to make you an elf—like Tinker *domi*?"

It was the one question that Olivia didn't want to answer the most. She knew that she couldn't explain it so Aiofe could understand. She could never explain to her stepsisters why she didn't just parrot the bastardized version of the Nicene Creed that the Ranch followed. It wasn't what she believed. To change what she believed was to change herself. To say the words would make it easier to lose herself against the pressure to be the creature that the Ranch wanted her to be.

She'd fought to stay true to herself for a third of her life. She didn't want to give herself up. All the whores on Liberty Avenue from Stateside would jump at the chance to be an elf; they would never understand her refusal to be transformed. Yet those women wouldn't allow just anyone to cut their hair, or give them a random piercing or tattoo. How could they not understand that having every cell in their body transformed would be more life altering than having their head shaved?

Olivia's faith was her bedrock. She knew through countless battles that her beliefs were built on a few thousand words. She'd protected those words because they protected her faith, which protected who she was at the very core. If she were transformed into an elf, what would happen to the person that she had fought so hard to protect? Would her soul bond to a body so foreign to the one that God gave her? Did elves have a soul? Did they go to heaven? Was there a separate heaven for elves? Elfhome existed in a different universe with a different sun and moon. She was terrified that changing something so fundamental about herself would wipe away everything that was her. Who would remain within her skin?

Even though it terrified her, she knew that most people would dismiss her fear. To them, she was like the little kid who was afraid they would slide down the drain when the bath water was let out. Yet, those who would belittle her fears couldn't know the truth. No one had ever seen a soul. Touched a soul. Kept it from going down a drain.

Luckily, Aiofe had too many questions to wait Olivia out. She followed up with, "Why did Windwolf do it? How did he make her an elf? He did do it—didn't he? I mean—she is genetically an elf—right? Or was it just an ear job?"

Olivia had been carefully questioning the marines about this for days. "The *domana* can use the Spell Stones because of something coded into their DNA. It's the key to their military power. It's against their laws to dilute *domana* bloodlines. They don't want any little bastards running around who may or may not be able to use the stones that could make more bastards that may or may not. Windwolf had to make Tinker *domana* in order for them to be together."

"And Forest Moss is going to...?"

"I want to stay myself."

"Tinker *domi* stayed herself."

Olivia bit down on "How would you know? You've never met her!" She said instead, "Did she? Really?

Why was she just a hoverbike racer, then? Why wasn't she someone influential before she was changed?"

"Life is always changing you," Aiofe answered. "It's like you're in an egg—it's nice and cozy and you know every millimeter of it and you think you know everything about the world. Then suddenly—boom! You hatch out into a different world. Then you're a little chick, all covered with fuzz in a nice cozy nest with a mom feeding you bits and pieces of raw meat and you think you know everything. Then boom! You grow these feathers and you can fly and your mom kicks you out of the nest and you realize that all that raw meat that she was feeding you are little animals that you now have to catch yourself. You don't know anything about the big massive world but you're one kick-ass falcon."

Olivia stared at her. That had to be the weirdest analogy she'd ever heard.

"When I grew up in Dublin, I thought I knew everything," Aiofe said. "I had it all figured out. But then I went off to uni and found out that I knew squat. Tinker *domi* was kidnapped by the oni and held prisoner, and made to work under the threat of torture. It changed her worldview. She might have only cared about racing before she got grabbed, but everything she's done since then proves that she was changed by what happened to her."

"I would argue that isn't necessarily a good thing," Olivia said.

"Life is a mixed bag of jellybeans. Good and bad. Change is inevitable."

The teakettle started to whistle.

Olivia didn't want to talk about her faith and her fears.

"I'm worried about some of the people that I know," she said instead. "Everyone in the city without family can easily fall through the cracks. People like you."

"I'm fine," Aiofe said. "I was worried about you. I got called in to translate and came home to find your house a pile of rubble. I knew that you were working night shifts but I still called the fire department and everything."

"I'm sorry," Olivia said. "The Wyverns showed up to collect Forest Moss. I was too scared to think about leaving a note."

"Ppfft!" Aiofe waved off the apology. "It's fine. I wouldn't have been thinking straight either."

"When I was talking to Tinker *domi*, one of her men reported that some kids from Stateside who work Downtown have disappeared." Olivia had gotten so used to editing what she said that she barely needed to think about not using the words "prostitutes" or "illegal immigrants." She wasn't totally sure if Tommy Chang could be called a "man" since that denoted "human." He seemed human enough to Olivia—certainly more humane than her ex-husband. "I know these missing kids. I want to check on them—make sure they're safe. I'm hoping that they're just staying home with all the fighting going on in the city. I know where they're squatting. The problem is that I think something bad might have happened to them, and if that's the case, I don't even know where to start finding that kind of stuff out. I need someone with a lot of resources to help me."

"And I work for the EIA!" Aiofe realized instantly why she was first on Olivia's list despite the fact that she was the one least at risk.

Olivia explained that while Tinker had had elves and tengu and a dragon at her enclave, there hadn't been any humans. "Tinker *domi* doesn't seem to utilize the EIA or the police."

"She doesn't have the same clout with them." Aiofe started to pick through a basket of clean laundry. "On Earth, the spouse of a ruler never has any real power. In Ireland, the president might be leader of the country but his wife can't do anything more political than host tea parties for charity. She certainly can't have people executed on the spot or thrown out of the country. Pittsburghers think of Tinker mostly as a muddy wee lassie on a hoverbike. Humans just don't get that she basically became a coruler with Windwolf when she agreed to become his *domi*."

Aiofe did a magic trick of pulling on a floral sundress and taking off her modest pajamas at the same time. A few days earlier Olivia would be totally shocked but the royal marines had worn away that response.

Olivia focused on the problem at hand instead of Aiofe changing her panties without flashing anyone. "These are humans that I'm looking for—not elves. The police or EIA will be the ones that know if they've been hurt and taken to Mercy Hospital, or arrested, or gathered up to be deported at some later date . . ."

"Oh, I'm thick!" Aiofe cried. "You're looking for *cute hoors*."

Olivia wasn't sure she had understood Aiofe correctly, especially since most of the prostitutes hadn't been particularly attractive. "Cute whores?"

"*Cute hoor*," Aiofe carefully pronounced the second word. "A person that engineers things quietly to their advantage. People that dropped out of school after coming to Pittsburgh on student visas or never had visas in the first place."

"Yes." Olivia braced herself for more negative comments.

"Well, the EIA hasn't been collecting anyone like that." Aiofe sat down at the table so she could type on her keyboard. "After the Viceroy was attacked, Maynard pulled everyone off rounding up people on the expired visa lists and focused on finding the oni."

"I see." Olivia had been hoping that the missing prostitutes had simply been arrested by the authorities.

"We keep lists of arrests, hospital admissions, and deaths." Aiofe pulled up the EIA system. "Before August, we rarely had to update any of them. Pittsburgh was a fairly safe town even with the jumpfish and the river sharks and strangle vines. We got lucky that the tengu learned of the attack on Oktoberfest. Station Square had been evacuated before the train derailment. There were, however, a lot of injuries and deaths from the confusion and the fighting that happened afterward. We just need to check for the names of your lads and lassies."

Tommy hadn't given any names, he'd only specified "prostitutes working Liberty Avenue." It seemed to imply that both the women and the men were missing. No one working the streets, though, used their real name, not even Olivia. The EIA lists would be useless for learning if people were accounted for or not. She didn't even know who had disappeared.

She did know, though, that all the prostitutes were a few years older than she. "We're looking for people between the ages of eighteen and twenty-five. They would have been admitted to the hospital or arrested after the keva bean handout."

Olivia had talked with all the prostitutes from Stateside the night before the handout, trying to convince them to join her in getting the free food. The streetwalkers were like the proverbial grasshopper, never worrying about tomorrow. Peanut Butter Pie had been the only one who'd come with Olivia.

Aiofe refined her search. "That does narrow things down. With Pitt on summer break, eighteen to twenty-five is the smallest age group in Pittsburgh. We can also see who they list as emergency contacts; normally locals our age give a landline that belongs to a older relative."

Olivia cringed with guilt; Aiofe didn't know that Olivia was only sixteen.

Aiofe pulled up two lists of names. "The police didn't arrest anyone since the handout. I guess that they were too busy to deal with minor offenders. The list from Mercy Hospital doesn't look promising. Everyone seems to have given emergency contact and doctor information. Since I don't have a general practitioner—something I should do something about—I doubt any illegal immigrant would have one."

That left a short list of the dead. At the very top was "Doe, John."

"That means he has no identification?" Olivia asked even though she was fairly sure of the answer.

"I'm sorry," Aiofe said. "It does."

Olivia steeled herself against the fear that was starting to grow in her. She really didn't want to go into a place filled with corpses and see someone that she knew lying dead. Who else would do it? None of the other prostitutes had the resources to find out what happened to one of their own. "I need you to take me to the morgue."

She needed Aiofe's help partially because she had no clue where the morgue was, but also because Aiofe had some pull as an EIA employee that Olivia lacked.

Aiofe typed on her keyboard a moment and then shook her head. "He's not at the morgue. The city ran out of space at their building on Penn Avenue. They've set up an overflow to handle all the dead with refrigerator trailers and are looking for other alternatives. I can take you to where he is."

Olivia had come across the border between Earth and Elfhome at midnight during the July Shutdown.

She'd learned that trucks carrying big construction equipment to Pittsburgh had first priority to cross. The vehicles were searched as soon as they arrived, kept in the most secure parking lot at the edge of the quarantine zone, and flagged through immediately after Shutdown started. All other trucks were subjected to multiple, random searches. With the exception of certain medical supplies, everything else was given permission to enter the quarantine zone only if traffic patterns allowed it. It meant that any other vehicle might not even reach Elfhome.

She had reached Monroeville a day and a half before Shutdown. She could see the huge fenced-in parking lots from her hidden advantage point. All the areas were filling up while a giant digital clock counted down. UN forces directed traffic, checked paperwork, and searched vehicles. In the first priority lot, there were three big yellow construction vehicles and a host of smaller backhoes and bulldozers and forklifts and skid loaders, all on trailers. While the parking lot was secure, drivers were allowed to come and go. Between the trucks entering and the drivers walking in and out, she should be able to slip through the checkpoint.

She'd hoped to hide inside one of the smaller bulldozers or backhoes, but the cabs were all glass. It provided the operators a full view of their surroundings but it meant that she wouldn't be hidden from scrutiny. She would have to hide under one of the bigger vehicles. Most had large wheels that gave the machine plenty of clearance but exposed anyone under them. Her best hope looked to be a John Deere logger with caterpillar treads. The cab created a long, narrow crawlspace under it. The logger sat on a lowboy trailer being pulled by an old blue Kenworth with a sleeper cab. BETTS FARMS was written on the Kenworth's door, along with a Pittsburgh address.

Olivia had studied the vehicle through her binoculars, wondering if the driver actually slept in his truck. There was a sprawling truck stop beside the larger nonpriority staging areas with showers and toilets. There were also many cheap motels within walking distance. She watched the Kenworth for nearly an hour but saw no signs of its driver. She knew that this meant nothing; he could be asleep. She also knew that her scrambling around on the trailer might be loud enough to alert anyone awake in the cab.

She had a narrow window of opportunity. She had to risk it. If she didn't find a hiding place during the cover of this night, it would be another month before she could attempt crossing the border. After years of sneaking around the Ranch, trying to keep hidden from all her various stepsisters and -brothers and extended family, it seemed ridiculously easy to ghost through security. The lowboy trailer's deck was only eighteen inches high. She stepped up onto wooden floorboards and then crawled between the caterpillar treads of the logger. Lying down, she had only inches of clearance above her head. It smelled of sawdust, engine oil, diesel fuel, and mud.

She was barely in place when the door to the Kenworth opened. There was the familiar jangle of a choke-chain collar. Her heart stopped. She hadn't considered that the sleeper cab would allow the driver to travel with a dog. She went still as possible, barely daring to breathe.

The dog raced around the truck, the jangle of its collar marking its fast loops. It was a big dog if it was wearing a choke chain. It came to a stop near where Olivia had scrambled onto the trailer. It was close enough for her to hear its loud snuffing.

"Shep!" the driver called to the dog. "Heel."

The dog bounded to the side of his master, who jogged away, singing a sea shanty in a rich bass voice. *"We are outward bound for Mobile town, with a heave-o, haul! An' we'll heave the ol' wheel round an' round, Good mornin' ladies all!"*

Olivia went limp with relief. She had thought the driver must have heard her scrambling around on the trailer. He must have just wanted a break after sitting in his truck all day. Mud covered the wooden floor of the trailer with hard uncomfortable lumps but she didn't dare brush them away. The driver might be back any minute. She would have to wait.

The driver came jogging back a half hour later, still humming the tune. The jingle of Shep's collar kept time with the sea shanty. There were mysterious noises of truck doors opening and closing and the rustle of plastic bags. Olivia had guessed that the driver must have gone to the truck stop and bought snacks for the following day. He had started to play fetch in the dimly lit parking lot. A ball thunked softly on the pavement and Shep raced back and forth alongside the trailer.

"Get that dog on a leash, you stupid Pitty!" one of the UN guards called from out of the night.

"He's on a leash," the driver cheerfully called back in his deep bass voice.

"You've got to hold onto one end of it, you DPshit!" The guard blurred "DP" for *displaced person* into an insult. "This isn't your backwater cesspool of a city! Get ahold of your dog or we'll impound it!"

"Will do!" the driver shouted back, still sounding cheerful. He whistled to his dog, and muttered quietly. "Don't fight with the off-worlders. Don't fight with the off-worlders."

The driver climbed back into his truck, hopefully for the night.

Olivia waited for nearly an hour, heart thumping, before deciding that the driver probably had gone to sleep. She spent a few minutes cleaning the wooden floor of the trailer under her, brushing aside the hard lumps of dried mud. She tried to sleep but her body refused.

Dawn came, exposing how little cover the caterpillar treads actually gave her. Anyone inspecting the trailer closely would see her. She huddled in the shadows, peering out of the hundreds of tiny spy holes in the treads. Luckily the morning brought rain, keeping everyone under covers. She spent all day tucked up into the machinery, staying as still as possible, carefully sipping water so she wouldn't need to pee but wouldn't end up dehydrated. There had been nothing to do but pray and feel bitter regrets about everything that she had said and done since she was eleven.

The driver exercised his dog several times, despite the rain. It was a big blue heeler like ones at the Ranch. An Australian cattle breed, it was a high-energy dog, good for a farm but not the confines of a truck.

With nothing else to do, Olivia made theories about what kind of man the driver was. He seemed to be in his early thirties. Assuming that the guard's designation of him was correct, the driver had been born in Pittsburgh before it went to Elfhome for the first time. An uneven tan on his face made it obvious that he'd recently shaved off a beard. He was a dishwater blond of Northern European extraction—not fair enough to be a Swede but maybe something just south of that country or perhaps muddied down in America's melting pot. He had the build of someone who worked hard in fields: tall, lean, strong. On the back of his neck was the farmer's brand: a suntan that bordered on burn. Both his baseball cap and T-shirt were blue with white lettering spelling out BETTS FARMS. Was it because he was so proud of his workplace or was it a way to allay UN guards' suspicion, showing that the man and the truck belonged together? Certainly, he closed to meet any roving guard before they could reach his trailer. He did it casually by using the dog as a distraction, making it seem as if he was coincidently stepping out of his truck to give the dog a few minutes of freedom. With his deep booming voice, he'd explain that the blue heeler normally herded the cattle on the Betts' family farm. He claimed that he brought the dog on a whim, wanting company while he searched out and bought a used logger. By the very nature of Pittsburgh being on Earth only one day a month, the trip would span weeks. During his search, he'd been able to exercise the dog as much as it needed. This long wait to cross the border, he said, was taxing Shep's patience. The well-trained dog would win the guards over with its friendly nature.

During these exchanges, Olivia learned that the driver's name was Gage Betts. His grandmother, Gertie, who was over a hundred years old, owned Betts Farms. Since she refused to abandon the land owned by her father and her grandfather and great-grandfather, the family had stayed put. Oddly there were no mention of parents, aunts, uncles, or other intervening family—but it could be that Olivia had been overly sensitized to such connections via the Ranch.

It wasn't until dusk that Olivia had realized what Gage had been doing all day.

Gage was keeping the guards from inspecting the trailer where she hid.

Had he spotted Olivia or was he hiding something else, something smaller, stashed within the machinery? If it was as simple as he'd seen her hidden between the treads, why hadn't he pointed her out to the guards? Was he afraid that he might be detained? Or did he have plans for the girl, completely alone on a strange planet?

The possibilities terrified her. As dusk deepened into night, she considered moving to one of the other trucks. The parking lot, though, became a kicked hive of activity as Shutdown approached. Drivers who had slept in the nearby hotels arrived. The ones like Gage who had stayed with their trucks made trips to the truck stop's showers and restaurants and toilets and convenience stores.

Just before midnight, the public address system kicked on. A woman announced in bored tones, "One hour to Shutdown. All priority drivers, please prepare for admission into the quarantine zone by your cue number. This call is for priority drivers only. All paperwork must be presented for final check as you enter the zone."

One by one, distant trucks rumbled to life and moved forward. Finally, Gage's Kenworth started up and lurched forward. The heavy shifting and rattling of the big equipment inches over her head scared her. There was nothing to do but wait.

At midnight, Pittsburgh arrived with a sudden huge clap of thunder, a wave of cool green air, and a chorus of truck horns.

Gage blasted his horn the longest.

The line of trucks surged forward, quickly building up to highway speeds.

She was committed.

She was terrified.

She fought to stay calm. She couldn't panic. She needed to get off the trailer safely before Gage reached his final destination. She moved her legs in the low space under the logger, working out pins and needles from lying still for an entire day. She needed to be ready to run the first time that Gage came to a stop. She knew that they were on Interstate 376 heading into Pittsburgh proper. At some point, though, he'd leave the main roads for his family's farm.

She could see by the headlights in the opposite lane that the outbound vehicles were at a standstill.

At some point, hopefully, the Kenworth would run afoul of the traffic heading toward Earth. The roads had remained clear for miles and miles. After twenty minutes of roaring at full speed, she was starting to despair. Where were they going?

The truck slowed finally, taking an off-ramp while the bulk of the traffic continued straight. The new route wasn't a limited access highway but an expressway through an inner-city neighborhood. Sidewalks and buildings lined the right hand side of the road. If she remembered the layout of Pittsburgh, this was Boulevard of the Allies and it led to other major highways heading out of the city with little or no stops. If she was going to get off, she needed to move soon!

She wriggled her way backward, out from under the big logger to stand behind it. The Kenworth slowed even more as it started into an insanely tight cloverleaf turn. The logger pulled tight on its tie-down chains, the equipment creaking loudly. Gage was downshifting, trying to bleed off speed to take the steep downhill turn. Olivia gripped the logger's cab as she pulled herself upright. Luckily there were no trucks taking the turn with the Kenworth. No one was behind them to see her.

Olivia risked leaning over the passenger side to see what was ahead of them. There was a red light stopping the ramp traffic. The truck shuddered and groaned at the effort to come to a full stop.

"Yes!" she breathed. She could jump safely off once the Kenworth stopped.

The light turned green.

She gasped. "Oh no!" The sign ahead read LIBERTY BRIDGE. If she remembered correctly, directly beyond the bridge were the Liberty Tunnels. She had made notes that whatever she did, she needed to avoid the tunnels and the sparsely settled areas beyond. She needed to jump now.

The Kenworth shifted gears, slowing to nearly a stop but no longer braking.

"It's just like the hay wagon," she whispered to steel herself. *If the hay wagon was under a dark overpass in a strange city filled with man-eating plants.* She pushed the fear aside and jumped.

She stumbled in the dark, going down to her knees. Her hands landed in gritty dirt. She stayed down, panting with her fear. If she stood up, Gage might see her in his mirrors.

The Kenworth rumbled forward, gaining speed. She crouched in the darkness, waiting, until it had disappeared over Liberty Bridge. It was the last time she'd seen the truck. For days the rumble of big trucks made her heart hammer in her chest.

The makeshift morgue was set up at the huge parking lot at the foot of Mount Washington. The EIA had erected a big white tent. She'd caught a glimpse of it on the way up the Duquesne Incline but she hadn't realized its significance. She'd thought it been set up for a wedding. Any little girl would dream of holding her reception within the crisp white canvas against the vibrant autumn leaves of the wooded hillside. Now that Olivia knew what the tent was, she noticed the line of refrigerator trailers parked beside it. Coolers for the dead.

Then she saw the Kenworth.

Olivia jerked to a halt at the sight of it. Around

her the royal marines shifted into combat model, reading her alarm.

"It's nothing." She motioned for them to stand down. She forced herself to keep walking. Maybe she was wrong, maybe it wasn't the same truck.

Blue Kenworth. Sleeper cab. Betts Farm. Blue heeler leaning out the window.

Yes, it was the same truck. The Kenworth was currently hooked up to a refrigerated trailer. She couldn't see Gage Betts; the person setting the chocks on the trailer, though, looked too young to be its driver. Did it mean that Gage was somewhere nearby?

"Jesus, Mary, and Joseph!" Aiofe whispered fiercely. "It's Director Maynard!"

Olivia tore her gaze away from the Kenworth to scan the area for the famous director of the EIA. She spotted Director Maynard talking with a tiny old woman dressed for church in a prim black pillbox hat, a russet housedress, white gloves, and black cane. What was riveting about the woman to Olivia was how prim and proper she looked—a counterpoint to the fact that every other word out of her mouth was a profanity.

"We normally fire up that goddamn ice rink up as soon as it gets hotter than fuck," the old woman said. "It's a son of a bitch to maintain and sucks energy like an expensive whore but the kids love it after pissing around in the hot sun all day. I don't like it myself, it freezes the tits off me. I can't take the cold like I could when I was younger. After the bullshit during the June Shutdown, we locked down and braced for war. Between that and Gage being off-world buying some equipment, we didn't fuck around with the ice rink."

"Can you gear up the ice rink to be a morgue, Mrs. Betts?" Director Maynard said.

Mrs. Betts? Was this Gage's grandmother? The woman certainly looked fragile enough to be over a hundred years old.

"We could but what's the fucking point?" Mrs. Betts said. "Most of the dead are elves or oni. Elves want cremated as soon as possible, not dropped on ice like a fucking Popsicle. The oni aren't going be coming around, wanting to identify their dead. My kids can just dig a fucking big hole for your people to drop them in."

"There are tens of thousands of people in Pittsburgh who aren't permanent residents," Director Maynard said gravely, as if he knew that Mrs. Betts had little sympathy for those who weren't locals. "They want to know that they will be returned to their families if the worst happens."

The old woman spat a curse so foul that Olivia blushed for having heard it. "They bitch and moan and do their damnedest to keep us locals from being together as a family. Serves them right to see what a bitter medicine it is to swallow."

"Grandma Gertie," Gage Betts said as he walked out of the big tent. He'd regrown his beard into a goatee. His dishwasher blond hair had been trimmed to a long crew cut. He was spiffed up to "farmer business" style with a button-down oxford shirt, new black jeans, and well-polished cowboy boots. He looked so much like one of the men from the Ranch that Olivia hated him on sight. All that was missing was a cowboy hat and a well-worn Bible carried like a weapon. "You know it's the treaty that screws us over, not the off-worlders."

The old woman cursed again. "The off-worlders are the ones that make it so hard to jump through the fucking hoops that the elves put in place. Two hundred pages of passports, visas, permits, and travel plans just to go to Earth for a month to buy a logger. What bullshit. When I was a little girl living on Earth, I could travel the planet with nothing more than a smile and nod."

"That might have been true in the nineteen thirties, but it wasn't true when I was a boy living in New York." Maynard noticed the royal marines. A slight frown marked his confusion as he scanned the squad. He spotted Olivia and his eyes went wide. He flicked his hand to a woman standing behind him. "I'm sorry, Mrs. Betts, I have to attend to this personally. My assistant, Mrs. Walker-Buckton, will handle things from here."

His assistant stepped forward with a clipboard. While her hair was dyed an unconventional deep blue, her demeanor was extremely professional. "I have the paperwork for the rental of your trailer and a check made out to Betts Farm to cover the agreed-upon deposit."

Mrs. Betts didn't take the unspoken clue. She eyed the assistant, grunting slightly. "What happened to that other girl, Maynard? The little twat that kept giving me the stink eye?"

Maynard glanced to his assistant, who did pick up the clue.

"She was an oni mole. I am not," Mrs. Walker-Buckton said in a matter-of-fact tone.

Mrs. Betts blocked Maynard's path with her cane. "She was? You sure? What did you do to her? Let those elves be judge, jury, and executor?"

"Taji Chiyo was part of the oni strike squad that

kidnapped Tinker *domi*," Mrs. Walker-Buckton said. "She was a kitsune; one of her ancestors was an oni spirit fox. Ms. Chiyo was part animal; she had fox ears and tail. At one point, Tinker *domi* nearly escaped while Ms. Chiyo was supposed to be guarding her. As punishment, the oni bred her to a warg."

"A warg?" Mrs. Betts gasped and then added a blazing string of profanity.

"If you'll come with me"—Mrs. Walker-Buckton motioned toward the Kenworth—"I can tell you all about it and we can discuss details pertaining to the ice rink."

Freed of the old woman, Maynard bore down on Olivia with "intent" written all over his face.

I can do this, she told herself. *I'm stronger than I think. If nothing else, this gets it over with fast—like tearing off a bandage.*

She had no idea how you greet the leader of your race on a foreign planet.

Maynard surprised her with a low, sweeping bow. "I am Derek Maynard, director of the Elfhome Interdimensional Agency. I take it that you are Forest Moss's new *domi* and they're with you."

He started in Elvish but the last sentence—much to her joy—was in English. It was so much harder to waltz around verbal traps in Elvish. By "they" he meant the royal marines, who were standing at attention in a line behind her.

"Yes, they are. I'm Olivia—" She caught herself before giving the rest. Her maiden name would be a lie but she wanted to abandon her husband's surname forever. "Prince True Flame recommended that I use the name Olive Branch over Stone."

Derek Maynard nodded slowly, giving her a slow once-over, probably trying to determine what kind of person he'd just been saddled with. "You're from Boston, aren't you?"

"How...how...how do you know?"

"You still have the accent. Not a lot; you probably moved away from it a few years ago, but the nasal short-A is still there. Strong enough that I'm guessing you're a Southie."

She blushed. Her mother had tried hard to erase the Southie accent but Olivia had clung to it, the only thing she had left of the family that she had been stolen away from. "Yes. I grew up in South Boston."

"So, you're not local," Maynard said.

He couldn't send her back to her husband. He couldn't send her back to Earth. Still, it was frightening to admit the truth. "I'm not."

He considered her in silence for so long that she found it nerve-racking. She could hear Dagger badgering Aiofe into translating for the marines. The girl seemed torn between reporting what her boss was saying and maintaining trust with her research subjects.

"What brings you here?" Maynard finally broke the silence. "Are you looking for me or have you lost someone?"

He gestured to the tent to imply the dead.

"Lost someone." Olivia wet her suddenly dry mouth. If the Wyverns were a big club to wield on the elves, then Tinker *domi* was the one to use on humans. "I spoke with Tinker *domi* this morning. She encouraged me to use my position for the good of others. I've learned that some people—some humans—have fallen through the cracks, much like the Stone Clan children had. I'm attempting to track them down. Make sure that they're safe."

Maynard frowned. "I didn't realize you were so young, but there's not much I can do. The *dau* mark makes you *domana* elf of the Stone Clan. I can offer you advice and limited assistance, but for the sake of all the humans within my care, I do not dare do much more than that—at least not until I know Sunder better."

"Why?" Olivia asked. The royal marines had told her the names of the incoming Stone Clan warlords but they knew little more than that. She wasn't sure if it was because they had been denied a decent education, or if they were indifferent to the history of other clans, or a combination of the two.

"I have known the Viceroy half my life and consider him a good friend, and yet he would not want me to overtly influence his *domi*. He would want me to protect her, yes, and offer sage advice, but I could not block her from any course of action that she chose. If she decided to borrow my construction vehicles to raze an entire hillside outside the city to build windmills, then I could do nothing but smooth any feathers that she ruffled among the humans. I know that because that is how he would expect me to react to his doing the same. I must see her the same as I see him; that is the nature of their union."

It would explain the instant obedience of everyone at the Poppymeadows enclave. It also explained why people kept warning Olivia that she didn't have the same level of power as Tinker *domi*. Windwolf was the Viceroy and head of the Wind Clan, which outnumbered the Stone Clan by a thousand to one.

Maynard continued his explanation. "Sunder is the

current head of the Stone Clan here in Pittsburgh. It means that both you and Forest Moss are under Sunder's domain. If Windwolf would not allow me to influence his *domi*, I have to assume that Sunder will allow even less freedom."

She nodded her understanding. The elder at the Ranch had an entire list of things that were forbidden, from phones to the internet to children's literature. She had packed up her favorite books in Boston only to watch the elders burn them all as too dangerous when she arrived at the Ranch. What was so dangerous about *The Wind in the Willows*? That "the other" was not to be feared? That vastly different people could be friends?

Maynard eyed the royal marines, who were still standing at attention because of Maynard's own guard. His mouth quirked slightly, as if he could see them as the puppies that they were. "You should know that these warriors would die to protect you. I urge you not to take any undue risk that would put them in harm's way. They could be considered children, high school age, and certainly they know nothing about human technology. Nothing about cars and trucks. Nothing about security cameras or phones and radios. Nothing about landmines or grenades. If they were to die while under your command, it would reflect badly on you. If your actions are judged to be pure stupidity and recklessness, the Wyvern will behead you. It's your responsibility to keep them safe. Do you understand that?"

"Yes," Olivia said despite the sudden lump in her throat.

"I've been told you're at Phipps Conservatory. Yes, it affords you access to the greenhouses, but I would strongly recommend you find a fallback location that is easier to defend." He fished a business card out of his suit's breast pocket. "This is my direct number. Do you have a phone?"

"No," she whispered. Every normal teenage girl had one on Earth. At the Ranch, though, only the men were allowed to own them. Since she'd had limited funds during her escape, she'd chosen not to purchase one before crossing the border. To her dismay, she'd discovered that cell phones were rare as hen's teeth on Elfhome.

He waved over one of his guards. "Find her a phone. Make sure it comes with a charger." The guard nodded and trotted away. "My guard will deliver a phone to you shortly. Keep it charged and keep it close. Call me if you need help or advice. Tinker *domi* had an advantage that you do not: she is a local. She knows Pittsburgh and she has a wide social network of friends. You should do whatever you can to build a network."

Which was the exact opposite of what she had done since she arrived in Pittsburgh, keeping almost everyone at arm's length. No one even knew her real name. Only the elves knew that she was pregnant. She had told no one of her abusive husband or the story of her dead stepson.

Maynard turned to Aiofe. "You work with my patrol squads as a translator? You're the Pitt anthology grad student intern?"

Aiofe nodded. "Yes, sir."

"You have a new job. Stay with her. Explain elf culture as you know it and act as a bridge when she needs to interact with city officials. I'm assuming that she will run afoul of them as often as Tinker *domi* does." He produced a second business card to give to Aiofe. "Call me if anyone picks a fight with her."

It would be more comforting to know that they had his backing if it didn't come with the knowledge that he expected them to need it.

The phone arrived moments later, just as Maynard was pulled away by news of power outages in Oakland. The Bettses drove away in the Kenworth, expressing concern about their extended family at their remote farmstead. Despite the alarming possibility of attack, Olivia felt relieved that everyone had left. It allowed her to fumble with the phone with a minimum of witnesses. It was one thing to know what other people could do with their phones and another to actually get the phone to do what she wanted.

Aiofe explained how the phone worked to Olivia and the fascinated royal marines. "These EIA models remind me of the toy phone I had when I was little. Just like these, it had big buttons, a green digital screen, and was virtually indestructible. I'm glad that I could use my own phone for work. My first year here, I went through three smartphones before I found one that worked in Pittsburgh."

"I've never had a smartphone," Olivia admitted reluctantly. If she was going to build a network, she had to stop keeping people at arm's length. "My mom had this really religious upbringing. It was like Amish, only worse. She was really strict about things like that."

Her mother had left the Ranch as a teenager but she hadn't escaped it. The brainwashing had gone too deep. She saw most "normal" American life as ungodly.

"That had to suck," Aiofe said.

"Not really—not at first. I didn't notice when I was really little. I had books and dolls and Legos. I don't think I noticed until I was about third grade that all the other girls wore pants or dresses without leggings. By the time I was in sixth grade, I would have killed for blue jeans. I wanted a phone because all the other kids had one."

"Me mum got me mine when I went off to boarding school so she could check in on me. She didn't like me going off so young. I saw it as my first chance to do a real anthropology study: the indigenous race of an Irish all-girl private school. She didn't like me coming to Elfhome either but here I am." Aiofe handed the phone to Olivia. "Here I'll stay until Tinker *domi* can figure out how to get us back."

Olivia nodded as she realized that she might be the only person in Pittsburgh who didn't want to go back to Earth. For the first time in her life, she was able to choose what she did. Even Maynard wouldn't—and perhaps couldn't—stop her.

"I want to get this over with," she said. "I want to see if I know this John Doe and then try to find out what happened to the others."

Aiofe stayed in the parking lot with the marines. The anthropology student was trying to explain human burial customs to the obviously horrified elves. The warriors were all shaking their heads and inching back.

It left Olivia alone amid the dead, steeling herself against the upcoming ordeal. *No one in that tent can hurt me,* she told herself. *They don't deserve to be feared. They have gone before God, nothing more.*

She'd expected bodies laid out on tables but there were only body bags being shuffled around via workers in hazmat suits. They had some kind of mobile air conditioner cooling the tent, making it at least twenty degrees cooler. The space smelled like the slaughter yard at the Ranch; all that was missing were the screams of frightened pigs.

Olivia didn't want to go around unzipping random body bags. She was sure that the bodies within would look like horror movie victims. Her stomach was already queasy from morning sickness. She didn't want to lose her lunch onto one of the dead.

The weirdly familiar feel of the slaughter yard made it possible for Olivia to walk up to the nearest worker and explain what she wanted. Either Maynard or his assistant, Mrs. Walker-Buckton, had spoken with the staff, or the presence of the nervous royal marines had convinced them to be helpful. It quickly became obvious that while the people working at the overflow morgue wanted to be helpful, they were so overwhelmed that they had an utter communication breakdown. Workers from the EIA, the coroner's office, and volunteers needed to discuss and consult paperwork over and over again as they tried to figure out where the John Doe body might have been stored.

A woman came trotting into the tent. She was short, had brown hair and eyes, and smelled of sunblock. There was something vaguely military about her, though she lacked any name badge or insignia. She wore a blue boonie hat, a khaki work shirt, black carpenter jeans and combat boots. They looked like a soldier's uniform made out of civilian clothes. "I heard you're here to identify our John Doe!"

"Actually, I hope not," Olivia said. "I only know a few people in Pittsburgh. Some of them are missing. I hope none of them are dead."

The woman nodded grimly. "I understand. I'm Linda Gaddy. My friends call me Gaddy. I'm working with the police. I'm the one that found our John Doe. I've been knocking on doors and such, hoping to put a name to the face."

"You're a police officer?" Olivia said.

"I'm kind of a jack-of-all-trades. I've got an eye for detail and a knack for being able to add two and two together. Sometimes I shuffle paperwork for someone that's trying to jump through the EIA hoops, and sometimes I'm a glorified meter maid during Shutdown, making sure off-worlders don't gum up the works by illegally parking."

Olivia had learned the hard way that the largest employers in Pittsburgh were the EIA, the University of Pittsburgh, and the city itself. The three paid well and had good benefits. Most of their coveted positions, however, went to off-worlders with post-doc college degrees. The police and fire fighters were the exception; neither required a college degree. It meant anyone who worked for them were locals.

Neither job description—accountant or meter maid—explained how and where Gaddy had found the unidentified body. Were those her normal street clothes or some kind of impromptu uniform?

"So currently you're . . . ?" Olivia said.

"Searching the back alleys for dead," Gaddy said. "The oni made a thousand elf bodies vanish into the wilderness. There's no telling how many humans are lying dead in the city. I won't lie to you, this is going to be grisly, but it would really help out solving this mystery."

"Mystery?" Olivia echoed.

"Who he is. How he got to where he was. Who or what killed him."

Olivia noticed that the questions didn't include "how he died." Apparently that had been obvious. "Where is he?"

"I figured that he wouldn't have anyone coming to claim him, so I had the last shift move him to that first trailer."

The body was already bloated from the heat. Someone had used the face for a punching bag, breaking the nose and smashing out two front teeth. Olivia cringed, forcing herself to look. Did she know this man? It was hard to tell with all the damage done. All the male prostitutes had short, blonde hair. The man had been shot in the neck, the neat hole just above his left collarbone leading to a massive wound where it exited. He definitely had been murdered.

She scanned downwards. His shapeless gray T-shirt used to have a decal from the University of Pittsburgh on it; the logo had partially worn away in the wash. He wore a pair of loose drawstring shorts. She gasped as she saw that he had LOVE and HATE tattooed on his fingers. She tugged aside the body bag to verify that he had the start of a sleeve tattoo on his left arm that looked vaguely like a *sekasha* protective spell.

"Do you know him?" Gaddy asked gently.

She nodded, blinking away sudden tears. "He liked looking sexy at all times; he would have never left his house in such ratty, loose clothes. I think he must have been home when he was shot."

"What's his name?" Gaddy pressed. "Where does he live?"

"I don't know his real name, just his street name." She knew that wouldn't help identify him to more than a handful of people. She knew that he had parents on Earth who thought he was still in college. She knew the agony of losing a child. Somehow his parents had to be told. "The reason he used a street name was because he'd used a student visa to get to Elfhome but it had expired. I do know that he turned twenty-one on August twentieth. They had a party for him."

"Oh, that helps a lot!" Gaddy shut the bag shut. "We just need someone with access to the list."

"Aiofe does," Olivia said, thinking of the birthday party that Peanut dragged her to. Peanut wanted her to move into the house, saying it would be safer. Olivia had fled as soon as it was polite to leave.

Out in the baking heat of the parking lot, Aiofe checked the expired visa list. "There's only one person with that birthday: Jevin Kay Kingston. He was here on a student visa. Oh, he was cute. Looks like he was a right cheeky one, though."

Aiofe shifted her tablet to show Olivia the photo attached to the visa. He was years younger in the picture but already smug.

"Yes, that's him." Olivia turned to Gaddy. "Where did you find him?"

Gaddy pointed downriver. "After the train derailment, I was scouting the rail lines. I found him down under the Fleming Park Bridge."

"Where?"

"Here." Gaddy took a well-worn map out of one of the carpenter pants pockets. She unfolded and folded it so that a small section was easily readable. Her fingernails were painted a neutral beige that nearly matched her skin tone. She tapped the words "West River Lot" and then traced along the river's edge for six or seven miles. "This is the Fleming Park Bridge. It joins Neville Island with the rest of the city. He was on the train tracks that run under the overpass but it's likely he started on the bridge. In the dark it would be hard to see that this part of the span is over train tracks and not the river proper. I think someone thought they were dumping him in the river."

"He lived on the North Side with a bunch of other kids." Olivia pointed out the general location on the opposite bank of the Ohio River. "I can't tell you the address. I could find it again by walking there but I didn't get any street names or house numbers. There were about nine kids living there, all about his age, all illegal. Either they had expired visas or snuck across the border during Shutdown."

Gaddy whispered a curse. She frowned at the North Side and then glanced downriver, toward where she found Jevin. "I was assuming that he had a run-in with oni troops after fleeing Oktoberfest. You sure about him being home?"

"He cared deeply about how he looked," Olivia said. "He liked looking sexy and clean and good smelling. If his clothes got ripped or stained, he'd go home to change. He would say things like 'I wouldn't be caught dead in that' when he saw someone in ratty clothing."

"Yeah," Gaddy said. "Someone like that doesn't go to a festival in that outfit."

"I'm going to the house," Olivia said. "I'm worried about the others."

Gaddy pursed her lips. She clearly didn't think it was a wise idea. She scanned the royal marines peering over Aiofe's shoulder, trying to follow the conversation that had been all in English. "I suppose you have plenty of firepower to wade into just about anything on the North Side. I'll come with you, just in case we need to call for backup."

Emboldened by the tale of Tinker *domi* and the construction vehicles, Olivia decided to commandeer a big six-wheeled UN cargo truck that they found sitting empty at Station Square.

"We can't just take it," Aiofe whispered, looking around.

"It's unlocked." Olivia leaned in to look at the ignition. It was an older model that still used keys. There was a chain to lock the steering wheel but it hadn't been engaged. Either someone had gotten sloppy or the truck had been left for her to find. "Maynard said that he would smooth over feathers ruffled by commandeering EIA property."

"That was just a random example of him not interfering with Tinker *domi*," Aiofe said. "If he wanted us to use it, he would said something more direct."

"Maybe," Olivia said, "but he's a politician. He might have to pretend he didn't know we were going to take it."

Aiofe squinted at her. After a few moments of thinking, she said, "That's stretching things a bit. I think he would have left a driver if he really wanted us to take it. It's manual transmission."

"He can't get a driver any more involved than himself." Olivia climbed up into the high driver seat. "I can drive it."

Maybe. She had learned to drive on the Ranch's big

equipment, but a Kansas hayfield was not the same as a major city street.

Olivia waved at the marines. "Get in. Get in."

The marines didn't need to be invited twice to a new adventure. They clambered into the back, laughing and shouting.

Aiofe remained on the sidewalk, looking torn. "I'm not sure this is a good idea."

Olivia thought enviously of Tinker's dining room filled with possibly stolen lamps. No one seemed to ever tell the older girl that something was a bad idea. "I'm not sure which bus to take to where Peanut Butter Pie and the others were living. The buses to North Side are few and far between. I don't want to get over there and then find out that we missed the last bus."

"It's easier to ask forgiveness than to get permission," Gaddy said. "I'll get my hoverbike and follow."

13: TEAM MISCHIEF! GO!

✦⇢◉⇠✦

Louise yipped in surprise and fear when something ran
up her bare leg. In theory she loved all things small
and furry, but not when they were running loose inside
her shorts. She jumped up from the concrete floor.

Jillian yelped in unison. "What is it?"

"There's something alive in here." Louise had been
sitting cross-legged, wiring together the luggage mules
through their maintenance ports. Whatever the small
furry thing had been, it had fallen out of her lap
and disappeared among the clutter scattered thick
around her.

"Alive?" Jillian pulled out her Taser. "Like what?
A steel spinner? A strangle vine?"

"I don't know!" Louise stepped up onto the luggage
mule's platform to get herself off the floor.

Crow Boy had gone to find food and information.
He believed that the bunker was safe, hidden as it
was in the middle of the secret tengu village. He was
thinking "oni invaders" not "deadly vermin."

Louise looked around for a weapon.

"It's me!" Nikola's voice called from inside a boot lying sideways on the floor. A white robotic mouse peeked out cautiously to wave at Louise. It wore Nikola's blue scarf. "Silly old bear. We were bored so we came to see what you are doing."

"Nikola!" Jillian squealed with happiness. She tucked away her Taser so she could scoop up the robotic mouse and nuzzle it. "I've missed you and the girls so much!"

Louise felt a flash of surprise and dismay. Didn't Jillian realize that the last thing they needed was bored babies?

On the heels of that impatient thought, she also realized that Jillian had spent most of the summer worried that she'd lose first the babies and then Louise. While Jillian had Louise walking and talking and plotting beside her, the babies had been dormant for a month. Jillian didn't have Louise's "sense" that the babies were safe and sound within their seven-pound eggs. The twins had marked the sky blue shells with the name of the baby they held but Louise supposed that wasn't the same as hearing Nikola's familiar Christopher Robin/little English boy voice.

"Are the girls here too?" Louise said.

"Of course we are!" Chuck answered as she park-oured across piles of camping gear. Her mouse had lost its pink scarf. Its right ear was torn and its face had dirt streaked across it like war paint.

"Chuck!" Jillian scooped up the battered robot to add to her mouse nuzzling. "You look so fierce!"

"Being in an egg is boring!" Red Jawbreaker stood on Louise's tablet three mules down. The Jawbreakers sounded nearly identical but Red wore a red gingham scarf. "There's nothing to do. Nothing to listen to. I want music! Let's drop the beat!"

Red must have opened up Louise's music folder as the deep thumping base of Imagine Dragons' "Believer" started to play. Red sang along with the words. "*First things first, I'mma say all the words inside my head! I'm fired up and tired of the way that things have been, oh-oohh!*"

"We want to race!" Green Jawbreaker scrambled up the next luggage mule down. Her scarf of green velvet was starting to fray at the ends. "We found our mice but we can't find our mini-bikes. We want to use the luggage mules instead!"

"No, no, no, no!" Louise cried. "Don't touch the mules! Why can't it ever be simple?"

When Crow Boy said that he would recharge things, Louise had assumed he would stop at useful things like the luggage mules and their computers. Apparently he'd also charged up the babies' robotic mice. How did he miss the babies' other toys?

Louise carefully picked her way toward the pile of items that were related to magic. After they had sorted everything and come up with a plan, they pulled most of the piles apart, resulting in the floor being covered with everything that might be useful now. Anything unneeded had stayed stacked together, mostly in cardboard boxes labeled with their contents. Back when they had geared up on Earth, they had tried to stay as organized as possible. "I'll find your . . . your what? Mini-bikes?"

"Chuck means the mini-hovercarts," Nikola said.

Did they even bring those? When did the babies start calling them mini-bikes? Back at the Waldorf Astoria, they called them mini-hovercarts because the small square platforms sort of looked like little shopping carts that hovered. The plastic railing kept the robotic mice bodies from falling off. The boxy design controlled by Wi-Fi interface had been easier to build than something that looked and operated like a motorcycle.

The babies had been on tiny hoverbikes in her dream. They'd been wearing racing goggles—something requested but the twins hadn't had time to create. In the dream, Chuck Norris had her pink scarf, there had been no war-paint-like dirt on her mouse, and its ears had been intact.

Oilcan "saw" the mice but not in a completely literal manner.

"How did you talk to Oilcan?" His real name was Orville but after seeing the world through his eyes, Louise couldn't bring herself to use it anymore.

"I told you that Lou would see us," Nikola said to his sisters.

"Dream walking is easy-peasy." Chuck Norris was unrepentant as always. "It was only a little harder talking to someone who is awake than someone who is asleep. Joy came with us."

"That explains the candy," Louise muttered to herself. Joy had been there, literally, while the babies had only projected themselves—somehow. The question became: How did Joy carry said candy back to Haven so quickly? Louise had a hazy notion that Pittsburgh proper was somewhere miles to the southeast, but she wasn't sure how far. She knew that Joy could phase through any solid wall, but could she teleport too?

"What are you talking about?" Jillian said.

"I told you that the girls didn't like the names that

we picked out for them," Louise said. "They went to talk to Oilcan to champion their cause."

"They did *what*?" Jillian cried. "And how did you 'see' them?"

"It's another weird genetic trick that some of us got from being from two dragon bloodlines," Louise said. "You can see magic. We both can cast *domana* spells. I can dream walk."

"And so can we!" Chuck said. "Charlene is a stupid name! I want to be Chuck Norris Dufae!"

"And I want to race!" Green's voice this time came from the luggage mule that her mouse had been sitting on. The mule unlocked its wheels.

"No!" the twins both shouted, pointing firmly at the mule just like their mother would have.

"If you try to move that, you'll rip out the cables and damage both mules' maintenance ports!" Louise said. "And then everyone will die! Just give me a minute! I'll find your mini-bikes. Just don't mess with the mules!"

"Everyone will die?" Nikola echoed.

"What is all this?" Chuck scrambled up onto the mule to examine the wiring. "What are you doing?"

"Can we help?" Nikola said.

"Of course we can help!" Chuck said. "Team Mischief! Go!"

Their trying to help would be almost as bad as their trying to race the mules.

"I don't think you'll understand what we're doing," Louise said truthfully.

Jillian, though, launched into an explanation. "We're using the neural engines of the luggage mules to build generative adversarial networks. If you look at the data that Dufae has in the Codex, he seemed to be trying to track subatomic particles. It appears that the elves don't have anything like Feynman diagrams or even calculators beyond a simple abacus, so Dufae was stuck crunching numbers the hard way."

"We can grind through his data fast with the mules, but only if you don't damage them," Louise said.

She hadn't seen the babies' toys when they sorted through everything but Jillian had dealt with most of the items that used magic to function. They had come to Elfhome loaded for bear, expecting to fight their way through the wilderness. While they had things like the Tasers, the twins' size, age, and the short time that they had to prepare meant that their most powerful weapon was their ability to combine magic and science. Using money that they had stolen from Desmarais, they had bought a hundred times what they could possibly use or carry on them, hence the fleet of luggage mules. The number of mules that they brought with them had been limited only by how many they could get drop-shipped to their Monroeville hotel.

"Can't you use your tablets?" Green Jawbreaker, thankfully, was back in her mouse again. "Don't they have neural engines? What about your phones?"

"Yes," Jillian said with more patience than Louise could have had. "They both have neural engines, but they're primitive compared to the luggage mules."

Louise started to shift the cardboard boxes of magical supplies. "Think of what the mules have to do: follow their owner through crowds, avoiding people while balancing any load across any terrain, be it indoor or outdoor, and in any weather condition. Wet grass. Deep snow. Icy stairs. Beach sand."

"What's a generative adversarial network?" Nikola said.

"It's when you set up two neural networks that 'play against each other' in a task." Jillian put down the mice and joined the search. "The concept evolved from game theory. The networks are competing but they're also learning from each other. We're pairing up the mules, two each as a team, and then feeding them the data sets that Dufae recorded within the Codex from his experiments with shield magic. Each team is trying to find the best possible spell."

"It's basically what Dufae was charting out with pen and paper in the Codex," Louise said.

"But the mules can work a zillion times faster than any normal person," Jillian said.

Louise found a box marked "Baby Toys." She opened it up to find everything related to the hovercarts piled on top of the broken robotic dog.

The flash of a muzzle in the darkness. The flare of pain. Tesla's deep angry growl.

"Oh." She whimpered at the memory.

"What is it?" Nikola tried to climb up the smooth side of the cardboard box and failed.

Louise blinked away the sudden tears. She didn't have time to break down and cry. She steeled herself to lift out the carts. "I found your mini-bikes. They need to be recharged before you can race."

Chuck parkoured across the luggage mules to land on the edge of the box. "Oh, it's Tesla. We should fix it."

"Yeah!" Nikola said. "It was useful to have a big body now and then."

"The mice are more fun!" Green Jawbreaker called. "Tesla was so crowded when we were all in it."

Her brother and sisters were not the bodies that she'd grown used to seeing them in, Louise reminded herself. They were four large eggs far above her head—from which God knew what would hatch out. Tesla was a broken machine; he was not Nikola.

"We don't have time to fix Tesla," Louise said. "We're working on a big, big problem. Besides, we don't have any spare parts for him."

"Can't we just print them?" Chuck said.

Louise glanced to Jillian, who shook her head. "Our printers aren't sophisticated enough. We would need something heavy duty like the ones at Perlman. We could barely do the prototype of the mice on ours. We don't have time to look for one."

"I wonder if we can find a printer in Pittsburgh that can do it," Green continued as if she hadn't heard Louise. It was hard to tell. She could be just ignoring Louise; the babies were good at ignoring things that they didn't like or understand.

"I'll look!" Red Jawbreaker cried. "Me! Me! I can do it!"

"Be careful!" Louise said instead of "No, don't!" because the babies were bored and frustrated and probably scared. Looking for big 3D printers that they could "borrow" was probably safer than doing something like trying to track down oni and evil elves.

"We'll be like ghosts!" the girls cried. Their robot mice bodies fell silent and still.

"I'll stay with you." Nikola climbed up onto her shoulder.

"How are you even controlling the mice?" Louise asked. "When you were in Tesla, it made sense—kind of—because he had a Wi-Fi connection that you could use to link with the robotic mice bodies."

"I'm not sure." Nikola cocked his head. "That's a

good question. We were bored. We could hear you talking about our names and the others were really annoyed with you. After you went to sleep, we decided to go talk to Orville. When we came back to Haven, someone had set up an internet connection. Over the last few hours, people have been sending hundreds of emails, coming and going. We skimmed the emails but they were boring. People we didn't know going off to places we can't get to. I'll connect your tablet."

The tengu were terrified at what the *nactka* could mean to their future. Jin Wong must have reversed his decision to keep Haven on a blackout in hopes that the improved communication would help in the war effort.

Louise hooked up the mini-hovercarts so that they would recharge and went back to her tablet. Nikola had logged her into a local network named Oneiroi. Being that the Oneiroi were the Greek personification of dreams, it might be a network that the tengu set up for Gracie. Louise resisted the urge to check on all of her favorite Pittsburgh sites that had been available to the twins only during Shutdown. She did stop the Imagine Dragons songlist that Red Jawbreaker had left playing and found the streaming signal from her favorite underground fusion radio station, WESA. "Sky Diving" was finishing up.

"*Nicadae Pitsubaug!*" the deejay shouted in pidgin Elvish and then switched over to English. "This is WESA and I'm Marti Wulfow, bringing you the best of new elf fusion music. A big shout-out to our sponsor, the Wool Shed, for all your knitting needs. The Wool Shed is a co-op of shepherds both here in Pittsburgh and in the Easternlands. It features *indi*, merino, and mohair wool.

They have dyed yarn skeins and bulk carded wool. I've started my wool socks—it's going to be a cold one this winter! And it's... I want to say a beautiful day here in Pittsburgh but I can see storm clouds rolling in. We could be in for all sorts of nasty weather out there, so take precautions: take your umbrellas if you're going out just in case! This is Naekanain with their new hit single, 'We Are Pittsburgh'!"

A song she'd never heard before started playing. Naekanain's lead singer was Carl Moser, who had a rough growling voice. "*Blood on the pavement, blood on the blade, blood flows through common veins.*"

It was odd knowing that musicians she'd spent a third of her life idolizing were suddenly a few miles south instead of in another universe, some impossible distance away. That she was going to meet the very people she used to make videos of using Barbie doll stand-ins. Windwolf. Wraith Arrow. Stormsong. Stormhorse. Maybe even Queen Soulful Ember. It made her feel a little giddy, mixed with something that could have been fear. All the kids at Perlman knowing about the Lemon-Lime videos had been a surprising revelation with weird, unexpected side effects. Surely the elves had never seen the videos. Hopefully. She wasn't sure if Queen Soulful Ember had a forgiving side. The queen they portrayed in their videos didn't. What if Louise's "future-seeing" ability had picked that up? What a terrifying thought. She pushed the thought from her mind and focused on the problem at hand.

Red Jawbreaker was the first to report back, but she hadn't found a printer. She hadn't even looked for a printer. Instead she had gone to raid the underground elf fusion rock radio station for information. "It's totally old school! They have an actual radio tower and everything. Marti Wulfow is awesome. She's part of the Resistance! That whole bit about the storm and the umbrella? That was code! She has a long list of words you don't say often that mean other things. Listen! Listen!"

"This is WESA and I'm Marti Wulfow, bringing you the best of new elf fusion music. It's the top of the hour weather report! We're looking at a huge storm blowing in, people! I hope you have your umbrellas with you. It's going to be raining cats and dogs, cows and zebras! And now here is 'First Hand,' written by our very own Orphan for our very own Tinker *domi*!"

"Did you hear?" Red cried with triumph. "'Umbrella' means combat weapons. 'Zebras' means all primary scouts should report to their cell leaders."

"What?" Louise shouted as Marti Wulfow started to play yet another Naekanain song that she hadn't heard before.

Red continued as if she hadn't heard the question. "If you meet someone and want to know if they're in the Resistance, you say, 'We are Pittsburgh' and they say, 'We are Team Tinker.' Isn't that cool? Oh, oh, oh and get this! Oilcan is Orphan. He wrote the song Marti is playing now and 'Sky Diving' and a lot of other songs that we like!"

"Really?" Nikola locked onto the least important part of Red's report.

"It's a secret but Marti is friends with both Oilcan and Carl Moser. I found an email where Marti was asking Carl if becoming an elf was going to stop

Oilcan from writing songs as Orphan and Carl didn't think so because Tinker is still the same girl that he's always known."

"Wait, wait, wait—Orville is an elf now?" Jillian cried.

"Please, try to keep up," Red said.

"Oh, I forgot to tell you about that," Louise said. "Dufae's father, Forge, is here in Pittsburgh and he made Oilcan an elf. It seems very messy, like Oilcan didn't ask to be an elf or something. I don't know the whole story but...we might have to live with Forge and it doesn't make Tinker happy."

"*And?*" Jillian shouted.

"And what?" Louise asked, confused. "I really didn't get the entire story. It was like walking into the middle of a very weird soap opera. Something horrible happened to these elf kids from the Stone Clan and Oilcan is their dad now or something..."

Jillian was staring at her with hurt and anger.

"I can't help it that our family is weird!" Louise shouted. "All of us! Just look at us!"

"Leave me out of this conversation," Red Jawbreaker said. "I'm not weird. I'm going to see what else I can find."

Red's mouse went silent.

Louise threw up her hands. "I really don't understand everything that happened in Pittsburgh since the last Shutdown. The last news reports that we had were from July's Shutdown and that was just that Windwolf survived the attack on him."

Jillian visibly struggled to keep her temper. "And he married our sister—after turning her into an elf."

"Exactly!" Louise said. "Our sister is now a full

elf! Esme is back from Alpha Centauri—and she's the same age as when she left eighteen years ago. That doesn't make any sense! Dufae's father is still alive after hundreds of years—and he's here in Pittsburgh, wanting to be grandpa to anyone descended from his son. And Oilcan is dad to a bunch of elf kids in some way that I totally don't understand. So much weirdness happened in a few months. We really need to be brought up to speed. Fast."

Jillian narrowed her eyes and studied Louise for a minute. "They're going to make us choose between them—aren't they?"

"Yes." Louise felt better for getting it out in the open.

Jillian threw up her hands. "How are we supposed to pick? We don't know them. None of them. Not really. How soon?"

"I don't know. There was a lot of stuff I didn't understand. Something about us being Stone Clan, not Wind Clan, and some scary people called Harbingers. What Tinker and Oilcan are most afraid of is that the Stone Clan might try to use us as pawns."

Jillian gave a short evil laugh. "Oh, they can try all they want but we're not going to be pawns."

"I don't think it's what we should be focusing on," Louise said. "Based on the rest of this summer, just about anything can happen the next week or so. We need to figure out Dufae's shield."

Green Jawbreaker's and Chuck's mice both suddenly stirred to life.

"I found a printer for Tesla!" Chuck reported. "It's plenty big enough and it's just sitting idle. No one has used it for a couple of weeks, probably since the gate fell."

"I found Tinker's secret base!" Green squeaked with excitement.

"Really?" Nikola asked.

"Where?" Chuck cried.

"I'll show you!" Green said. "Follow me!"

"Wait!" Louise cried. "You can't go breaking in on her private stuff."

"We're not breaking in," Green said with labored patience. "Someone put this massive backdoor into her system. Her security is wide open. Since the door is hanging open, we should be able to go in and look around—right? She's got very nice computer systems with a very helpful AI. She named it Sparks. I had lots of fun playing with him. You should see some of the things she's invented. Talk about mad-scientist genius! She's got detailed schematics and print files and everything—though Sparks says there's no devices attached . . ."

"Show us! Show us!" Chuck and Nikola squeaked.

"Who hacked her system?" Louise cried before all four could virtually run off.

"I don't know," Green said as if it was little importance. She cocked her head as if listening to some distant voice. "Sparks says it was someone using an IP registered to a company called Midas Exploration, L.L.C. Is that like LOL? It has lots of employees. Any one of them could have hacked her system."

Chuck was frantically waving her paws in impatience. "Show me Tinker's secret base! I want to see."

"Come on!" Green said even as Louise and Jillian both cried out, "No!" The mice both went still again as the babies went off to explore Tinker's computer systems.

"We really need to find a way to put them into time out without mentally traumatizing them," Jillian said.

Crow Boy returned with a small flock of winged tengu children and a basket full of food. The three older kids were dressed as warriors even though they were probably only seventh or eighth graders. They wore sharp metal claws on their crow feet, and war paint. They were obviously trying to look fierce despite their age. Louise would have thought it a joke except she had seen Crow Boy fight for his life. The two boys in normal street clothes were younger, one about the twins' age and the other looked like a kindergartener—if kindergarteners had large black crow wings.

"Why did you bring them?" Louise whispered to Crow Boy as he unloaded several pork cutlet bento boxes out of the basket. The twins didn't deal well with normal kids; they'd been social outcasts at school. Things had improved during the class play but that was more because of the other kids changing their attitudes after they found out that the twins were Lemon-Lime JEl-Lo. The twins had their hands full just dealing with the babies. They didn't need more chaos. At least the tengu kids were not bouncing off the walls or picking through the clutter on the floor. They stood in a line and stared at the twins with dark brown eyes.

For some reason, Louise could only think of barn owls, but those were the mortal enemies of crows. It was interesting to note that the tengu wings scaled to the child's size as the spell that triggered the magical constructs seemed identical on all the children.

"They have been on Elfhome all summer," Crow Boy whispered in reply. "I could ask them about what they know and report to you what they said, but I might not ask them the right questions."

"Fair enough," Jillian said, although she didn't look any happier than Louise felt.

It had been a whispered conversation and the tengu children's faces didn't change but Louise had a feeling that they had heard every word. It meant that the twins had to be careful not to leak out their secrets while trying to learn all they could from the children.

"Do they know anything useful?" Louise realized how rude that sounded. "I mean, what we need to know is complicated magic stuff and what our family is like."

One of the teenage girls snorted. "She's right. Even Riki couldn't keep up with Tinker *domi*. I should be out fighting with the other warriors, not babysitting."

"Suit yourself." Jillian made shooing motions. "We don't need babysitters."

The girl made a face and glanced meaningfully at the kindergartener. She hadn't meant the twins when she complained about babysitting duty.

"The Chosen are leaders, Keiko, before they are warriors," Crow Boy said. "Else they could never lead us to peace."

Keiko took a deep breath and growled it out. "Yes, I know. Not all the Nestlings have their wings and they'll need practice flying. Until everyone can flee Haven safely under their own power, someone of the Chosen bloodline needs to stay to coordinate an evacuation."

The other girl looked a little surprised that Keiko

had backed down so easily. "Only you could have gotten away with saying that to her face, Daffodil."

Crow Boy frowned at the girl for using his hated nickname. "We should mind our manners." He gave a slight bowing wave toward the twins. "These are the Chosen of Joy, daughters of Jin Wong's savior, Esme Shanske, and sisters to our *domi*: the honorable Jillian and Louise Mayer."

He turned to bow and wave toward the teenage girl, the boy who seemed to be the twins' age, and the kindergartener. "These are the Chosen of Providence, nieces and nephews of our leader, Jin Wong: the honorable Keiko, Mickey, and Joey Shoji."

Crow Boy had told the twins that he lived next door to the Shoji family, pretending to be a mild-mannered American suburbanite while secretly protecting the Chosen bloodline. He'd gotten Keiko and Mickey to safety after the house had been attacked, but Joey had been kidnapped by the oni. At some point, while Crow Boy was on Earth with the twins, Joey been found and rescued. It gave new meaning to "babysitting" duty and the face paint: If Haven was attacked, the older children would fight to death to protect the younger ones.

Keiko bowed. "Honored to meet you."

Mickey waved nervously and said, "Heyo!"

Joey whispered, "They look just like her—only shorter."

"Hush," Keiko whispered even as Mickey nodded in agreement.

If they had met Tinker, then they might be able to answer the twins' questions about her.

"This is Hoshi and Mai Sessai." Crow Boy gave another polite bow and wave toward the other two kids. Hoshi was a teenage boy with feathers braided into his long hair; he was slightly taller than Crow Boy so he might have been older. Mai was a girl whose black hair been cropped into a pixie cut. They both nodded in greeting.

"They are *yamabushi*, like I am," Crow Boy said. "They were raised here on Elfhome. There is little that they do not know of Pittsburgh or the surrounding wilderness or the oni forces that we face."

"Okay," Jillian drew the word out to emphasize the twins' confusion. "We do need to know about our family—"

"Eventually," Louise finished the thought. "What we really need to stay focused on is the shield."

Crow Boy nodded. "As the Chosen, the Shoji family has been taught the language of the Ryu dragons. They might be able to talk to Joy."

"Do we really want to talk to Joy?" Jillian said what Louise was thinking. "She's just a baby."

Which was the nice way of saying that Joy was hopelessly self-centered, often rude, and generally not helpful.

"She might be, or she not be," Keiko said.

"What is that supposed to mean?" Louise said.

"While we have been under Providence's protection for thousands of years, there is much we do not know about the dragons of Ryu," Keiko said. "At one point in time, we had all that Providence's child could tell us about her father's people written down, but it was decided to burn all our records when we were enslaved, lest they fall into the hands of our captors. What remains is an oral history, passed from parent to child."

"It's full of holes," Mickey complained. "Like who was Providence's mate? Why wasn't she looking for their missing kid? Did they have any other kids? How many babies do dragons have at a time? Are they born live like boa constrictors or hatched from eggs like alligators?"

"Mickey, I'm trying to condense." Keiko motioned that he should stay quiet. "But yes, there are holes in what we know. Since the appearance of Impatience, we've been looking closer at our legends and realizing how little we know. What we know for sure was that Providence's child originally was a dragon by the name of Nirvana. Our legends imply that she was young, and thus not held accountable for breaking some of the rules of draconic society, namely the edict covering travel to Elfhome. We believe that she was trying to rescue other dragons that had gone missing. Providence asked Wong Jin to rescue his daughter from the elves. We know that Wong Jin was too late to save the dragon, but found shattered pieces of Nirvana, including a young female who was 'made from what had been stolen from Nirvana,' who took the name of Huan, which means 'happiness.'"

"Nirvana. Happiness." Mickey made a rolling motion. "Joy?"

"We named Joy—" Louise said.

"*You* named Joy." Jillian corrected her. Unsaid was that Louise came up with the name while the magic generator was running. "I wanted to call her Greedy Gut or Bottomless Pit. She turned down all the other names we came up with. We tried dozens of them."

"I think Joy understands more English than what she actually uses to communicate," Crow Boy said.

"It's possible that since the dragons can project their minds outside their bodies that they actually have some type of telepathy."

Like the babies "talking" to Oilcan, Louise thought.

"Our legends imply that Wong Jin found all the pieces of Nirvana," Keiko said. "But our legends could be wrong."

"I see what you're implying," Louise said carefully. It did seem plausible that Joy was a missing fragment of Nirvana. Did the tengu think this gave them some claim to Joy? "But I'm not sure what point you're trying to get to."

"Dragons have a complex and powerful set of written spells that they can use to supplement their natural abilities. Impatience taught some to Tinker *domi* and he inscribed others on Esme's ship to keep it stable against the forces of wind and gravity. If Joy has Nirvana's memories, then she should know a great deal about magic."

"Wow! Okay, that makes sense." Louise looked around the cluttered bunker. The baby dragon was nowhere to be seen. "Joy used to be anchored to us via the magic generators. Since we got to Elfhome, she comes and goes as she pleases. I haven't seen her for a while."

"I brought cookies," Crow Boy said loudly.

"Cookies!" Joy squealed, suddenly on Louise's shoulder.

Yes, Joy could teleport. The question remained how far could she teleport? And could she teach it to the babies once they were born? Oh God, if the babies could teleport themselves out of cribs, the future was going to be nightmarish.

The tengu children had surprising reactions.

The two *yamabushi* stepped forward, spreading their wings to shield Keiko, Mickey, and Joey. Keiko sputtered from the sudden face full of feathers.

Mickey cried "Whoa! Cool!"

Joey ducked under the *yamabushi*'s wings to bow and call out a flowing greeting in a strange language.

"Be nice." Louise sensed that Joy was about to be Joy. "Or no cookies."

"Tengu belong to Providence," Joy grumbled. "Double stupid poopy face."

Louise remembered it was the same thing Joy had said when they first met Crow Boy. The little dragon had instantly recognized the winged boy as someone who belonged to Providence. If Joy was a leftover fragment of Nirvana, though, she couldn't have known about Providence becoming the guardian spirit of the tengu. That had happened after Nirvana had been "shattered" by the elves. "How do you know?"

Joy blew a raspberry. "Says so."

"Says so?" Louise echoed in confusion.

Joy reared up, holding onto Louise's ear to stabilize herself. Her mane bristled out, each tendril writhing, seeming more like a nest of snakes than hair. Louise felt something warm wash over her, like someone had opened a door to a desert. The dry heat lifted the hairs on her arm but didn't shift any of the lightweight clutter strewn about her feet. A glowing line appeared on the left hands of all the tengu, running up their arms to disappear under their shirts. The children gasped and peered closely at the line.

"It's tiny little letters," Joey said.

"Dragon runes," Mickey gasped. "It's cool! It's like an ultrasecret magical tattoo."

The older kids glanced at one another, obviously uneasy by the discovery.

"This part is Providence's name." Keiko traced out part of the gleaming line of runes. "I can't read the rest. I'm not sure how I feel about this."

"Yeah, it's kind of like finding out you're a Build-A-Bear." Mai tented her shirt to see where the writing led even as it faded away.

Hoshi shook his head. "We've always known that Providence interceded. He did what he could to protect us."

The realization that Providence hadn't been able to wholly protect the tengu filled Louise with disquiet. It meant that the dragons didn't know a spell that could shield Pittsburgh from whatever the oni planned.

14: ONCE MORE WITH FEELING

Oilcan wasn't sure how he ended up taking *all* the kids at the enclave shopping.

It started out small. He wanted to buy two of everything for a little girl's bedroom: bed, nightstand, dresser, bookcase, desk, and chair. Tinker would be persuaded by a furnished room faster than by an empty space and vague promises. Oilcan hoped that her sisters would be similarly inclined. There were also things his enclave still needed, especially if it was to seem like a home to children raised on Earth. His pickup wouldn't be able to handle all the furniture he hoped to buy. He could swing past the salvage yard and pick up the flat bed, but that would leave his pickup on the other side of the city. A second driver would be the easiest way to get everything back to the enclave.

It had seemed simple to grab Blue Sky Montana and take him along. The little half-elf might look ten years old, but he was eighteen and thus legally old enough to drive. What's more, his *sekasha* bloodline meant that if they got separated, none of the royal marines who were patrolling the city in droves would give him grief.

Blue Sky had been painting bedrooms on the second floor with a handful of kids. Some of them belonged to Oilcan. Some of them were just visiting.

One thing led to another and before Oilcan knew it, an entire herd of kids and the three dogs were spilling out onto the sidewalk on the South Side from three separate vehicles. All five of his kids came along, even Barley, who was rarely out of the kitchen. His kids had also brought along their elfhound, Repeat, who they thought had been killed in the oni attack. Since Repeat had mysteriously reappeared, the kids had refused to go anywhere without the puppy. Oilcan had also somehow picked up the half-oni Spot, a tengu girl named Rebecca Brotman, a random *sekasha*, Guy Kryskill, Andy Roach, and two of the Roach family elfhounds, Pete and Bruno.

The mini-circus had gotten started when everyone that wanted to come wouldn't fit in Oilcan's truck. Guy had been at Sacred Heart, helping Team Tinker install the new custom-built front gate. Guy volunteered his fiery red Ford pickup with a long bed, but apparently that required his cousin Andy and the dogs to come with him. (The truck was older than the boy, who turned sixteen in the spring. Oilcan and Tinker had spent part of the winter helping Roach refurbish the Ford what now seemed a lifetime ago.)

The other three additions—an elf, a tengu, and a half-oni—were a mystery. Oilcan hadn't been aware that they'd picked up random spare people somewhere along the way until they unloaded in the South Side.

"Stay." Andy pointed at the dogs and then sidewalk beside Guy's Ford. "Guard."

The bear-sized adult dogs sat down in the shade casted by the pickup. Repeat glanced between Andy and Baby Duck, but the little female was entranced by the flashing neon sign over the door. The puppy decided to obey its former master and join the other dogs. It made Oilcan happy since both pickups had rifles in their gunracks and the *sekasha* were stashing their bows, arrows, and other backup weapons into the weapons crate strapped to the back of the flatbed.

"*Quiee*," Baby Duck quacked at the gaudy display. "What does it say?"

Blue Sky blushed, self-conscious that his Elvish was not as good as one expected for a half-elf. He liked being the voice of authority for the other children, so he fumbled through the translation. He'd spent enough time in Oilcan's wake to know the reference. "Once More With Feeling. It's something a..." He paused to consider how to translate "conductor" and settled for "...leader says to his musicians so that they'll play the same song a second time but less mechanically. It's because they sell used furniture and music... stuff. Instruments—and the paper with songs written on them..." Blue Sky stumbled to a halt and then switched topics by pointing to the store across the street. "See! That's the ice cream shop I was talking about. It serves Reinhold's ice cream and things like whipped cream and hot fudge to put on top."

"Furniture first," Oilcan said loudly as all the kids except Merry and Rustle surged toward the curb. He didn't want the group splitting up. "We'll get the ice cream afterward."

The kids swarmed into Once More With Feeling. The shop was currently the biggest furniture store in Pittsburgh. The title of "biggest" used to be held by its sister store, Once Upon A Mattress. Located in Market Square, with big storefront windows, Once Upon A Mattress had handled only new merchandise, which it leased at insane prices to off-world personnel: UN peacekeeping forces, embassy employees, and private corporation employees. Locals would window-shop the displays of matched furniture sets but never actually buy anything. They knew that off-worlders rarely *stayed* on Elfhome. After a year or two, most workers would finish their duty and rotate back to Earth. Once Upon A Mattress would collect the leased furniture to sell at Once More With Feeling for pennies on the dollar.

Once Upon A Mattress, though, had gone down in a blaze of glory when someone shot several thousand bullets through it. Six forty-foot-long walking electric catfish, a police car, and the store's entire inventory had been reduced to Swiss cheese by the gunfire.

Once More With Feeling was a thrift store in theory. It was, however, very expensive compared to the others of its kind due to the quality of its stock. Oilcan hadn't been able to afford it, not with the amount of furniture that he needed for his enclave. He had avoided the store while he'd scoured the city for tables and chairs for his enclave's dining room.

He'd picked clean all the nearby abandoned buildings and cheap thrift stores and still needed a lot more furniture for his enclave. It was one of the many reasons Oilcan had decided to become Beholden to the Wind Clan. With backing from Tinker, he could simply do a massive purchase of everything he needed.

The front door of Once More With Feeling opened

to a football-field-sized showroom. His kids stood for a full minute staring openmouthed in awe.

Blue Sky broke the silence. "It's just a furniture store, not the Grand Canyon."

"Elves custom-make all their furniture to last for centuries." Guy Kryskill's brother apprenticed under one the elf furniture makers, so he could speak with authority. "They don't have stores like this, not even in their big cities."

"So . . ." Blue Sky mimed "mind blown" while looking meaningfully at the stunned elves around him.

"Yup." Guy started toward the back corner of the showroom. "The cooking stuff is all back in the corner. Gas ranges. Grills. Pots and pans. It's all hit or miss but sometimes you get lucky."

Guy triggered a sudden scattering of kids, each pursuing their own interest. Barley followed Guy and Andy to the cookware department, deep in a discussion about smoking meat. Merry and Rustle headed to the opposite corner for a wall display of guitars. Cattail Reeds and the tengu girl, Rebecca, beelined upstairs where bridal wear and vintage dresses were sold, talking about Earth fashion trends. Baby Duck started to critique all the overstuffed couches lining the store's center aisle in a twisted elf version of Goldilocks.

"Too black. Too ugly. Too black." Baby Duck ticked quickly down the row. "*Quiee!* This one is beautiful! Let's get this one!"

Her choice was a small pink French country love seat with wood accents. It was very cute but very small.

"We need lots of seating." Oilcan pointed at the largest piece on the floor, a huge U-shaped leather sectional. They didn't have a family-only communal space at the enclave yet. If he could get Jewel Tear moved to the second floor, though, they could use her current room. The American ideal of family was one who gathered in a living room on a couch. The twins might find comfort in that familiar arrangement.

Baby Duck eyed the sectional doubtfully. "It's too black."

Again? It took Oilcan a moment to realize that she meant Stone Clan black. The kids had spent their whole life identifying themselves with the color—only to have their clan betray them. Baby Duck was wearing a man's chambray work shirt in Wind Clan blue as a dress with rainbow leggings. Under a very thin veneer of "I'm fine," the kids were still traumatized.

Blue Sky and Spot closed ranks with Baby Duck to lend their support. The three were the youngest and had become fast friends over the last week.

"Too smelly," Spot whispered in English. It was the first time Oilcan had ever heard Spot talk; he'd been wondering if the half-oni wasn't able to speak. The boy looked as if his father had been a Labrador retriever instead of an oni. Spot had big amber eyes, long floppy ears, dark fur, and a wedge-shaped black nose. According to Tommy Chang, the boy had spent his entire life hidden away because of his appearance. It might have made him too shy to talk, or maybe he didn't follow Elvish, since the other half-oni kids seemed to know only English, Chinese, and Oni.

Spot wrinkled his black nose and whispered, "Cat peed on it."

Oilcan smelled nothing but a lavender-based cleaning product that the store apparently used by the gallon. "Are you sure?"

Spot cringed back behind Blue Sky, nodding.

"You don't want an ugly, black, peed-on couch." Blue Sky championed both Baby Duck and Spot.

"This one is big!" Baby Duck dashed over to a long white couch that looked like stitched-together clouds. She flopped down and the massive puffy pillows swallowed her. "*Quiee!* Too soft! Too soft!"

Spot and Blue Sky rescued her from the couch.

"What about this one?" Oilcan moved to a half-moon sectional behind the first row of couches. It wasn't his style. The tufted cushions and curved sections seemed too pretentiousness to him, but it was a misty blue color in a soft micro-suede fabric.

"Oh, that one is just right!" Baby Duck cried. She and Spot tumbled onto the couch to test it out.

Blue Sky went into alert mode as the other *sekasha* drifted closer. Oilcan recognized the hard look on the boy's face; they were seconds away from Blue Sky launching himself at the interloper.

"We're getting this couch!" Oilcan announced, catching Blue by the shoulder. He turned the boy around and pushed him toward the distant service counter. "You three go find an employee. I want to start the process of getting this stuff loaded."

Blue resisted enough for Oilcan to know that he wasn't going willingly. "He's looking at Spot weird. No one invited him. He just added himself. He doesn't have any right to be here. He's not one of us."

Not one of us?

Oilcan had been aware that they'd picked up a second armed guard just as everyone piled out of the vehicles outside of the store. Oilcan had assumed it was one of Forge's people; they'd provided backup to

Thorne on previous shopping trips. Who exactly had they picked up? Oilcan glanced at the male *sekasha* drifting toward them.

"Shit," Oilcan breathed in English. The *sekasha* was a complete stranger. "I'll deal with it." Oilcan gave Blue Sky another nudge. "Trust me."

Blue Sky was a good kid. He'd spent most his life trusting Oilcan and Tinker. He gave Oilcan an unhappy look but he obeyed. The boy caught Baby Duck and Spot by the hand and dragged them off.

It was hard to tell with elves, but the *sekasha* seemed "teenage" young. The male was shorter than the warriors in Tinker's Hand, but so were all of Forge's. His armor and tattoos were Stone Clan black but the ribbon in his braid was an emerald green. He was watching the children, just as Blue Sky claimed. He had his face set in the emotionally neutral "warrior's mask" that the *sekasha* had perfected; there was no way to tell what the male was thinking.

Whatever his interest in the kids was, it was derailed by a La-Z-Boy recliner with its footrest raised. The warrior squatted to closely eye the mechanical pieces of the chair.

"Who is that?" Oilcan whispered to Thorne Scratch, pointing discretely at the *sekasha*.

He didn't understand any of the words that she used as a reply. He really wasn't as fluent in Elvish as he thought.

"I don't know what those words mean," he whispered.

"I'll try to break his name down to more common words," Thorne said, then paused to think it through. "On certain nights, when the moon is bright, there appears to be two smaller lights that bracket it. It's been determined that they're reflections of the moon-light off of thin wispy clouds. I'm not sure if you can see them in Pittsburgh; the conditions must be right for them to appear. I have yet to see them here in the Westernlands."

"Paraselene." Oilcan gave the scientific name, which meant "beside the moon." The elves had determined the true nature of the optical illusion, although he wasn't sure how. It was a very specific refraction of moonlight through ice crystals found in cirrus clouds that were shaped like hexagonal plates.

Thorne Scratch gave an uncertain nod, probably because she didn't know Latin. "His full name means 'the ghost white gleams to either side of a full moon when it is nearest to Elfhome in its elliptic orbit, and thus its brightest, in the middle of winter over foreign mountains.'"

Her original phrase had been much shorter. Oilcan didn't know the Elvish for "supermoon" or "paraselene" or whatever "foreign mountains" denoted. They needed an idiom that they both easily understood.

"We sometimes call the illusion 'moon dog' instead of paraselene," Oilcan said.

Thorne looked slightly surprised. "We use that phrase too. In old legends, the moon dog was thought to be the greyhound of Huunou. It is believed that it was rare to catch sight of the dog in the sky because Huunou often gifts it to those who have his favor."

Oilcan had heard of Huunou's greyhound. The dog was a weirdly seasonal mythological creature, like Santa's reindeer, if his reindeer tortured anyone who didn't put out cookies. The elves made a big production of "feeding sky's greyhound" around Winter Solstice by putting out brightly decorated suet, much to the delight of the local bird population.

Moon Dog's name, however, really didn't explain who he was, and more specifically, what he was doing with Oilcan's little group of shoppers. Thorne Scratch sounded like she knew the young male, but he hadn't been part of Earth Son's or Jewel Tear's households. "Where did he come from?"

Thorne shook her head to indicate that she didn't know. "He was not on the list that Little Horse gave to me, yet the last time I saw him was at Cold Mountain Temple. It is possible that he is not here officially, much the way he was not at Cold Mountain Temple formally. Most of his life has been shaped by his dangerously odd name. Perhaps, once again, he's let it take him on a wild hunt."

Huunou was the god of a weird collection of things, starting with everything in the sky and working down to laundry. The moon was often referred to his palace where he slept and the sun was his blazing red horse. He was the "Santa" of the winter solstice celebration. The weeklong festival was like Christmas for the elves, but with little weird hints of Halloween thrown in. It made for a bright, joyous, but a little creepy celebration. All the elves he knew looked forward to it. None of what Oilcan knew would indicate "dangerously odd."

He had to be missing something in the translation. "What is so odd about his name?"

Thorne gave him a strange look, as if he'd asked, "What's odd about the sky being polka dot?"

"Until this summer, I was friends with only a handful of elves." Oilcan ticked them off on his fingers as he gave their full Elvish names. Briar Rose. Snapdragon.

Windchime. Misty. Owl. Raindrop. Their real names were long and complicated; it was one of the reasons that humans gave their elf friends English nicknames.

"Ah, I see." Thorne pursed her lips together. "How to explain? When a child is born, it's taken to a priestess to be named. She will see the shape of its future and give the child a name to guide it on that path. For example, I was given the name of Thorne Scratch, which suggests that I will bring harm to anyone that gets too close to me. Some would point at Earth Son's death as proof that the priestess was correct with her warning. I would argue, though, that I did not have many choices as to who I could become Beholden to, since most heeded the warning of my name. One's name is a double-edged sword, especially if it is filled with bad omens. It gives you direction but at the same time, it can hamper you at every step."

"Moon Dog in winter over foreign mountains is a bad-omen name?" Oilcan guessed.

"It is filled with portents. It is believed the earthquakes and volcano eruptions happen most often when the moon is large in the night sky. The phrase 'foreign mountains' is an ancient term for a mountainous area that is unmapped and unknown and home to a powerful enemy. Lastly, winter is when Huunou decides if the souls he's gathered are fit to be reborn into our world again. He is the god of death. That is why we burn our dead, so their souls are free to join Huunou in the sky. His hounds are said to escort souls to his palace for judgement."

That would explain the "Halloween" part of the midwinter festival.

"His dogs are said to be divine and noble but ruthless," Thorne Scratch continued. "They will ignore all pleas of the dying to carry out their mission. In the past, they were given to heroes to help them fight demonic beasts, change the course of rivers, throw down mountains, and slay evil gods. To be given such a name is to say that the course of your life will be legendary. You will be given an impossible task and will be expected to succeed. He has worked hard to live up to it. At the age of seventy, he decided to leave the temple he was born in and walk completely across the South Plateau and the Hill Region—three full *mei*—to study under Tempered Steel."

Cold Mountain Temple was rumored to be in the same region as the Himalayan Plateau, which made a three-thousand-mile trek even more impressive.

"You will have to talk to him alone," Thorne said. "To offer and accept—that is a very private thing that no one should come between. Not even as your First can I interfere."

Oilcan stared at her, trying to understand what she meant until the light went on. "You think he came with us because he's thinking of offering to me?"

Thorne's mouth quirked into a frown that was instantly smoothed away. She was too on-edge to be natural; she was hiding behind a warrior mask. "I don't know him well; he arrived at Cold Mountain Temple after I won my sword and left. He was there when I returned to the temple a few years ago; I was too wrapped up in my own concerns with Earth Son to give him proper notice. People like to talk, though, of the odd and mysterious. From what they told me, I thought nothing could pry him away from Tempered Steel's side. He was driven to learn all that Tempered Steel could teach."

In other words: I doubt he will offer to you, but I can't think of any other reason for *him* to be *here*.

The holy warrior in question was sitting in a burgundy La-Z-Boy recliner, raising and lowering the leg rest.

After such a monumental effort to get to Cold Mountain Temple, why would Moon Dog leave? Why travel halfway around the world? It was possible that if Thorne had difficulty finding someone to take her because of her name, Moon Dog might be having the same problem. Did he hope to become Beholden to Oilcan?

The Harbingers had arrived while Tinker was playing hide-and-seek with Chloe Polanski, just hours after Forge transformed Oilcan into a full *domana* elf. Last week, Oilcan had been human with some residual *domana* powers. Last month, no one knew that the Dufaes had been originally elves. Last spring, only a handful of Wind Clan elves even knew that Oilcan existed.

The young warrior hadn't traveled to Pittsburgh to seek out Oilcan.

Moon Dog could have possibly planned to offer to the three *domana* initially sent by the Stone Clan. He would have arrived a day or two ago to find Earth Son dead, Forest Moss clinically insane, and Jewel Tear captured by the oni. He probably didn't know that Forest Moss had recovered enough to rejoin the war effort. He might not have heard that Jewel Tear had been rescued, depending on how long he'd been at Sacred Heart before joining the shopping trip. It was possible that Moon Dog didn't realize that Oilcan had joined forces with the Wind Clan. It only happened yesterday. There had been no formal declaration beyond Oilcan painting his door blue.

The young warrior might not have gotten as far as

Sacred Heart's front door, considering everything that was going on outside.

That was a lot of "maybe" and "possibly" and "probably." It made Oilcan uneasy. There was no clear, logical chain of events that would lead Moon Dog to the thrift store. Oilcan took a deep breath and flexed his hands. If it came to a fight, he should be ready. Still, his stomach was roiling as he moved toward Moon Dog.

The warrior seemed fixated on the chair, but as Oilcan closed on him, he said, "*Kau*, I was *ikudae* confused by this place. I thought it was a *garorou* but where is the *chaviyau*? And I always thought that a chair was a chair unless it was *boudu* or *daeni*. I never imagined that you could make chairs in so many assorted ways. These *baviali* move! Is that not *waya*?"

Moon Dog had an accent thicker than any elf Oilcan had ever met. He had heard echoes of it in Forge and at times Thorne and the kids, but nothing like this. Oilcan wasn't totally sure what the warrior had said.

"This is a furniture store," Oilcan said cautiously. "We're here to purchase chairs and beds and such for my enclave. These children—most of these children— are part of my household." He was careful to be exact because it could be considered lying if he made a mistake. He made a motion to indicate the kids scattered throughout the building. "Those that are not my Beholden are my *domi*'s Beholden and some of my close friends. Why did you come with us?"

Moon Dog paused, obviously thinking hard, before saying in what might have been English, "Size king?"

"What?"

"The frozen milk with sweets and fruit." Moon Dog pointed toward the ice cream store.

"Ice cream?" That still didn't explain why he was half a world away from his home, or what he was doing in the furniture store.

"*Sebeyou* made it sound very good. I wanted to try it. I have coin."

"*Sebeyou*?" Oilcan echoed.

Thorne must have decided that Oilcan was in over his head. She drifted in to the conversation. "*Sebeyou* is what we call the warriors at the temple who have not yet earned their sword. He means Blue Sky."

"Boo sky." Moon Dog mangled the English. "What does it mean? No one could tell me."

Oilcan translated it into Elvish, not bothering with Blue Sky's last name of Montana as it would be too difficult to explain.

"That's it? Nothing else? No indication of time of day? The color of the morning sky is not the same as the late afternoon. Morning is full of bright expectations while the evening is somber with failure. Did the priestess not say?"

"I believe he was named by his mother; she is a human." Oilcan had never met the woman; she'd gotten sick and left for Earth before Oilcan came to Elfhome. John Montana wasn't the type to pick fancy names—his pets were called Stray Mama Cat, Gray Kitten, and Guppy Fish.

"*Waya!*" Moon Dog said. "It is an *inios* name. 'The color of the sky without clouds.' There are no omens there. It is a name that is at peace with itself."

Blue Sky was returning with an extremely old man. The store manager was bent with age. His white puff of thin hair looked like the head of a dandelion about to go to seed.

The manager glanced briefly at Oilcan and the seated Moon Dog before focusing on Thorne in the more reassuring Wind Clan blue. Judging by the widening of his eyes and his step backward, the man recognized that Thorne Scratch was a *sekasha*. "I don't speak Elvish," he said to Blue Sky. "Do they know that I don't take elf coins? Our books aren't set up to deal with it. Up one day. Down the next. You never know the real value of the gold coins."

"I'm—" Oilcan caught himself before he claimed that he was really a human, at least in his own head. He needed to stop feeling the need to explain to others about the complications in his life. What was, was. Others didn't need to understand or sympathize. "I'm the one buying the furniture. I speak English and I have American currency."

Oilcan took out the bills that he'd gotten yesterday after Tinker bankrolled him. "I want this blue sectional and the pink French country love seat to start." Baby Duck only had a mattress in her room. The twins probably could use a love seat as they might want their room to be a refuge from all the strangers, He scanned the couches selection for a second small piece. "And that other tufted white settee."

The old man blew out his breath. "I don't have anyone right now to load these pieces. My stock boys are off playing spy or hero or something. It's all hush-hush and code words stupidity. All I know is their 'cell leader' called them about an hour ago about a 'recon mission' and they took off."

"We'll handle it," Oilcan said. They'd come with enough people to move anything. "How much for the three?"

"Hold on, let me tally it." The store manager took out a paper waiter's pad that looked nearly as old as the man. He flipped a grubby cover over, took a stub of pencil out, and started to scratch out numbers. "Three and five and three is eleven. Carry the one."

Oilcan glanced at Blue Sky to find the boy glaring at Moon Dog. Luckily the young warrior was fixated on the store manager.

"What's wrong with him?" Moon Dog asked in Elvish.

Wrong? Oilcan eyed the man again. Then it dawned on him. "Oh, he's just very old."

"Old?" Moon Dog echoed. He clearly had never seen any living being that could classify as "old" before. Even the elfhounds lived ten times longer than an Earth dog.

"Yes," Oilcan said.

"*Waya!*" Moon Dog breathed softly.

Oilcan still didn't know why Moon Dog was in Pittsburgh, but it was obvious that everything in the city was new and amazing to the young *sekasha*. Hopefully it would mean that the holy warrior wouldn't be dangerous to anyone. Still, the faster that they got done, the sooner they could gracefully scrape off the male.

Oilcan switched to English to tell the manager, "We need a bunch of beds too. The whole package: headboards, mattresses, sheets, and such."

The manager paused to wave toward the far wall. "Bed frames, headboards, linens, and the rest are over there. None of our mattresses are new, but they're cleaned and verified that they don't have bedbugs or lice or whatnot. We're not allowed to sell them during Shutdown, but that hasn't been an issue for a month or so."

"Go find a bed that you like," Oilcan said in Elvish. He pointed at Baby Duck but included Spot and Blue Sky with a wiggle of his finger. He switched back to English for Spot's sake. "Explain to her 'twin-size.' We really can't handle a lot of big beds for everyone."

"Yes, *sama*!" Baby Duck skipped off, the picture of sunshine and happiness. Of all the kids, she was rebounding the best, but it could be because she had literally wiped the memories of everything from her mind—who she was, where she was from, why she had come to Pittsburgh, along with all the torture that the oni had inflicted on her.

Blue Sky nodded like a commando given orders and followed Baby Duck. Spot looked puzzled but trailed after them. Perhaps the half-oni boy was too young to know the difference in bed sizes, or maybe the half-oni living situation didn't afford the children separate beds. Oilcan really should find out since the half-oni were now his responsibility in name. It begged the question as to how he could fix any problems they had without stepping on Tommy Chang's toes.

The manager eyed the cash in Oilcan's hand. "I'll tag these as sold and keep a running tally of what you want."

Tagging the pieces apparently involved getting supplies from somewhere else in the store, as the old man headed off at a slow shuffle.

Oilcan considered the overstuffed chairs. Should he get more for his other kids? The oni had taken everything that the kids had brought with them to Pittsburgh. Other than their mattresses, the kids' bedrooms were empty.

They'd painted the rooms in cheerful colors that the kids had picked out. Cattail Reeds was making bright curtains for the tall windows. Oilcan had provided paintings to scatter through the building; each kid had chosen a favorite from his collection to hang in their room. It seemed too little, especially since Oilcan planned to fill up the twins' bedroom with furniture.

He should check to see if the others wanted a chair.

"I'd like a worktable, if we can find one." Cattail Reeds had been trying on clothes with Rebecca. They both wore long, flowing bohemian dresses in shades of red. "As wide and long as possible so I can lay out pieces of any outfits I'm working on. Also, if we can, a rack like one of these." She gestured to the metal display rack holding the dresses on hangers. "And some better lights. It's hard to sew with just the elf shines."

The two musicians had tucked themselves into the corner with all the instruments and sheet music and couldn't be budged.

"No. No chairs!" Merry said. The two had found drumsticks and were taking turns testing them out on a practice pad. "I like having the space to work on my instrument. A worktable, maybe, and some lights. Humans have good lights."

Rustle twirled his drumstick with his left hand. His right arm was still broken. "Me too. If we want to sit, we can use the common room. I'm glad for the space, though, to get away. The dormitories we had at Court were tiny and crowded. It always felt like we were stacked like pickled herrings."

"I would love more of these dishes." Barley held out a sleek, modern soup bowl in a cobalt blue with a gold-plated rim. "We need at least a hundred sets to run an enclave. This would be perfect for us, but there's just this one."

Andy and Guy had been helping Barley root through the mismatched dishes. For some reason, Andy had a pot on his head like a helmet. With Andy it was hard to tell if he was fooling around or he had put the pot in the one place where he couldn't misplace it. Probably the latter. Guy seemed to be working in earnest despite the fact he was listening to the radio. One earbud dangled on his chest, broadcasting Marti Wulfow's afternoon show on WESA. The other was firmly in his ear.

Barley picked up a white square plate. "There's thirty sets of this. I like the simplicity of it but I do wish it had a little more decoration—a band of gold or blue or something to offset the stark white. It will work for now. China never lasts more than a hundred years at an enclave no matter how careful you are with it. Thirty is too few but it is a start."

"There are some Wind Clan potters here in town," Guy said. "They make good quality dishes. They normally sell to *five-star* restaurants on Earth."

"Five-star?" Barley echoed the English words planted squarely in the otherwise all-Elvish sentence.

"It means that they're..." Guy glanced to Oilcan for help with his Elvish.

"Of the highest quality," Oilcan said. "They're very refined."

"The potters can make you something to your exact specification." Guy took out his phone and paged through photos he had stored. "I know when I open up my own restaurant, I'll have to make do with whatever I can afford but I would love to have my own line of dishes. Something like these."

He held out his phone showing a picture of a bold, black, square plate with a crescent design along one rim that looked almost like golden brown bark.

"That's beautiful," Oilcan said.

"Oh, I have never seen such wonderful plates!" Barley said. "Are they expensive?"

Guy shrugged. "I found the photo on Earth's internet late at night during Shutdown. Startup happened before I could figure out how much they cost. I kept a picture for reference."

"They look expensive," Barley said.

"Something to dream on," Guy said. "My mom says that to get anywhere, you need to know what direction to head. This picture is a road sign."

Oilcan wished he had a picture of his future. Lately he seemed to be roaring down a pitch-black road without any signs.

15: SNAKE HUNT

❖━━◉◯◉━━❖

"Even if I wanted to join Usagi's household, I couldn't," Bare Snow whispered in Law's ear. "Do you think that's Kajo?"

Law felt like she'd spent the morning crawling through a minefield. Usagi had asked them to join her commune. The discussion with Bare Snow on whether or not they would accept the offer had been filled with a lot of abrupt starts and stops as Law tried to detect and disarm emotional bombs. This one stopped her cold: why *couldn't* Bare Snow do it?

Law knew all the reasons she herself wasn't in love with the idea, but she thought that Bare Snow was overjoyed at the offer. Perhaps the weird hiccups in the conversation weren't Law's reservations fighting the logic of it all. They were speaking Elvish, so it wasn't Bare Snow making a mistake with English. Was Law's understanding of Elvish at fault? Law considered the statement. No, the word that Bare Snow used definitely meant "couldn't."

If Bare Snow was agreeing with her, could Law tell

Usagi "thanks, but no thanks"? Should she ignore all the good reasons just because Bare Snow gave her a quick out? Certainly the proposal was a mixed bag of good and bad.

It was easier to focus on Bare Snow's question about the small masked figure in the valley below.

Law clicked her tongue softly in an elf version of a shrug. "If Yumiko was right about the mask: maybe."

The woods east of Pittsburgh were crawling with oni. In theory there should be elves too, hunting said oni, but the two obviously weren't colliding in the virgin ironwood forest.

"Should I kill him?" Bare Snow stripped off her camouflage T-shirt without waiting for an answer. In the dim light, her pale spell tattoo was too faint to pick out against her creamy white skin. The female didn't seem to own a bra. Did elves not have such things? It always made Law question what she had been told about undergarments.

"It's not worth the risk," Law whispered. *Focus, woman, focus!* Law studied the valley encampment. The oni were breaking camp, taking down a dozen large green Coleman tents. "There's a hundred or more warriors down there and we don't even know for sure if that's him."

Yumiko only had a drawing of a mask and a vague description of the secret overlord of the oni forces. The person in charge of the encampment in the valley below seemed to fit the bill. He looked like he was only five and a half feet tall. His fearsome mask was lacquered red with black accents. The long fangs, scowling eyes, and sharp horns were gilded with gold leaf. A flowing mane of white horsehair hid even his natural hair color. It looked exactly like the drawing that Yumiko had shown Law.

There was one small problem.

A second oni wearing a nearly identical mask came out of the last tent. It was slightly shorter than the first one but only by two or three inches. They wore matching outfits of elaborate black silk robes with red highlights. Law couldn't tell which of them was "in charge" even though it was clear that they were the ranking officers of the encampment. Both gestured and pointed and were obeyed by the lesser blood oni.

"Oh, great." Law scanned the camp. Even if there was only one possible Kajo, she and Bare Snow wouldn't have survived taking on all the oni in the valley. The warriors were armed with assault rifles and rocket launchers. There were a dozen wargs, muzzled and chained. They were outnumbered and outgunned.

Bare Snow might be able to evade the warriors but not the wargs. Worse, Law wasn't sure where they were exactly. She normally hunted in the South Hills, near where she'd grown up. East of Pittsburgh, she needed a compass and map to stay on track. The tengu's holy spaceship in Turtle Creek changed that somewhat. It was a mile-high exclamation point covered with magical dragon runes. It was impossible to miss, even at three miles away.

She believed that they were near Churchill. She would need to take out her map to check but she didn't want to take her eyes off the oni or Bare Snow.

"It's possible that neither one of them are Kajo," Law said to make sure Bare Snow didn't try a suicide run. She repeated it in Elvish to be sure that the female understood. "Yumiko said that all the tengu familiar with Kajo were killed. She's working off secondhand reports. It's possible that Kajo was playing some kind of shell game with the tengu."

"Shell game?"

Law winced. She'd used the Elvish word for walnut shell as that was what her grandfather used when he taught the game to Law. She'd seen variations of it using bent playing cards. Did elves have playing cards? Law was fairly sure playing Three-card Monte with the elves was a good way to get killed. Elves hated liars. "It's a trick to fool people. You pretend to hide something under a walnut shell—like a pea—but secretly you put the pea someplace else. It's like the game of hide-and-seek that you play with the Bunny children, but instead of actually hiding, the kids left the house while you were counting to one hundred."

"Why would the children do that?"

"I'm explaining this badly." Law considered while she watched the tents being packed away. "Kajo always wore a mask when dealing with the tengu. He was hiding something. It might have been that the person under the mask changed; there could have been several fake 'Kajos' to serve as decoys. The tengu might have never met the real Kajo."

"Ah, yes, to foil assassination attempts by the tengu since he didn't trust them."

"Something like that." Law ducked down to think.

Kajo wasn't the target; the magical genetic bombs were. So far, she hadn't seen the eleven bowling-ball-sized eggs but there were many pieces of luggage large enough to fit one. The oni seemed as if they planned to head west after leaving the clearing. That would take them in the direction of Oakland. If the real Kajo was playing a true shell game, it was possible he was hiding within the city, passing as human.

"If these two aren't Kajo," Law said, "then they might be going to meet up with him."

"We should follow them!" Bare Snow bounced in a very distracting way.

"Put your shirt on," Law said. "They look like they're gearing up for a hike."

Law considered the hunt before them. Staying ahead of the oni would be dangerous as they could walk into any hidden war camp that the two "Kajos" were heading to. Trailing behind, though, would mean they might lose the oni if Kajo had vehicles waiting someplace.

Should she call Alton?

No, not yet. It would get the tengu involved. Yumiko implied Kajo had some magical ability that let him dance around the elves, but it might be simply an old-fashioned, well-placed mole. Sparrow had been the second highest Wind Clan leader and a Skin Clan lackey. Any one of the tengu might be a turncoat. Kajo hadn't been that hard to find. There were twenty thousand tengu in Pittsburgh; why hadn't one of them spotted him?

Law had stolen a rail car from the Charleroi train depot to give chase after the oni-filled train. She'd crashed the vehicle at Station Square, leaving her with no way to get back to her Dodge Power Wagon, still parked at the depot. It seemed logical to ask Usagi to give her and Bare Snow a lift to Charleroi so they could get back the Dodge and her pet Elfhome porcupine, Brisbane.

Usagi had used the child-free drive to propose the merger of households. She'd been very compelling. Bare Snow was technically still a child at ninety-four years old; she would be approximately seventeen if she were human. The half-elf children were maturing slowly; they might not be adults for decades to come. Law and all the Bunnies were human, which meant that they could vanish out of the lives of the children before they were full grown, especially with the war raging around them. It forced Law to realize that if she got herself killed, Bare Snow would be totally alone. The children already called Bare Snow "Big Sister." Law loved all the Bunnies dearly—but she wasn't sure if she could stand living with them.

After Usagi drove away, Law scouted around for Brisbane. She found him tucked up in a big spruce tree near the river, happily eating bark.

He was "her pet" in that he normally cooperated in her ownership of him. There was no forcing something that was a third her size and came loaded with thirty thousand foot-long barbed spikes.

Law was trying to talk him out of a tree when she spotted a herd of elk on the opposite bank of the Monongahela River. The big animals rarely came that near to the jumpfish-infested waters. They would only venture that close to a bank if they were trying to avoid something even more dangerous. Law guessed that it meant that a large number of oni might be pushing the elk in front of them.

"Okay, just stay up there," Law said to Brisbane, who seemed to be ignoring her. "I'll be back later." (Being that porcupines lived most of their life in trees, she was fairly sure he wouldn't move until she produced apples or something to lure him down.)

Law drove across the river via the Rankin Bridge, hid her Dodge in an empty warehouse, and then on foot, backtracked the herd to this ridge. Three hours after her meeting with Alton, she had eyes on Kajo.

Why hadn't anyone else found him?

Was it because Kajo guessed that none of the tengu would expect him so close to the city? Yumiko had refused to give Law any more guidance than the drawing. She seemed to think that any suggestion from her would unduly influence Law. Certainly, Law hadn't even seriously considered where Kajo might be hiding; she was just trying to retrieve her Dodge.

Law decided that they'd follow the oni to see where they were going. If they reached the city, she would call for backup.

There was nothing to do but wait for the oni to move.

It left her time to think. All she could think about, though, was Usagi's proposal.

"Why can't you?" Law whispered to Bare Snow. "Why can't you be part of Usagi Sensei's household?"

Bare Snow looked at her with surprise in her eyes. "My family has a death sentence on it. After Howling's assassination, the *sekasha* hunted down everyone in my grandfather's household and killed all that they could find."

"But they're all dead now," Law said.

"*I'm* still alive."

"You weren't even alive when Howling was killed. Your mother lived on a deserted island for years in hiding before she even met your father."

"It does not matter. We were wrong. We were Beholden to Howling; we betrayed him and our clan when we believed the worse of him. We nearly destroyed all hope of peace. If the Clan War was still waging when the oni first attacked, we would have fallen to the Skin Clan. My family deserved the punishment that the *sekasha* dealt out."

"You had nothing to do with it."

"My mother trained me; she wanted me to seek revenge on those that wronged my family."

"That's the Skin Clan!"

"As far as the *sekasha* know, we acted alone. To them, the *domana* would be my natural target."

Law sputtered in the face of Bare Snow's calm acceptance. "No one knows who you are. You were born after your mother went into hiding. There are no Water Clan in Pittsburgh; they don't have Spell Stones for their *domana* to tap. How would anyone even know?"

"If someone asked me the name of my mother, I would have to tell them the truth. It is much too dangerous for the Bunnies."

Law wanted to argue the point but she wasn't even sure that she could stand being a permanent part of the Bunny household. She enjoyed the controlled chaos of the commune but only because she could escape the moment she got overwhelmed.

"The oni are moving," Bare Snow whispered, ending the discussion.

They followed the oni cross the Rim into Pittsburgh proper. All around them were abandoned houses and shops. The oni went slower, keeping to the cover of the trees rather than using the weed-choked city streets.

Law wondered if she was doing the right thing. This could quickly escalate out of her control. What if the oni planned to stage an attack on Oakland? The

Pittsburghers were still recovering from the attack on Oktoberfest. Many of the royal marines were taking care of their dead, far to the north. Others were scattered all over the South Side, looking for any stray oni troops who survived the train derailment. Prince True Flame was deep in the forest to the east, looking for the oni camps that Tommy Chang had rescued Jewel Tear from. There was no large Elvish force in Oakland.

The oni hit the tangled knot of the Edgewood exit on I-376 and stopped.

Law crouched behind the brick rubble of a collapsed garage. She made sure that Bare Snow was safely beside her before taking out her binoculars.

The taller of the two Kajos seemed to be the ultimate head of the group. He split the oni into two groups. He sent a handful north along the Rim with all of their gear. He kept the rest of his heavily armed escort with him and the second Kajo and turned west.

"Shit, shit, shit," Law whispered. If the two Kajo continued in the same direction, they would head into Frick Park. The area around Nine Mile Run was extremely marshy. Over the years, it had filled with black willows. Any sane person avoided it at all costs. Yet it put the oni just a few miles from the elf enclave's back door. "Don't go west. Don't go west."

The taller Kajo led his group toward the Braddock Trail, which led through the heart of Frick Park.

Law didn't know what Kajo planned but she didn't want to follow the oni into Frick Park. Black willows hunted via vibration on the ground; they could feel even something as light as a two-pound rabbit at a hundred paces. The oni could find a safe path through the park, but that would leave only unsafe ground for her and

Bare Snow. Guns and knives and even machetes were useless against the giant man-eating trees.

Maybe Kajo didn't know about the black willows.

There was an odd high-pitched whistle.

It sounded again.

Bare Snow hissed and crouched lower.

"What is that?" Law whispered.

"It's a monster call!" Bare Snow whispered. "They're directing all monsters to head toward the sun."

Toward the sun? It was past noon. The sun was in the west. That would lead all monsters in the area toward Oakland. There was a distant loud creak of wood followed by a hollow thud: the unmistakable noise of a black willow stirring to life.

"Oh, shit." Law pulled out her phone. This officially had become larger than what she and Bare Snow could handle. She'd call Alton, drop it in his lap, and go after Kajo's gear. Maybe the bombs were with his equipment.

16: BLACK WILLOW STOMP

❧══◉══❧

Jane Kryskill hated black willows. Hated them with a passion. They scared the piss out of her because she couldn't hurt them with anything short of dynamite. That they scared her made her angry at the world, which meant she was tempted to shoot anything that crossed her path. Thus she nearly killed Corg Durrack—again—when he suddenly appeared beside her.

"Hey, hey, hey! It's just me!" Corg had taken hard cover just in case she took another shot at him.

"Didn't you learn not to do that after the last time?" Jane lowered her pistol. They were near the Rim in an abandoned part of Squirrel Hill. She had Chesty locked in the *Chased by Monsters* production truck to keep him safe; she knew that meant her back was unprotected. The man should know that between the two facts, Jane would be even more prone to shoot first, ask questions later.

"I thought I was being obvious." Durrack stuck out his hand to show that he was unarmed.

Jane snorted. It was Durrack's left hand, not his

right. Durrack acted like a Boy Scout, but he looked like a muscle-bound superhero and fought like a Navy SEAL. If he had been anyone else, Jane's first instinct would have been shoot him anyhow. The mere fact that he'd shown up at their remote location was suspicious. Everyone from Maynard to Yumiko to Taggart, though, had vouched for the man. Besides, his partner, Hannah Briggs, was probably hidden somewhere nearby.

Jane wasn't sure which government branch the two agents originally worked for. Taggart had said that the pair had saved him and some other journalists in Syria shortly before he quit being a war correspondent. Jane had managed to learn that the two had come to Elfhome on loan to the NSA. They'd been ordered to find, protect, and extract the one technical genius who could build a world gate before the oni could kidnap the person. It was an operation that a typical NSA agent wasn't prepared for. Durrack and Briggs ham-handed the extraction so badly that they'd been arrested by the EIA and nearly executed by the elves. (To be fair, they hadn't known that they were after a young girl, let alone that Tinker *domi* was the Viceroy's new bride. Bad intelligence can kill a good operative.) By the time the agents had gotten out of that mess, they were stranded on Elfhome with the rest of Pittsburgh. This hadn't stopped Durrack and Briggs from pursuing truth, justice, and the American way. Time and time again they had thrown themselves into the thick of the heaviest fighting to protect Pittsburgh.

Their paths had crisscrossed all summer. Jane's team would help the pair deal with Elfhome flora and fauna while trading intelligence on the oni. It was a mutually useful friendship.

Durrack shook his outstretched left hand while still hidden behind his hard cover. "Are we good?"

"Yes, we're good." Jane tucked away her pistol.

Interacting with Durrack meant she'd taken her eyes off Hal and Nigel. Hal had taken advantage of the distraction to move closer to the black willow. Grinning hugely, Nigel was scurrying to join Hal. It forced Taggart to shift closer too. The men should be safe as long as they kept out of range of its writhing tentacle-like branches.

It wasn't the first black willow that the *Chased by Monsters* crew had encountered. For some insane reason, Tinker had had one on ice at Reinhold's. It had been before the tengu became her Beholden, so they could only guess at her logic, or lack of it. The tree had broken out and gone on a rampage through the North Side. Jane and her crew had arrived seconds ahead of Prince True Flame. It meant that they got no establishing shots, and had lousy framing, bad lighting, and no direct interaction with the tree. They could only stand back and film the prince reducing the monster to a charred stump. It was safe footage: none of their secrets made it to video. It just hadn't seemed good enough for their show. Jane had dumped what they had to WQED to use on the evening news and moved on.

If they combined it with what they filmed today, however, there might be enough for a full episode. They just needed to be sure to get enough footage without anyone getting hurt. By "anyone" Jane meant Hal. He knew to keep out of range of its branches, but Hal had the self-preservation instincts of a toddler.

"What are you doing here?" Jane asked without taking her eyes off Hal.

"Maynard sent us to check on this area," Durrack said. "There were reports of multiple black willows moving thru this neighborhood."

"Multiple?" Jane cursed softly. She had called Duff and had him deploy some of the scouts within the militia to find something Jane could film. He'd gotten back to her at noon, saying Alton had forwarded a report that a black willow had been spotted in Squirrel Hill. (Jane wasn't sure how Alton got involved. With the additional load of the Harbingers and their households, the enclaves had all the foragers in Pittsburgh scrambling for fish and game. Jane thought that Alton had gone hunting with Boo in tow.) Somewhere along the lines of communication, the fact that there was more than one tree had been lost.

She scanned the neighborhood around her for more black willows. The Rim cut an arcing path through this area. It ran from the Allegheny River in the Northwest to the Monongahela River in the Southeast. To the south was the collection of neighborhoods now known as Oakland, and the downtown triangle. A few blocks west from her current location was the back end of the enclaves. Virgin forest lay just a few blocks north.

In theory, the tree could have come from anywhere beyond the Rim. A walking tree, though, left a wide trail of torn dirt, shattered sidewalk, and downed (and hopefully not live) power lines. As she studied the area, it was clear that the tree had come through the cemetery at Jane's back. A trail of overturned granite tombstones and statues made it easy to plot the tree's course. It had smashed its way in a straight line through the graveyard, hit the stone wall at the cemetery edge, and followed the fence out to the street.

In the distance, Jane could see the bobbing foliage of a second black willow. The incoming tree seemed to be on the same course but it either had found something large to eat or had gotten caught up on some obstacle in its path. She had an unknown amount of time before her team would be dealing with two trees at once. Clearly both black willows were from Frick Park. The flesh-eating plants thrived in the marshy ground around Nine Mile Run. Normally black willows avoided the paved city streets and other rocky outcroppings. Why had they left the marsh?

"How many?" Jane asked. "And are they all heading toward Oakland?"

"That's what we're trying to determine," Durrack said. "We have the small problem that on Earth trees don't walk. We're kind of out of our element here."

It was becoming Durrack's catch phrase as the Earth-raised agents tried to deal with the dangerous Elfhome flora and fauna.

When Jane glanced back at Durrack, he was standing beside her with Hannah Briggs.

Durrack was in blue jeans and a Team Tinker T-shirt stretched tight across his muscled chest; he could have passed as a local. Briggs wore something that resembled a superhero outfit, made from a matte-black fabric that looked sprayed onto her highly toned body. Both had on blue Hal's Heroes boonie hats.

"Stop doing that!" Jane lowered the pistol that she had raised out of habit.

"I hate that I have to keep asking this question, but how do you kill that?" Durrack had asked the question every time Maynard sent them to check on their filming. (Apparently Maynard didn't like them blowing up local landmarks, regardless of what the elves said.) Briggs said that the vespers gave Durrack nightmares afterward.

"Dynamite and chickens," Jane said. She waved toward the crate of large white leghorns that they had managed to buy on short notice. "Unless you have a grenade launcher handy."

She kind of hoped Durrack did have access to a grenade launcher or something similar. Nigel had made unhappy noises at the idea of using the chickens. She'd ignored him, thinking that there was only one tree to bait. She was clenching down on her own unhappy noises at the idea of having to deal with multiple trees.

Durrack didn't volunteer a grenade launcher. "Chickens?"

"They're bait. You kill the chicken, tie on a stick of dynamite, light it up, and throw it into the path of the black willow."

It was horrible delivery system with a hundred things that could go wrong with it. They couldn't possibly survive doing it multiple times. Perhaps they should fall back and find another weapon.

"I suppose that's humane," Durrack said. "Since you kill the chicken first."

"You don't want a frightened chicken with a lit stick of dynamite tied to it running around." Jane decided not to explain how they had learned this. (Yes, it had been Hal's idea but she'd been desperate enough to try it. At least it hadn't been an entire flock of chickens like Hal had first suggested.)

"Why a chicken?" Briggs said.

"They're easy to get. Rabbits work too," Jane said. "Anything small and recently dead. It's either body

heat or smell of blood or something. The black willow
will eat it, dynamite and all."

"Fresh out of chickens and rabbits." Durrack dodged
being volunteered for the duty. "I take it that the
dynamite doesn't work all by itself?"

"We're usually called in when a black willow has
hunkered down in someone's backyard. It gives us a
lot less room to move around in." Jane didn't mention
that there was also structural damage to buildings
to consider. "The tree can sense the vibration in the
ground from any movement, so it's usually moving
toward you as you try to get into position to hit it. It's
slow moving, but it usually can walk past anything you
throw with a long enough fuse to let you stay out of
range of its branches. The tree has a reach of nearly
a hundred and fifty feet. It can reach over, around,
and into anything you try to use as cover."

Durrack whistled softly. "Getting close enough to
toss a stick of dynamite where it will actually damage
the tree must be nearly impossible without getting
yourself killed."

"That's our experience." It had been a difficult
learning curve. "We need to get footage for both
Monsters in Our Midst and *Chased by Monsters* and
then we'll start in on the chickens."

"Can't you use the same footage?"

"Two different hosts. We're still filming Nigel's show
for when Pittsburgh is reconnected with Earth." While
replacing the "lost" footage was their first priority,
Jane didn't want to lose momentum on *Chased by
Monsters*. It was still shy of a full season. The oni
couldn't have known that Tinker was going to crash
the orbital gate. Some were still on Earth, telling

the humans only God knew what. Sooner or later, Pittsburgh would be reconnected to Earth. Nigel's show could be important propaganda to counter the oni influence in United States.

Durrack grunted and tugged on the brim of his boonie hat. "Good thinking."

Hal had awarded the two NSA agents their Hal's Heroes hats last week, off-camera, as they didn't want to be filmed. Jane hadn't expected Durrack and Briggs to actually wear them.

"Are you really that short on hats?" Jane asked.

Durrack looked confused by the question.

"You guys do good work," Briggs said quietly. "We're fans."

The woman turned away before Jane could be sure if the color on her cheeks was a blush or not.

Briggs had the silent-bitch routine perfected but Jane had caught glimpses of a naturally quiet and shy woman underneath the tough exterior. Jane imagined that she would be a lot like Briggs if she'd waded through the war zones that the two agents had worked in.

"Thanks," Jane said. "Let me check with my sources and see if I can get a lead on the other black willows. We're almost ready to fire up this tree. If you stick around, we can team up on the rest."

Durrack and Briggs nodded their agreement to the plan.

"It's me," Jane said when Duff answered his phone. "We've got a problem. EIA is saying that there's more than—oh shit! Hal! Hal!"

Hal had produced a sling made out of paracord. She thought she had confiscated and burned it long ago. The idiot must have made a new one. As she shouted at him, he lit the fuse on a piece of dynamite tucked into the sling's pouch.

"Don't you dare!" she shouted.

"What's he doing?" Duff asked.

Hal helicoptered the sling over his head, the fuse leaving a smoke contrail.

This was why she hated black willows. They were dangerous to kill before you added dynamite and Hal into the equation.

"Get back!" she yelled at Taggart and Nigel. "Fire in the hole!"

Hal flung the dynamite. It went wide, smashed thru the front window of a house beside the black willow, and exploded.

"Jesus Christ, Mary, Joseph, and all the carpenters!" Jane swore.

"Did Hal just blow himself up?" Duff asked. "Should I send an ambulance to your location?"

"No!" Jane snapped as she pointed at Hal. "Search him! Make sure he doesn't have any more dynamite!"

Durrack glanced behind him as if he thought she was talking to someone else. Realizing that she *did* mean him, he dashed across the street. Jane scanned the now-windowless house with smoke leaking out of it. Did anyone live there? It looked abandoned. The yard hadn't been mowed in years. The door was a peeling green. There didn't seem to be any obvious takens. Maybe they got lucky. It was a big, brick house with a driveway on either side of it. Even if it went up in flames, they weren't going to set the entire neighborhood on fire.

Probably.

Jane eyed the smoke, trying to decide whether

they should call their favorite accidentally reoccurring guest star, the fire marshal. This was one of the many reasons she hated black willows.

Duff took the delegation of tasks to mean that Jane was free to talk. "Hey, I just got off the phone with Mom. She wanted to know if I have a girlfriend."

"What?" Jane's mind was on the house—possibly not abandoned—possibly about to burn down. The smoke had gotten thicker.

"She says you need two more girls for the party," Duff clarified only slightly.

Party? Shit, the wedding party! Jane had totally forgotten about the bridesmaids.

Hal's yelp of pain dragged her attention back. Durrack had him professionally pinned to the ground. The tree had shifted to the house, lured by the vibration of the explosion. Its branches explored the façade, looking for food.

"Watch the tree! Don't mess up his face, Durrack! We still have close-ups to shoot!" Jane shouted as she waved her team away from the house. If it did catch fire, hopefully the tree would go up with it. "Well? *Do* you have a girlfriend?"

"Not currently," Duff said. "You know that most of the people where I work are either related to us or are—you know—pregnant." He meant the Bunny household members. "There's one girl—kind of—but we haven't actually even hung out, let alone dated. I told Mom to call Marc—he's the person that gets out and about and talks to people. Well—not talk-talk—the Stone being stonelike."

Marc's nickname was "Stone" because he rarely spoke. That and because he was built like a stone wall.

Durrack dragged Hal back to Jane. The tree was still exploring the smoking house; maybe it was picking up a panicked squirrel or raccoon trapped inside. Jane waved to Taggart and Nigel and indicated that they all should follow her back to the production truck to get a chicken and more dynamite. (She wasn't sure why Hal hadn't used a chicken but it could be because Nigel didn't like killing things. Unfortunately, most of their summer had involved killing things. Dangerous things.)

The thought reminded her why she called Duff in the first place.

"EIA is here and says there might be more than one tree. Can you confirm?"

"Yes. Bam-Bam called Alton and said that the oni sicced an unknown number of monsters on Oakland. BW have been deployed."

BW—or black wing—was this week's code word for tengu. Who was Bam-Bam? It took Jane a moment to remember Bam-Bam was what the kids at school used to call Lawrie Munroe. Law was legendary for saving girls in trouble, usually using baseball bats and random pieces of lumber instead of something sane, like a handgun. It had earned her the nickname based on the old *Flintstones* cartoon character. Law wasn't part of their scout network but she could be trusted to pass on accurate information.

Jane glanced toward the distant, oncoming black willow. It hadn't gotten any closer but she could see a third tree had appeared behind it.

Black willows reproduced via seeds that found root in swampy areas. In marshes, there would be swarms of saplings that fed in packs like piranha, finding safety in numbers. Once the saplings grew as tall as a man, though, they would spread out, seeking less crowded hunting grounds. All the black willows that she and Hal had ever dealt with had been individual trees that had drifted into yards near streams or swampy areas. It was unheard-of for them to march so far from water in one day.

"I've got a bad feeling about this, especially with the blackout in Oakland," Jane said. "Activate all our scouts to do a full city sweep. Let's check all the backwaters for a buildup of oni forces. The entire eastern front might be a ghost army to keep the elves tied up while the main attack comes from another direction."

"Will do," Duff said. "Anything else?"

"Not now," Jane said. "I'll let you know how this goes."

"Yo!" Briggs called to someone.

Jane realized that Yumiko had joined them. The tengu *yamabushi* wore skinny jeans and a Team Tinker tank top. Was that how the good guys were telling one another apart from the bad guys now—Team Tinker T-shirts? Yumiko folded her massive black wings, panting slightly from her flight.

Briggs greeted Yumiko with a fist bump.

"My people are spread thin, so I called in the guardians of the *Dahe Hao*." Yumiko pointed eastward.

The tall, slender spaceship was five miles away as the crow flew. It was a giant black stroke against the gray overcast sky. The tengu considered it holy since it had delivered their leader, Jin Wong, from space via dragon intervention. Said dragon had covered it with spell runes to keep it from collapsing under its own weight.

"It leaves the *Dahe Hao* unguarded, but only someone with wings could access the interior." Yumiko sounded like someone who had made a decision that they hated.

"The ship should be fine until I can get backup. It gave me four *yamabushi* to cover Frick Park."

"Where's Alton?" Jane figured from Duff's various comments that Alton and Yumiko had been together all morning. The entire family had members of the tengu elite keeping an eye on them at all times. By accident or design, Yumiko usually paired up with Alton.

Yumiko gestured toward the south. "He's in Schenley Park with Xiao Chen, making sure there are no black willows in Panther Hollow."

Jane didn't like the idea of Alton out hunting black willows, but as a forager he was well versed in Elfhome's deadly flora and fauna. Nor was he alone. Xiao Chen was one of the returning tengu astronauts and part of Jin Wong's most trusted inner circle.

"There are a score of trees moving in our direction," Yumiko said. "One of our operatives said that a person fitting Kajo's description used a whistle that started the black willows heading west."

The name "Kajo" spiked anger and fear through Jane. The oni leader had been the one who kidnapped Boo and kept her alive as his personal plaything. In the end, he'd transformed her into a tengu, changing her down to the DNA level. It would explain why Yumiko and the other *yamabushi* were handling the search. He was a clever and powerful enemy.

"Jane?" Hal whined. Durrack had him pinned to the side of the production truck. "We really should kill the tree before it gets bored with the house."

Jane sighed. Hal was right but that would mean letting him play with dynamite again. When PB&G first experimented with killing black willows, they'd determined that Hal was better at throwing than

Jane. He'd played lacrosse in college, developing the hand-eye coordination that Jane had never honed. Nigel had demonstrated that he was woefully out of his element. Not that he wasn't athletic, but cricket "pitching" was more like bowling than baseball, rugby players rarely threw the ball more than a few yards, and Nigel had never played goalie in soccer.

"You have a way of killing trees?" Yumiko asked.

"Dynamite." Jane glanced at the cage. She had two chickens, giving her the excuse to bring only two sticks of dynamite with them. (She had left the nearly full crate with her cousin, Roach, for safekeeping.) Hal had just used up one.

"I can get more dynamite," she told Yumiko. "It's the delivery system that's a problem. I only have two chickens. I'm not sure where to get more on short notice."

And she didn't relish the idea of trying to fling explosive dead chickens at a horde of black willows. There were so many things that could go wrong.

"If you have the dynamite, my people can drop it from above the black willows," Yumiko said.

It was one of the few times in Jane's life where the phrase "Praise God" seemed appropriate. The last thing she wanted to do was dodge a swarm of man-eating trees while Hal juggled dynamite.

One of those "only in Pittsburgh" discussions followed as to whether or not they needed to attach chickens to the dynamite being dropped on the mobile trees. (At least, Jane assumed it was a "never on Earth" conversation based by the number of times that Durrack, Briggs, Taggart, or Nigel shook their heads to denote ignorance of the subject.)

Briggs suggested that Yumiko do some test runs.

"It's not like the tree will be shooting at you. As long as you stay out of its reach, you can drop rocks on it until you feel ready for the real thing."

"What's your ceiling height?" Taggart asked while keeping the camera trained on the tree.

"I can keep out of its reach," Yumiko said. "Getting too high would make targeting harder."

The black willow had found something small and furry inside the house. It dragged out the squealing animal and dropped it into its maw.

Durrack muttered an impressively inventive string of profanities.

Jane shook her head. They weren't going to be able to use any of the audio after Durrack's arrival. At least it was easier to edit out audio than white wings in a reflection. "Let's give it a try with just the dynamite. If it doesn't work, I'll track down more chickens."

Jane confiscated their lighter from Hal and gave it to Yumiko, along with their remaining stick of dynamite. She moved her team behind the truck so they wouldn't be in blast range if the stick bounced or got swatted in their direction.

As Yumiko made test drops with small rocks, Jane called her cousin.

"How did it go?" Roach said when he answered his phone.

"Fire in the hole!" Hal yelled as Yumiko dropped the lit stick.

It was a perfect hit. The stick landed inside the tree's open maw. There was a deep thud, like a big bass drum being hit. With a long splintering crack, the black willow's trunk split open and gravity took over, tearing the smoking pieces apart.

Jane took a deep breath, feeling like a massive load had been lifted off her. Clearly the tengu could safely deal with the black willows, freeing her team from the task.

"One down," Jane reported. "I need the rest of the dynamite."

"The entire crate?" Roach said with clear reservation in his voice.

"There's a wave of black willows coming toward Oakland. We're going to need a lot of dynamite to stop them."

"I'll be right there." Roach hung up after getting her location.

Yumiko landed beside Jane.

"Great job," Briggs said.

Yumiko and Briggs fist bumped.

Jane realized that she had two women she trusted right under her nose. Yes, she had had reservations about them when she first met them, but they had risked their lives to protect her family more than once in the last two months. "Could the two of you be in my wedding? Please?"

"Yes!" Briggs eyes lit up with joy that was quickly hidden away. "Sure. I'm free."

"Me?" Yumiko said. "I thought the police officer was your maid of honor."

"We're making it bigger." Jane winced as she realized that she should have talked with Taggart but he'd seemed fine with whatever her mother decided. He only wanted to get married. "My brothers are going to be part of the wedding party. I need more women to balance out the numbers."

"So, Alton and the others?" Yumiko asked. "All cleaned up? In a tux?"

Jane nodded.

"Okay," Yumiko said. "It might be fun."

Like a circus, Jane almost said, but she didn't want to scare off her volunteers.

"The dynamite is on its way." Jane took out her phone to call her mother with the "good" news. "Until then, I'm going to need your dress sizes."

The entire summer had been an insane series of deadly events, starting in July when the oni's secret war had boiled to the surface. Jane had had to constantly juggle information to keep all the little parts of her life from knowing about the whole. WQED had no idea that she and her team had triggered the destruction of the oni encampment at Sandcastle Water Park, days before open warfare had broken out. They didn't know about Boo being rescued or how she had been transformed into a tengu of the Chosen bloodline. Nor did the station know that Jane's team had purposely gone to Mercy Hospital to rescue Yumiko, and that setting fire to her EIA guard hadn't been an accident but a planned distraction. WQED knew that it was her film crew that shot up downtown and blew up parts of the Carnegie Museum. Both gunfights triggered meetings with Dmitri but became "we will not talk about these events" at the station when the EIA hadn't pressed charges. The station didn't "know" that Jane's team was using *Monsters in Our Midst* to organize a human resistance army—although Dmitri probably suspected.

Likewise, Jane had kept the NSA agents—and with them the EIA—at arm's length. It was quite possible that they knew nothing about Boo or Sandcastle. She had to assume that they knew about the fight that ended at the stadium and the museum shoot-out, as the EIA had been present during both. If they didn't know about the Resistance, they weren't much in terms of intelligence operatives. But up to this moment, she hadn't taken them into her confidence.

If the oni were on the move, it was time to get everyone on the same page.

"We're not sure what Kajo is planning." Yumiko had been bringing the agents up to speed as Jane relayed the dress sizes to her mother. "He always works with layers of deception. Smoke and mirrors. It's how he has stayed hidden for so many years."

"You said these Eyes can magically see things." Durrack twiddled his fingers in front of his eyes as if X-rays were shooting out of his sockets. "Even without them, Kajo has to know the main elven force is closing on his encampments. You would think that he would want to be commanding their withdrawal or ambush or pincer movement—whatever he has planned."

Yumiko nervously tapped out a cigarette, nodding. "Our operative reports seeing two people matching the description that we gave them of Kajo. It is quite possible neither of them were the real Kajo."

"How experienced is your operative?" Durrack asked. "Can they tell one oni from another?"

"The less we talk about my operative, the better." Yumiko twiddled her fingers in front of her face, copying Durrack's mime. "Kajo's eyes."

That explained why Duff had used Law's nickname on the phone.

With the rumble of a big engine, Roach turned onto the street in one of his big dumpster hauler trucks. He pulled to a stop behind the production truck. He sat a moment, studying Jane and the strangers around her, assessing her body language before getting out.

"Hey," he called. He locked his truck after getting out. There was an unasked question posed in the tilt of his head.

"This is my cousin." Jane started introductions for the more dangerous side of the equation. Roach was the smartest and most charismatic person in her entire family. Considering his older brother was a popular deejay for KDKA radio, that was saying a lot. It was unlikely Roach would do anything to get himself shot, but she wanted it clear that no matter what happened, he was off-limits to being hurt. "You can trust him completely."

For reasons that Jane never understood, her aunt had named her middle son after her husband without sticking a Junior on the backend. She'd made things worse by giving him the middle name of Angus. Roach started out as "Billy." Around eleven, he tried to use the more adult "Bill," which resulted in a lot of "Big Bill or Little Bill?" confusion. Sometime in high school, he decided just to only use his last name. It was a testament to his salesmanship that he'd gotten even his brothers to agree to this. "Everyone just calls him Roach. He's Team Tinker's business manager and he handles the Hal's Heroes merchandising."

Jane let the others introduce themselves because she wasn't sure how they wanted to be known. They nodded at the name; their lives had interwoven with Tinker enough to recognize someone she trusted implicitly.

Briggs, being secretly shy, let Durrack do most of the talking.

Durrack was built like a pro wrestler but could be surprisingly charming. He claimed to be "working with Maynard" without mentioning EIA or NSA. He handed Roach a business card that gave contact info, including an office whose street address put it in the EIA building downtown.

Yumiko simply said, "Yumiko Sessai."

"Is it dead?" Roach pointed toward the shattered the black willow that Hal, Nigel, and Taggart were cautiously filming.

"It's like a Christmas tree after you cut it down," Hal called. "It's not quite alive but it's not completely dead."

"I would not advise getting close to it," Nigel said even as he was cautiously edging closer to it to get some wrap-up shots.

"I brought the dynamite." Roach pointed toward his locked truck. "What did you mean by 'a wave' of black willows?"

Jane pointed out the oncoming trees and caught Roach up to speed the best she could without mentioning Lawrie Munroe.

"How sure are we that this is the work of Kajo?" Durrack looped the conversation back to where they were before Roach showed up.

Yumiko explained how Kajo had always worn a mask anytime he interacted with the tengu. "Kajo has killed everyone that might have seen him unmasked. All we have is this."

The female took out her phone to show Durrack a picture of a red scowling demon face.

Jane studied the photo instead of staring at Yumiko as she tried to remember who knew what. Was Yumiko keeping info from the NSA to protect Boo? It wasn't like the female had to admit where the information came from. Her family had told Yumiko that Boo was a prisoner of Kajo for years—hadn't they? Maybe? Maybe not?

"What about Jin Wong's nephew?" Jane said cautiously. Did Durrack and Briggs know about Joey? Roach didn't. "The one that Kajo was using?"

Was that vague enough? Most people only knew about Riki, although the NSA might know about Riki's other young cousins, Keiko and Mickey.

Yumiko shook her head. "We already asked him. He never saw Kajo without the mask."

Then Boo was the only person who could identify Kajo.

Briggs caught the dismay on Jane's face. "What?"

This was not how she wanted to break the news to Roach. The good guys, though, all needed to get onto the same page. *Monsters in Our Midst* was an information gathering and dispersal tool so that everyone who stood against the oni knew what they were fighting. If the oni were making their move soon, she couldn't worry about her cousin's feelings.

"I can get a description of Kajo," Jane said. "He kidnapped my baby sister, Boo, when she was six. He kept her as his personal plaything for eight years."

"Wait," Roach said. "What?"

Jane ignored the question; she trusted Roach to catch up without her having to explain everything. That said, though, there was very little she knew about the oni male. "I've avoided asking her questions about the time she was with him. We all avoid talking about it. There's nothing we can do to change the past. Nothing we can do to make things better for her—except kill him. I already planned to do that if I have the chance. As much as I want Kajo dead, I don't want one of my little brothers to be the one that pulls the trigger. I've already got blood on my hands; a little more won't make much difference to me."

Yumiko made a face as she realized that she'd missed the obvious. "Joey said that she'd been brought to Sandcastle the same time he was. I didn't consider that she might have been moved from someplace else. I should have realized that she was editing what she told Joey so he would be less frightened, especially since she didn't tell him that his aunt and uncle had been murdered. Kajo kept her hidden but we knew he had a concubine; our people caught glimpses of her. They called her the White Bride of Death because if anyone that saw more than a glimpse of her, Kajo would kill them."

The word "concubine" put a dagger through Jane's heart. Roach breathed out a curse.

"You need to talk to her," Briggs said. "You don't just walk away from something like that and be alright. You need to get her medical treatment."

Jane shook her head. "Pittsburgh doesn't have shrinks. We checked. Being officially diagnosed as mentally unbalanced got you exported, so nobody dared to go to a doctor, even if they desperately needed one. All the psychologists left within the first two years of the treaty being signed."

"Some of our people are therapists," Yumiko said. "Our centuries of enslavement left deep scars. Many of them are quite fresh."

Jane winced as guilt lanced through her. It felt like

she'd just found Boo a few days ago but it had been nearly two months. Two insane months of fighting a secret war. This was a set of cards that she couldn't play close to her chest anymore. They might have lost valuable time in not bringing the tengu into the loop.

With the crate of dynamite, the tengu could deal with the black willows. The real threat was Kajo. Law had two possible suspects but no way to determine if either person was the real oni commander.

"I'll talk to Boo about Kajo; I'll try to get a description out of her. Gently. Roach, can you give the dynamite to Yumiko?"

Roach nodded, looking somewhat shell-shocked.

"You're not giving her *all* our dynamite?" Hal cried. "We need it for...emergencies."

Jane wanted to say no but Hal had gotten them out of a tight jam at the museum with a stick. "Roach, how many sticks are left in the crate?"

"Forty," Roach said.

Yumiko said there was a score of black willows heading to Oakland. The tengu might need more than one stick to destroy a tree.

"Hold back ten sticks," Jane said.

Roach nodded. "I want to see Boo."

"I'll have to call Duff," Jane said. "I'm not sure who has babysitting duty today. I thought it was Alton."

"Not Guy or Geoffrey." Roach jerked his thumb in the direction of Oakland. "They're both at Oilcan's installing the security gate that Geoffrey made. That's why I have the dumpster hauler. The gate didn't fit on either Guy's or Geoffrey's pickups so they called me and I called Team Tinker to help move it since it weighs a ton."

Her mother was at her café downtown. Duff was at the bakery. Alton was in Schenley Park, looking for black willows. She doubted that Alton would drag Boo through that.

"Boo is probably with Marc, then," Jane said.

Roach nodded and kept nodding, obviously mentally checking boxes for seeing Boo. "I need to swap trucks. This dumpster loader stands out too much. People might wonder. I should change clothes too; I didn't take a shower this morning. Maybe I should grab donuts or something...?"

Swapping vehicles was a smart idea. The *Chased by Monsters* production truck was the gaudiest thing in Pittsburgh. She should swap back to her SUV. "If you tell Andy about Boo..."

"God, no, not yet," Roach said. "I'll have to figure out some way to keep him from blurting it out without thinking."

"That was one of the reasons we didn't tell your family," Jane admitted.

"Andy might be Andy," Roach and Jane said at the same time.

"He and Guy went off to help Oilcan move something anyhow," Roach said.

Jane continued. "We need to backtrack to WQED for my SUV. We'll meet you at Marc's."

17: TOAD HALL

The Mexican War Streets was a housing development that had been built a century ago on the North Side. The brick town houses weren't cookie-cutter copies of one another but were all of a similar style, so that every building was slightly different from its neighbor. What all of the houses did have in common was a narrow window over the front door with the house number painted in gold leaf. The district had only a handful of streets running parallel to one another, starting at 1200 and going up.

In the photo that Knickknack had given Mokoto, the house number of 1225 was clearly painted over his head. It took Tommy only a few minutes on a hoverbike to find the right building.

There was a dusty boot print by the doorknob of the red painted door. The century-old jam had splintered under the force.

Tommy glanced about as he dismounted his hoverbike.

The North Side used to be one of the more heavily populated neighborhoods of Pittsburgh. It was nicknamed Chinatown because of the number of "Chinese" who lived in the area. Most of the population, though, hadn't been human. The gutters had run with blood as the elves had gone door to door, killing any nonhuman that they found. Tommy had managed to get most of the half-oni to safety, but the true bloods disguised as humans had been wiped out.

It meant that the area had been nearly deserted for weeks. It was unlikely that anyone had seen or heard the front door of Number 1225 being kicked in.

The foyer had been painted white. Someone had been hit hard enough to spray the wall with small droplets of blood. Stairs led up to a second floor. A bloody handprint marked the wall at the top of the steps, as if someone going up had steadied themselves.

Tommy shook his head. Why run up the stairs? That would trap you in the building with whoever kicked down the front door. Someone had gotten wise—the back door was hanging open at the end of the long hallway.

He pulled the bandana off his ears. They twitched back and forth as he listened closely. The house seemed empty. He could only pick up the distant rumble of traffic. He pulled his knife and cautiously went through the front door.

Tommy had never been in the home of a pure human. He hadn't been sure what to expect.

Not this.

The room to the left of the foyer had been painted brilliant red. "Toad Hall" had been spelled out on the far wall in big mismatched letters stolen from store signs, mostly from closed McDonalds. The archway into the room was half blocked off with wood from shipping pallets, and the entire space had been filled with colorful three-inch-diameter plastic balls. The connecting windowless room had been painted with a big gleaming mural of a starscape of planets, stars, and rimfire done in ultraviolet paint on black. Every inch of floor was covered with couches or mattresses, like a big sleeping pit, except there were no real sheets or blankets. Tommy couldn't think of any reason for the dark bed-like area except for sex, but it seemed too public.

He paused in the foyer, listening, as he puzzled over all the scents washing over him. Did human houses always stink this bad? The smell of garbage was the strongest, coming from the kitchen. From where he was standing, he could see that every counter was covered with unwashed dishes and several big overflowing black trash bags sat on the floor. This was nearly as bad as a whelping pen. Did true humans actually live this way? His aunts would beat these people with a wooden spoon for not keeping the kitchen clean.

Under the stench of standing dishwater and garbage, he could pick out the smell of death. It wasn't strong enough for a full dead body to be rotting in the heat, but definitely something had died in the building. Then there was another, faintly sweet flowery smell that he couldn't place.

The stairs were as old as the house and would probably creak and groan as he climbed them. Was anyone hiding upstairs? All his senses said no. He climbed the steps as quietly as he could but they still seemed dangerously loud to his sensitive ears.

At some point in the past, the second floor had been made into one big room. He couldn't imagine why. The space had been divided down into "rooms" via clotheslines strung above eyelevel and draped with old blankets, American flags, and sheets. It seemed as if the girls had claimed this area. Each fabric-defined cubby was stuffed to the brim with the most unlikely items. A massive stuffed giraffe. Photo collages. A sex blowup doll. A stunning number of shoes. Frilly clothing. A small shrine to something called "Lemon-Lime" with posters proclaiming "Blast it all" and "Prince Yardstick Rules" and bobble-head elves. Mismatched chairs. Road signs. Street signs. Stop signs. It seemed as if the girls would loot anything that they could carry away, even if they had to pry it up.

In the corner farthest from the stairs, there was an oddly placed door. Someone had run to the doorway but had been killed before they reached it. The body was missing but the blood spray on the wall beside the door indicated that an artery had been hit. The person had collapsed onto a mattress and bled out. The stench of death was coming from the blood soaked into the bedding.

Where were they running to?

Tommy opened the door. Someone had knocked a hole into the neighboring townhouse via the shared wall. The connecting building had been gutted and set up as a giant three-story trampoline pit. The front door and first-floor windows were boarded over so that the door between the houses was the only way in and out. It was unlikely that the work had been done this summer, not with the war going into full swing. Toad had expanded into the second building long ago, before Knickknack and the other Undefended moved in with him.

More and more Toad seemed like a giant child instead of an adult male.

The flowery scent was even stronger in the second building, despite all the second- and third-story windows being wide open. Tommy followed the smell down to the basement door. There were respirators hanging by the door.

What in the world did Toad have in the basement? Tommy fitted one of the respirators over his face and opened the door.

The basement was filled with glowing plants in long raised wooden planters. Tommy recognized the gleaming gold flowers from running medical supplies for his father. *Saijin* was used by both the elves and the oni as an anesthetic.

How the hell did Toad figure out how to grow *saijin*?

The oni had long complained that the drug needed to be smuggled in from Onihida as they hadn't been able to get it to grow in Pittsburgh. They had tried everything. What had Toad done differently? Tommy went down the steps to investigate closer.

Big industrial-sized grow lights, like the ones marijuana farmers used, hung from the rafters. The oni had tried those and failed. There were containers of various fertilizers set under planters, but the oni had used those too. There was a homemade computer-controlled watering system, but it seemed only to turn the faucet on and off with a timer. The water flowed through plastic tubing with tiny holes drilled in the bottom.

The only thing different from the failed farms that Tommy had seen in the past was that Toad had affixed ceramic tiles onto the wooden planters. The tiles were etched with a spell that gleamed faintly as a sign that the magic was active.

Tommy had seen something like the tile before. Lord Tomtom had dozens of oni true bloods disguised as humans working on Tinker's gate. Most of them were carpenters who knew how to work ironwood, but a few had learned the rudiments of electrical wiring. After Tinker melted down Turtle Creek, some had come to Chang's restaurant in Oakland, carrying what they could quickly salvage before the entire valley turned into a weird, cold blue soup. One had a box of ceramic tiles printed with a spell. Aunt Flo had chased them out, saying that the elves would track them to the restaurant. The tiles had been left behind. At some point the little ones got into them and were playing with them in the backrooms.

Then Malice had leveled the restaurant. His family had taken what survived—clothing, pots and pans, and dishes—and fled. Again, the tiles were left behind in the chaos.

Knickknack was a college student. A smart boy. Had he gone to the restaurant looking for Mokoto and found the tiles instead?

Tommy realized that the edges of his vision were going white. He stumbled upstairs and slammed the door shut. No wonder Toad had set the farm up in a separate house. One flower was safe but not a basement full of them.

Tommy backtracked to the door on the second floor of the first house, taking deep breaths to clear his mind.

Who had attacked Toad Hall?

It didn't feel like an oni attack. The oni would want

the women unharmed and the men rendered harmless fast. They wouldn't have wounded a woman and a man wouldn't have left the foyer alive. The time of day was odd too. The oni would have would attacked late with the cover of night, long after even the night owls had gone to sleep. Based on what lights were on in the house, it would have been easy to see that at least one of the Undefended had been on the first floor, awake. Also the oni wouldn't have ignored the door to the second building, even after capturing the humans. The oni would have searched, found and taken the *saijin*. It wasn't hidden and it was worth its weight in gold.

The elves had searched the North Side earlier in the summer, killing any disguised oni that they found. The sidewalks had been stacked with dead. More than one half-oni had been caught up in the search and executed. Tommy hadn't heard of any new searches. The elves wouldn't have left the second building unsearched, and they too would have taken the *saijin*. Ditto for the tengu.

That left a city full of humans as possible attackers. The streetwalkers had little of value beyond the *saijin*. Secondhand mattresses. Worn linens. Thrift-store clothes. Theirs was a plastic and cardboard existence.

Tommy climbed the narrow, creaking stairs to the third floor in search of answers. The top floor had three proper bedrooms. By the musky male scent that lingered in all of the rooms, this was where the boys had been sleeping. Unlike the girls, the boys had actual furniture. Dressers. Desks. Beds with headboards and frames to lift the mattresses off the floor. Like the girls, the boys had posters, photographs, and stolen signs covering the walls.

One of the rooms had shelves built out of cinder blocks and wooden boards. Whatever had sat on the shelves was gone. A cork board had been hung over the desk. Push tacks still held down torn corners of paper, evidence that someone had ripped down everything pinned onto the board. The desk was cleared but the dresser still had some clothing.

Tommy knelt down beside the bed. His family hid things under their pillows and mattresses and in among their blankets, as their beds were the only private space in the warren. He was guessing in a houseful of streetwalkers, the lack of privacy would be much the same. A quick search of the bed uncovered a phone and a familiar T-shirt. It was one of Mokoto's favorite shirts. It had been tucked under the pillow and still held his scent.

This had been Knickknack's bedroom.

Tommy scanned the room. Everything that a person would need while in hiding hadn't been taken: the clothes, the bedding, the phone. Someone else had stripped Knickknack's room. What did a streetwalker have that was so valuable? Why had they taken everything pinned to the bulletin board?

He thought of Tinker's war room at Poppymeadows. She had lists, maps, and pictures taped to the walls of the dining room. Oilcan had something similar at his enclave, tracking the work on their nightclub. Was that how crazy smart people tracked what they knew?

Someone walked onto the back porch of the house and into the kitchen.

Tommy froze. Knickknack's bedroom was on the third floor with only one way down to street level. A single person was easy prey for Tommy's mind-clouding abilities. If he had to deal with more than one attacker while trapped on the third floor, things could get hairy.

He tucked away Knickknack's cell phone and listened closely.

The person in the kitchen opened the refrigerator and clinked together glass bottles. Tommy's keen ears caught the unmistakable hiss of a beer being opened. The cap fell to the kitchen floor with a quiet jingle. There were no other footsteps to indicate there was more than one person.

Tommy reached out with his mind. The person was attempting a fearless swagger while filled with nervous fear. Tommy pulled his bandana back on just in case "one" became "many." Feeding the illusion of the peaceful silence of an empty house into the mind of the person in the kitchen, Tommy started down the creaky stairs.

Toad was standing in the back doorway, drinking a cold beer while eyeing the dim hallway to the foyer. He was an ugly guy even to Tommy's half-oni standards, his face too wide and his eyes bulging slightly. He wore loose cut-off jeans shorts, a bright yellow Hawaiian shirt, and red flip-flops. Watching Toad trying to psych himself up to go deeper into the house, though, it was easy to see that his "appeal" was his personality.

"I am one with the force and the force is with me. I am one with the force and the force is with me. Deep breath. Ghost in. Ghost out. Ninja style." He made some karate-like motions with his hand, nearly dropping his beer. Despite his brave words, he continued to hover in the doorway. "Oh, Joyboy, if you got yourself killed being a drama queen, please don't haunt me for this. I told you to run, not stand and be a mega bitch."

Toad tried to press his hands together into a prayer but the attempt was ruined by his beer. He muttered a couple of curse words as he tried to decide what to do with the half-full bottle. In the end, he chugged the contents and then put the glass bottle on the floor with a loud clink. He pressed his hands together, whispered a prayer, and bowed. He wobbled while bowing; apparently it hadn't been his first beer of the day.

Tommy wanted Toad away from a quick exit before he braced the man. He was guessing that Toad had come back because of the *saijin*-filled basement. It meant that the man probably would head upstairs to the connecting door on the second floor.

It took several minutes for Toad to gather his courage; he mostly jogged in place while huffing and puffing. His flip-flops squeaked loudly with each step. Tommy shook his head; it was a crime scene, not a prizefight.

Toad eyed the refrigerator as if considering another beer to boost his courage and then—finally—slowly headed upstairs. Tommy erased himself from the other man's awareness even as Toad passed inches away from him. Tommy followed Toad up the steps. The man headed straight for the *saijin* but staggered to a stop at the pool of blood.

Tommy dropped his illusion and grabbed Toad. He slammed the smaller man against the wall.

"Tommy!" Toad cried in surprise and slight relief. "Shit! Where the hell did you come from? What are you doing here?"

Tommy ignored the questions and asked his own. "What happened here?"

Toad worked his mouth while his eyes flicked right and left, trying to come up with a reasonable lie. "I-I-I don't know. I wasn't here."

Tommy bounced Toad off the wall. "Yes, you were! You ran! You told the others to run! What happened?"

"S-s-s-some guys broke the door," Toad stuttered. "I don't know who they were. Jonnie sold me out. That's all I know."

"Jonnie?"

"Jonnie Be Good. He's an ambulance driver. If he knows that you're cool, he'll sell you drugs on the side."

Tommy knew the slimewad in question. The man was local born and raised. His real name was Jurek Beiger. He was slightly older than Tommy. When he was younger, people called him Jerk Booger. Jurek remade himself after going off-world for college and washing out. He came back with his ears surgically pointed and enough medical training to be an EMT. He grew his hair long, dressed in elf hand-me-downs, and told people that his name was Jonnie Be Good. Since most of the kids Jonnie's age had left Pittsburgh, the new generation took him at his word. Elves didn't lie, after all.

Tommy knew that Jonnie sold drugs in Oakland to college students but Jonnie was a cowardly little shit. He'd run back to Pittsburgh because he couldn't take being a little fish in a big pond.

"He knew about the *saijin* in the basement?" Tommy guessed.

Toad nodded unhappily. "I needed to get seeds off of Jonnie to grow it. I tried once or twice before I got

Knicknack to help me with the planters. I knew the elves would pay dear for it—or the college students trapped on Elfhome who are desperate for any kind of escape. It's a sweet trip—breathe it in and it's all good. Jonnie, though, is like duct tape; it's nearly impossible to peel him off once he gets stuck to you. He'd show up with little bribes to get in the door. Hash brownies. Moonshine. Whippets. If you passed out while partying with him, though, you would wake up royally used. It didn't matter who you were. He'd poke himself in any unprotected hole. I think the only one of us that he hadn't screwed was Knickknack. At least Jonnie is superhot, so most of us don't mind. Much. The whole reason he comes here—a house full of illegal immigrants—is that we can't do shit if we're pissed off that he rapes us while we're passed out."

They could kill the bastard. Tommy knew it was easy for him to consider killing someone but in truth it wasn't so simple. His aunts and cousins needed Tommy to secretly kill the worst of Lord Tomtom's warriors who used them too roughly. Only Tommy could quietly kill an adult male oni and ditch the body without getting caught.

"You're saying Jonnie was responsible for this?" Tommy pointed to the pool of blood.

Toad nodded for a few seconds, like once he started, he couldn't stop. "I wasn't here. I mean, I was here when it started but I got out. I'm not sure what happened after I left. I heard gunshots and I just kept running."

"Who was here when you ran?"

"Everyone. It's all been so crazy. The Wyverns going house to house, finding hidden oni that they chop up and leave stacked on the sidewalk. Your surly neighbor turns out to be from another planet that you never heard of. Giant dragons fighting wooden attack helicopters. Where the hell did the elves get *those*? Then one night none of your people showed up to work Liberty Avenue. It was like your entire stable dropped off the face of the planet. It was just us with no idea what happened to Mokoto and Babe and all your girls. We freaked out. We packed up for the night and went home, scared shitless. If something took out your stable, what was going to happen to us? Knickknack was out all night, asking around, trying to find out what happened to you. No one knew anything."

Mokoto and Babe had been busy alongside Bingo, shifting their people to the William Penn Hotel after the Wyverns raided their old warren. They had sat tight, waiting to find out if Tommy could clear their name by finding Jewel Tear. That had taken him days and he returned just hours before the train derailment. His family had stayed hidden until he'd managed to rescue Oilcan and help kill Iron Mace and Chloe Polanski. Sometime during that time, the Undefended had been attacked. September had been hotter than normal but based on the smell, the blood pool had been festering at least a day.

"How long ago were you attacked?" Tommy said.

"Night before last," Toad said. "It was getting to be the time that we normally head to Liberty Avenue. None of us had made any money since your stable disappeared. We were trying to decide if it was safe. Me and Knickknack didn't think it was a good idea but the girls have us outnumbered and they're all into

elves like you can't believe. They act like the royal
marines are a candy shop on feet. Personally I'm not
into heavily armed redheads.

"While we were hashing it out, Jonnie suddenly
showed up. He rang the doorbell and was yelling for
us to let him in. There was something weird about
it; he was being too loud and too pushy. Usually he's
all careful to be nice until he's in the door and we're
all high as a kite. What's more, Jonnie kept going,
'Hey, Knickknack, are you in there?' like they were
best friends or something. There's a good reason why
Knickknack is the only one of us that Jonnie hasn't
screwed over: he really hates the man. What Jonnie
didn't know was that Knickknack had put a camera up
on the roof so we could see the entire street. Jonnie
had a bunch of guys with him. Big guys. I was like,
'Run! Hide!' and I took off. Before I could even get
out the back door, I heard Joyboy shouting insults at
Jonnie. The stupid little boi bitch! The front door got
kicked in. Everyone was screaming. Then there were
gunshots. I just ran."

The invaders had taken the dead body, everyone
who witnessed the murder, and everything in Knickknack's room—but not the drugs. It had to mean that
Knickknack had been the target of the raid.

Downstairs, the front door creaked open and several
people entered the house, their bootsteps echoing up
the stairwell.

Tommy whispered a curse. In cornering Toad on the
second floor, he'd cornered himself. The stairs were
the only exit but the newcomers were already in the
foyer at the bottom of the steps. Tommy's father could
have clouded the mind of a full army, but Tommy

could only control one person completely. With each added person, his ability frayed.

"No! No!" a female cried out in Elvish from the street. Her voice got louder as she neared the front door. Her Elvish was really bad, marking her as possibly a human, possibly someone from off-world. "You just can't walk into someone's house."

"The door has been broken down," a male with a Fire Clan accent replied in fluent Elvish. "There might be hostiles inside—stay back."

All the Wyverns had gone east with Prince True Flame. The only Fire Clan elves in the city were royal marines. Judging by the number of heavy bootsteps downstairs, an entire squad had just flooded into the house. Were they searching the North Side for hidden oni again? All they were going to find was Tommy.

None of the windows on the second floor were open, despite the oppressive heat of the last month. It probably meant they were all painted shut. Had there been windows open on the third floor? Could Tommy get to the third floor unseen? Maybe, if he shoved Toad down the steps as a distraction.

"Why is this room filled with balls?" a male voice asked. By the sound, the elf had stepped into the thigh-deep sea of balls that took up the front room.

"Eeewww, so much garbage!" a third female voice from deep in the kitchen called out in Elvish. "Look at all the dirty dishes! Are we sure this is a human's house? This looks like that oni whelping pen!"

Someone open and closed the refrigerator several times before a male voice called out, "Does the light in the cold box stay on all the time?"

"Wait! Just wait!" the woman said. "We can't just

dance into people's homes. Someone might still be home! Hello? Peanut? Chardonnay? Hello?"

"Who is that?" Toad whispered as if Tommy should know.

"Dance?" A male echoed the woman in a puzzled tone. "We are not dancing. Are you sure that you're saying that right?"

"Is that Red?" Toad whispered and then called out before Tommy could stop him, "Red? Is that you?"

Mokoto had showed Tommy a picture of Red. She had been the tall, busty redhead who showed up at Poppymeadows during his meeting with Oilcan, surprisingly pretty and young to be a streetwalker. What was the name that she used? Olive Branch? It wasn't her real name but it was probably safer to call her Olive Branch than use the nickname that she used as a whore.

Tommy had watched Tinker and Oilcan grow up at the racetrack. He'd known them enough to trust them. He didn't know Olive Branch. He didn't even know her real name. He didn't trust her. With twenty marines at her beck and call, though, he couldn't hide. He made sure his catlike ears were covered before the first marine reached the top of the stairs.

He was glad to see that Olive Branch was close behind the royal marine leader. She was in the same blue gingham sundress that she had worn at Poppymeadows. The only addition was a rifle slung across her back.

Olive Branch spotted Tommy and her eyes went to his bandana, then to the red-coated elf beside her. "This is one of Tinker *domi*'s people." She pointed at Tommy. "He can be trusted."

She said nothing about Toad as she scanned the room around them.

Tommy felt surprise and then relief go through him like a bolt of electricity. He hadn't dared to hope that she was a clever girl but she had no doubt realized that as a half-oni, Tommy was in immediate danger from the marines. He wasn't about to correct her about Tinker vs. Oilcan. The marines nodded and focused their attention on Toad.

Mokoto said that Toad could talk his way out of anything. Toad grinned and blushed and scratched his head in a way that seemed natural and endearing, but Tommy could smell the nervous sweat pouring off the man.

"Hey, Red!" Toad said in passable Elvish, focusing not on the girl but the tall marine beside her. "We've been worried sick about you! You just disappeared off the streets and no one knew where you lived."

"Yeah, well, shit happened," Olive Branch said in English.

Downstairs, the royal marines seemed to be thoroughly exploring the room filled with balls. A female voice explained that it was a play space for human children, often found at restaurants geared toward families on Earth. The information suggested that the female had been raised off-planet and could be human. Her Elvish sounded like Wind Clan with an odd foreign lilt to it. There was another person moving around downstairs other than the female who was also explaining the ball pit; they carried a radio playing the local elf fusion music station. Who had Olive Branch added to her marine escort?

Olive Branch pointed at the congealed blood pool. "Who was killed here?"

Toad puffed up his cheeks as he shrugged, looking even more toad-like. "I think Joyboy was shot. He was being Joyboy like usual—drama queen on overdrive. I don't know if he was killed. Maybe he was only winged."

Olive Branch shook her head. "No. Too much blood. Whoever was shot bled out like a stuck pig. Joyboy is dead; I just identified his body at the morgue. He had been shot, so this was probably where he died. What happened to Peanut Butter and the others?"

Tommy would have thought she had nerves of steel the way that she moved on past the murder, but there were tears shimmering in her eyes.

"Oh, God, Joyboy is dead?" Toad looked shell-shocked. "I was sure he was but I didn't want it to be true."

"Toad," Olive Branch said with cold steel in her voice. "What happened to Peanut Butter and the others?"

The man seemed close to breaking down. He repeated what he'd told Tommy but slower, stumbling in places.

Olive Branch held up her hand, stopping Toad when he got to the information about the camera that Knickknack had installed. "A camera? Was it recording?"

"Shit! The camera!" Toad patted his pockets to find his phone. "Yeah. Hold on. Let me find it."

Tommy stood mystified as Toad fiddled with his phone. He knew that off-world phones had more functions than those normally found in Pittsburgh, but he didn't realize that you could link them to security cameras.

Toad found the recording and rolled it back to the night before last. "Yeah, yeah, see? There's Jonnie pulling up and then the guys are in the van behind—Hey!"

This was because Tommy had snatched the phone

out of Toad's hands. Olive Branch leaned in close to watch the video with Tommy.

The camera had been positioned so that it could see the street for fifty feet on either side of the front door. Jonnie arrived in a pickup with a lift kit that raised the vehicle to stupid heights. The paramedic waved to a van that parked behind him as if it had followed him to Toad Hall. Six men got out of the van and glanced around as if looking for possible witnesses to what was about to unfold.

The camera had a microphone and it picked up Jonnie shouting to the Undefended as he rang the doorbell and then banged on the door. The men from the van kept tight against the wall, flanking the front entrance, so they were hidden from anyone within the house using the spyhole mounted on the door.

No wonder Toad ran once he saw what was outside his front door.

The camera picked up Toad's shouted warning and then someone cursing out Jonnie. One of the hidden men lost his patience, took a running start, and kicked open the door. Jonnie drifted backward, seemingly startled by the violence. After the men poured into the building, there was screaming and gunshots. Jonnie ran to his pickup and drove away. The house filled with frightened screaming as a man shouted, "Shut up!" over and over again. Minutes later Knickknack and six women were herded out of the building. Their hands were tied and they were gagged. A body wrapped in a blanket and stacks of books followed.

"They're still alive," Olive Branch murmured. She shook her head as the van drove away. "You can't see the license plate." She backed the video up to where the six men had flanked the door and paused it. She showed the image to Toad. "Do you know any of these men?"

"Just Jonnie Be Good." Toad pointed at the paramedic.

"Jonnie Be Good?" a woman echoed from downstairs. "That gobshite? May the Lamb of God stir his hoof through the roof of heaven and kick him in the arse down to hell. That one is all hands and won't take no as an answer."

"That's Jonnie, alright," Toad said.

"Where can I can find him?" Tommy intended to flee whatever circus Olive Branch had following along behind her.

Toad blew his breath out and spread his hand. "He always comes here. I don't know where he squats."

"I can find out where the little gobshite lives," the woman downstairs called. "He works for the city. Anyone who works for them needs to provide a real address within the city limits; it's some old rule from before the first Startup. I know an old geezer who works over in their HR that owes me a favor. I'll give him a ring and see if he can give me Jonnie's home address."

Whoever Olive Branch had picked up, they had better access to information than Tommy and perhaps even Oilcan. Tommy couldn't cloud the mind of six men during a fight. Perhaps it would be better to stick with Olive Branch and her marine escort.

18: OLLY OLLY OXEN FREE!

Having seen Tommy Chang's cat ears at Poppymeadows, Olivia could not erase the image from her mind. At the Ranch, there had been a big black feral barn cat that always stood aloof from everyone and everything. The other cats would seek out humans, rub against ankles and beg for milk. The black would find a safe perch to watch Olivia at her chores and glare at her when she tried to approach him.

Now that Olivia had seen Tommy's ears, even though he'd hidden them away under his signature bandana, he seemed very much like the black barn cat. He had said little while she talked to Toad and even less as she gathered up her marines and herded them outside. He tucked himself into corners and watched intently with his golden eyes. Where the other girls who worked Liberty Avenue called him dangerous and unfriendly, Olivia sensed only that he was leery of strangers.

She worked for years to win the barn cat over. The first thing she'd learned was to be patient and give the black tom space. Trying to catch him and hold onto him only made him more feral. She half-expected Tommy to leave immediately but he stayed, watching.

She wanted him to stay. The royal marines had some combat experience but they knew nothing about Pittsburgh. Aiofe knew modern technology but not the city or the darker side of human nature. Olivia had no real reason to trust Gaddy. Toad was a charismatic idiot who could sway people into stupid things. Olivia didn't want this rescue mission to depend on her skills alone.

Tommy cultivated a dangerous bad-boy image: the black bandana, the tank top that showed off his muscled arms, a corded leather bracelet, knobby jungle boots, and a cigarette dangling from his lips. Even the way he lit the cigarette seemed menacing and cool. How did he do that? Did he practice when he was young or was it somehow just ingrained?

And did he have a tail?

Olivia fought her curiosity to keep her eyes off his butt. The jeans he wore weren't tight enough to make it obvious, although the front suggested that the man was well endowed.

"Jonnie Be Good," Aiofe was saying into her phone. "Tall. Blond ponytail. He had some kind of crop job done to his ears so they're pointed."

"His real name is Jurek Beiger," Tommy said.

"You got to be kidding," Toad said.

A dark look from Tommy sent Toad climbing into the back of the cargo truck with the marines for protection. The marines greeted Toad with enthusiasm, pelting him with questions about his loud Hawaiian shirt and plastic flip-flop sandals. (She hadn't noticed

Toad's footwear but based on the marines' exclamations, apparently the sandals looked like red lobsters.)

Aiofe repeated the name. "2208 East Street, Pittsburgh, 15212? Okay, thanks!"

"Is there more than one East Street?" Gaddy murmured as she checked her map. "No. Okay. That's odd." She pointed down the street that they were standing in. "Well, at the end of this street turn left onto North Avenue, go over I-279 and turn left onto Madison Avenue. Madison becomes East Street."

"We're that close?" Olivia asked as she climbed up into the truck's driver's seat.

"Maybe," Gaddy continued to frown at her map. "I'll go ahead on my hoverbike and check house numbers—if I can find any."

Tommy pointed at another hoverbike tucked into a narrow alley between two row houses. "I'll follow you."

The barn cat was coming too? That surprised Olivia and made her happy.

Olivia nodded, trying not to look pleased. Tommy might find her joy alarming; it would be like rushing the barn cat before it was actually willing to trust her.

Olivia had assumed Gaddy's "if I can find any" to mean that most of the homes in the area were abandoned and thus without house numbers. As they turned onto East Street, it became apparent that Gaddy had meant "if I can find any houses" as the street seemed utterly devoid of buildings. It made the address of 2208 odd, considering the area was empty.

"Oh, I've heard about this," Aiofe said from the seat beside Olivia. "An old geezer that grew up near here said that there used to be a neighborhood here until the middle of last century. They decided to put this highway in and needed to bulldoze all the houses that were in this valley. He said that when he was growing up, this area was covered with basements left behind after the houses above them had been torn down."

Half a century had been long enough to erase all evidence of a once-thriving neighborhood. Maples grew thick on steep hillsides, dressing the valley with reds and brilliant yellows. As they headed north toward the Rim, the trees slowly changed from maples to ironwoods. In the distance, the top of the hill had been cleared and windmills churned in the afternoon sun.

"Is that where Tinker *domi* razed the area?" Olivia asked.

"Yeah, it was a complete *hames*! No one even knew that she and the Viceroy were back in the city as they hadn't been in town before Shutdown. She was out at the crack of dawn, swooping down on construction crews with a *sekasha* at her back, saying that they had to come help her build infrastructure. I got a dozen calls telling me to grab a *jo maxi* and hurry out to the job site before someone got beheaded."

The road rounded a curve, revealing a large, beautiful, pale limestone cathedral. Gaddy was coming back toward them; she had scouted ahead. The woman pointed at the cathedral and turned into the parking lot.

"Oh, he didn't." Olivia growled in anger, slowing down. "Oh, the bastard! He squatted in a cathedral?"

"St. Boniface—technically—isn't a cathedral, it's just a church," Aiofe said. "It was never the seat of the Pittsburgh bishop."

"It looks like a cathedral," Olivia murmured in

defiance, still angry that a slimewad like Jonnie Be Good had taken over holy ground.

As she slowed, she noticed that there was a driveway between the church and a second pale limestone building that seemed to be some kind of office or residence for the priest. She pulled to a stop where she could peer down the drive. It led to a small enclosed courtyard with a two-stall carport. She recognized the truck parked in the second stall: it was the pickup with a lift kit that Jonnie had driven to Toad Hall. He'd obviously hidden it from anyone who might drive past the church.

"He's here." She pulled into the driveway to block the pickup in.

There seemed to be a third building behind the church. It was made of red bricks, not limestone, but from its shape and bell tower, it seemed to be a religious school or a secondary chapel. She couldn't tell from the driveway how the three buildings were connected or where the entrance to the red structure was. She had already spotted six different doors to the church and office building. There were sure to be more, not counting all the windows.

Even with twenty marines, it was going to be difficult to keep Jonnie Be Good from rabbiting. She made sure to pocket the cargo truck's keys. The royal marines had been waiting for orders. Seeing her, they spilled out of the back, surprisingly quiet and tense, like bird dogs before the start of the hunt.

"We're trying to find a human male," Olivia said. "He's tall and blond. He . . . He . . ." What was the word for "surgery"? "He cut his ears so he could look more like an elf."

The marines fingered their pointed ears with various expressions of uncertainty, confusion and horror on their faces. She understood their feelings; it was how she felt about the idea of being transformed into an elf.

"He may not be alone here," Olivia said. "Your main objective is to stop anyone from fleeing this area." Olivia pointed at the door from the office building to the courtyard. "Break into teams. Go quietly. Circle the . . ." What was the word for church? "Circle these buildings." She pointed at the sprawling church and its various outbuildings. "Make sure no one can escape out a back door. We need whoever is inside alive to question them. Try not to break anything—this is a holy place."

Maynard's warning flashed through her mind. She added, "Be careful as there may be traps."

Dagger took command, splitting the warriors into teams to the four quadrants of the map. "Go, go, go," the female commanded quietly.

Olivia checked the nearest door, which seemed to be a handicapped entrance into the church. It was neither trapped nor unlocked. She swung around to the front of the church where three sets of double doors faced the street. The middle set were unlocked.

The doors opened to a shadowed narthex with another set of doors leading to a huge nave. She slipped cautiously through both sets of doors. The pendant lights were off. The only illumination came from the high stained-glass windows, filling the space with light and deep shadows. It was at once comfortingly familiar and yet disquietingly strange. It was a massive nave, much bigger than her grandmother's Presbyterian church. It had a huge domed ceiling inset with stained glass windows. The floor was tiled instead of carpeted. With its randomly colored square pieces of stone, the wide aisle reminded her of stained glass. The altar was heavily adorned with gold leaf. A massive painting of a crowned Jesus, belted in gold, holding a solid gold scepter hung above it. This was a princely Jesus—not her poor carpenter turned rabbi. A phrase in Latin ran along the top of the wall behind Jesus. She didn't know what it meant. The ceiling was a vast dome covered in mosaics. Saints with gold halos gazed down at her. It was the twelve apostles although Judas the Betrayer had been swapped out for Paul. Somehow the addition of the word "saint" before their names made the disciples distant and unknowable.

Tommy ghosted in after her, followed by Toad, who sounded like a demented penguin in his flip-flops. (And yes, they looked like red lobsters complete with antennae, eyes, nubbly shells, and oversized claws. Why would anyone wear those?)

"Do you think he's here?" Toad whispered.

"Shh!" Olivia pointed fiercely at the pew nearest Toad. "Sit. Wait."

Toad sat, looking bug-eyed in surprise. She was vaguely surprised that Toad obeyed her; he normally attempted to walk all over her. The rifle on her back and the marines at her beck and call might have changed his mind.

Olivia caught sight of an unmade bed on the floor behind the altar; all thoughts of Toad vanished. It was a big queen-size air mattress pumped up to nearly two feet thick, with sheets of fairy silk and a faux red fox fur blanket. A can of beer sat next to the unmade bed, sweat beading down its side. Someone had been in bed until recently.

The sight of it made her furious. "All this space! Three buildings' worth! And he's sleeping right on top of the altar?"

Tommy wrinkled his nose. "Yeah, that's Jonnie's bed. It reeks of him." Tommy walked in a wide circle, sniffing. "He was here recently. He probably heard us pull up. He's crawled into a hole. I can't get a bead on him—too many people."

"So it's hide-and-seek?" Olivia said. "Okay, we can play that."

Olivia's mother married a man with five other wives. All told there were ten boys and fourteen girls, not counting Olivia. The Ranch overflowed with children but it lacked toys. It meant that playground games were the only distraction. Red Rover. Red Light Green Light. Double Dutch. But in the winter, when snow and sleet kept everyone inside, there was only Hide and Seek.

Since Olivia always started as "It," she had gotten very good at the game. Of course, this triggered her stepbrothers to insist that she was cheating somehow. What they never realized was all the little tiny clues someone hiding left behind. Dirty footprints on clean floors. Furniture moved ever so slightly from its normal position. Floors whispering that they were bearing a nervously shifting weight. The faint scent of a dirty boy. The gentle sigh of a breath released when the searcher turned away.

The hide-and-seek games at the Ranch had pitted her against her twenty-two stepsiblings. Their family used the rules that anyone who touched home base would be "free" and if Olivia didn't tag at least one person before they could reach home, she would be "It" a second time. With twenty-two possible full-out panic runs for freedom, she discovered the number one rule for winning: until you had the hidden person cornered, never let them know that they'd been found. Cornering someone required moving quietly, pretending that you hadn't spotted their hiding place, and taking the appropriate measures to block their escape.

Olivia scanned the area. The outer doors had all been shut. There were two doors at the front of the nave. The left one was closed but the right was open halfway. She walked quietly to the door, keeping to the hinge side. She paused at the doorway to peer through the crack between the hinge and the frame. The sacristy lay beyond, although it seemed as if the priest had taken the vestments when the church was abandoned. There was no place large enough to hide a full-grown man within. She slipped inside, careful not to touch the door that might squeak.

A window looked out over a second courtyard between the church and the mystery redbrick building and a baseball field. Two marines stood staring through the high fence, obliviously mystified by the baseball diamond still visible through the tall grass. They hadn't noticed the hoverbike parked in the courtyard. To be fair, they hadn't been warned to keep watch for one.

If Jonnie had heard the cargo truck, he could have realized his pickup was blocked in. He might have headed toward the bike. Had he seen the marines and decided to hide instead? She needed to get between Jonnie and his bike.

Olivia tiptoed through the sacristy. The far door opened to a long dusty hallway. There were three doorways on the left. The passage ended with a stairway down. A sign explained that the stairs led to a basement locker room and the baseball diamond. From what Olivia had seen from the window, going out to the ball field would have trapped Jonnie within the tall fence. He probably hadn't gone that way.

The first two doorways on the left had beautiful wood paneled interior doors with leaded glass transom windows above them that spilled sunlight into the hallway. They seemed original to the century-old church. The last doorway had an ugly modern exterior steel security door that was so new, Jonnie must have installed it himself. If he'd gone through the last door, he'd be at the hoverbike already.

He was behind one of the wood paneled doors. Which one?

The hallway had a layer of dust bunnies covering the floor. While Jonnie hadn't cleaned the passage, he used it enough that there were no helpful fresh tracks. As she stood considering the two interior doors, she noticed that more dust motes were dancing in the sunlight coming through the far transom window. Jonnie must have kicked up the dust as he ducked into the room.

If she tiptoed carefully to the exit, she could step outside, wave over the marines, and have them tackle Jonnie.

Squeakie, squeakie, squeakie. Toad came up behind her, his lobster flip-flops making a horrible noise in the silent church.

Olivia motioned him to be still and quiet.

He pulled out his phone, mouthed, "I can call him" and pushed a button.

From the far room, music started to play. *"Why*

did you go out on the road? You were my friend and now you're dead. You wear the mark of tire tread."

The door burst open and Jonnie was on the run.

Olivia ran after him. If he got to the hoverbike, he could escape before any of them got to a vehicle to give chase. He was halfway across the courtyard when she reached the door. The marines were turning from the fence, surprised and confused. Jonnie was going to get away.

Like hell he was.

She brought her rifle around, took aim and fired. Jonnie went down with a yelp.

"You shot him!" Toad cried with shock.

"Yes, I did!" Olivia shouted. "If he doesn't stop running, I'm going to shoot him again."

That checked Jonnie's limping run. He swore loudly as he checked his wound. "You stupid bitch! You could have killed me."

Olivia lowered the rifle slightly and fired a round into the soft ground beside Jonnie. "I might still kill you if you keep calling me a bitch. You're going to tell me where Peanut Butter Pie and the others are, and you better tell me the truth because you're not going to the hospital until we find them."

"I'm bleeding!" Jonnie cried.

"Yes, you are! One tends to do that after being shot!" Olivia advanced on the downed EMT with rifle leveled. "You're going to be fine unless you keep screwing around with me. Where is Peanut Butter Pie?"

"I had nothing to do with that!" Jonnie cried.

"You brought those men to Toad Hall. Because of you, Joyboy is dead. You know who took the others. Where did they take them?"

"They didn't tell me that they were going to break down the door like a murder squad. They said that they just wanted to talk to Knickknack about a business project."

"Where. Are. They?" Olivia closed to just out of lunging distance and pointed the rifle directly at Jonnie's face. She was aware that the marines had come to flank her but they didn't have their weapons out. They must have thought she had the situation handled.

"I don't know!" Jonnie shouted. "They were wussy off-world businessmen—the kind that walk around downtown in their stupid skinny-leg suits looking like dorky schoolboys. You know the type with the waxed-down hair, enough cologne to choke a cow, and their frat-boy rings. I know you know—I've seen them cruising Liberty Avenue in their town cars. I didn't think they would have guns. I didn't think they would hurt anyone. That was my honey pot. My hoes and my drugs. I wouldn't have taken them there if I didn't think they were harmless douchebags."

"They're the most dangerous of men," Olivia said. "The ones that can do anything and walk away clean because people think they're respectable 'God-fearing' men."

"I thought they were safe or I wouldn't have taken them to Toad's," Jonnie whined.

"Fine, we'll pretend that you didn't recognize the top of the food chain when you saw it," Olivia said. "What did they want with Knickknack? What business project?"

"I didn't ask. That's not how it works. I provide what my customers want, no awkward questions asked. They're here on visas; it's a ticking clock. They don't have time to figure shit out for themselves. If they want a bag of weed, I sell it to them. If they want a blonde in a tight red dress at their hotel room at eight, I set it up. Don't ask, don't tell."

"They told you *something*," Olivia growled. "Why Knickknack?"

"They said they just wanted to talk to people who knew how to do magic like Tinker for a business project." Jonnie laughed. "Like Tinker? Like Tinker? I told them that they were shit outta luck—the creature doesn't exist. They offered me a bounty if I could produce someone to help them with their project, so I dug around. I told them about Oilcan but he dropped off the face of the planet just before the black willow tore up Reinhold's. When he popped back up, he either had a dragon or a *sekasha* with him. I suggested Tooloo—she does some magic out of her store in McKees Rocks, but that didn't pan out. Every time they went to see her, no one would be at her place except some crazy attack chicken. I even suggested that guy that makes the ironwood furniture but that got fucked up somehow. Then out of the blue, I stop by Toad's to find out our little Knickknack is a freaking magical genius. He had printed a spell onto these ceramic plates that did some weird voodoo on the *saijin* seeds so they would grow."

"You sold out Knickknack?" Toad growled.

"I thought they just wanted to hire him!" Jonnie said.

"Job interviews don't include the recruiters kicking down your door," Olivia said.

Jonnie shook his head. "The furniture guy made them jumpy. They wanted to be ready if someone else pulled a gun. I didn't think they would do anything—they were afraid of a chicken, for Christ's sake!"

"Who are 'they'? Where do we find them?" Olivia said.

Jonnie looked away, obviously trying to decide if he could get away with lying. What a man-child.

"You're going to hide from them the rest of your life?" Olivia asked.

"They found me anytime they wanted something," Jonnie admitted in a low voice. "I don't even know how they knew about me in the first place. First time I met them was about two years ago—they came to the station and were waiting by my truck when I got off work. I thought they were cops at first. It really spooked me; that's why I moved my squat to this place. I didn't think anyone knew where I lived. How did you find me?"

If Aoife could find Jonnie by asking the city, then anyone with the right connections could find him. They just needed the right name. Aoife and Gaddy came running around the corner with the last of the marines.

"They had all the goods on you and you didn't even know who they worked for?" Olivia asked with disdain.

"They pay me not to ask." Jonnie sulked. "That how it works. All I know is their company logo. They put it on everything."

Jonnie pulled out a ballpoint pen. It was a big fat thing done in matte black, stamped with the golden image of a crowned lion's head and the word EROB-ERN. She'd seen the logo before, somewhere—maybe on the side of a delivery truck. It was familiar but she couldn't place it.

Aoife took the pen from Olivia. "Erobern is German. It means 'conquer' but I haven't heard of any company using that name here in Pittsburgh. It's possibly a company slogan."

"They've got offices downtown," Jonnie said. "But I'm not sure where. They just call it 'the office' but they've made it clear that I'm not to show up there."

The company wouldn't be holding whores hostage in their corporate offices. Being that Toad Hall was on the North Side and Joyboy had been found on the opposite bank, miles downriver, it was probable that they stopped along the way to dump Joyboy's body.

"Does the company have anything downriver?" Olivia said. "Almost to the Rim?"

"Yeah," Jonnie said as if he hadn't expected the question. "They've got a shipyard down on Neville Island."

"The old Dravo shipyards?" Gaddy said.

"You know where it is?" Olivia said.

"My grandfather worked for Dravo as a shipfitter until the nineteen eighties," Gaddy said. "They hired him as a consultant after Startup to build ships to sell to the elves. There was a massive fire at the shipyard a few years after they launched their first boats. It gutted the place. I thought it closed for good after that."

Jonnie shrugged. "I don't know anything about it except they retooled the place a little while back and it was supposed to start up production again."

"They might have Knickknack and the others there," Olivia said.

They got Jonnie to the back of his pickup and left it to Toad to drive him to Mercy Hospital. Olivia took Jonnie's phone and then made sure Toad understood that Jonnie wasn't to be given access to any way of warning the kidnappers.

"We need to scout the area to ascertain the enemy force that is guarding the kids," Olivia said.

"You really think they're still alive?" Tommy asked.

"Yes," Olivia said. "They probably didn't set out to kill Joyboy; it feels like a random act triggered by an escalation of violence. Once Joyboy was dead, though, how do you get Knickknack to cooperate with you? You take hostages. If nothing else, they're following the oni blueprint on how to get a working gate. Knickknack is a smart boy, he's probably stalling in the most cooperative manner that he can."

"He's trying to actually build a gate?" Tommy asked with doubt clear in his voice.

"He's making it look as if he is," Olivia said. "He probably can't but he's not going to tell them that he can't at this point."

Tommy tilted his head as if to say, "It's possible."

Gaddy took out her map and spread it out on the tailgate of the cargo truck. "This is Neville Island. It's largely abandoned; the shipyard was one of the last businesses down there still operating." According to the map scale, the island was nearly five miles long. The narrow strip of land sat in the middle of the Ohio River. "I found Jevin's body under this bridge across the back channel here. This notch here on the northern bank—that's the ramp they use to slide the boats down into the river after they're finished. The fire took out the buildings attached to the shipyard, so I'm not sure what's there now."

Tommy grunted. "I was down in this area a couple of times after Tinker first invented the hoverbikes. It was a complete no-man's-land. Her team had the run of the island. Tinker had set up jumps and such to make an insane course where one missed jump landed you in the river. Everyone was more than happy to move to my racetrack when I set it up. A few days ago, we had a fight with the oni and Iron Mace at the hotel where Oilcan used to live. Oilcan killed Iron Mace at the dam." Tommy pointed to a line drawn across the main channel of the Ohio River about a mile from the notch. "After the fighting, I was trying to stay out of the elves' way." He drifted his finger toward the notch. "I noticed that something was going on here. There were buildings that looked new but what really stood out was the big electric chain link fence all around it and prison-level guard detail. The Wyverns checked to see if the people were humans or oni. There was no mass beheading, so I'm assuming that they were happy with whatever they found."

A high-security human business site. It sounded like the perfect place to hold whores prisoner.

"We should go to the hotel," Olivia said. "There was activity there recently. If we're spotted, then they probably will assume that we're there because of something that happened during the fight. From there, we can make an attack plan."

Tommy gave her a surprised look but nodded. "That sounds smart."

Neville Island looked like something out of a postapocalypse film. Industrial buildings crumbling with disrepair. Weed-choked parking lots. Rusting vehicles with flat tires. Random trash everywhere. A chair. A desk. A filing cabinet. It was like someone put them on the street to take and then abandoned them. Scattered here and there were also remnants of a hoverbike race course. Near the bridge where Joyboy's body had been found was a large berm turn of packed dirt along with homemade arrows outlining the lip. Anyone who overshot the turn would end up in the river. Part of the sidewalk along the road had dirt jump rhythm section. Beside the driveway to the collapsed hotel was a high tabletop jump. Knowing that Tinker had been thirteen when she invented the hoverbike, the race course construction was even more impressive. It would have required dump trucks full of dirt from someplace, dug up by backhoes and packed down with bulldozers.

It was telling, too, that Tommy had managed to replicate it someplace else and had lured the racing circuit out to it. The man had mad people skills despite his barn cat ways.

The battle at Tinker's childhood home had leveled the abandoned hotel. It made an impressive mound of debris. There was some yellow tape, fluttering in the wind, put in place by the police or the EIA. Judging by the fresh footprints in the mud, the tape failed to keep the curious from picking through the rubble.

Olivia pulled the cargo truck into the hotel's driveway, running over the tape. Parking and pocketing the keys to the truck, she pulled the binocular case out of her purse, once again glad that she had thought to steal them from her husband. She looped their strap over her head as she waved the marines out of the truck.

"Secure the immediate area," she said.

Once the marines were fanning out, Olivia scrambled up onto the tabletop jump to scan the area with her binoculars. The area was as flat as one expected for an island in the middle of a large river that flooded often. It had probably started life as a sandbar in some prehistoric time. While the tabletop gave her a vantage point, there were still dozens of warehouse buildings blocking her view of the entire island.

Gaddy muscled her hoverbike up the steep slope to stop beside Olivia.

"Where is the shipyard?" Olivia asked.

"We're facing west on Neville Road." Gaddy indicated the street beside them. She pointed out a dam with two locks along the far riverbank. "To the north, that's the Emsworth Locks and Dam on the main channel of the Ohio. That's where Oilcan fought with Iron Mace." She pointed south to the other side of the island. "Okay, follow Neville Road west and you'll see that there's a second dam on the Ohio's back branch. It's smaller and it doesn't have any locks."

Olivia found it. The road seemed to come within fifty feet of the southern bank at that spot. "I see it."

"Right there, a second street splits away from Neville Road, goes north, and turns to run parallel to it. That's Grand Avenue, which always seemed to me to be too fancy a name for such an industrial area. The shipyard is off of Grand Avenue, along the northern bank. Tommy is right; there's a big new building there, right where the shipyard should be."

Olivia found the massive steel building, longer than a football field. It was difficult to tell how tall it was as there were no windows to mark off floors. It seemed three or four stories high. A gold crown and the word "Midas" had been painted onto the side of the building.

"I always thought you built a ship outside," she murmured. "Not indoors."

Perhaps the shipbuilding was a cover story for

something else. There seemed to be smaller buildings beyond the big one but it was hard to tell from their angle. A tall chain-link fence surrounded the buildings.

Tommy popped his hoverbike up to land beside her. Aiofe stayed with the marines, still peppering them with anthropology questions about the Fire Clan in general. Olivia really had to admire the girl for her diligence.

"What is your plan?" Tommy said. "Storm in? Guns blazing?"

Olivia shook her head. By his tone, it sounded like he'd leave if she came up with that sketchy of a plan. The Ranch had police raid drills based on the assumption that the children would be seen as helpless pawns, not well-trained soldiers. She wasn't sure who had the flawed worldview—the police or the elders. Working backward, it was fairly easy to tell a standard hostage rescue mission required a distraction.

They had too little information, though. They were assuming that the shipyard had been the kidnappers' destination. That Knickknack and the others had been kept together. That they were still alive and hadn't done anything stupid and the violence hadn't escalated after the men moved their hostages. Olivia didn't want to blindly charge in to discover that there was no one to save. She didn't want to risk the marines for nothing.

How could they get more information?

"Why don't the two of you do a lap on the race-track? Make it seem like you're just two kids, messing around, but see if you can spot anything that can tell us exactly who is at the shipyard?"

Gaddy laughed. "Yeah, sure, I'll race against a Delta but I'm not going to win."

19: SIGNED, SEALED, AND DELIVERED

Tinker vividly remembered the day that Tooloo stole her mail. It was in April. It was a few days before she turned eighteen and no longer had to be afraid of being deported as an underaged orphan. It was roughly eight weeks before she saved Windwolf's life or met Pony. It was three months before she knew about the oni army hidden in and around the city.

Pittsburgh used to travel back and forth between Elfhome and Earth. While Pittsburgh was on Elfhome, all the mail on Earth addressed to the city was collected in a warehouse in Cranberry just on the other side of the Rim. The massive collection of letters and packages was shuffled across the border during Shutdown. Home delivery within Pittsburgh was suspended for forty-eight hours while the post office workers sorted through the monthly flood of mail. Two days after Startup, the mail carriers would stuff her mailbox with magazines, catalogs, junk mail, and a

variety of small boxes that represented items impossible
to find in Pittsburgh ordered over the internet during
the last Shutdown. Thus she knew exactly what day it
was when she caught Tooloo cleaning out her mailbox.
April 25, six days before her eighteenth birthday.

It meant the birthday card would have been terrifyingly timely. How had the twins known what day
she was born when she knew nothing about them?

The morning Tooloo had stolen her mail, Tinker had
hiked down to her salvage yard, caught between annoyance and giggling madly. She had woken up insanely
early from a weird and crazy dream. It started as a
nightmare where she'd built a teleporting device that
had gone haywire, spitting out duplicates of herself like
something out of *The Fly*. Some of her copies were
half-size. Some had black crow wings. Others were
tiny as mice. She was hip-deep in weirdness before
she'd gotten the machine turned off. In the dream
she'd been frustrated that the copies had decided to
throw a weird combination of birthday party and circus
with everything from giant wingless birds to a large
talking dog that spoke only in Japanese.

As if that wasn't enough, the copies had decided
to put up posters everywhere advertising that Tinker
was still only seventeen and an orphan living alone.
Shadowy men had taken notice and were coming
with cages for the entire crazy mess. It was a stupid
unsettling dream with bits of silliness that made her
laugh all the while checking over her shoulder.

It had been a day designed to annoy her. April in
Pittsburgh was normally a fragile, warm month as the
city crept out of the hold of winter. The crab apple
trees that hugged the river's banks were all beginning

to bloom, filling the air with their sweetness. This morning, though, had decided to turn bitter cold and damp. It wasn't quite raining but dampness hung in the air like mist. To top it off, Tooloo had been at the mailbox of Pittsburgh Salvage, going through her mail.

"Tooloo!" Tinker shouted as she closed on the old half-elf.

The tall female was dressed in a threadbare fairy silk gown that came down to her ankles. The ragged hem showed off her worn red high-top sneakers. Her white hair was braided into a thick cord that hung down the middle of her back. Tooloo had her huge rooster, Box, hooked up to his little cart—that she was filling with Tinker's mail.

"That's mine!" Tinker tried to snatch a box out of the cart. Box pecked the back of her hand. "Ow! Tooloo! What do you think you're doing?"

"I'm keeping a certain little monkey from chasing its own tail." Tooloo dropped a handful of packages and magazines into Box's cart. "It only leads to trouble."

"No! Stop that!" Tinker tried to grab a small Amazon box—probably the replacement motherboard she ordered—out of the wagon.

Box puffed up, readying himself for battle. He was a huge buff Orpington rooster, fifteen pounds of pure golden orange fury. She had seen him take on cats, dogs, foxes, and coyotes. He was a fearless and vicious warrior. He was, though, also fairly stupid—being a chicken and all.

Tinker had bought a loaf of raisin bread from the Jenny Lind bakery before Shutdown and then forgotten it. It was rock hard and possibly moldy (the raisins making it impossible to be sure). She'd brought it with

her, thinking there was an off chance she would see
Roach with his elfhounds. She pulled the loaf out, tore
it into large chunks, and flung them onto the ground
in front of Box. While the rooster was busy pecking
at the bread, Tinker snatched up her packages.

"You can't steal people's mail!" Tinker said. "It's
against the law!"

"Pft! Moral obligations outweigh laws," Tooloo said.
"If you see a bomb in someone's mailbox, you take
it out."

"Bomb? What bomb?" Tinker eyed the packages in
her arms. She'd ordered a lot of odd things, some of
which could be used for bomb making, but she hadn't
ordered anything explosive. At least, she was fairly
sure she hadn't. It had been a month or more since
she ordered most of the items in the boxes.

"One can never be sure with off-world surprises.
They arrive without warning to blow up in your face.
That's always been the problem."

"There's no bomb in my mail," Tinker decided.
"You just want some weird excuse to take it. If you
need something, like packing material, just tell me."

"You don't explain a fire to a blind woman using
colors. You just tell her that she's going to get burned.
The problem with monkeys is that they never listen.
Give them to me."

"Wait until I open them!" Tinker danced out of
Tooloo's reach. Thankfully the old elf didn't follow.
"I'll bring them to you tonight."

"Whatever." Tooloo turned and walked away.

Box pecked up the last of the bread and strutted
after Tooloo.

Tinker thought she had gotten everything off of

Tooloo. Certainly everything she expected to find in her mail was there. She hadn't been expecting a birthday card from her baby sisters, so she hadn't realized that it was missing from her mailbox. Tooloo must have secreted it away while Tinker fought with Box. Tooloo had come armed to take everything but settled for the only "bomb" in Tinker's mail.

Tinker stormed out of Lain's house. She'd suffered a constant barrage of rough emotions since the tengu dragged her out of bed in the middle of the night. Fear of what the oni might do with the contents of Dufae's box. Terror that she might have to act as parent to her twin sisters, who already outstripped her in insanely dangerous and impossible feats. Anger and jealousy toward Esme. Deep hurt that Lain hadn't trusted her with the truth for so many years. After being tumbled through those many abrasive emotions all morning, Tinker had been polished down to pure rage.

Rainlily had caught up to them on Stormsong's Delta, directed by Lemonseed as to where to find them. Tinker was too angry to ask how the female's mission had gone. Pony and Stormsong had warned her that Windwolf wouldn't be able to leave the battlefront. The fact that they were obviously right only fueled Tinker's rage more. She caught flashes of blade talk as the *sekasha* filled one another in. She ignored it; Pony could tell her later about how useless Rainlily's trip had been.

Tinker stomped to their big Rolls-Royce limo. Pony was the best driver of the five; he'd driven them to Lain's. Tinker was too angry to be chauffeured; she got in behind the wheel. The *sekasha* gathered at her door, unhappy about her intended destination.

"If Tooloo is truly Vision," Stormsong said quietly, "she will know that you are coming."

"I don't care." Tinker held her hand out to Pony. The Rolls-Royce had been gifted to the elves near the turn of the century; it still used manual keys.

Stormsong pressed on even as Pony surrendered the keys. "If you think Lain and Esme are cruel and heartless for what they've done to you, know that they are just pale shadows of the ruthlessness that is Pure Radiance and Vision. I spent a hundred years begging my mother to tell me why she had me. Why a mixed caste? Why after thousands of years of being chaste, did she sleep with my father? Why him? Her answer had always been that if I could not envision the world that she was trying to create, then I was just a stumbling block for her to remove."

Tinker paused in sliding the seat forward so she could reach the pedals. Pony might be the shortest and stockiest of the *sekasha* but he was still a foot taller than she. "Remove? Like kill you?"

It was telling that Stormsong had to consider the question for a moment. "I believe she would if she felt it was necessary. She is ruthless. She had a disagreement with Vision. She betrayed her own mother to the Skin Clan to make the world that we now live in. It was by her action that Vision was bound hand and foot in the first place."

Tinker growled in frustration at the truth. Her grandfather could outthink her when she was a child with limited experience about how the world worked. He had a harder time as she got older. Lain and

Tooloo, though, never had trouble keeping two steps ahead of her. "Well...your mother didn't do a very good job if Vision got away."

"Which should terrify you at the thought of going against Vision," Stormsong said.

Tinker doubted that Tooloo would kill her. The female had been her babysitter; that had to count for something. Tinker wasn't sure, though, that her Hand was safe from the old elf. Tinker frowned at the warriors who were patiently waiting for her to give orders. All five would willingly die to keep her safe. During the summer, she had come close to killing them several times over. They would go wherever she led; she had to be sure that she didn't lead them into danger. Or at least...unnecessary danger.

Tinker had to assume that Tooloo was as clever and dangerous as Chloe. Tinker had trapped Chloe by doing abstruse things, like designing traps using both little known science and magic. Tinker didn't want to kill Tooloo. Trapping her would be pointless. Tinker imagined that Tooloo would sit calmly in the trap, give her a slow clap, and then ask, "Now what, little monkey?"

Now what indeed?

Tinker handed the keys back to Pony and climbed over the center console to the back. She needed to think about this.

At one time, Tinker's whole world had been the narrow five-mile-long island in the middle of the Ohio River. She and her grandfather had claimed most of Neville Island for themselves, living in a huge empty hotel at the edge of the rusting hulks of industry.

Pittsburgh's steel-town legacy had started to crumble after the Second World War, but the deathblow had been the city being kidnapped to Elfhome. The only company on Neville Island that survived the first Startup had burned to the ground a few years later.

Downtown had been a place that the adults talked about. Tinker could see the tips of its skyscrapers over the trees that grew thick along the river's edge. Since she and her grandfather never visited the city proper, Downtown seemed like a far-off fantasy castle. They left the island for only two exceptions: every few days, without rhyme or reason, her grandfather would take Tinker to Lain's on Observatory Hill or across the river to Tooloo's store in McKees Rocks.

At least, it seemed without logic to Tinker as a child. Lain felt like a random stranger that her grandfather didn't particularly like but decided to entrust his granddaughter with. He referred to Lain as "that woman," especially when Lain tried to influence how he was raising Tinker. The two fought over her education, diet, hygiene, and safety. More than once Lain had shown up at Neville Island during the spring floods to drag Tinker off to high ground as if it was her God-given right to kidnap small children out of their beds. Tinker thought that her grandfather only grudgingly permitted Lain's attitude because Lain had been an astronaut, one of the few scientists on Observatory Hill who had actually been in space, and a force of nature when opposed.

It was all so clear now that her grandfather allowed it because Lain was her aunt.

But if Lain wasn't an arbitrary stranger, then who was Tooloo?

Her grandfather didn't trust strangers or elves, but he'd trusted Tooloo.

Oilcan had arrived on Elfhome knowing Elvish. He spoke High Elvish better than Tinker. He'd learned it from his mother, who had learned it from her great-aunt Josephina Dufae. Tinker never wondered how her great-great-aunt knew Elvish; she accepted it as one of the universal truths, like the Earth circling a different sun from the one she normally saw in the sky. Unbounded Brilliance, though, had died while his son was an infant. Etienne Dufae and his children might have had access to the Dufae Codex but that wouldn't have taught them how to speak Elvish.

Had Tooloo been watching over the Dufae children for generations?

If she had been, it would explain so much. Why would Unbounded Brilliance break into his uncle's private lockbox? How did infant Etienne get safely to Boston after Unbounded Brilliance had been swept up in the French Revolution? Why had her grandfather been living in Pittsburgh in the days prior to the city being kidnapped to Elfhome? How did Esme find out about Leonardo's stored sperm and arrange for Tinker to be born?

Tooloo.

Vision.

Whoever she was.

The twins had warned the tengu about the Dufae box. It meant that the twins probably had an unedited copy of the Dufae Codex. Tooloo had given Esme a digital version of the journal to pass on to her children, most likely because she had foreseen that the twins would need magic to escape to Elfhome.

But Tooloo hadn't given it to Tinker. She had let Tinker work with the highly edited version, fully knowing that Tinker was heading into a perfect storm of oni and elves.

How did Tinker get her to cough it up now?

Tinker sat in the back of the Rolls-Royce, blowing raspberries, as she came up with nothing.

The problem was that for Tinker's entire life, Tooloo had defied all logic. The old elf almost never answered a direct question; when she did, she often refuted it within minutes. How old was she? Who were her parents? When was her birthday? Tooloo had given dozens of conflicting answers.

To be fair, some of the questions might have been impossible to answer. Vision had been created out of dragon DNA. Were Tooloo's "parents" elves or dragons? Genetically she was both and neither. She'd been born a slave; her birthday probably hadn't been celebrated with a frosted cake and lit candles. Even if Tooloo somehow knew the exact day, over the last few thousand years, humans had changed their calendar multiple times. September was no longer the seventh month. At one point, ten days were simply dropped from the calendar. Every four years, they added an extra day. How could anyone keep track?

The truth was, though, that Tooloo refused to be known. Even with something as simple as her favorite color, the female had answered with the entire spectrum of the rainbow, starting with red and ending with violet. Tinker used it to her advantage when she was little, discovering that a barrage of personal questions was the fastest way to trigger a magic lesson. Tinker knew that she was being derailed from learning anything about the old elf. Tooloo knew that Tinker knew. Had Tooloo ignored the personal questions simply to cut to what Tinker truly wanted in the first place?

Tinker had the unedited paper copy of the Dufae Codex. It would take days for her to plow through it alone. She could cut it up, give the pages to all the elves at Poppymeadows, and have them find every reference to the box. She really hated the idea of tearing apart the two-hundred-year-old family heirloom, especially knowing now that she and Oilcan only had a portion of it saved to computer memory.

She could look into how her grandfather managed to create the digital copy that he gave her; maybe one of his old computers had the unedited version on it. None of his machines, though, had been in the storage unit where she found the paper copy. Oilcan might have left the ancient computers at the now-leveled hotel. She couldn't remember seeing them there either but she had been focused on getting her own machines up and running. She could call and ask Oilcan where the machines went, but that felt like a waste of time. Even if she could get the ancient machines to boot up, she would then have to hack past her grandfather's security and dig through a mountain of purposely confusing file names. (She was never sure if her grandfather's levels of encryptions were because of his paranoia of strangers or because of her curiosity.)

Maybe the tengu could finagle a copy from the twins. Actually, that wouldn't be a bad idea. It would be faster and less painful than dealing with Tooloo.

Pony, she realized, was pulling into the parking space beside Tooloo's seedy storefront.

BREAD, BUTTER, EGGS, FISH, FOWL, HONEY, PITTSBURGH INTERNET ACCESS, MILK, SPELLCASTING, TELEPHONE, TRANSLATIONS, VIDEO RENTALS was written under the glass block windows in English and Elvish. Tinker had painted the words and runes there herself when she was eight. It hadn't occurred to her until now that the advertising would pull in every spectrum of people within Pittsburgh. The locals wanting food and help with magic. The human newcomers who needed a public telephone and internet access. Elves who didn't speak English. Was there ever a better information-gathering nest for a spider to sit in?

They sat in the car, its cooling engine ticking loudly in the silence.

Tinker stared at the OPEN sign in window of the store's front door. Tooloo kept random hours as she worked both her store and her farm alone. She was religious about flipping the sign to CLOSED when she wasn't in the building. It was swaying slightly. Even as Tinker watched, the sign came to a stop.

If Tooloo knew that Tinker was coming with five *sekasha* in tow, she wasn't hiding. She had closed up her store to keep out other customers until Tinker arrived, and then flipped the sign as if to welcome her in. Maybe. Assuming that Tooloo was that good at seeing the future.

"*Domi?*" Pony spoke for all the *sekasha* who were all looking at her.

Was it worth getting out? Tinker had a ton of questions for Tooloo but would the female answer any of them? Was this a futile exercise? Or was the "Open" sign an indication that Tooloo was finally willing to talk?

Tinker wasn't going to find out sitting in the car.

The bell above the door jangled as Pony went through ahead of Tinker.

Tooloo's always seemed impossibly big on the inside. It wasn't readily apparent from the outside but the female had built a hodgepodge of additions that also served to connect her store to nearby abandoned buildings. It had overhead lights but Tooloo rarely turned them on, preferring the sunlight that streamed through the glass block windows. Display shelves and clothing racks and antique furniture created an endless dim maze filled with junk that Tooloo had collected over decades, if not centuries.

Cloudwalker, Rainlily, and Little Egret spread out to search for hidden assassins, leaving Stormsong and Pony to guard over Tinker.

"Wood sprites," Tooloo called from the big room in the back of the store that served as her living quarters. "They never have much common sense but they never lack for courage."

Wood sprites! Tinker growled, pushing Pony aside to charge in the direction of the voice. Damn the old elf. The female had called her "wood sprite" all her life without explaining what it truly meant. Tooloo had known full well that Forge was still alive and grieving over his lost son, unaware that he had great-great-great-great-grandchildren.

Tinker paused at the threshold into the back room. The polished cherrywood planks glimmered with magic. She'd forgotten about the ley line running through Tooloo's home. It had been invisible to her until she became a *domana*. She'd had nothing to compare it with when she had visited Tooloo just days after her transformation into an elf. Now that she had more experience with sensing magic, she realized that the old elf had camped on a *fiutana*. It wasn't as powerful as the one at Reinhold's, but it beat everything else that Tinker had seen in the last few months.

Tooloo was sitting in one of her two wing-backed chairs. Her big rooster, Box, stood in the other. Between them was a small chess table with pieces arrayed across the board. For all the world, it was like Tinker was interrupting an game. She knew, though, that Tooloo disliked chess with a passion and that none of the chickens were normally allowed in the house, not even Box. The female had staged the scene—but what was it supposed to mean? Tinker couldn't guess. That dealing with Tinker was like playing chess with a chicken?

Box pecked at crumbs that had been sprinkled on the chess table to ensure his participation in the tableau.

Tinker clamped down on the questions that wanted to pour out of her. She might get only one real answer out of Tooloo, so it needed to be the right one. "Do you have—" No, no, Tooloo could claim to have the copy and then refuse to give it to her. "I need the digital copy of the Dufae Codex that you gave to Esme."

"You have all you need," Tooloo said. "I've made sure of that. You're just wasting time, running around like a headless chicken. The hours are ticking down to minutes."

"No, I don't!" Tinker shouted, losing hold of the anger she'd been struggling to keep in. "Grandpa edited my copy. I didn't know anything about the box or the *nactka* or the baby dragons or what the oni plan to do with them. I know that you know that I know that you know..." Tinker got lost in her sentence.

"I haven't known anything from the start and you've known that I haven't all along."

"You never listened when I warned you in the past." Tooloo gave Box a little push toward the open door. "Shoo! I'm done with you for now."

"*Bok caw!*" Box resisted to peck up two more crumbs and then turned his head sideways to eye the tabletop closely.

"You're wasting time here," Tooloo repeated, although it was difficult to tell if she was talking to Box or Tinker. Perhaps she was addressing them both. "I know you're clever; you can figure this out without me showing you how the pieces are arrayed in this deadly game and reminding you how they move."

She was definitely talking to Tinker.

Tinker chased the rooster off the chair and sat down. She eyed the chessboard warily. All the games she had ever played with Tooloo had ended in tears of frustration. Not because Tinker was bad at the game—she beat any other adult she ever played—but because Tooloo would "cheat" by having all the pieces—Tinker's and her own—take on human personalities. Pawns would desert the game out of fear. Queens would fall in love with knights and run off with them. Bishops would assassinate their own kings. Chaos would reign.

Tooloo wasn't some random crazy old elf but the most powerful oracle ever born to the elves. She had spent centuries carefully carrying out some kind of detailed plot. She had carefully set up this display. Why? What did it mean? Did it mean anything at all?

The board was turned so that Tinker seemed to be assigned black, and thus the second to move. The pieces weren't all chessmen. At a casual glance, it would seem that Tooloo had just substituted random things for missing pieces. Tinker's king was a miniature bottle of Heinz ketchup. A Superman mini-action-figure stood in for one of her bishops. Her rooks were miniature chicken figurines. All of Tinker's pawns were Minnie and Mickey Mouse statues. Tooloo's queen, one of her bishops, and four of her pawns were plastic monkeys in a variety of cute poses.

The pieces were arranged in the classic Queen's Gambit, with white moving one of its monkey pawns to D4. Black mirrored the move, blocking any further advance. White continued the classic opening with a second monkey to C4, which black had captured. The arrangement of the pieces on the chessboard would seem like just random noise except Esme had called her half brothers "Flying Monkeys Four and Five." Wouldn't that make Chloe "Flying Monkey Six"? Who were all the other monkeys? Could the Heinz bottle be Pittsburgh itself? Were the Disney mice supposed to be her little sisters? And why all the chickens? Were all the changed pieces some kind of silent code that Tinker should already know?

"Bok caw!" Box complained, staring up at Tinker from the floor.

"I don't understand," Tinker said. "You may think you've told me everything but-but-but I don't always listen!"

Tooloo laughed bitterly at the truth of the statement.

Tinker pressed on. "Why is it even up to me? You've had years and years. Centuries! Couldn't you have stopped the Skin Clan before this?"

"You sound like my daughter," Tooloo said. "Simple revenge, fast and bloody. It's one thing to stop an object in motion. It's quite another to change someone's heart."

"Whose heart are you trying to change?" Tinker asked.

Tooloo snorted. "You want a list? It's quite long. You are on it. Things would be easier if you'd stayed hidden. But no, you plowed on through all the obstacles I put in your path. You gave yourself to my daughter and she made you into a baited trap. You have no idea how tiring it is to see something coming and no matter how hard you try, the ones you love best ignore your warnings. The only reason you escaped them that first time was because they didn't know what they'd gotten hold of. They know now."

"It would help if you actually explained things in a plain, straightforward way," Tinker grumbled. "Something that didn't involve chessboards and chickens and double-talk."

"I have centuries of experience that say otherwise." Tooloo waved away the complaint.

This was the Tooloo that Tinker expected to talk to.

Tinker looped back to her original attack plan. "I need the original digital copy of the Dufae Codex."

Tooloo gave a tired laugh. "See? The world's greatest oracle has told you that you don't need it, but you persist instead of stopping and actually using that clever brain of yours."

Tinker gritted her teeth against the urge to scream in frustration. "The Skin Clan has what Dufae— Unbounded Brilliance—stole from Iron Mace. They might use—"

"Oh, they will." Tooloo closed her eyes. "Shortly. The clock is ticking. You're wasting time."

"Then give me the Codex!"

"I've seen what giving you the Codex now will do. You'll waste time flipping pages and coming to conclusions already reached. Do you think that Unbounded Brilliance did nothing in France for all those years and years that he lived on Earth?"

"I think he found a solution!" Tinker shouted.

"Would he not have returned home if he had?" Tooloo asked calmly.

Tinker threw up her hands in frustration. "The gateways were closed behind him, cutting him off!"

"Would that stop you?" Tooloo asked. "Would you stay in place if you knew the answer to save your world?"

"No," Tinker huffed, because the truth was a gut-punch. She eyed the chessboard. "How much time?"

Tooloo spread her hands. "You are not playing against me. There are others in the game. It could be as soon as an hour or as late as tomorrow. The less said, the better."

Other *intanyai seyosa* who could see the future. Tinker eyed the chessboard. Stormsong had said that one of the twins shared her *nuenae*. Lain had said that Chloe was probably the result of the same type of mass fertilization of eggs that created the twins. How many sisters did Chloe have?

Tinker eyed the white pieces on the chessboard. Was Tooloo saying, in so many words, that at this moment the "monkeys" could be spying on this conversation? Tinker pulled out her tablet and took a picture of the board. If the substituted pieces were some kind of code, it was going to take a while for her to figure out. If she had time...

If she was going to fight her shadow again, she'd better start by hiding where she couldn't be found until she had a game plan. Someplace where she had access to all sorts of things she could turn into unexpected weapons.

20: I AM A BEING CAPABLE OF DOING TERRIBLE THINGS. RUN.

The shopping trip had been a mistake. Oilcan was beginning to realize that he'd committed a cascade of blunders. He probably should have waited until the *domana* were back in the city. He could have asked someone to buy the furniture for him; half of Team Tinker had been at Sacred Heart. He should have started small—just beds for the twins. He shouldn't have brought all the kids. He should have left Once More With Feeling the moment he found out that the ancient manager was the only employee in the store. He felt like he was stuck in resin that was slowly turning to amber.

They'd been there for hours as he bought out full sections of the store. Seven beds. Seven mattresses. All the linens. (Cattail Reeds added "fabric" to her list when she saw what the store had in stock for sheets and blankets.) Four dining room tables and dozens of chairs. Two dress racks. Two student desks. Every lamp that they could find. Even with three trucks, it was going to take more than one trip to ferry everything back to Sacred Heart.

The manager moved frustratingly slow. He wanted to tag their purchases as "sold," do math by hand, twice, then fill out stock inventory sheets. The last step Oilcan was certain should have been done at the end of the day when customers weren't standing and waiting. Bored, the kids investigated other parts of the store and started to bring him impulse buys. A garden gnome statue. An old leather suitcase. A singing fish. A giant German beer stein. A Raggedy Ann doll. A picture of Jeff Goldbloom in a delicate metal rose frame. (The last mystified Oilcan as he wasn't sure if Cattail realized that the photograph could be swapped out of the beautiful frame.)

Oilcan didn't mind the kids buying the random odd things except he wanted to be done with the "buying" and move on to "loading." Each new purchase jumped the process backward as the manager would stop everything to find the "sold" tags. It was already well past noon and they were going to need to make two round trips to get all the furniture to Sacred Heart. Everything would need to be loaded and unloaded and dragged up three flights of stairs. It was quite possible that after going through the grueling process once, Andy, Guy, Rebecca, and possibly Blue Sky would bail. Postponing the second load might be a wise decision but it meant picking what went on the first load became all important. He wanted to make sure each of his kids got something today that they truly wanted.

"Can we start loading the big pieces?" Oilcan asked. It would keep the kids from finding new things.

The manager shook his head. "I need to supervise loading to make sure you only take what you're paying for. Store policy. That's why we normally have employees load up purchases."

Oilcan realized that he was clenching his hands into fists out of frustration.

"We could go get ice cream," Blue Sky said.

There were cheers and more than one "I'm hungry" made Oilcan realize that they'd missed lunch.

"You will be back?" the old man said in a voice full of suspicion.

"Yes." Oilcan peeled off bills from his roll of cash to cover all that the manager had totaled up so far. It was an alarming amount but Tinker had promised to cover his expenses for a year. "You could hold onto this as good-faith money."

The manager sighed deeply. "I'll get you a receipt."

As Oilcan crossed East Carson Street, there was a distant *boom* of an explosion, muffled by the hills and trees to the point that it became a barely audible thud. He paused on the opposite sidewalk to scan the horizon. A flock of birds rose from the far bank of the Monongahela River, startled by the explosion. A thick plume of black smoke went up against the gray blanket of clouds that covered the sky. It looked miles away, visible only because the explosion occurred on a hilltop.

"What do you think it is?" Oilcan asked Rebecca and Guy, who were pointing at the dark smoke and discussing it in whispers.

"I think it's a black willow," the tengu girl said. "There was a report of several trees moving toward Oakland. Don't worry; the tengu are dealing with the situation. They must have dropped some kind of explosive on it."

"Dynamite," Guy murmured but didn't offer any more information.

Tinker had said that Windwolf and the other *domana* were far to the east, miles from the city, with a majority of the elf forces. It left the city defended only by a small force of royal marines, the EIA, the local police, and the tengu. It was a lot of land to cover for a small force. The bridges created choke points and Oilcan was in the South Side, on the wrong side of the Monongahela River.

Maybe they should leave after they got the ice cream. They could come back tomorrow. He would say leave now, but all his kids were excited about their first taste of the human treat. Ten minutes shouldn't make any difference.

He walked into the ice cream shop where his kids were gazing at the selections in wonder and confusion. The shop was an assault on the senses. The walls and ceiling were painted in pink stripes. Gaudy beaded chandeliers provided the light. A brightly colored toy train ran along a track near the ceiling. The sound system was playing "Lucy in the Sky with Diamonds." It had a long, glass-enclosed, refrigerated counter displaying dozens of different flavors of ice cream in five-gallon tubs and then, at the far end, little bins of possible toppings like peanuts, gummy bears, M&M candies, and brightly colored sprinkles. The employees were two teenage girls in cute blue aprons. They had swooned at the sight of ruggedly handsome Guy

Kryskill and seemed oblivious to the fact that there were two *sekasha*, four visibly battered elf children, and seven assorted "others" standing in front of them.

"Cotton Candy?" Barley read the Elvish runes that had been hand-scrawled under the English labels. Whoever had done the signs had simply used direct translation of the words without realizing that most of the names were utter nonsense to elves. "White House?"

Blue Sky did his best to describe the flavors. "White House is vanilla with cherries in it. I'm not sure how to describe Cotton Candy except as very sweet." Blue Sky eyed the tubs sitting next to Cotton Candy: Moose Tracks and Muddy Sneakers. He pointed to a tub at the far end of the counter, probably to avoid having to explain the oddly named flavors. "I usually get the chocolate peanut butter."

"Peanut butter?" Thorne and the kids said with excitement. Oilcan's lone jar of peanut butter had been scraped and then licked clean within minutes of the elves discovering the spread. He hadn't been able to find a second jar; the stores had been picked clean of pantry staples since the gate failed.

The type of cones had to be explained: waffle, sugar, cake, pretzel, or chocolate-dipped. All fifty different possible toppings were named and some of them needed to be described and/or sampled. The process of getting ice cream ground to a halt as everyone considered the hundreds of combinations.

Oilcan normally got his mother's favorite of Rocky Road. He wasn't sure what being transformed into an elf had done to his sense of taste. Tinker had been dismayed by the change. He wasn't sure he wanted to find out that he no longer liked Rocky Road with all his kids to witness his disappointment. "I'll take a waffle cone with two scoops of chocolate peanut butter, please. No toppings." He handed across enough money to cover a dozen of their most expensive cones. "I'm paying for everyone."

The taste was different. Better. Amazing even, but in a weird way, since with every bite he expected normal chocolate peanut butter.

Moon Dog was digging out dime-sized gold coins from a leather pouch and looking puzzled.

Most Pittsburghers wouldn't take gold coinage; the exchange rate fluctuated wildly every Shutdown since it was based on the amount of rare metals within the coins. (To be fair, most currency fluctuated but most Pittsburghers weren't aware that humans had anything but American dollars.) Nor did the elves completely trust the human cash. What ended up happening was that the enclaves acted as banks for the Wind Clan elves living within the city. They would exchange gold coins for dollars that they earned from their human customers.

Someone should have explained it to Moon Dog. Had he not stayed in an enclave since he arrived in Pittsburgh? Or had the Wind Clan elves turned a blind eye to the Stone Clan *sekasha*? It was doubtful since Tinker threatened to exile anyone who refused to help incoming elves because they weren't Wind Clan.

It could be possible, though, that the Wind Clan elves were more scared of the young warrior than they were of being exiled.

Oilcan's ice cream cone had started to melt down over his hand.

"I am paying for everyone's ice cream," Oilcan said between licks to control the melting. "Please consider it as a gift. It is the least I can do for the help that everyone is giving me and my household."

"You are so kind." Moon Dog put away his coins. "Thank you."

Despite being young and obviously smitten with Guy, the teenage girls were fast and efficient. Whenever anyone finally decided what they wanted, the girls put together the ice cream combination of flavor, size, container, and toppings with practiced speed. In a matter of minutes, they had served all eleven people with Oilcan plus created three "doggy bowls" for the elfhounds guarding the trucks. According to Andy, chocolate was off-limits for the dogs, so they got plain vanilla with a bottle of water as a chaser.

"Shit!" the taller girl suddenly hissed as she jerked back from the glass counter. The girl fumbled with the various serving utensils, whispering fiercely, "A rat! Don't let the customers see."

All the *sekasha* had gone to full alert at her abrupt motion.

"I don't think that's a rat," the other girl whispered back. "It's pink and long and snaky."

A weirdly familiar squeal of delight came from the counter. The baby dragon accompanying the talking mice had been pink and snaky.

"Wait, wait, wait!" Oilcan waved at Thorne and Moon Dog and Blue Sky to stand down. "I think it might be Joy. She's a dragon."

"A dragon?" everyone in the store echoed.

"Yummy!" a baby-girl voice cried in English from the tub of Cotton Candy flavor. The tiny pink dragon popped up to put her cream-covered paws against the glass. "Knock, knock! Who's there?"

Everyone started to talk at once. Because Oilcan had named the dragon aloud, the counter girls were under the impression that it was his dragon and were not pleased. Guy and Andy wanted to know how Oilcan kept finding dragons; they seemed to think that the dragons were like scaly talking elfhounds. Thorne wanted to know if this was a good dragon like Impatience or a bad dragon like Malice. His kids were freaking out, thinking that it meant there were some oni somewhere close by. Moon Dog seemed to be the only one unimpressed.

"*Waya!*" Moon Dog had gotten a three-scoop cone with chocolate peanut butter, cotton candy, and cookie dough. "And this ice cream is *waya* too."

"She's ruined that entire tub!" The tall girl pointed at Joy while keeping as far back as she could get. "It was nearly full! I just opened it this morning."

"I'll pay for it." Oilcan handed over the cash and then ducked behind the counter to lift the cotton candy flavor's tub out of the freezer.

The baby dragon continued to happily shove fistfuls of blue-and-pink ice cream into her mouth. "Nom, nom, nom."

"You are not taking that dangerous beast back to our enclave," Thorne said firmly and then seemed to realize how it sounded. "Are you?"

Was he? Oilcan didn't know what he was going to do with the baby dragon. This wasn't like finding Impatience at his barn, far away from any other person who could be harmed by Oilcan's curiosity about the strange beast. There were more than a dozen people crowded into the small shop, counting the frightened counter girls. According to the tengu, though, the baby dragon had come to Elfhome with the twins and was claiming them as her Chosen. Surely Joy wasn't that dangerous.

Since Joy had spoken English, he decided that asking questions might be an intelligent thing to do. "Hi, there. What are you doing here? Were you looking for me?"

"Ice cream! Yummy!" Joy said in her baby-girl voice.

"Oilcan! Oilcan!" someone squeaked.

It was the four white mice from his odd waking dream. They sat astride their tiny hoverbikes on top of the ice cream counter. Instead of racing goggles, they wore wide-brim hats like the ones that Roach had tried to get for Team Tinker. Their hats were different colors: pink, red, green, and blue. Based on everyone's surprised reaction, the squeaking mice were real, not a figment of Oilcan's imagination.

Realizing that they'd caught his attention, the mice all started to talk at once with excited gesturing.

"We've been looking all over the city for you..."

"...we can't find Alexander anywhere!"

"You're in danger..."

"...so you need to cast it right away."

"Whoa! Whoa! Whoa!" Oilcan motioned for them to stop talking. "One at a time. I can't understand you when you all talk at once."

They paused for a few seconds—and then all started to talk again, only faster and louder. This triggered a sudden fistfight, with three of the four mice flailing at one another while squeaking, "I was talking! Just shut up and let me talk! I'll do it! Me!"

The fourth—the one that sounded like Christopher Robin—stood to one side, going, "This isn't helping!"

Oilcan leaned closer to the mice, peering down

at them. They weren't living animals but small, well-articulated robots. What made it difficult to tell which mouse was talking was that their mouths didn't move and at least two—the red and the green—were using the same computer-generated voice. Oilcan struggled to remember the names that went to the various colors. Nikola Tesla Dufae had been the one that sounded like Christopher Robin and he wore blue, marking him as the only boy. The pink one had a girl's voice but was named Chuck Norris. Red and Green were the Jawbreakers.

Baby Duck edged closer to the mice. Robotic or not, she was barely controlling her greedy hands from scooping up the new cute little animals. The rest of his kids were attempting to hide behind Thorne, staring with confused fear.

"Westernlands mice can talk?" Merry whispered.

"I'm not sure they're really mice," Blue Sky answered her.

Nikola's mouse suddenly transformed into a very large dog. "We don't have time for this!"

Everyone shouted with surprise. The three mice blew raspberries at the dog.

"How . . . how are you doing this?" Oilcan asked. These were his new baby cousins? *Oh, Tinker is going to totally freak out.*

"We're dream walking!" Chuck Norris cried. "Joy taught us how!"

"We're baby dragons!" Green Jawbreaker stated firmly, but then added less surely, "Kind of. Wood sprites. *Intanyai seyosa.* It's all kind of the same thing."

"We can be anything we want while dream walking," Red said. "We're just used to being mice, that's all."

"It's a comfortable size," Nikola said as he turned back into a mouse. "Tesla feels too big to be just one of us."

"We're here, but we're not really here," Red Jawbreaker said. "We're like a figment of your imagination but less so."

Green smacked her sister. "That was a stupid analogy."

"It doesn't matter!" Chuck Norris cried. "You're all in danger! We're here to warn you and give you top secret information!"

"Yeah! We're part of the Resistance now!" Red pointed at her wide-brim hat.

"The Resistance?" Oilcan echoed. "What's that?"

Guy looked a mix of confused and horrified. "We are Pittsburgh?"

"We are Team Tinker!" the mice squeaked.

"Hooyah!" Chuck Norris added in.

"The Flying Monkeys are setting a trap for the *domana*!" Nikola said. "It's a spell using one of the *nactka* that was in the Dufae spell-locked box! They've got troops moving into position to attack the moment that the spell is cast. They know where you are right now. They're coming for you! You need to get to a place where you can cast a shield spell."

"I'm a *domana* now," Oilcan said. "I can just use my hands to cast—"

"It won't work!" the mice shouted in chorus.

"It needs to be the special spell that Lou and Jilly made up!" Chuck cried.

"They've made the luggage mules fight until they found what Dufae was looking for!" Red said.

Green grumbled, "They wouldn't let us race the mules while they working on them."

"Joy has the printout of the..." Nikola paused to look around. "Joy, where's the printout?"

"Quick! We need to find it!" Chuck Norris cried.

The mice started up their hoverbikes to fly around the room. They were fearless, making jumps that put Oilcan's heart into his throat until he remembered that the mice weren't really there—that the hoverbikes were some kind of illusion. Chuck Norris jumped past him and he realized the mouse was making the engine noise for the little hoverbike.

"Here it is!" Green called from inside the ice cream counter.

Everyone leaned in close to see that a full-size piece of paper was tucked between the ice cream barrels, covered with the metal ink of a computer-printed spell and some handwritten notes in crayon along the margins. The other mice landed their miniature hoverbikes beside Green.

"The oni are coming! Now!" Nikola said. "The main force is hitting Oakland but there are troops coming from the boat ramp at the dog park."

"What?" Oilcan said.

This triggered all the mice to talk at the same time.

"You've got to run!" the mice cried. "You need to get someplace safe with a casting circle!"

"Bong!" Green had suddenly made an odd chiming noise.

"What was that?" the other mice cried.

Green threw up her hands. "Print job is done!"

"Hooyah!" Chuck Norris cried and vanished. Red and Green blinked out of existence.

"You need to go," Nikola said. "You need to go now. Run."

Then he too was gone.

Joy climbed up onto Oilcan's shoulder. She grabbed the ice cream bucket from his hands and vanished, taking the ice cream with her.

"Holy. Shit." Andy muttered exactly what Oilcan was feeling.

"We're leaving," Oilcan announced. "Everyone to the trucks."

Oilcan waved toward the door as he took out his phone. He needed to call Tinker and warn her. The mice claimed not to be able to find her. He wasn't sure where she'd gone; he'd seen the Rolls-Royce leaving Poppymeadows while he was in Oakland. She didn't answer her phone. Guessing that Tinker might have gone to tell Esme about the twins, he called Lain.

"Hey, kiddo," Esme answered the phone and started to talk without even asking who was calling and why. Lain and Tinker both did it all the time; until recently he hadn't questioned it. "She was here but she left a while ago."

"I need to talk to her," Oilcan said.

"I think she's gone dark," Esme said. "I'm not sure where she's at."

"Okay. Thanks." He hung up. Tinker had gone into hiding again? Why would she do that? Had she realized that the oni were about to attack Oakland? No, if she did, she would be heading back to Poppymeadows. Something else made her run and hide.

His kids were out the door but the two high-school-aged clerks were still behind the counter, looking scared and uncertain. The oni were coming for Oilcan and his kids, but they might grab the girls for the whelping pens.

"You should close down early." Oilcan motioned for

them to follow him. "Your boss will understand. You shouldn't be here when the oni sweep into this area. You can come with us if you want."

The girls looked through the big storefront window to Guy standing by his flashy pickup, glanced at each other, and nodded.

"We need to lock up first." The taller girl opened the cash register, took out the bigger bills, and dropped them in the store's safe. The shorter girl started to close lids on bins and to turn off lights. "It will just take us three minutes!"

"We'll wait for you." Oilcan walked across the street to their convoy of three pickup trucks. The kids were deciding who would ride where. Thorne and Moon Dog had gotten their range weapons out of the crate strapped onto the back of the flatbed. They were standing guard, scanning the area, bows in hand.

Oilcan did a head count and came up short. Who was missing? He ticked through who they'd brought: his five kids, Blue Sky, Spot, Thorne, Moon Dog, Guy, and Andy. "Where's Rebecca?"

"Scouting." Guy pointed skyward. "Ninja-like."

Oilcan pointed toward the ice cream shop. "Those girls are coming with us. Let them ride with you."

The teenaged cousins both nodded. Andy was older by two years but, judging by his expression, was confused by what was going on. Guy was only sixteen yet he looked as solemn and determined as a veteran soldier. Oilcan was glad that Guy would be driving. He seemed to have a better grasp of the risks involved.

Blue Sky unlocked the driver's door of the flatbed. "Where are we going to?" He shook his head even as he asked, "Back to Sacred Heart?"

It was a bad sign that even Blue Sky recognized that as a horrible idea. By his tone, though, he was willing to try if Oilcan committed to it.

"No, not back to Oakland," Oilcan said. If the oni were hunting down *domana*, then Forge and Jewel Tear's presence at Sacred Heart was going to make it a prime target. Oilcan and his kids would have to cut through the thickest of the fighting to get to questionable safety of the half-finished enclave. "We need a casting circle."

"Tinker blew the one at the hotel to hell along with Chloe Polanski," Blue Sky said.

"Yeah, I know." Oilcan held out his keys. "Why don't you drive my pickup?"

Blue Sky gave the key ring a wary look. "Why switch?"

"If we get in a running fight, I want to be in the heavier truck," Oilcan said.

"Okay." Blue Sky tossed Oilcan the flatbed's keys. "Then I'll have all the other kids with me?"

"Most of them." Oilcan trusted Blue Sky to cut and run if he knew that the others depended on him. "I'm counting on you to get them someplace safe if the shit hits the fan."

The boy nodded solemnly.

"If you need a casting circle," Guy called, "my brother has one at his shop."

"Okay, we're going there, then," Oilcan said. One problem solved. But how did he get the spell to Tinker? He needed to copy it first. He grabbed his tablet out of his pickup. He put the paper on the flatbed and photographed it several times, focusing first on the tangled knot that was the spell he never seen before and then instructions written in crayon around it.

He emailed the photographs of the spell to Tinker

with a note to cast it immediately. He didn't bother to explain how he got it. The problem was Tinker would only get the pictures if she knew to check her email. She could be literally anywhere in the city; knowing her, it was someplace with an internet connection. Email, though, was probably the last thing on her mind. He might be able to count on her to *know*, the same way that Esme *knew* it was him on the phone looking for Tinker without being told. He didn't like the idea of leaving it to some weird magical talent. Tinker could get laser focused on her own goals and ignore the rest of the universe until something whacked her hard.

He needed something to catch her attention. Wait, he could try a version of the "battle code" that the Harbingers were doing that morning.

He tapped the Spell Stones, summoning power. He dismissed it after a second. He tapped it a second time, holding it longer, dismissed it, repeated it. Short and long. Two shorts. One extra-long. He waited a minute and repeated the cycle. *Email.*

From somewhere north, a flare of power flashed. Held for a long moment. Another short flash. *Roger.*

Good. Another problem down. He just needed all his chicks gathered together so they could flee the area.

The ice cream girls came out of their shop, locked the door, and then hurried across the street. As they climbed into Guy's cab, Oilcan double-checked who was in his pickup with Blue Sky. Rustle was in the cab since he had the broken arm, with Merry taking up the middle of the bench seat. Spot and Baby Duck were in the bed with the puppy Repeat. It put all the younger kids in one vehicle, but Barley and Cattail Reeds had gotten into the bed of Guy's pickup.

Oilcan wished he could send someone older with the little kids. Neither Barley nor Cattail Reeds would be much of a help in a battle. Moon Dog was a possible addition but Oilcan couldn't trust Blue Sky to keep his temper around the outsider. At least they were only ten minutes or so from Gryffin Doors.

Oilcan patted the door. "Go to Geoff's place. We'll catch up. If Geoff's isn't good, head to your brother's place."

Blue Sky nodded understanding. He started up the pickup and headed west.

Where was Rebecca? Oilcan didn't want to leave her.

Moon Dog suddenly sprinted away, heading east, nocking an arrow even as he dashed down the street.

Chaos came around the corner, a confusion of bodies and wings. Oilcan wasn't sure where the swarm of wolf-sized hornets came from but at its heart was the tengu female, fleeing for her life. Moon Dog raced to meet Rebecca halfway, firing spell arrows. The wooden shafts transformed to light as they left the bow. The brilliance lanced through the swarm, cutting through several hornets at once. One or two dropped from the sky, but many of the others merely flashed translucence, revealing that the creatures were magical constructs. The massive insects were a solid illusion projected by a smaller creature within the puppet shell.

They were like the foo dogs that had attacked the salvage yard. Illusion or not, the hornets would be dangerously strong and hard to hurt.

"Go, go, go!" Oilcan yelled at Guy.

Guy didn't like it, but he understood he was responsible for Barley, Cattail Reeds, and Andy. He roared off even as Andy shouted, "What? Wait! Rebecca!"

Oilcan ran toward Moon Dog. The *sekasha's* personal protective shield haloed the warrior with a dark gleam. The spell couldn't take fast repeated hits over a short period of time. A machine gun could eat its way through the shield. The swarm of giant hornets might be able to breach it. Nor would Moon Dog's shield protect Rebecca; the spell only extended a hand's width from the male's body. Oilcan needed to get close enough to cast a *domana* shield on the two.

It will be just like playing backup for a band, coming in for the chorus, Oilcan thought to calm himself. *Prepare for the chord.* He tapped the Spell Stones, pulling power to him as he ran. *Wait for the beat.* As he closed on Moon Dog, Rebecca cried out in pain and tumbled onto the ground by the elf's feet. A hornet clung to her leg, lancing her with a glistening black stinger the size of a butcher knife. She whimpered as it struck her again even as she tried to wrestle it off her. Behind her was a dark flood of giant hornets, loud as an entire orchestra of angry violins.

Now! Oilcan stepped in front of Moon Dog and cast his shield.

The swarm crashed on the invisible edge of the spell's dome. They recovered to circle around the shield, a hundred alien faces staring at him. Oilcan never thought he was scared of insects but fear washed through him at the sight.

Thorne Scratch had kept pace with him despite being able to outrun him. She had shouldered her bow. As his shield went up, she drew her sword and stabbed through the giant hornet puppet on Rebecca to pierce the insect within. "Aim for the center of their thorax!"

Elfhome hornets were normally "Pittsburgh colors" of mostly black with touches of gold and only the size of a man's thumb. Their stings were extremely painful but not normally deadly. Oilcan had burned their cone-shaped paper nests whenever they had taken up residence at the salvage yard or out at his barn.

The oni's attack hornets were amber with stripes of black and, judging by the flash impressions of when the puppet-shell went translucent, large as a rat. Oilcan had no idea how deadly their poison was.

Oilcan's shield had stopped the bulk of the swarm but three hornets had been close enough to be included inside his shield. Oilcan held the spell, trusting the others to deal with them. Moon Dog and Thorne killed the insects with quick, efficient stabs.

"We should reserve arrows." Thorne sheathed her sword to check Rebecca's wound. "Use force strike while holding the shield."

"Oh damn, that burns!" Rebecca hissed in pain. "We've got to move. They're off-loading an entire platoon from a barge. The hornets are just the first wave."

"Can you walk?" Oilcan asked, as Rebecca hadn't gotten off the ground.

"I can fly," she said through gritted teeth.

Oilcan steeled himself to do a force strike into the swarm without dropping his shield. This would be a bad time to mess up his fingering. *Hold the shield steady. Force strike!* The spell smashed away from him, reducing the hornets in its path to small wet splatters on the broken pavement. It also took out a stop sign and part of a building behind the insects. "Oops."

"Only lives matter in war," Thorne said.

He nodded but still aimed his force strikes with more care. It took three tries, but he smashed the insects to pulp. He dropped his shield and cried, "Let's go!"

"I need a boost to get off the ground," Rebecca said. The two *sekasha* hauled her to her feet.

"On three," Thorne said. "One. Two. Three."

They flung the tengu girl up higher than Oilcan thought possible. Her great black wings swept downward and she climbed higher.

"They're coming!" Rebecca cried as she rose above the third-story buildings.

"Run!" Thorne commanded.

They ran back to the flatbed. Oilcan scrambled into the driver's seat and turned the key. The big engine rumbled to life. Oilcan had never heard anything so reassuring sounding. Thorne climbed in the passenger side. Moon Dog vaulted onto the back. A moment later, Rebecca landed beside the male elf.

"Hold on, this might get crazy!" Oilcan stomped on the accelerator. He'd have to be careful on turns and stops. The flatbed didn't have any sides or safety belts to keep the two in the back on the truck. It was one of the main reasons why he'd put the little kids in his pickup. The other problem was that the flatbed was a beast to drive. Blue Sky had mad skills at driving but the truck needed someone tall enough to work the stiff double-clutch manual transmission. Oilcan practically had to stand on the clutch to shift into second. It would have been unfair to expect the little half-elf to do it in a panic situation.

Oilcan was roaring up to fourth gear when Moon Dog called, "Here they come! On fast little chariots!"

On what? Oilcan glanced into his driver's side mirror. The oni had hoverbikes. Of course they did! There seemed to be a baker's dozen. A menacing black Jaguar sports car growled around the corner and joined the pack. The oni hoverbikes weren't racing machines; street bikes became highly unstable over ninety miles per hour. The sports car wasn't much better. The flatbed was stable as a rock and had a powerful V8 engine. Sheer physics were on Oilcan's side.

Rebecca suddenly slid across the weapons crate and in through the back window. She'd dismissed her wings. Sweat covered her face. "The poison is setting in. I don't know how much longer I'm going to be upright."

"You're fine," Oilcan said to calm himself, shifting into fifth. If he ignored the guns, it was just a simple street race. He'd been racing since he was ten, just not with so many lives on the line. "It's fine. Everything is fine."

"I'll deal with them." Thorne pushed Rebecca down onto the floor to get her out of the way, and went out the window.

If Oilcan wasn't so scared, he would probably feel sorry for the oni. Hoverbikes did not offer a lot of protection in the best of times. Also, the only people in Pittsburgh who knew their limits better than him were Tinker and Blue Sky. "Hold on, we're making a right-hand turn!"

"We're braced!" Thorne shouted back.

He made the turn as fast as he dared onto Tenth Street, shifting back down to fourth to give him more control. Two blocks ahead, the Tenth Street Bridge rose up to cross the Monongahela River. Hoverbikes couldn't cross wide bodies of water; the magic involved in the lift drive required a high surface tension that rivers didn't afford. If the oni wanted to give chase, they were going to have to stick to the straight, narrow shot of the road. Nothing to hide behind. Limited weaving and bobbing.

More importantly, it would lead the oni forces away from Oilcan's kids.

The narrow, three-lane suspension bridge painted Pittsburgh gold ran fifty feet above the river with a span of a quarter mile. Oilcan floored the accelerator, shifting up through fifth to sixth gear. The big flatbed truck had a powerful engine meant to carry heavy loads at highway speeds, but it meant that without a load, the rig could fly. He wanted to get as far ahead of the pack as he could. His mind was racing even further ahead, mapping out a course. He heard Thorne get her rifle out of the weapon's crate.

"Hold steady!" Thorne shouted.

Oilcan checked his side mirrors. The hoverbikes and Jaguar fanned out behind them, taking up all three lanes. There was a crack of a rifle. One of the bikes disintegrated at eighty miles per hour as the wounded rider allowed part of the machine to touch the pavement. The bikes started to weave back and forth in the narrow lane, which was a horrible plan at that speed with those vehicles. Two collided, made contact with the bridge's side barrier, and instantly became tumbling bits and pieces. One tried to pop up onto the arching main cable. It missed the landing, hit the railing of the pedestrian walk, lost its balance, and slid off the side. The oni rider fell screaming into the river far below.

Thorne shot again, taking out another. Eight hover-bikes closed quickly.

"I'm taking another right turn ahead!" Oilcan warned as they neared the end of the bridge. He downshifted to gain more control over the flatbed. "Going into a tunnel."

"Tunnel?" Thorne repeated to confirm.

"Yes! A short tunnel!" Oilcan shouted. "We'll only be in it a few minutes at this speed!"

The end of the bridge was a confusing mess as there were various levels of road crossing their line of sight. The four lanes of the Parkway crossed directly overhead at the end of the bridge. It obscured the fact that on the other side of the intersection, the century-old Armstrong Tunnel cut through the base of the bluff, directly under Mercy Hospital.

"Hang on!" Oilcan called as they hit the end of the bridge and ducked under the Parkway. The bridge and the tunnel didn't match up completely, creating the need to swerve slightly. His wheels squealed in complaint as he entered the tunnel at nearly a hundred miles per hour.

A single line of antique lights dimly lit the old tunnel. The dark arching limestone roof and the bend in the middle made the tunnels seem claustrophobic despite their fifteen-foot clearance. Oilcan rarely used the tunnels. He couldn't remember exactly how long they were. He was fairly sure that the tunnels were short. The upcoming exit definitely was onto a T-shaped intersection. Making a ninety-degree turn at his speed could be deadly, especially to the unsecured warriors on the back.

Oilcan glanced in the side mirrors. All the remaining hoverbikes were just entering the tunnel. He'd worried slightly that they would split up, using the outbound tunnel instead of entering the close quarters of the inbound tunnel. Apparently they weren't thinking that far ahead.

He slowed as much as he dared, downshifting to fifth gear. "We're going to turn shortly! Hard left!"

Rebecca surprised him by suddenly leaning across him to secure his seat belt.

"Stop at the end of the tunnel," Thorne said.

"What?" Oilcan said as Thorne's rifle cracked again, echoing loudly in the stone tunnel. Another hoverbike disintegrated with a horrifying noise as its wounded or dead rider lost control.

"She said stop at the end of the tunnel!" Rebecca said while putting on her own seat belt.

What was Thorne planning? Certainly the tunnel took away the hoverbikes' maneuverability but they were still moving at close to seventy miles per hour. Oilcan slowed more, downshifting to fourth. If he was making a full stop, he had to slow even more. He only had at maximum forty feet of road at the end of the tunnel before he hit a literal wall.

The hoverbikes closed fast even as he neared the end of the tunnel.

He glanced into his rearview mirror to check on the *sekasha*. The two warriors leapt from the back, shields gleaming, swords drawn. The hoverbikes were roaring down on them. The Jaguar, however, was nowhere to be seen.

"Shit!" Oilcan hissed. He stomped down on the brakes. The sports car had taken the outbound tunnel instead of following directly behind them. The wheels squealed as the big truck slid forward. He fought to control the slide, downshifting so the engine wouldn't stall. He couldn't let the truck turn too soon. The bed alone was twenty-six feet long and the tunnel was only twenty-two feet wide. If he lost control, he'd wedge the truck sideways in the narrow passage. Once he was clear of the tunnel, though, he needed to turn to face the sports car that was trying to outmaneuver him by taking the outbound tube.

The oni in the car had guns.

Oilcan had a powerful heavy truck and a ram-prow front bumper.

As the flatbed's cab slid past the tunnel opening, he could hear the roar of the oncoming Jaguar. The outbound tube was a mere six feet from him. A narrow traffic island separated the two lanes. Oilcan checked his mirrors. His tail wasn't clear yet. He let the truck continue to slide forward, the air thick with black smoke from his tires. The snarl of the Jaguar grew louder. Not clear yet. He saw the running lights of the oncoming car reflected in the white tile walls.

Clear!

He floored the accelerator. The big truck leapt forward just as the Jaguar came roaring out of the tunnel. The driver wasn't familiar with the road; he tried a panic stop as he realized that there was a building directly ahead of him, in less than forty feet. The Jaguar started to swing right, aiming for the driveway beside the building. The flatbed jumped the curb, and plowed into the Jaguar square in the passenger door. His seat belt bit deep into Oilcan's chest as the impact checked their speed. He kept the accelerator nailed to the floor.

The Jaguar tried to pull away but Oilcan wrenched

the flatbed's steering wheel, turning with the Jaguar as he shoved it across the road. He slammed it through a low railing and into the retaining wall beyond. Its aluminum body crumpled like a beer can. Its horn went off in an unending death wail.

Behind him, bits and pieces of hoverbikes rained out of the inbound tunnel. There was no sign of the riders.

Oilcan put the flatbed into reverse and backed away from the crumpled Jaguar.

"You going to hit it again?" Rebecca was holding a pistol ready.

"It's not going to be following us." Oilcan didn't want to think of its trapped and probably dead occupants. "That's all that matters."

Thorne and Moon Dog came running out of the tunnel and leapt onto the flatbed.

"Go!" Thorne said.

Oilcan turned and headed for Gryffin Doors, praying that his kids had arrived there safely.

21: KNICKKNACK PADDYWHACK GIVE A DOG A BONE

Tommy started cautiously around the old racetrack on Neville. He'd studied it closely while building his own course but it had been years since he had taken its insane jumps and sharp, unexpected turns. Everything was in better shape than he expected. The banks were clear of weeds and the jumps had been recently reinforced.

Someone had to be using it for practice. Was it workers from the shipyard? If they were rabid hover-bike fans, they would recognize Tommy. They would know that he kept a stable of prostitutes who worked Liberty Avenue.

The track went under the interstate and split. The main branch looped back but a small section followed an older go-kart track through the maze of side streets. On the turn's inside wall, someone had painted a black crow on a bloodred field.

Tommy hugged the inside curve to get a better

look at it. It was definitely Team Providence's tag. They must have fixed up the old course in order to secretly train their rider. It meant that the off-worlders at the shipyard probably wouldn't recognize Tommy.

As he came looping back, he saw Gaddy had faked a breakdown just before the shipyard's driveway. He pulled to a stop beside her, careful to place an electric pole between him and the armed guards inside the fence.

"I hit a ley line!" Gaddy called to Tommy, louder than necessary. "It made my spell chain slip. I'm just adjusting it."

Like that would ever happen, but it sounded feasible to anyone who didn't know real bike mechanics. The guards didn't seem to be paying much attention. They were gathering in groups, pointing toward the tall windowless building and shaking their heads.

Tommy scanned the shipyard looking for ways into the compound and signs of the kidnapped Undefended. Most of the vehicles in the parking lot had some version of the crowned lion logo on them. Some had the word "Midas" under the logo or "Midas Exploration," while others had the German word *Erobern*. It was hard to tell if there were multiple companies represented or just one with a branding problem. The unmarked van that the attackers had used at Toad Hall sat near the gate. In the mud, just behind the back tire, was a black flannel stuffed cat. It looked like a typical Mokoto handmade special: big derpy eyes, a green heart stitched onto its flank, and a body filled with lavender that Tommy could smell from the street.

Knickknack definitely had been brought to the shipyard.

"You good?" he asked Gaddy.

"Yeah, I'm good." She started her bike back up.

They headed back toward the cargo truck.

Tommy had very limited experience with average human teenage girls. His cousins didn't qualify because their half-oni status made their lives anything but normal.

Makoto had said, "*Something nasty happened to Red on Earth. She kept walls up around her. Massive stone fortress walls. Nobody got in.*"

The EIA intern, Aiofe, kept a constant flow of information going between her and the elves. So far Tommy had learned indirectly most of her life story including the fact she had three older sisters, went to an all-girls school in Ireland, and was far from comfortable with the male side of any species.

All that Tommy had learned from "Olive Branch" herself was that her human name was Olivia. No last name. No clue to why a teenage girl had been walking the streets as a prostitute last month and was now acting like a drill sergeant to a herd of juvenile elves. Nothing about her made sense. While tall and curvy with beautiful long flame-colored hair, she was modestly dressed in a sundress and sensible shoes. Her hips and ample bust said she could be as old as sixteen but, now and then, her face could be as doe-eyed innocent as a twelve-year old's. Her baby bump said that she was close to three months pregnant by someone other than Forest Moss, who had arrived in Pittsburgh a month ago. Given that Mokoto hadn't seen Olivia on Liberty Avenue prior to a month ago, the pregnancy might be why she was on Elfhome, running from whoever preyed on innocent children.

Tommy could understand running from something like that.

It was becoming obvious that Olivia was clever and cautious but in over her head. She was smart enough to know that they needed to recon the shipyard before using the strength that the royal marines gave them, but she wasn't sure how to do that. She didn't have Tinker's knowledge and control of magic nor her knowledge of the Pittsburgh area and its people. She didn't know about Tommy's powers. Sooner or later she would probably turn to the EIA, which would mean that all the Undefended would probably be detained and deported once Tinker did get her gate up and running.

There was no one on the planet that Tommy trusted more than Mokoto. His little cousin might not be a brute force like Bingo, but he was fearless, clever, and ruthless. More importantly, Mokoto could pass as human. At any point, he could have walked away and left it all to Tommy and Bingo to protect the family. He could have even escaped to Earth and vanished completely. But he hadn't. He'd stayed, backing Tommy at every step, always putting family first, always taking whatever shit life threw at them.

Knickknack was an off-worlder stranger but Mokoto loved him. Tommy knew how shitty it was to fall in love with the wrong person. Annoying as it was to have to sneak around to be with Jewel Tear, at least he had the comfort of knowing that she was safe and sound.

Olivia waved as he and Gaddy roared up to the cargo truck.

"The kids were taken to the shipyard," Tommy said. "We still don't know if they're actually alive or not. The place is heavily guarded."

"From what I overheard, a machine that isn't supposed to be running got turned on and no one seems to know how to turn it off," Gaddy said. "They're not even sure if they should attempt it. They're distracted. Now would be a good time to move."

"How many guards?" Olivia asked.

"I saw at least two dozen different men," Gaddy said. "Not all of them were armed. It seemed to be a mix of workers and guards. Technically we outnumber them."

"Barely," Olivia murmured, still studying the distant building. "Violence will beget violence. It could escalate out of our control quickly. They have the home advantage and solid cover. We would need to breach first the fence and then the buildings. There could be booby traps. They could kill the hostages before we found them. This is like hide-and-seek but in reverse. You can't pull the trigger until you're sure you have the person hiding trapped or you have to race every player to home."

It was an odd way of putting it, but she was right. If the kidnappers wanted Knickknack to build a gate and he was cooperating to keep the girls safe, then it was unlikely that the boy was being held with the others. While Tommy's focus was Knickknack, Olivia had made it clear that saving Peanut Butter Pie was her priority.

Tommy didn't want to walk alone into the armed camp. He didn't like having the women—young, inexperienced, and complete strangers to him—as backup. He considered calling Bingo or Babe but they looked too much like their oni fathers. He couldn't be sure that the royal marines wouldn't kill them. Most of his cousins who could pass as human were still teenagers or younger. Much as he didn't want to go in alone, he couldn't see another way to save Knickknack where the boy wasn't immediately locked up by the EIA. "I noticed a ramp down that dirt side road. I can use it to get over the fence behind the building. If you create a distraction at the front, I can go over the fence and scout for the kids."

Olivia considered and then nodded in agreement.

"I'll move out first," Olivia said as she waved to the marines to get into the back of the truck. "Gaddy, keep pace with him until he slows down to stop, then keep going around the track. Anyone not paying attention to me will probably keep an eye on the moving bike over the one that has stopped."

"Sounds good," Gaddy said.

"Godspeed." Olivia said it like a blessing.

They moved out with the truck in the lead.

This wasn't as insane as taking on a pack of oni warriors by himself in the middle of the forest. It was his experience that humans normally didn't react instantly or fight to the death. They didn't come from a kill-or-be-killed culture. Among the more beast-like lesser oni, the winner often ate the loser. It meant that humans at the shipyard probably wouldn't shoot to kill if they saw him. Probably. He never liked the word "probably." Too often it really meant "you thought wrong."

The big truck trundled the mile to the shipyard, occasionally jumping the curb and riding on the sidewalk. Olivia wasn't the best of drivers although she hadn't stalled the big truck once. The shipyard had two driveways. The first was a dirt road that led back to the small jump Tommy had spotted earlier. Rusty signs stated NO PARKING OR TURNING AROUND. Judging by the weeds, it was last used when Neville Island was still on Earth. Three hundred feet farther on, the shipyard's gate stood guard on a wide paved driveway.

Tommy veered onto the dirt road. Gaddy roared on, passing the big cargo truck as it put on its turn-right signal and slowed to awkwardly make the turn into the driveway. Olivia either misjudged the stopping distance or intentionally didn't stop in time, bending the front gate with her reinforced front bumper. She beeped once, quickly, perhaps hitting the horn by mistake.

By mistake or on purpose, she got what she wanted: everyone in the compound focused on Olivia as she leaned out of the truck's window. Aiofe wasn't in the front cab with her; the translator must have gotten in the back with the marines.

"Sorry!" Olivia called and waved at the guards. "Hello? I'm sorry about your gate! I'm not used to driving something this big through a city."

Olivia was going with a hapless female ploy. With her modest sundress and often childlike face, she was going to throw the men for a loop. She didn't look like someone who had shot a man just minutes ago.

Tommy popped up and over the fence. He slid across the compound where tarps covered pallets loaded with spools of structured fiber filament and five-gallon buckets of gloss white marine paint. He tucked his hoverbike between pallets of paint and pulled the tarp over it. No one seemed to notice his arrival but it could be because Olivia had just put the truck the rest of way through the front gate—slowly—while claiming that she was attempting to back up. She was doing a great job of grinding gears, making it seem like she had no idea what she was doing. Certainly Tommy would buy it if he hadn't just followed her around the city for over an hour. Her steering had been rough but her shifting was fine.

"Whoa, whoa, whoa!" a man was shouting in a tone that was annoyed but not furious.

A squawk of a radio warned Tommy that someone was coming around the far corner of the building. He reached out with his mind and erased himself from the compound. A man carrying a rifle rounded the corner and walked past Tommy without checking his stride. The man swore softly as he saw the truck parked on the remains of the gate with Olivia picking her way down out of the cab going, "Sorry, sorry, sorry."

The rifleman hadn't been in the back lot as Tommy popped over the fence so he must have come out of the building. Unless the door locked behind the man, there was a way in.

Tommy slipped around the corner. There was an unremarkable steel door on the windowless wall. He tried the handle. The latch clicked. The guard hadn't locked it behind him.

He opened the door.

The inside surprised him. He hadn't considered what might be within the building but he would have never imagined what he found.

It was a huge pure white space. The walls and ceiling were all a smooth, slick whiteness. It was like being inside a massive, very clean bathtub. Lights blasted the area. A huge complicated machine was running, humming and whirling and buzzing. It had robotic arms that were placing and removing items. He couldn't guess what it was making. The unfinished item didn't look very boat-like.

There was a path painted on the floor, indicating where it was safe to walk and not be hit by moving machinery.

A man was talking loudly on the far side of the massive room. "I can't tell what's it doing. You know how complicated it is. Some of the pieces in the assembly bins were quite small; it might have been processing for hours before anyone noticed." The man paused as if listening to someone. Tommy's sensitive ears didn't pick up the other person. The man continued as if in response. "No, the kid doesn't have access to anything that can connect with it. I've tried that. And that. And that too."

Moving machine parts obscured the person as Tommy threaded his way through the room. He reached out with his mind. He encountered two different knots of emotions. One person was irritated and considering violence. The other was filled with fear.

The speaker sounded angry. Was the terrified person an Undefended? Tommy's gut feeling was that he'd found one of the missing whores. Tommy focused on locking his mind-clouding ability on the angry person.

After he dodged three massive rolling robotic arms trailing wires, he spotted his target on the opposite side of the building. A big man paced back and forth while talking on a smart phone. Knickknack sat at a table with a laptop, trying to ignore the angry man behind him. The boy was shackled to the floor by a ten-foot chain. The girls were nowhere in sight.

Tommy could cut the big man's throat before the

brute realized he was there but there was the problem of whoever was on the other end of the phone. Was the person someone close by or on the other side of town? With Knickknack chained to the floor and the girls possibly chained elsewhere, Tommy didn't want to be dealing with reinforcements.

Tommy erased himself from the man's mind as he stalked toward the table. The shackle on Knickknack's ankle was jury-rigged from a heavy chain bolted to the floor and a padlock. As Tommy neared the two, he noticed that Knickknack's eyes kept going to the key ring at the big man's side. Did it have the key needed to free the boy?

The boy noticed Tommy. "What the—"

Tommy put a hand over Knickknack's mouth. Tommy shook his head. He could cloud the mind of the man beside him but not the person on the other end of the telephone conversation. He reached over and plucked the key ring from the man's side. He handed the keys to Knickknack and pointed down at the padlock.

The boy's brows knitted together in annoyed confusion. Knickknack glanced at the man, who was clearly unconcerned by Tommy's presence—not realizing that it was because the man was unaware of him.

Was Tommy going to have to beat the boy into unlocking himself?

Tommy's irritation must have shown on his face. Knickknack's eyes went wide and the boy knelt quickly to fumble with the padlock.

There was a crash in the direction of the front gate. What was that Olivia doing now?

"What the hell was that?" The big man glanced toward the table but Tommy made sure that all he saw was Knickknack still typing on the laptop. "I need to go. I'll call you later."

The man strode off as Knickknack carefully placed the unlocked padlock quietly on the floor.

The boy had a black eye but otherwise seemed fine. He was a hair taller than Tommy, dressed in shorts and T-shirt that read YOU MATTER, UNLESS YOU MULTIPLY YOURSELF BY THE SPEED OF LIGHT . . . THEN YOU ENERGY. Tommy wasn't sure what it meant; was it supposed to be funny? Knickknack had on bright yellow tennis shoes that had Japanese lettering written on them. He smelled like he hadn't showered or changed his clothes for days.

"Where's the girls?" Tommy whispered.

"What are you doing here?" Knickknack whispered fiercely. "Are you working with these assholes?"

"This is a rescue, idiot. Where are the girls?"

"A rescue? Is Mokoto here?"

Tommy bounced the boy against the nearest wall. "Where are the girls?"

"They're in the female employee locker room." Knickknack fumbled through the key ring. "I think this key unlocks the door."

The keys jingled softly, betraying the fact that the kid was shaking in fear. It made Tommy angry.

"We're here to save you," Tommy snarled as he took the keys.

"Mokoto is here?" Knickknack repeated.

Tommy bounced him again. "Take me to the locker room where the girls are."

Knickknack indicated the door that the big man had taken. "There's a guard on the girls."

"I'll take care of him," Tommy said.

"Wait." Knickknack started to gather up stuff on the table. "I tried to talk sense into these assholes but it was like talking to a brick wall. They don't understand the danger. There's multiple worlds out there. I have no idea how you key to the right world. I could have been opening a doorway to literally anywhere. There could be massive colonies of man-eating ants, or AI-driven death machines, or diseases that make the Ebola seem like the common cold, or a literal black hole that will use the doorway to tear Pittsburgh into little pieces of matter."

"Just leave it," Tommy said.

"No, I can't. They set up a backdoor to all of Tinker's files. I want to be able to block them after we get out of here—or they'll just do this with someone else."

"We need to hurry," Tommy said.

"Got it!" Knickknack took off running.

A fireproof door led to a maze of hallways and offices.

Knickknack paused at one turn to whisper and point. "The guard is around the corner."

Tommy reached out with his mind. There were lots of minds around the corner. He couldn't tell the girls from their guard. They were too close together and they were all bored.

He signaled Knickknack to get closer to him.

"What are you going to do?" Knickknack whispered. "Shoot him? Everyone will hear the—"

Tommy shoved Knickknack out into the hallway.

Knickknack yelped in surprise, nearly falling on his face before he recovered his balance.

One mind stopped being bored. "What are you doing here, kid?"

"Hey, Zhukov! I need to use a real toilet, not just a

piss jar." Knickknack pointed back behind him. "Mulligan said I could come down here and go proper-like."

Tommy locked his thoughts onto the guard and erased Knickknack from his vision.

"What the hell?" Zhukov said as Tommy stepped around the corner. He was a beefy man with a full beard. "Where did you go, kid?"

Knickknack looked at Tommy walking toward him, back at Zhukov who was turning in circles, and then back at Tommy. He spread his hands with a silent "What?"

Zhukov had a radio and sidearm and probably combat training. Tommy couldn't just whisk the girls away and not count on the man summoning help.

"Take the keys." Tommy handed the keyring to Knickknack. "Free the girls, get them headed back to where you were chained."

"What are you going to do?" Knickknack whispered.

"Focus on the girls." Tommy checked the door to the men's locker room. He wanted to keep the Undefended females out of the fight. They were like alley cats when it came to fighting: painted claws out and scratching while howling curses. It might be effective against other girls on street corners, but not against men armed with guns.

The door swung inward. Zhukov was bigger than Tommy but not braced for an attack from the rear. Tommy caught the man by the collar and dragged him fast through the door.

The locker room was an assault on Tommy's nose, of piss and damp and mold. Nor was it empty; two men stood by the wash sinks on the far back wall, looking surprised. Zhukov spun out of Tommy's hold and pulled his gun.

Tommy stepped back. He fed into Zhukov's mind

the image of two lesser blood oni warriors standing in place of the men: the ones that were over six feet tall with a pig-snout nose and tusks. Their sharp nasal grunting. Their musky reek. Zhukov shouted with surprise and emptied his gun into his coworkers.

"*Blyat!*" Zhukov shouted the word like a curse. The gun shook as he kept it aimed at the dead bodies. "What the hell are those? How did they get in here?"

There was a sudden barrage of gunfire outside the building. The cargo truck's loud horn sounded long and urgent. Tommy had never heard a more clear "come now" signal.

The door opened behind Zhukov. Knickknack stood in the doorway, looking shocked.

The guard whirled and pulled the trigger on his gun. Luckily, it was empty.

"Stupid fuck!" Tommy cut Zhukov's throat. "I told you to focus on the girls!"

Knickknack backed out of the door, mouth open, eyes wide. "I-I-I thought you might need help."

Tommy wiped his knife on Zhukov's clothes and sheathed it. The gunfire outside was only increasing in volume. What the hell was happening out there? "Come on."

The hallway was crowded with frightened girls. They apparently had afforded themselves use of the showers in the woman's locker room: they smelled of cheap hand soap and clean flesh. Without their heavy streetwalker makeup, they all appeared young and innocent. He might have been wrong about their ages; none of them looked older than eighteen. All the kids were bruised and battered. Knickknack wasn't the only one with a black eye and the girls all had marks on their arms to show that they had been roughly held by men with large, strong hands.

An alarm started to sound as they headed cautiously through the maze of hallways back toward the big machine room.

"Is that a fire alarm?" Peanut Butter Pie said.

"Maybe," Knickknack said.

Tommy wanted to get back to his hoverbike without running into any more groups of armed guards.

In the machine room, the far wall was slowly lifting. He hadn't noticed before but it was actually a huge airplane hangar-like door. The entire massive wall was folding up in four separate sections. Beyond the gleaming white manufacturing room, rails led down a steep concrete slope to the water. The muddy scent of the river was spilling in through the opening doorway.

The loud alarm might be to warn people that a boat was launching. Certainly the freshly created machine seemed to be preparing to leave—arms and clamps were retracting and the hum of a motor was coming from the thing. There was a weird chiming noise, similar to a hoverbike's spell chain spinning up.

Bullets pinged off the side wall. Tommy glanced out toward the river. There was a tugboat maneuvering a river barge filled with oni warriors toward the boat ramp.

"Shit," Tommy hissed. "Run!"

Loud elf fusion music started to play on a loudspeaker and a squeaky girly voice announced in English, "We are Pittsburgh! We are Team Tinker! Hooyah! Launching Tesla Mark Two Point Oh! Team Mischief, Go!"

The large newly fabricated machine lifted up and roared sideways out the opening. It had been a spell chain spinning up that he had been hearing.

"What the hell is happening?" one of the girls shouted.

That was what Tommy wanted to know. He wasn't sure what the giant mongrel hoverbike thing was but it seemed to be on their side.

Olivia was desperately honking the cargo truck's horn again as Tommy led the Undefended out of the big building and around the corner to where he had left his bike. He was glad to see she'd shifted the big vehicle so that it was protected by the building. The marines were behind heavy cover, returning fire at the oni. There was no sign of the Midas *Erobern* people; the rats had piled into their cars and fled. At some point Gaddy had slipped through the trashed gate and now sat on her hoverbike beside the truck.

The Undefended skittered in circles, not wanting to get closer to the gunfight.

Olivia spotted them and scrambled out of the cab to wave the Undefended toward her. "Come on! Get in the truck!"

"Go!" Tommy ordered, shoving them. He stopped at his hoverbike. All the Undefended except Knickknack ran to the truck.

The boy paused to look around. "Is Mokoto here? It's all my fault that Joyboy is dead. I don't want Mokoto hurt because I was stupid. None of this would have happened if I didn't let Toad talk me into growing those drugs. If I hadn't started to work Liberty. Hell, I should have just gone home for the summer! Mokoto didn't come, did he? He's not getting shot at?"

"He's not here!" Tommy roared. "He sent me, okay?"

Knickknack looked relieved and pleased. "Oh! Good! Okay. Right. I'll get in the truck, then."

"They're setting up a heavy machine gun!" Dagger shouted. "We cannot hold this position!"

"Pull back!" Olivia ordered. "Get in the truck! We're leaving!"

The marines dashed back, covering one another as they retreated. The machine gun opened fire, chewing through the pallets that the marines had been hiding behind. The truck had heavy cover behind the building but they needed to pull into the oni firing range to clear the gate.

"Hold on!" Tommy called as he pulled his hoverbike up beside the cargo truck. "We need to take out the machine gun before driving through its line of fire!"

"I can try ramming the fence," Olivia said.

Tommy scanned the fence line. Yes, the truck could probably easily ram through the chain-link fence but the jumps for Tinker's racetrack blocked the sidewalk beyond.

The large flying vehicle suddenly swooped down to hover beside Tommy. Up close and without all the fabricating machines attached to it, the thing looked more like a tank, with a long tube barrel sticking out in front. "We are Pittsburgh!"

"We are Team Tinker?" Gaddy said even though she wasn't on Tinker's hoverbike racing team.

"Hooyah!" the hovertank said in its little girl voice. "Leave that barge to us!"

"Okay," Tommy said when it became obvious that everyone else was speechless.

The hovertank swooped around the corner of the building with the speed of a hummingbird. There was a quiet *poof* and a small white ball went sailing out of the cannon. A foot or two from the muzzle, the ball transformed into a massive ray of white-hot energy that flashed forward. The beam hit the machine gun and sliced through the deck of the barge.

"Chi-chi-chi!" one of the marines cried. "Spell arrow!"

Tommy had never seen a spell arrow do that kind of damage. How did anyone get it ramped up to do that? Why was the hovertank using something akin to a spitball? How?

The hovertank ducked back behind cover as the oni used rifles to shoot at it. The barge was already listing as it took on water. The oni warriors rushed toward the smaller tugboat as the water became thick with feeding river sharks. A true blood was trying to detach the barge before it dragged the tug down with it.

"There," the little-girl voice said from hovertank. "No more problem! You should go someplace safer. The oni are launching an attack on Oakland. Okay, got to go, bye!"

The tank soared off.

"We should go," Olivia said after a moment of stunned silence. "Somewhere. Someplace safe."

Tommy doubted that anywhere in Pittsburgh was safe. He needed to get back to his family. Mokoto and Babe would still be asleep. Bingo and the others were distracted by the hotel; they might not notice the incoming oni until it was too late. At least with the human businessmen coming and going, no one who couldn't pass for human should be in the lobby. They could discuss tactics after he warned his family.

He revved the engine on his hoverbike, adding power to the lift engines so he drifted upward to cruising height. "Follow me."

22: GRANDVIEW

❖━━◉⊂❖⊱

Jane's little brother Marc had lucked into an insanely beautiful modern house on Grandview Avenue near the Monongahela Incline. Perched on the edge of Mount Washington, it had an unobstructed view for ten or twenty miles. The house was a blocky, white-walled, space-age-looking thing with multiple terraces and giant windows to make the most of the vista.

Jane had called Duff to let him know where she was headed and to double-check that Boo was actually with Marc. Duff had put her on hold, checked on Marc's location, and let her know that Marc had just gotten home. The call had forewarned Marc; he opened up his garage doors as Jane pulled into the driveway. His repaired Hummer sat in the right bay, leaving the left bay empty for Jane's SUV. Before Marc could close his garage doors, though, Nigel and Taggart and Hal walked out of the garage, heading across the street to the far sidewalk at the cliff's edge. Chesty stoically stood beside Jane despite the fact that he'd spent most of the day so far penned up. The elfhound glanced up hopefully at Jane.

"Hal!" Jane snapped even though all three of the men were guilty. It was probably Hal's idea.

"It's the first time Taggart has seen Pittsburgh like this!" Hal gestured to the vista even as he continued to walk toward the iron fence that lined the far sidewalk.

It was a stunning view. The cliffs of Mount Washington dropped off beyond the sidewalk, leaving nothing to obstruct the vista. In a single glance, one could see from Point State Park—where the Allegheny River met the Monongahela River to form the Ohio—all the way to the Cathedral of Learning rising over Oakland. At the foot of the cliff was Station Square, currently littered with train cars after the Oktoberfest derailment. Across the Monongahela River rose all the skyscrapers of Downtown. On the hilltops beyond the Allegheny River was the solid wall of green that was the virgin ironwood forest. Rainclouds blanketed the sky, threatening, dimming the entire vista.

Much to Chesty's delight, Jane walked across to view it with the men. The big elfhound trotted in a wide circle around her, burning energy, tail wagging.

"We can see it even better from Marc's," Jane said, aware that Marc was following them across the street as if Hal had the gravity of a black hole. "It's going to rain soon."

Hal looked pained. "I wanted Taggart to get shots of the tower. From the street. It's more impressive that way."

"The tower?" Jane echoed in confusion. The only tower in the area was a block down the street from Marc's house. It was a tall, anemic, Eiffel-Tower-looking thing painted white and red. There was a little flat building tucked under it, housing WESA, which used to be the Pittsburgh NPR station. The public radio station had lost its US government funding, just like WQED. Whereas private investors had stepped in to take control of the public television station, the radio station had been abandoned. What was operating in its place was a pirate station, run by locals as young as twelve and as old as thirty.

Jane pointed just to be sure they were talking about the same thing. "The radio tower?"

Hal nodded and grinned in the way he had when he was trying to keep a secret.

"Why?" Jane let her voice to drop to a threatening level. All of the kids running the pirate station had joined the militia. Since the militia was using the spy cell model, Hal hadn't been told that it was one of their communications hubs. Although it was possible that he'd guessed; he wasn't a total idiot and the coded broadcasts were accessible by any radio.

Hal grinned tighter. "WESA appeals to a younger audience."

Jane glared at him and he lost the grin.

Hal lowered his voice to a whisper. "Jane, I've been doing lots of research on successful rebellions. Historically, communication is key to any successful resistance. Radios have always played an important part in organizing coordinated action. KDKA is nice but it's very public and very vulnerable and very... cowardly. Really. I haven't been able to get in to see any of KDKA's staff beyond your cousin. They're afraid I'll set the place on fire. Again."

She was wrong. He hadn't realized that they'd

already taken over WESA. She shook her head. "I don't want you drawing attention to the station."

Nigel shifted to stand shoulder to shoulder with Hal.

"No, no, no, don't evil dead twins on me," Jane growled.

Nigel gave her an apologetic look for siding against her. "Elf fusion music is blowing up on Earth. It's part of what is fueling people's interest in Elfhome. If Tinker *domi* does manage to open up a path back to Earth, an episode on a pirate radio station devoted to the music would be huge."

Jane hadn't considered that the radio station could be anything more than a communication hub for the militia. This was the problem of having two hosts. Hal alone was easy to ignore; his way normally led to madness, fueled by his overconfident ego. Nigel, on the other hand, was so reasonable that it was hard to counter him.

"We're here to talk to Boo," Jane said.

"We could split up," Taggart said. "It's probably better that only you deal with this."

"This" being *find out exactly what Kajo did to Boo.* Yes, it would be better if Boo had privacy for this.

"I can cover your crew." Marc wore his kidney holster under his tank top. He held out his keys to show that he wouldn't be locked out if she closed the garage doors.

"We can take Chesty with us." Taggart gave her a smile that did warm fluttery things to her heart. "He would enjoy the walk."

"Okay. Fine." She was trying to get Chesty used to the idea that Taggart was part of the family now. She pointed at Taggart. "Chesty. Obey."

Taggart patted his leg. Chesty went without hesitation, which was an improvement since they had first started working on it two months ago.

"Good boy!" Taggart rewarded Chesty with affection. Jane walked back to the garage and hit the wall switch to close the big doors.

It was a good thing that Marc's place was all windows and outside views because it was minimalist bare. He had no art on the wall or rugs on the polished hardwood floors. The only furniture on the first floor was an ironwood coffee table made by Geoffrey and a leather recliner bought at the thrift store Once More With Feeling.

Jane grabbed a cold beer out of the kitchen's refrigerator; she needed something to focus on other than her feelings. She didn't want to have this talk with Boo. She didn't want to drag Boo through the emotional minefield of her kidnapping. Jane didn't trust herself not to react yet; Boo didn't need her anger and revulsion. After a moment's thought, she took a beer for Boo too. Her baby sister wasn't a baby anymore. All the Kryskills started to drink alcohol when they were ten or eleven, probably on the theory that if it wasn't forbidden, it wasn't as enticing.

Boo wasn't on the first-floor terrace off the living room, nor the second-floor one off the spartan master bedroom. She was up on the roof terrace, under the protection of the lattice roof, her new wings flaring from her back in snow-white perfection. Her spill of curls was just as white, to the point where it was hard to tell where her hair stopped and her feathers started.

Boo had her eyes closed as she folded and extended her wings. While she had resisted the offer of getting her wings immediately after being rescued in July, she had decided to agree in August, when little Joey Shoji got his. The tengu created the spell tattoo with magic, impregnating the skin with ink, in what Boo described as "instant sunburn." While the spell gave her wings, it didn't instantly give her the muscle memory or the strength to use them efficiently. The tengu explained that flying was like learning any endurance sport; practice would be what made flight effortless, not magic.

"Fold," Boo whispered as her wings closed. "Extend."

In a rustle of white features, her massive wings spread.

She looked like a battered angel, dressed in a backless tank top and cut off shorts, and sporting vivid bruises on her alabaster skin after countless bad landings.

"Hey." Jane held out one of the bottles. "Do you want a beer?"

"Sure!" Boo cried, opening her eyes.

Jane had just grabbed what was in the refrigerator. She hadn't really looked at the label until she cracked hers open. It was a Church Brew Works Blue Valentine. It was a stout beer with chocolate and fudge undertones. It was a good beer, but strong. From experience Jane knew that kids rarely liked the more robust beers right out of the gate. But then, maybe the oni had been giving Boo beer to drink since she was little. Boo seemed excited by the prospect of drinking it.

Boo was sniffing her opened beer. "Wow, it smells like some kind of dessert."

"Beer takes a little time to get used to," Jane said to warn her.

It was nearly comical to watch Boo soldier through the first few sips. No, the oni hadn't weaned her on beer.

"I normally have things like hard cider," Boo said when she realized that Jane was watching her. "Or wine coolers."

"You don't have to drink it."

"I want to," Boo said. "He liked sweet drinks. Girly drinks. You guys all drink beer."

"Kajo?" Jane said.

Boo nodded.

Jane took a long chug on her beer to give herself courage to dive into the conversation that she didn't want to bring up. The one that she'd unconsciously avoided for over a month. "Boo, if we're going to stop Kajo, we need to know everything about him. What does he look like? Where is his main camp? What you think the oni might be doing? Anything you can give us will help."

Boo hesitated for a moment before saying, "Kajo's a little taller than me. Just enough that I need to tilt my head up a little to look him in the eye."

That made him damn short, as Boo hadn't shot up like most Kryskills. She was only about five foot two.

"His hair is long and blond," Boo continued, frowning in concentration. "Not white blond like mine but still very pale. He normally wears it in a ponytail but sometimes he braids it or he wears it in a man-bun. He doesn't like having his hair so long but he was told to let it grow. His eyes are very green—they almost don't seem real. You know in movies, when the actors use contacts to make their eyes really vivid? They're like that. When I was little I used to dream that he had little emeralds instead of real eyes."

Boo fell silent for a minute. She took another sip of the beer and cringed. "Oh, this tastes like a chocolate tart that's gone bad."

"Being a tengu might have changed how things taste to you," Jane said.

Boo visibly braced herself to take another sip. "Kajo actually looks like a Disney prince. The chin. The cheeks. The nose. He's beautiful. So beautiful I could never understand why he kept me. He could have anyone."

Jane finished her beer as she struggled to keep her anger in check. The "beautiful" bastard who "could have anyone" had stolen a first grader who weighed less than fifty pounds. What kind of pervert wanted a girl that young?

"Five and a half feet tall, roughly. Long blond hair. Green eyes." Jane focused on the important details. The hair could be changed but not the eyes or height. "Looks human?"

Boo nodded. "Yes, he looks like a normal person. He could walk down the street and no one would think, 'Oh, there's an oni.' That's why he wears the mask. No one would be scared of him otherwise, at least on first meeting him. Once you got to know him, you realized that he could be so ruthless. Sometimes it seemed like he had no heart—but then he would look at me so sad and say he loved me. Sometimes I believed him."

It wasn't much but at least it was more than they had before. She wondered if Marc knew a police sketch artist that he could trust.

Jane moved on. They needed to find the two possible Kajos before they could identify the real one.

"Do you have any idea why Kajo would be moving around black willows? Did he put the trees in Frick Park so he could use them in some master plan?"

Boo shook her head. "The trees were here before everything. Before the oni reached Pittsburgh. Before Pittsburgh came to Elfhome. The elves surveyed this area extensively and monitored it for decades before the first Startup. Pure Radiance knew that something big was going to show up here. The Viceroy mapped out the ley lines, the springs, and all the wetlands that were infested with black willow. The seeds of the black willow are like those of a dandelion: real fluffy. Based on their DNA and the genetic drift, Kajo thought that some seeds got blown up into the jet stream during the Rebellion and came down somewhere in the Westernlands. He sees them as a mixed blessing. They've made moving around the virgin forest more difficult for the oni but they deterred the humans and elves from exploring extensively."

Jane took out her phone and started to take notes. There was a lot to unpack from the statement, perhaps more than Boo realized. Her baby sister had been on the inside so long that she didn't know what was common knowledge and what wasn't.

Nigel and Hal theorized that the monster-call whistle took advantage of instincts encoded into creatures at a genetic level. For it to work, the beast had to have been doctored at some point with magic to reinforce those instincts into a behavior that could be quickly and readily commanded. Nigel and Hal had experimented with the whistle—carefully—to discover that while most wild creatures—songbirds, small mammals like squirrels, and most fish—didn't respond, bioengineered animals like elfhounds did. (Chesty was not amused by the experiment but he would obey the monster call.)

Sparrow had betrayed her kind by working with the oni. Kajo must have received all his information about the black willows and the local area from her.

"Kajo is taking advantage of the fact that the trees are in the area but they're not part of his plans," Jane said to confirm she correctly understood what Boo reported.

"Kajo said that during the Rebellion they found that the black willows were too vulnerable to the Fire Clan and Stone Clan, especially if the two clans joined forces," Boo said. "Nor are the trees really an urban warfare weapon—they're slow moving and have trouble navigating around houses."

Jane had to agree that if she and Hal had been able to deal with lone black willows in the past, then no, the trees weren't really ideal weapons. Jane frowned at what she had just written. The Stone Clan hadn't arrived until after Sparrow was dead; the female elf's intelligence reports must have been extensive.

"Kajo had creatures he called horrors," Boo said with uncertainty.

"Horrors?" Jane echoed.

"We were watching a movie one time. I didn't like it. It was this little girl who was taken by a monster and her family was trying to save her. Danni came in and asked what we were watching. Kajo said, 'A movie about a *kaiju*' and Danni didn't know what a *kaiju* was, so Kajo said, 'It's a horror—a river horror.' Danni saw how much the movie upset me and made me watch it to the end. She had figured out that the little girl in the movie would die."

The more Jane learned about this bitch Danni, the more she wanted to kill her.

Boo continued. "The oni had been developing monsters on Onihida. They couldn't get them from their world to Elfhome—not with half the Earth between their two access points. That's why they kidnapped Tinker *domi*. If they had managed to keep her gate to Onihida open, they could have brought all their monsters and troops through the gate. Before they came up with the idea for the gate, they focused on smuggling in genetic material to build monsters with."

"Were the *namazu* the only horrors Kajo has here in Pittsburgh?"

Boo gave her a look that said that she didn't know for sure. She whispered, "Kajo never trusted me. He said he couldn't tell me because the Eyes would kill me if I knew too much."

Jane wanted to be sure that Danni died slowly. She tried to coax out a little more information. "You think there are more horrors than just the *namazu*?"

"They would let things slip." Boo said. "Little things. By themselves, it meant nothing, but after a while, you could piece things together. Every Shutdown, the oni would ship a vast amount of goods to Pittsburgh. A lot of it was legal to import like food, blankets, clothing, and building materials. Kajo had underlings that handled those shipments. He was never involved unless it was some luxury item that he thought his underlings would keep for themselves. Caviar. Kobe steak. European chocolate. Cashmere sweaters. Silk sheets. If was something illegal, like guns, Lord Tomtom handled the deliveries on the theory that if something went wrong, only his people would take the fall. Now and then, though, the oni would bring something in that required everyone to work together to make sure it crossed safely."

Boo reached out and gripped Jane's hand tightly. "That's what Kajo was doing in the Strip District the day I saw him with Danni. The day he took me. He was supervising the delivery of something too important to trust to Lord Tomtom. It was in this big shadowy warehouse. After I'd been tied up and gagged, they gathered across the room where there was a large animal in a wooden crate. It was hurt. I could smell blood and hear it making sounds of pain. They were talking in Oni and I didn't know the language yet. There's a lot of words, though, that Oni doesn't have. Truck. Gun. Highway. Computer. Internet. When you're talking in Oni and you hit one of those words, sometimes the rest of the sentence comes out in English. Kajo and Lord Tomtom flowed in and out of English as they talked about what to do with what was in the crate. The conversation made no sense to me, but helpless as I was, it is forever etched into my mind.

"They smuggle genetic material for horrors onto Elfhome inside large pregnant animals, like cows or horses. They decided to kill whatever was in the crate because it was making so much noise. I think it was a cow. I didn't see whatever came out of it. Lord Tomtom was unimpressed by it. 'It's just a building block,' Kajo said. 'A tiny piece for something bigger.' That made Lord Tomtom laugh and say, 'Tiny? Yes! Everything you've made is far too small to be a horror.' Kajo dismissed his complaint with, 'We can make them bigger anytime. Temperament is more important than size.' Danni took possession of whatever it was to get it safely out of the city; I don't know what she did with it. I know that Kajo went several times down to the Strip District during Shutdown to handle something that he didn't trust Lord Tomtom with, but I never went with him and he would never talk about it later."

Jane took deep breaths, not wanting to rage in front of Boo. Her baby sister didn't need her anger. She couldn't imagine the terror that Boo had gone through that day, unsure if the oni would slaughter her as casually as they killed the animal in the crate.

"I'm sorry I'm so useless." Boo's voice broke with emotion. "I knew that in the end everyone in Pittsburgh would be in danger. They would talk casually about how they would deal with the police and the EIA. I should have worked harder to learn what they were doing but I was too scared. Anytime I tried to learn more, one of the Eyes would say, 'I know what you're doing,' and then tell me exactly what I had planned. It was if they crawled into my head and listened to my thoughts. They always knew. I couldn't do anything."

"Oh, baby!" Jane gathered Boo into her arms and held her tight. "You stayed alive! That's all that matters! That's all we wanted! We just wanted you back, safe and sound."

Boo tried not to cry but slowly her defenses crumbled until she was wailing ugly tears. "I'm so useless! Useless!"

Jane rocked her, trying to figure out how to make this right. Boo was a deep well of knowledge, but it was so fragmented and every "I don't know" would cut deep. Worse, Boo would feel responsible for every death and disaster that happened in the upcoming conflict. She would feel like she could have prevented it. This was Jane's fault for letting the fear of what she might learn keep her from trying to pump Boo for information. She should have just opened the taps, let everything pour out. It would have let Boo feel useful.

"You're not useless," Jane said. "We should have been asking you more questions. You have no idea what we need to know, so how can you know what to tell us? Let's see what we can figure out about what is happening now with the trees."

Boo nodded, sniffing loudly, but at least she stopped crying.

"Let's start simply," Jane said. "It's okay if you can't answer me. I need to know where the holes are before we can try to fill them. Okay? Now, where did you live when you were with Kajo?"

Boo sniffed again and wiped at her nose with the back of her hand. "We moved around a lot—usually during Shutdown. I think it was so that Pure Radiance couldn't 'see' what we were doing. The Eyes were blind to what was happening on Earth when they were on Elfhome and vice versa. During the winter we lived someplace in the city, usually somewhere fairly deserted. The nicest place was a cul-de-sac in Mount Lebanon; Kajo and I lived in a big stone house with fairy-tale-sized fireplaces and lattice windows. I felt like Rapunzel or Belle—a girl who wasn't a princess being held captive in a castle by a monster. The worst place was a hotel downtown. It should have been the nicest; it was deluxe three-bedroom suite. I could see all of Downtown from the windows. They put bars on the inside of the windows and doors, though, making it one big prison cell. I wasn't allowed out all winter.

There was a television but it didn't work. All I could do during the day was sleep or read or do homework."

"Homework?" Jane echoed in surprise.

Boo puffed up her cheeks in embarrassed anger. "Kajo made me do schoolwork. He got these workbooks from Earth: one hundred and eighty days of boring stuff that I'd never get to use because I was never going to get away from him. I had to do six pages every day. I was up to eighth grade before he transformed me into a tengu and abandoned me at Sandcastle. In the evenings, if he didn't have to go out and oversee something, we would play shogi."

"What's shogi?"

"It's a stupidly complicated game. You've got eight different types of pieces that all move differently. Most of the pieces can get promoted and that changes how they can be played. I always lost. I was getting better. Kajo said he didn't like playing against the Eyes because he always had to lose. While we played, we'd talk about his favorite books."

Jane had been avoiding this talk because she hadn't wanted to hear how Kajo sexually assaulted her baby sister. Their daily routine sounded fairly innocuous. There were so many questions she pushed down. She didn't want Boo to relive the bad. She didn't really want to hear the answer and not be able to immediately kill Kajo.

What was a safe question? One that Boo could answer? *Had to lose.* Did that mean he lost on purpose? Boo probably didn't know the answer to that either.

"What kind of books?" Jane asked to keep the flow going.

"*Where the Wild Things Are. Treasure Island.*

Charlie and the Chocolate Factory. Phantom Toll-booth. Redwall."

"Those were his favorite books?" They were all children's books written in English. It was a weird choice for an oni.

"Kajo grew up on Earth. His people had been trapped there for thousands of years. They knew from the beginning that they needed to move slowly when they invaded Elfhome. Stay hidden. They couldn't take on all the elves; not with how powerful the *domana* are. Windwolf proved that during the first Startup when he kicked the Americans' asses. Every time we moved, it would be dark enough to cloak us but not so late to make people wonder why we were out in the streets. Any house we used was emptied of everything, scrubbed clean, and then burned to the ground. We only stayed in the city when tracks in the snow would betray our movements. For most of the year, we lived deep in the forest."

Jane nodded, her mind racing. She could see why Boo thought her information was useless. Kajo had been good at covering his movements. Boo had been transformed into a tengu in the spring and given into the care of an underling at Sandcastle. Kajo probably changed camps immediately afterward, nullifying any secrets that Boo had about his current location.

The important fact was that Kajo didn't stay with the main oni force. He and Boo always lived in a small separate encampment. A couple floors of a hotel. A house. It meant that if the larger camps were found, Kajo remained hidden. It also meant that he probably wasn't at the camps that Prince True Flame, Windwolf, and the Harbingers were attacking. Law most likely had spotted Kajo, possibly with Boo's replacement.

It was autumn. If Kajo kept to his pattern, his camp was still hidden deep in the forest. He probably wouldn't be able to move back into the city for winter. Things had changed. Humans were now aware that the oni existed. Jane's family had spent the last two months organizing Pittsburghers into a secret militia scattered throughout the city. The oni couldn't move about as easily as when Pittsburgh was routinely flooded with off-worlders. The humans who had been previously unaware of the danger would be alarmed if strangers suddenly moved into or even through their neighborhood. There would be dangerous questions raised.

"Tell me about the forest camps," Jane said.

"What about them?"

"Were they north, south, east, or west of Pittsburgh? How far from the Rim were they? How many oni were there? Anything you can tell me is useful."

Boo looked doubtful. "I know that the main camps were in the east so that they could use the train or the Monongahela River to transport bulk goods beyond the Rim. We normally camped in the west or the south. Our camps would almost always have these stones with spells chiseled into them that were anchored into a strong ley line or a magical spring. They created illusions of an empty forest. People could walk into our camp and not see the buildings or tents or even our guards. It made it a little wonky, though, trying to find the outhouse. There was one time we drove all the way down I-79 to I-70 and then across to the Rim to outside where Wheeling used to be—or at least still is, kind of. Anyhow, we took barges downriver from there to where a small river they called the Muskingum joined the Ohio. It was my favorite camp. They didn't set up a cloaking spell because we were so far away from Pittsburgh. They could tuck the barges up the Muskingum, out of view of anyone using the Ohio. The ironwoods screened the camp. Kajo had them make us this really big compound that had a stream, and a garden, and a swing and even a treehouse. I felt sad when we left because they always dismantled any camp we set up. I liked the treehouse."

"How many oni were at that compound?" Jane asked.

Boo cringed, shrugging. "I was never allowed out of our private area."

"I'm guessing about a hundred," Jane said to test a theory. "Just to ballpark it."

Boo made a face. "I suppose it would have been around a hundred warriors when we were in the forest. Kajo always had a full guard while we were out where a pack of saurus might be. They're not spell-worked, so there's no controlling them with a monster call. When we were in the city, we would have little more than a dozen people, counting me. Most of them were greater bloods like Kajo. There would always be one of the Eyes with us, usually Danni, but sometimes Adele or Felicie. Kajo did most of his work while we were in the forest, so we would make camp in March and strike it in late October."

"So the only time that the tengu came to where you might have seen them was in the forest?" Jane said.

Boo nodded. "I don't think they ever saw me but I'd catch glimpses of them as they flew in and took off."

Pieces were fitting together; Jane didn't like the picture that was forming. Kajo kept separate from the main force, sometimes putting as much as a hundred miles between them and himself. He kept hidden at all times, leaving his camp only to oversee something that couldn't be trusted to an underling. Law had reported seeing Kajo with about a hundred oni breaking camp and heading toward the river. Yumiko said that the male used smoke and mirror tactics. Combining the two, the black willows had to be a distraction. But for whom? Most of the elves were in the east, fighting what they saw as the main oni force. The only human who spotted Kajo was Law. The female forager had been outnumbered a hundred to one. If Kajo had been aware of Law, he could have killed her easily. Jane wouldn't have been called in if the black willows hadn't been roaming where they shouldn't be. The same for the EIA. That left just the tengu.

"My people are spread thin," Yumiko had said. *"So I called in the guardians of the* Dahe Hao.*"*

Was that Kajo's real goal? To distract the tengu from the *Dahe Hao*? What would Kajo want with a spaceship? Or was it something other than the ship that he was after? Jane and her team had filmed in Turtle Creek shortly after Tinker escaped from the oni camp that been located inside the old Westinghouse Air Brake factory. It had been a careful tightrope walk of explaining the inexplicable condition of the valley to their viewers without letting out any of the information that the tengu had told Jane. Yumiko had mentioned a cloaking spell, saying it might be the source of the odd freezing blue haze filling the area. It wasn't until Boo talked about not being able to find the outhouse because of an illusion cast on Kajo's camps that Jane fully realized the implications. To keep the illusion constantly running and covering the entire mile length of the old Westinghouse Air Brake building would have required a great deal of power.

To cast a spell that was able to transform an entire species of people into another would also need a great deal of power.

Was Kajo looking for a place to use the contents of the box?

"Shit!" Jane breathed out the curse, her mind racing. She pulled out her phone, dialing Duff, even as she charged downstairs.

Boo followed behind her. "Jane? Jane? What is Kajo going to do?"

Duff answered his phone with, "You know, I got to thinking, I could ask her—the girl I kind of like. It would be a weird first date but then she would know what she was getting into—although she probably knew that after the entire *namazu* thing—"

"Duff, activate all our troops!" Jane ordered.

"What?" Duff and Boo both cried.

"Kajo works in layers. The black willows were to distract the tengu out of Turtle Creek, but the trees would have walked right into the back of the enclaves. He wanted the black willows to soften up the elves' defenses prior to his push into Oakland."

"Putting out the blast," Duff said. "Activating all troops. What's happening?"

"Kajo is looking for a large source of magic," Jane said. "He was heading to Turtle Creek first. I think he plans to target the spell at the elves. Once he triggers the spell, he's probably going to unleash an attack on Oakland to take out the enclaves."

"You don't think he's going to target humans?" Duff

said. "We're heavily armed and outnumber almost everything on this continent."

"It's a genetically keyed bomb. The humans in Pittsburgh range from Chinese to African to Vikings with even some Neanderthal randomly mixed in. If he's smart—and he is—he'll use the first bomb to take out the elves' heavy hitters: the *domana*."

Duff cursed. "Windwolf is deep in the forest surrounded by the entire oni army."

"Not all of it." Jane paused in Marc's living room. Through the massive windows, she could see down the Ohio River to Brunot Island and up the Monongahela to Panther Hollow. The only movement on the water was from schools of jump fish. The skies were heavily overcast with rain clouds creating a thick blanket of gray. "Kajo probably has a platoon or a full company that has come upriver from somewhere around Wheeling. He's got barges, so he has at least one tugboat."

"They would have to get past . . . I don't know—a half dozen lock and dams?" Duff said. "A dozen?"

Jane closed her eyes and thought hard. She'd spent an entire week in July looking for the *namazu* nests. She'd gotten to know the three rivers intimately. There was a lock and dam on the Ohio at Neville Island. The Allegheny's lock-and-dam system had remained on Earth. Monongahela's first dam was near Turtle Creek. Law had spotted Kajo in the forest north of Turtle Creek, heading south. It wouldn't make sense for him to boat up to the first dam and then hike in a huge circle. It would make sense if he'd cut through the forest north of Oakland, heading west to east.

Where would she put a large attack force in the west, where it wouldn't be easily stumbled over by humans or spotted by tengu who would have been flying up the Allegheny to reach Haven?

"Did any of our scouts go out to Herr Island?" Jane said.

"Where's that?" Duff said, which meant that the answer was probably "No."

"It's on the Allegheny River, under the Thirty-First Street Bridge," Jane said. "The Rim cuts right across it. Half of it is a bunch of abandoned office buildings and other half is virgin forest."

"If it's that's close to the city, then it might still be connected to the traffic cameras," Duff said. "Hold on!"

"Wait!" But the line had gone quiet as Duff put her on hold. Duff was using the phone system at the bakery that had multiple landlines with the ability to have several lines connected at once. He was probably calling his computer guru bunny.

Jane pulled out her ancient pocket radio and turned it on. Marti Wulfow was spilling out coded orders for all militia troops to assemble in Oakland. Duff had gotten the blast out before checking the cameras. "Good boy!"

"Boo, the others went to the radio station." Jane trotted down to the garage stairs. Boo followed her, wings fluttering nervously. "I'm going to pick them up. Stay here, wait for Marc."

Jane hit the power button on the garage door. It rattled upward. "I won't have time to fill Marc in completely. I need you to—"

"Hello?" Roach ducked down to look under the rising garage door. His hair was still damp from a shower and he was holding a stuffed bear and a box of candy. He stared at Boo's wings with stunned surprise. "Oh. Um. Hi."

Oh, shit, she had forgotten Roach was meeting her at Marc's.

"Billy!" Boo cried and leapt at him.

Roach's dismay vanished to a huge grin. "Baby Boo!" He dropped the presents to swing her around in a circle. "Baby Boo, you're found! You're found!"

"We have incoming!" Duff suddenly came back on the line. "Incoming on Liberty Avenue heading east toward—"

The line went dead.

"Duff? Duff?" She checked her signal. No bars. The cell phone network was down. Jane realized that her pocket radio had gone to static. "Shit, shit, shit."

The automatic light on the garage door had gone off too. Jane flipped the light switch beside the power button. The big shop lights stayed dark. The power had gone out. WQED might have a backup generator but the underground pirate station of WESA probably didn't.

"Damn, damn, damn, damn," Jane swore as she scrambled into her SUV. In the glove box were the radio headsets that they'd pulled together just for this type of emergency. "This is Beater One, are we good?"

"Oh, thank God!" Duff said over the headset. "Power is out here. I don't know what to do."

They had had to return the headsets that they'd borrowed from Team Tinker in July but had spent the last two months finding replacements. Only a handful of their team leaders had one and they wouldn't be able to contact their squad members if the phones were out.

"I'll see what can be done about Bullhorn." Jane used their code word for WESA. She dug out her map of Pittsburgh. There was a steep ravine between the river and the enclaves. There were only two bridges across it until Liberty Avenue climbed high enough to meet the plateau that Oakland rested on. "Have our teams head for Orphan's."

"Roger that," Duff said.

Her team came jogging up the street, saving her from having to decide what to do with Boo.

"Duff pulled the trigger," Taggart said. "He didn't give a rendezvous point past Oakland. What's up?"

Jane explained the oni attack. "They've taken out the cell phone towers and the power system. They're going to attack the enclaves. I'm having Duff send our people to Sacred Heart."

"Wait, what?" Roach said. "Oakland is under attack? Andy, Guy, and Geoffrey are at—oh, wait—Andy and Guy were going with Oilcan to move something heavy. They said something about ice cream. I think they're on the South Side. Maybe. Depends on how long the trip took. Geoff wanted to watch the elves build the wall."

Jane cursed. "I'm going to Oakland."

"I'm coming with you," Taggart said. Her dismay must have shown on her face. "Surprise attacks by insurgents used to be my morning wake-up call."

Jane nodded and turned to Marc. She wanted to head off her little brother from trying to come with her. If he did, Boo would want to come too. "Find a generator and get it hooked up to Bullhorn. We need them back on the air."

"I can help," Roach said.

As Jane made sure that her little brother nodded in compliance, she realized that Hal had detoured to the back of her SUV. He was getting something out of his backup bag. "Hal, what are you doing?"

"I realized long ago that our technical prowess was also our greatest weakness. I decided to rely on a more primitive and thus more robust method to spread the news of attack."

"Hal, what did you do?" Jane said.

"Sheer genius is what I've done!" Hal pulled out a flare gun, pointed it skyward, and pulled the trigger. "Light the signal fires!"

The flare shot up into the sky and flashed to orange against the gray storm clouds.

"Damn it, Hal, all you did was tell the enemy our position!"

"Wait for it," he murmured.

There was a flare of color in the skies over Oakland as fireworks exploded against the clouds. A moment later another went up over Hill District. Even as the two sites fired their second rounds, a rocket lifted off from the Steel Building.

"See!" Hal shouted. "The beacons of Oakland are alight, calling for aid. War is kindled. See, there are the fireworks on the Cathedral and the Hill District, and flame on the Steel Building, and there they go speeding south: Mount Washington, Beechview, Dormont, and Castle Shannon on the borders of the Rim."

Behind them, a string of fireworks went up, just a handful from each site but enough to mark a line heading deep into South Hills. Jane had no idea how he'd arranged it.

"It was glorious, wasn't it?" Hal breathed out as the last firework faded away.

"Brilliant!" Nigel agreed.

Naturalists!

"Come on," Jane said. "Let's go."

23: A SNAKE IN THE GRASS

The spaceship made Tristan's older brother laugh and laugh. Lucien sat, laughing, on the roof of the two-story stone piers that once anchored the Washington Bridge over Turtle Creek. He'd perched on the stone's edge, kicking his feet like a child.

"Oh, you should have seen it," Lucien said. "Even Danni was blindsided. I tell you, Esme's changeling daughter is a hoot. Before the spaceship, this entire valley was ice-cold blue soup. The weirdest freaking thing I've ever seen. I have no idea how she did it, but that stupid cat was toast. I'm glad Father made the decision to trust him with the changeling because I'd be totally screwed by now."

While Tristan could pass as a very tall nine-year-old and be enrolled into fifth grade, his brother looked like he could be as old as thirteen or fourteen. Lucien was growing up faster than Tristan; it seemed like his brother had inherited more of their mother's genes. The irony was that they hadn't seen each other for over twenty years. It had been a joyful reunion in

July. As the days stretched on, though, Tristan realized that Lucien was keeping him at arm's length and isolated in his deep forest camp. He was starting to worry something was drastically wrong.

What did this mean? Bringing him to the site of a major failure for their side to laugh like the children that they were?

"They said she opened a gate to Onihida," Tristan said, repeating the rumors around camp. "You could see our troops gathered on the other side—half a million strong—waiting for the chance to cross through it. It would have been an instant victory for us."

"Danni said it would fail but she wasn't sure how." Lucien waved at the spaceship. "Not even the Eyes could see this coming! Danni said it would get that damn cat out of my hair, so I let it run its course."

"Didn't we need Lord Tomtom?"

"Father might think we did but Danni said he was getting to be a liability. Certainly it's his mistakes that we've been tripping over all summer, starting with that stupid gunfight on Veterans Bridge. He was sloppy and ambitious. He had no sense of delicacy. It's because of him we lost all advantage of surprise. It was best to let the stupid cat get burned on the fire that is Esme's changeling daughter. Oh, she burns so hot."

Tristan turned back to the spaceship standing tail down in the valley below. There were glyphs of draconic magic scrawled up its side. He guessed that the spell inscribed on the hull was what was keeping the mile-long ship from collapsing under the weight of gravity and wind shear. Written in giant Chinese letters was the name of the spaceship. *Dahe Hao.* He'd watched it jump out of Earth's orbit eighteen years ago. He was sure that he'd never see it again. He was sure that his older half sister was dead. "It's Esme's ship."

"Yeah," Lucien laughed. "It's so like her, coming out of nowhere to kick Father in the nuts as hard as she can."

"She's alive?"

"Yes. She's at Lain's. She looks the same as when she left. It's like she's half-elf too. Dufae had left a booby trap in his design. All the ships that went through the gate were trapped in time until his daughter ripped it out of the sky."

"How did she . . ." Tristan paused, mind boggled to the point that he couldn't even form a question.

"Make the valley blue soup? Rip the gate out of the sky? Find her mother? Teleport her here?" Lucien laughed and flung himself backward to lie staring up at the gray sky threatening to rain. He'd abandoned his oni robes for this exploration of the bridge and was wearing blue jeans and a dark gray hoodie. For the first time since Tristan arrived, Lucien seemed like the boy that he was. It almost seemed like they were back on Earth again, just normal kids, out exploring the woods around their father's estate. "Only the gods know! I certainly don't. I've given up trying to guess because even the Eyes can't see her next weird wiggle. She's like her mother that way. Who would have guessed that Esme would suddenly want to be a spaceship captain? She was all angst and steampunk when she lived at the mansion."

Tristan thought of his two nine-year-old nieces now living in their mother's bedroom. He felt guilty that he'd left them there—unknowing, unprotected. They were far too clever not to realize something was off about everyone at his father's estate. Would they realize that all the servants were ancient elves, camping on the edge of a pinprick gateway between the worlds?

"They say that Esme made more than this changeling." His brother said it as fact but it was a question, as if he guessed Tristan's thoughts. They had some of their mother's intuition, just not enough to please their father.

Tristan struggled to keep his tone factual. "After the first implantation was successful, Esme had the remaining genetic material frozen. An employee of the lab noticed that the material had been abandoned and stole it. He and his wife had twins." Tristan felt another guilty twist. He couldn't be sure if his father had a hand in the death of the girls' parents but it felt too unlikely to be a coincidence. He knew what it was like to be torn away from your mother at a young age. He wouldn't wish it on anyone—and yet, the twins were now orphans trapped at his father's estate. "Father seems unsatisfied with them. I think it's because they remind him of Esme and how hard she fought him. He has our people looking to see if there was more material in storage. Something he can mold into a more useful tool."

"Twins?" Lucien sounded genuinely surprised. Had Father told Lucien nothing? "Oh, the horror! Two more like this changeling? I'm glad they're on Earth and not here."

"With the gate gone, there's no way Father can have them brought to Elfhome now." Tristan was glad that they were on Earth with his mother, but still he wasn't completely sure that they were safe.

Yves had been left on Earth to oversee their efforts there. Their older brother had always made it clear that Lucien and Tristan were beneath his notice. They were half-elves and would only live a few hundred years. Maybe. Or they might live for thousands of years. No one was sure. Yves still saw his younger half brothers as disposable tools. What would Yves do to the twins? Would he see them as a valuable commodity or a dangerous nuisance?

"There's always a way." Lucien said that as if he knew something Tristan had never been told. "Yves is long overdue but Father expects big brother any time now."

With the orbital gate gone, there should be no way for Yves to get to Elfhome. Lucien made it sound like it was only a matter of time.

Tristan wasn't sure what their father planned for him. He hadn't seen his father since he'd been sent away from the mansion in the middle of the night. They had crossed during the July Shutdown in separate vehicles. His father hadn't summoned him during the last two months; it almost seemed like he'd forgotten about Tristan. It did not bode well.

"Don't worry," Lucien said. "I've made myself indispensable here. I'll keep you safe until you can establish your own worth. You found the tengu Chosen bloodline. You figured out how to find the box that Unbounded Brilliance stole hundreds of years ago. Even if Father can't see the value of that, don't worry, little brother. You're one of the two things I plan to claim for myself once Pittsburgh has fallen."

"Two? What's the other?"

Lucien blushed and sat up. "There's a girl I want. I found her one day, down in the Strip District. She's like an angel. I had to put her aside until the fighting was over. Danni said that she was too dangerous to keep. Danni was right, she has a very audacious family—but I want her. If I am the ying—the darkness—then she is my yang. My light. Once we bring the elves to their knees, I want you to help me recapture her."

Tristan nodded even as he inwardly winced at the word "recapture." It was not a word one should use regarding a beloved. It was weird to think of his brother even having a lover. Tristan was too young physically to consider taking one. His body wasn't showing any of the signs of puberty. There was also the problem that as a half-elf, he aged much slower than any of the humans he'd ever known.

"Will you make her an elf?" Tristan said. "So she can stay young as you?"

His brother waved aside the concern. "I made her immortal when I made her a tengu. Transforming her was a way to keep Danni from fiddling with her. The Eyes are tricky to work with. They can see what you're about to do unless you're very...indirect. It makes them infuriatingly independent. Chloe would not be dead if she hadn't been so sure she could dance rings around the changeling. I'd warned her to be careful but she was too confident of her own skills. Danni would have killed my Boo if I hadn't made Boo irreplaceable as part of the Chosen bloodline." His brother grinned. "Danni and the others always underestimate me. They forget I'm of Clarity's bloodline too."

Lucien had all the tengu in his camp killed shortly after Tristan arrived. He'd *known* that he was going to lose all leverage with the Flock even before Joey Shoji had been rescued.

"If you made her tengu," Tristan said, "where is she now?"

Lucien waved lazily as if this wasn't important. "I'm not sure. I dare not ask the Eyes to fetch her, lest they take it upon themselves to kill her. Joey Shoji is back with his people—he was spotted at Poppymeadows when the tengu summoned their dead guardian spirit. Boo wasn't with the other Chosen. She might be at the tengu base, wherever they have that hidden. Or she might have gone back to her family. I don't trust my normal spies. They're too bloodthirsty to fetch someone you love. I need your skills and finesse."

Someone you love. That must be nice. Tristan was glad but a little jealous that Lucien wasn't alone like him. "I'll find her for you."

"Good lad!" His brother bounded to his feet.

Somewhere nearby, something exploded. Birds rose up from the forest like a startled cloud.

"So much for our distraction," Lucien said. "The tengu got their hands on some explosives. The black willows will be sitting ducks for an aerial assault. We need to go before the ship's guards return."

"We're not using this site, then?" Tristan asked.

"It doesn't suit our needs anymore. There was a strong *fiutana* in this valley but it is gone. Either the changeling drained it dry when she turned this area into blue soup or the spell that Impatience put on the spaceship is redirecting the magic to the point that this area matches normal levels of magic. Either way, even if our casting circle survived everything that the changeling did to this valley, the spaceship is now sitting on top of it."

They climbed down the ladder inside the stone

pier to the bridge deck. There a host of true blood oni waited. Just before stepping outside, Lucien said "Masks."

Lucien pulled his on—a scowling red black lacquer demon's face with horns and fangs. It was a fierce façade that covered his child face. It was a grim reminder that his brother had been fighting on Elfhome for over two decades. Tristan's mask was a hand-me-down with a deep scratch where some enemy had gotten too close to his brother.

"Lord Kajo." The true bloods bowed in greeting to Lucien. "What is your will?"

"We're shifting to the second camp. Bring the weapon. If the *fiutana* is intact, we'll set it off there."

Malice had raided the second camp after the spell-worked dragon temporarily slipped out of their control. The dragon had smashed open half of the cabins like piñatas, and feasted on the oni inside. There were scattered bones everywhere, cracking under foot like dried branches. The cloaking spell had been blasted from their crude spell stone, evidence that the elves had followed close behind Malice. It was depressing proof that they were backed into a corner, fighting for their lives.

Things had been so different before the first Startup, so many years ago. Elfhome was this impossibly distant fairyland and they were the exiled rightful rulers. Life is so much cheerier when you're the long-lost prince of a mythical empire; when your "possibly fatal disease" was "a ruse designed to disguise your immortality."

Just when Tristan started to doubt it—thinking it was like Santa Claus but something you told dying children—Pittsburgh vanished. In its place had been a forest of ironwoods just like his father's stories. He was an elf. He was a prince.

He would live forever.

His euphoria lasted for three days until he realized that the people he loved most were pure human.

Those who would be with him for the rest of his life were his father and his brothers. He'd spent decades trying to win their love and trust. He'd done so many questionable things for his father—things he didn't allow himself to ponder deeply. One more distasteful thing—this time to secure Lucien's love—and then, hopefully, it would be the end of it. They would have won the war and there would be others better suited to be tools than himself.

"Here." Lucien handed a leather messenger bag to Tristan. He was speaking in English, something his troops didn't understand, so he wanted Tristan's activities to be secret. "I'll see if the casting circle is intact. I want you to focus on this."

Tristan nodded. He took shelter in one of the undamaged cabins. The camp had housed a small unit of elite true blood warriors. They were the more civilized oni. Their buildings were vaguely Tudor-style in appearance, with thatched roofs, magic-hewed ironwood timbers, and walls of wattle and daub that had been whitewashed with lime. The floors were covered with mats of woven reeds, much like the Japanese *tatami*. Tristan had lived in rougher buildings while pursuing his father's work on Earth. It was ironic that his father's people who had lived in New York for decades now considered these houses too rough to live in. The troops who survived Malice's attack had stripped the building of food, weapons, and bedding. They had left behind only a long plank table and a set of benches. Something smelled faintly like cat urine—perhaps the daub. In the privacy of the cabin, though, Tristan could remove the demon mask without Lucien's troops seeing him.

He could hear that Lucien was ordering his less trusted people away from the buildings on the pretense of setting up a secure perimeter. It meant that the casting circle was intact and Lucien wanted the freedom to inscribe the spell without a mask.

Tristan made sure the table was dry and shifted one of the benches into the sunlight streaming through a set of arrow slits. He sat down, slid up his mask, and opened the leather messenger bag to see what had Lucien handed him.

Lucien had given Tristan information to use in finding his beloved: Carla Marie "Boo" Kryskill.

Their ancient father didn't trust human technology, not so much because he thought it was temperamental, but because it was transitory. During their father's life on Earth, the language of the educated had changed from Greek to Latin to English. He'd lived through the rise and fall of printed newspapers. He'd recently lamented that even handwriting was falling out of use. He'd urged his sons not to get dependent on anything more complex than a pen and paper. It had been advice that Tristan ignored on Earth. He saw no point of not using all the human tools available to accomplish the impossible tasks that his father gave him. Lucien walked a fine line between the two.

The contents of the messenger bag reflected Lucien's balanced approach. There was a thick folder of paper and an iPad. Tristan flipped quickly through the folder. It contained newspaper clippings about the Kryskill family and an odd collection of handwritten notes. Tristan ignored the paper in favor of the tablet. The iPad had hundreds of photographs and videos.

Lucien had kidnapped Boo when the girl was in first grade. Her white-blond hair reminded Tristan of their half sisters, the Eyes, when they were little. They had been sweet children, once upon a time. Boo's hair started to darken to gold as the girl grew older but suddenly returned to its pure white state. Tristan suspected that Lucien had done something to "fix" her hair. It would have needed a deft touch, as spell-working on a child was a delicate procedure.

Lucien liked dressing Boo in white gowns for a look that was filled with ethereal innocence. He must have had the dresses all handsewn for her out of delicate, gauze-like fabrics. He liked to crown her with little bright flowers woven into rings, usually out of blue and yellow. There was always one red note in her outfits, like a splotch of blood on the pure white. It was a disturbing detail, which could not be unseen once Tristan had noticed it.

In the earliest videos, the girl had looked at the camera with wide-eyed fear. The look softened over the years to something that could be sweetness. After Lucien transformed the girl into a tengu female, though, she glared at the lens in rage.

"You have a mountain to climb there, brother, if you want to win that heart."

Beyond Lucien's home movies, there were a lot of other videos to weed through—a majority of them were local TV shows and news broadcasts, most from eight years ago. Tristan skipped them, suddenly aware he'd spent over an hour watching the videos. There didn't seem to be anything else saved on the iPad. He reluctantly opened the thick folder. As he sorted through the paper within it, he wondered about his brother's motivation.

Lucien had tweaked Boo's hair color when she was eight or nine. He allowed the girl to age to sexual maturity before making her immortal. Boo had the tengu crow feet, but had retained her pure white coloring. Lucien had gotten very good at transformational spellcasting. What Lucien had done to the girl had been a mix of fetish and need. Where did one stop and the other begin? When Tristan captured Boo, would Lucien leave her as a tengu or did he plan to quietly make her an elf later?

Did Lucien plan to make himself pure elf?

Lucien was maturing faster than Tristan, despite the fact that Tristan had spent the last two decades on magic-poor Earth instead of Elfhome. It seemed to indicate that while Lucien would be extremely long lived, chances were good that he would not be immortal. If Lucien could so easily change his beloved from human to tengu, going from half-elf to full elf would be a minor tweak in comparison. Knowing his brother, Lucien probably planned to "fix" both of them once they reached full maturity.

Did Tristan want to be full elf? He gained no benefits from being half-human. His humanity, though, was all he had left of his mother. She had been past her prime when he was born. He'd known for years that any visit with her might be the last one. He hadn't wanted to come to Elfhome, afraid that she might die alone while all her remaining children were stuck on another planet.

He pushed aside the morbid thoughts and the ache that they caused within his heart.

He'd divided the papers into several piles. The largest was an unruly mass of old newspaper clippings. Boo's disappearance had been headline news. The search for her had taken up full pages, and then, as time went by, several columns, and finally just small paragraphs.

"These are useless," Tristan muttered as he set them aside. The clippings were ancient history. He'd only resort to them if he hit an utter dead end.

Here was a surprise. Lucien had communicated with Chloe via email. He'd asked simply, "Where is she?" It was a safe enough question, the vagueness itself a code. Chloe had printed out the email and wrote her reply by hand, a dutiful daughter to a technophobe father.

"Little Taipan," Chloe had written in her beautiful, well-practiced script, "taking a doll and turning it inside out renders it invisible. There's a hole in its heart where you used to reside. Eyes that were turned inward look out beyond itself. The landscape it considers is alien to me. By your hand, I am unable to help."

Taipan was Earth's deadliest snake. It was at once a riff on Lucien's oni name and an insult as it underscored Lucien's connection to Earth as half-human. "Little" was a sneer at how short the brothers were compared to their younger sisters. Chloe—and perhaps the others—hadn't realized that their height and apparent age were proof that Father had done something to the girls to make them more human than their older brothers.

That was Chloe for you. Poor, dead, snarky Chloe.

His father's servants had tried to explain the abilities of a trained seer. They were going by what they knew from several thousand years before when his father had an entire stable of well-groomed *intanyai seyosa*. They were hampered by the fact that none of them had the capability to see the future, so it was much like blind people trying to explain moonlight. According to them, a seer's ability worked strongest with someone who was closely associated with them. It was the reason his father married his mother instead of just working with her as a business partner.

What Chloe must have meant was that by making Boo a tengu, Lucien had utterly changed how Boo saw the world. It wiped clean all the connections Chloe had with Boo through Lucien. The other Eyes would be equally hampered.

The date on the email caught Tristan's eye. It was shortly after Tristan arrived on Elfhome with their father. That explained much. Lucien had lost his beloved just as he'd gone from the voice of god to their father's second oldest son. While Lucien was still the main war commander, he could no longer move troops without answering to a higher authority. Since today was the first time Tristan had heard tell of Boo, Lucien must have removed all mentions of her from the official reports. Tristan could guess why—their father would consider Lucien's fixation on the girl as a threat to their success. The Eyes had, hence the entire reason Lucien had needed to transform Boo into a tengu of the Chosen bloodline.

Tristan flipped through the handwritten notes in Lucien's sloppy schoolboy writing. Judging by the condition of the paper they were written on, most of them seemed to have been made years ago, as if Lucien realized early on that he couldn't keep Boo a prisoner for eternity. Perhaps he'd planned to give her more freedom after he was sure that she would freely return to him. He had summaries of every member of Boo's extended family. Grandparents. Parents. Siblings. Aunts. Uncles. Cousins. As Tristan scanned the notes, he couldn't help but shake his head. Lucien couldn't have found a worse set of people to steal a baby girl from. The Kryskills were a large, well-connected, heavily armed family with a colorful history on both sides of the law.

Lucien had set up methods to remotely monitor the Kryskill family. He had tracked them compulsively over years; he had even had someone attending their church and playing bingo every week for eight years. Immediately after Boo's disappearance from the fish hatchery in July, the family showed no real deviations from their normal pattern. Boo's mother, Amanda Kryskill, owned a coffee shop downtown. She worked long hours on weekdays, opening at the crack of dawn and closing at six. It made it easy to keep tabs on her. Their people who worked as moles in the EIA would stop for coffee several times a day in July—until Maynard arrested most of their spies in his organization. The only recent change in Amanda's routine had been an increase of phone use during work hours and marathon cookie baking sessions with her sisters every weekend.

Boo's oldest brother, Alton, foraged for fish, game, and produce to sell to the enclaves. He was the hardest to keep track of. He still officially lived at home with his mother but camped out in the South Hills during the warmer months. Lucien had only monitored Alton via a true blood oni squatting in an abandoned Catholic high school across the street from the enclaves. Reports showed that Alton made all his deliveries—until the Wyverns ferreted out all the disguised oni in Oakland, ending reports on Alton.

According to Lucien's notes, the furniture-maker brother, Geoffrey, had claimed a stately Victorian mansion near his mother's house but didn't seem to actually live there. Since last year, he had been keeping odd hours, often working late at his workshop, sometimes falling asleep at his desk, sometimes driving to an artists' commune in the Strip District to sleep there. His change of pattern seemed to be due to his success at selling his furniture to a high-end showroom on Earth.

The police officer brother, Marc, had been at roll call without fail all through July, August, and into September. The baker brother, Duff, had clocked into work every weekday before the crack of dawn. The teenager brother, Guy, had gotten into trouble at summer school as normal until the end of July, and then spent most of August hanging out with his cousins and brothers.

The older sister, Jane, worked on a television gardening show that seemed to routinely set buildings and people on fire. The notes on the various episodes across eight years made the host sound like an arsonist—several employees, the station's break room, a score of shooting sites, and various homeowners had fallen victim to the man. There been two noteworthy incidents in July. The first had been on Startup when he set himself on fire and landed in Mercy Hospital, allowing him to film Tinker's kidnapping.

The second arson victim had been an EIA private guarding a female tengu who had been found trapped within the ruins of the fish hatchery. The female obviously had been searching for Joey Shoji and the boy had obviously been found by the tengu at some point, but not that day. Lucien's people in the EIA had reported that the television crew had been attempting to get an interview with the prisoner, and while the fire helped to distract the guards, the prisoner had escaped under her own power.

Another elegant note written by Chloe, this time replying to a more direct email asking "Is there a connection between the hatchery and the television show?" Chloe was less poetic this time, reporting that she personally witnessed Maynard calling Jane's crew in as biology experts and giving them the job of killing the *namazu*. Chloe was sure that it was mere chance that put Jane at Sandcastle. Chloe had a deadly flaw, though, of underestimating her enemy. The resources that the Kryskills had mustered to kill the adult *namazu* and the zeal that they put into finding every last egg highlighted how dangerous they could be. Had Chloe been wrong?

Lucien's reports slowly fragmented after that point as their father shifted resources and the EIA dug out their moles. What Lucien did have seemed to indicate that the family hadn't changed their behavior. The only deviation from normal could be explained by an upcoming wedding. Lucien's people had intercepted a wedding invitation addressed to a woman named Cesia Cwiklinski. Jane Kryskill was getting married to a man with the unlikely name of Keaweaheulu Ka'ihikapu Taggart.

"How did you pronounce that?" Tristan muttered. "What ethnic group is that? Wait a minute. I *know* him."

Tristan dug out his own tablet to check his records. Keaweaheulu Taggart was the cameraman for the world-famous naturalist Nigel Reid. The two men had been at the NBC mid-summer gala in New York City. While Tristan had no verification of it, the twins most likely met Nigel there. (Tristan hadn't been able to attend since his mother was there.) The event was set up to bring wealthy fans together with their favorite NBC stars. Considering his mother's plans for the evening, it was possible that Nigel might have been unwitting bait to guarantee that she got her way.

Still, it seemed fishy to Tristan that Taggart had been at the gala and now here, on a totally different world, getting married to Boo's sister. Tristan didn't trust coincidences; he'd set up too many for him to believe that pure chance dictated people's movements. "People without motivation sit at home, watching television. Everyone else has ulterior motives."

As he reviewed his notes on Taggart, he couldn't see any real connection between the twins and the man. Yes, the twins' silly videos had triggered a huge interest in Elfhome, too large to be ignored by the American television networks. *Chased by Monsters* was given the greenlight, though by a network that had no idea who the twins were. Someone managed to bypass his father's gatekeepers and gotten Taggart's and Reid's visa applications approved. His mother had invited the Mayers to the gala in order to get the entire family out of their house so it could be searched. Tristan knew that the twins were huge fans of the naturalist even though Tristan had tried to ignore their personal interests. He had been assigned to protect them, not be their friend.

It had been hard. The twins had reminded him of Esme. The way that they laughed. The set of their mouths when they were angry. The way they took life head-on. The way they plowed through adults. Even the weird little cat noise that they made when they sneezed was like Esme. Everything about them made him mourn his lost sister.

He knew that their father would see the twins as disposable tools.

He also knew how much it hurt his mother to have lost all her children. Tristan hadn't been able to give his mother flowers that last time he went to see her, but he'd been able to give her two granddaughters.

He was wasting time thinking about the twins; there was nothing he could do now. They were on Earth and their older sister, the changeling, had trapped him on Elfhome. His mother would be able to keep the twins safe until they could fend for themselves. Judging by their older sister, that wouldn't take long.

He should be thinking about Boo. Within hours, their main attack would start. He needed a plan of action. He opened a new folder on his own tablet and started to photograph Lucien's handwritten notes on the Kryskills. If Tristan was going to be chasing after the girl, he couldn't carry the incriminating newspaper clippings with him, nor the unsecure iPad filled with damning video.

Chloe had dismissed the fact that Jane Kryskill had been at Sandcastle hours after Boo and Joey Shoji vanished. Tristan didn't believe in coincidence. That Jane interacted with the female tengu searching for Joey was too much for him to overlook.

Tristan's best bet was to infiltrate the family. Normally this would be difficult but once the main attack started, the city would be filled with chaos. He could show up, pretend to be separated from his own family, and stay close. The Kryskills probably would be touching base with one another as they were currently scattered through the city. At some point, someone would probably mention Boo if she had rejoined her family.

Lucien wouldn't have told Boo about his family on Earth, so she wouldn't know about Tristan, Yves, or their father. Boo might have warned her family about "teenage Kajo" but couldn't have warned them about an even younger brother.

Tristan considered making contact with Boo's youngest male cousin, Andy Roach. Lucien's notes indicated that the boy was known to be naïve, trusting, and the worst person to keep a secret. There was a possibility, though, that the Kryskills hadn't trusted the boy with the truth.

Boo's mother was another possible entry into the family. She was downtown at the coffee shop, making her easy to find. A mother who lost one of her children would probably have a weak spot for a child in distress. It would be tricky to put together a solid backstory on such short notice, but he'd dealt with worse conditions.

24: HIDE

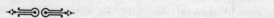

Geoffrey Kryskill's workshop was in McKees Rocks Bottoms, not far from Tinker's junkyard. Geoffrey was worried about thieves breaking in and stealing his stockpile of kiln-dried ironwood lumber, his extensive collection of power tools, and his handmade furniture, so he kept a low profile. The old warehouse was a massive block-long structure that at first glance seemed abandoned.

Oilcan's heart sunk as he pulled into the parking lot. There was no sign of the kids. Where had they gone? Directly to John Montana's gas station? Or had they been stopped before reaching McKees Rocks?

He sat idling in the muddy parking lot, trying to decide what to do. He hadn't circled back to the South Side, since Rebecca said that there had been dozens of oni on foot behind the hornet swarm. Oilcan had cut over to the North Side instead and headed up to the McKees Rocks Bridge.

Rebecca looked horrible. The hornet had stung her twice in the left thigh. The entire leg was swelling up and she was having trouble breathing. Should he trust that the kids were safe...someplace and go... somewhere to get Rebecca's wounds treated? She was tengu—could Mercy Hospital even help her? He couldn't drive to Haven, there were no roads between Pittsburgh and the tengu village.

"Oilcan!" Blue Sky called from one of the upper windows that overlooked the parking lot. "Hey! We pulled inside. Hold on, we'll open the door."

The big doors rattled open, letting out a flood of cooler air heavily scented with sawdust. Oilcan pulled the flatbed into the huge dim warehouse that was Geoffrey's woodshop. The pickups were parked where stacks of rough-cut and kiln-dried lumber usually sat.

The kids gathered around the truck, all asking questions at once. Guy opened the passenger door and lifted Rebecca out. The three big elfhounds gathered around Andy, snuffling and grumbling about Rebecca's scent.

"Stop." Andy waved his hand flat with floor. "Down." The dogs grumbled but settled by the flatbed.

"She has been stung twice by a death hornet." Thorne pointed Guy toward a worktable. "Its venom is brutally painful but not deadly. We need to get her pants and fighting spurs off. The poison makes her limbs swell and tight clothing can restrict her blood flow."

Guy had been acting very adult. After this announcement, though, he put Rebecca down on the worktable and backed away, hands raised, very much a teenage boy.

Cattail Reeds and Barley leapt to undress the girl in a quick and careful manner. Cattail dressed people for a living, but normally they were healthy and upright. Judging by the murmured instructions from Barley, stripping sick and drunk customers of their clothes was something enclave elves learned young.

Thorne pulled out a small handbound book and flipped through it. "I have a spell that can neutralize the poison. The wound should be washed. Ice would be helpful to reduce the swelling if there is a means to make water frozen. We also need to control the bleeding; put pressure on the wounds."

"I can do ice!" Andy dashed off to the workshop's makeshift kitchen, which was a collection of random appliances clumped together next to a big stainless steel bar sink.

"Burn her clothes," Moon Dog added. "The Skin Clan used to use scent markers to indicate a target for a swarm. It will make any hornet in the area attack."

Spot nodded solemnly, wrinkling his nose. It explained the elfhounds' reaction.

"I can burn them." Merry held out her hands for the offending clothing.

Trusting that the kids and the *sekasha* could care for Rebecca better than he could hope to, Oilcan turned to Blue Sky.

"Blue, can you make sure that the casting circle is clean and ready?"

"We can help," Baby Duck said for her and Spot.

As they hurried off, Oilcan turned to Guy. "I know Geoffrey has printers for printing out spells. It would be really useful if I can use them."

"Yeah, sure." Guy led the way to his older brother's printing area. Oilcan and Tinker had helped Geoffrey set up his original system since they were the only ones in the city who understood the mix of spellcasting and technology. The computer workstation had shifted locations and expanded greatly since Oilcan last worked with it.

"I might have to hack his system," Oilcan said when the computer powered on to a login screen.

"Wait." Guy entered a password. "He's been swamped since last year. I come down after school to help Geoffrey out, so I have an account that can access the printers."

Oilcan nodded. Geoffrey had cleared his schedule to make the gates for Sacred Heart. Geoffrey had said that the security of the enclaves trumped all the other projects he had outstanding.

Guy got Oilcan into the computer system and then stood back as he copied the images on his tablet. As the spells printed out, Oilcan glanced around. Andy was carrying a cooking pot full of ice and some clean dishtowels to Rebecca. Thorne and Moon Dog were prepping the tengu girl for a healing spell. All of his kids were accounted for. Someone was missing. It took him a moment to figure out who.

"What happened to the girls from the ice cream shop?" Oilcan said.

Guy pointed up hill toward McKees Rocks proper. "They live over on Church Avenue, across from Saint John's, so we dropped them off. John Montana wasn't home or I would have tried talking Blue Sky into staying there with the little kids. I figured they'd be better off with John than with..." He paused to put his hand to his earbud and listened intently. "They're blasting general quarters. Oakland."

The printer spat out the spell. Oilcan felt a moment

of relief. He and Tinker had the spell. They were out of harm's way. Then he realized that Forge and Geoffrey were still at Sacred Heart.

"I should make a second copy and see if I can get it to Oakland somehow," Oilcan said despite not being sure how. He didn't want Blue Sky taking it despite the fact that the half-elf was the most logical choice.

"I could take it," Guy volunteered.

Oilcan shook his head. Guy was technically younger than Blue Sky and didn't have his *sekasha* immunity with the royal marines. Andy was older than his cousin but lacked all common sense in the face of danger. Thorne wouldn't leave Oilcan. Moon Dog didn't know his way around...

The lights went out.

Could he even print a second copy?

The computer was on a UPS that started to complain. Oilcan eyed the battery unit; it looked too small to be able to power the printer. He tried anyhow and the printer powered up. Then a warning message appeared on the computer screen about exceeding the wattage rating and the entire system shut down.

Oilcan silenced the UPS so it wouldn't continue chirping.

Guy fiddled with his earbud. "The radio station is off the air. The oni must have cut the power." He checked his cell phone. "They cut the cell phones too."

"The circle is clean," Blue called, "but we're going to need lights to trace the spell."

"Geoff has elf shines." Guy scrambled to break out the backup lighting.

The casting circle was under a tall, fifty-foot-square ironwood shelter out the back of the warehouse.

Building it had been a massive group effort four or five years ago. Team Tinker along with members of Carl Moser's enclave and Geoffrey's friends from his high school woodworking club had helped to clear the area of metal, lay the marble onto the tamped sand, and build the shelter without nails. The simple design and the number of people who had turned out to help meant that the work went fast; they'd finished in one day. Afterward they had an amazing pig roast potluck (Geoffrey's family apparently were some type of food gods). They ate and played music and danced on the newly constructed casting circle. It had been a good day. Oilcan was afraid that there wouldn't be days like it in the future if they lost to the oni today.

The "no metal" restriction meant that the shelter had no wires or batteries for lamps. The area was normally lit by sunlight shining through plexiglass skylights. While sunset was hours off, heavy rain clouds blanketed the sky in dark gray. Under the shelter, the casting circle was dark except for the dim purple haze of magic, probably not strong enough for anyone but Oilcan to see.

Guy came out with a wicker cage full of gleaming elf shines and a shimmering bottle of lure. He went around the shelter dabbing the support beams with lure and then released the big shimmering bugs. The elf shines floated overhead, casting dappled light down onto the white marble.

Oilcan inspected the stone, making sure that the kids had actually gotten all traces of old spells scrubbed away. Blue Sky knew the work after a childhood of chasing Tinker's whims, but Baby Duck and Spot didn't know the drill. He was glad to see that despite the lack of experience, the stone looked spotless.

"Good job." Oilcan patted Spot on the head since the boy looked fearful.

There was a deep boom like thunder. It echoed down the river basin, bouncing off the steep hills that flanked the Ohio River. An odd crackling sound followed it.

Spot turned toward the sound and cocked his head. "That's fireworks."

"It is?" Guy said.

They all paused to look up through the skylights. A firework bloomed in the cloud-shrouded sky. The rocket had been fired off from somewhere downtown and then another followed from Mount Washington.

"It means fighting has broken out in Oakland," Guy said.

"We better work fast," Oilcan said as he knelt in the dappled light of the elf shines. He was keenly aware that he was surrounded by children whose lives depended on what he did in the next few hours.

25: OH, THE HORRORS

-->==○==<--

Between Pittsburgh and the East Coast were ancient mountains, worn down by time and weather into tall ridges separated by long, continuous valleys. A virgin forest of ironwood trees blanketed the land in unending green when viewed from the air and a vast dim cathedral of moss and fern rose from the ground. The rich dark smell of earth seemed overwhelming after the baked asphalt of Pittsburgh, but after hours of hiking up and over the steep ridge, it faded from Wolf's senses enough that he started to catch the stench of the large oni camp. It was a smell like that of a slaughter yard mixed with an open latrine. As he led his people down the ridge into the valley, he started to hear noises from the fortification. There were command whistles blowing, drums beating out instructions, and deep, rough voices barking out orders. It sounded like the oni were on high alert.

Wolf came to a rocky outcrop covered with moss. Ahead the trees stopped at the edge of a marshy area. The rocks made a good viewing platform. Wolf crouched at the cliff edge to study the valley. His warriors took up positions around him, careful to keep down so as not to be silhouetted on the summit.

The forest stopped a few yards beyond the foot of the cliff where the land leveled. A beaver dam had been built across the stream that cut through the heart of the valley. The brook had been too small and the land too uneven to make one large pond. A dozen small pools were linked together by a maze of meandering channels. The water had killed all the valley's trees, creating a wide marshy meadow full of denuded stumps and thick clumps of cattail reeds. On the far western side of the marsh, the land sloped up to a stockade wall. The oni had left enough ironwoods standing within the camp so that Wolf couldn't see into it clearly from his elevated perch. Even with the green leafy screen, the scale of it was intimidating. The oni had built a fort of ironwood, a quarter mile square. Wolf could pick out hundreds of tents and cages that once held wargs. Like a kicked anthill, the camp swarmed with creatures. Oni of all sizes moved with intent, some controlling packs of wargs on leashes.

Wolf scanned the ground his people would need to cover to reach the fort. It made a hellish obstacle course. He considered the dam. Would blasting it make the crossing less dangerous? The weather was right for call-lightning, with heavy clouds hanging overhead. The dam seemed poorly made, suggesting that there been a great deal of engineering—although poorly executed—to turn the valley floor into a swamp. "No beaver would make something that sloppy looking."

"Marshes like this one were a common Skin Clan defense," Wraith Arrow murmured. "There will be black willows someplace close. They guard against large predators and keep would-be deserters from fleeing their post."

Wolf cast a fire scry. He picked out a score of black willows currently standing motionless among scrub trees at the far southern end of the marsh. The lack of cover, the unstable ground, and the black willows made the meadow a death trap. Even if he removed the dam, he couldn't make the area safe to cross.

He kept his scry active, studying the signatures returned by the spell. While it couldn't have been seen from where they stood, the oni had dug a narrow trench before the wall, filled with wood spikes coated with something organic that was no doubt poisonous. The seething fort was filled with a confusion of potential magic. There was something huge and covered with active spells trapped within a magically reinforced ironwood cage at the heart of camp. Wolf guessed that it was a horror by the size. Wolf ignored it for now, searching for sign of the *nactka*. There didn't seem to be anything like them within the camp. He focused back on the horror.

Even as he considered the signatures of the huge creature, the horror's presence faded from his scry.

He recast the scry. The giant horror appeared again, easily large as a wyvern with more limbs. Was it some kind of spider? No, it seemed to have some type of wings. He noticed that there were faint echoes of similar creatures in small cages near the western wall.

All the signatures from the horror and smaller versions of it faded away a second time.

What was happening? The fire scry picked up on the combustion potential of everything in an area.

Most organics burned at different rates. He should be able to feel the differences as long as he maintained the scry. Were the reinforcement spells on the cages' timbers absorbing the magic?

Wolf switched to a wind scry. The signature was full of confusion as the thousands of shifting bodies echoed back as a chaotic chop of charged particles. While he could determine little of the horror sheltered by the cage, the power of the scry didn't change as he held it.

"What's wrong?" Wraith Arrow asked as Wolf changed back to a fire scry.

"I think there's more than one horror in this camp. There's a big one but there're several smaller creatures of a similar type on the west end. They're all fading from my scry as if...." He hissed as curse as he realized what it could mean. "I think they're phoenix scorpions."

"Are you sure?" Wraith Arrow said. "The Fire *esva* is worse than useless against them. Fire empowers them."

"It matches with what I've been told of them."

All the Skin Clan's horrors like the phoenix scorpions had been hunted down and killed long before Wolf's father was even born. Maybe even before True Flame had been born.

Had his older cousin noticed the results of Wolf's scry? Would he realize what it meant? Wolf's scry would be nearly invisible to the Stone Clan *domana*; they would only be aware that he was casting spells. Not that it mattered much—they were at a point of no return. The oni were arming themselves. If no attack came, they could pursue the elves, vastly outnumbering them.

"How many of the smaller scorpions?" Wraith Arrow asked. "How much smaller?"

"Four about the size of a horse." Wolf felt True Flame pull from the Spell Stones and cast a scry. He sensed the signatures as if he'd cast the spell himself. He focused on the smaller scorpions covered in the odd runes. There was something disturbingly familiar with them. "Get the *laedin* away. I'm not going to be able to protect them while fighting. I'm casting call-lightning on the horror." The spell needed two hands to cast, which meant he couldn't keep a shield up. He doubted he could kill the horror in a single shot and it was known to be smart enough to rush its attacker. "Have the *laedin* swing south and join Sunder. They'll be safer with the Stone Clan with phoenix scorpions on the loose."

He could feel True Flame recast his scry. The male wasn't attacking, which probably meant he'd identified the horror.

Darkness's gossamer came soaring over the ridge. The oni armed with rifles opened fire on the airship in a panic. Cana Lily, though, was holding a Stone Clan shield on the entire craft.

The gossamer dived toward the camp, its machicolations opening to drop war fire down on the oni.

"No, no, no!" Wolf cast wind blast, trying to shift the chemicals away from the phoenix scorpion.

Flames erupted as the chemicals mixed, water igniting the naphtha and quicklime mixture. The sheets of fire roared up and then snuffed out as the energy of the flame was sucked in by the giant phoenix scorpion. The horror started to glow like a landbound sun. It shattered its cage. It was a nightmare taken form with a scorpion-curled stinger tail, large crab-like pinchers, and transparent wasp wings.

The gossamer paused over the eastern edge of the camp. Its gondola hatch opened. Darkness and his people dropped down, in among the oni, shielded by Darkness. The *laedin* and *sekasha* were all armed with spell arrows. They landed and released their arrows. The spells printed on the shafts were activated by the whistle of them cutting through the air, changing the bolts into brilliant piercing energy.

"Is he mad?" Wolf cried. "Why would he not abort? How could he miss the phoenix scorpion?"

"He's dropped into the heart of the enemy a thousand times before," Wraith Arrow said. "He would not see any reason to not do it again. Here, put this in your ears."

"What is this?" Wolf asked.

"Beeswax and cotton." Wraith Arrow held out two plugs that he had made from his medicine kit. "Be quick about it."

Wolf pushed the wax into his ears. All sound became muffled like he was under water. A moment later, the scorpion began to make a horrific noise. It was like the song of a cicada, only louder than a hundred human sirens combined. Even with the plugs in his ear, the sound seemed to pierce through his head.

"Ready shields!" Wraith Arrow signed using blade talk.

The *sekasha* gathered close around Wolf.

Wolf called on the winds in order to summon his lightning. Magic thrummed around him, ready to be used. He shifted through his call-lightning spell. His right hand primed the clouds as his left hand readied the ground. Magic flooded over the rocky outcrop on a hot wave. The hairs on his arms rose as the magic shifted into potential. He felt it reach its critical point and brought his hands together, aiming the channel through which the lightning would run. The faint leader flashed downward out of the belly of the clouds, and then the return stroke leapt from on top of the scorpion, up to meet the leader with a deafening clap of thunder. The blinding column of light flared the area around the scorpion to white haze, and the thunder rumbled as the stroke climbed up into the sky.

The horror shrieked in pain. The lightning licked the sky, as leader and return stroke danced back and forth over the open channel. There was a strange magical pulse from the scorpion, something akin to a fire scry, but filled with static. It washed over Wolf, identifying him as holding an active attack spell.

"Here it comes!" Wolf shouted and started another call.

It had been huge at the distance of a quarter mile. It grew in scale as it winged toward them. Its chitin exterior glowed molten gold with stored magic; it set fire to the cattails when it landed in the center of the marsh. Steam rose hissing where each of its eight legs touched the damp earth. The keening noise it made grew louder as it neared. Wolf could feel the vibration of it in his bones and under his feet. It felt like nails were being stabbed into his head through his ears.

Wolf brought his hands together, bringing down another leader at the horror. It was his last chance to hit it. Call-lightning was a wildly inaccurate weapon. He couldn't risk hitting his own people once the beast closed with them.

The lightning flared again and again. The flash within a few yards from the rocky outcrop was blinding. Thunder followed instantly, loud enough to feel. Wolf cast call-lightning again, rushing through the motions, hoping for one last hit as it visibly staggered.

Wolf could feel Darkness in the heart of the fort, maintaining a shield around his people as he slammed force strike after force strike through the oni. True Flame had started to blast oni escaping to the north. Where were Sunder and Cana Lily? As if in answer, Cana Lily cast a large inclusive scry that let even non-Stone-Clan *domana* sense what was going on in a one-mile radius.

The horror rushed forward, its eight long legs propelling it like an arrow released from a bow. It was on them faster than Wolf could even follow. The horror was so massive that it towered over the rocky outcrop. Wolf dropped the call-lightning and started to cast a wind shield as it slammed into his *sekasha*. Their shields weren't strong enough to stop the monster, but his people overlapped as they fell back, so the warriors behind them protected those in front even as their spells failed. Even as they slid sideways and back, they slashed at the massive claws that hammered down at them. Wolf had trusted his people to know what to do; still, the tactic surprised him.

The massive barbed tail, the size of an automobile, came slashing forward.

Wolf jumped backward and shouted the activation of his shield. It snapped into existence, buffering the head-splitting noise that the horror was making.

He paused, panting, holding his shield.

The horror was staggering even though there seemed

to be no visible damage to it. All the *sekasha*'s hacking slashes at the claws had done nothing to mar the gleaming gold chitin. The delicate transparent wings weren't even scorched. The only markings were odd yet familiar spell runes.

"Oh, no!" Wolf whispered as he recognized it.

Wraith Arrow couldn't have heard Wolf but a glance at his face made Wraith Arrow flash "What is it?" in blade talk.

Wolf signed: "Conference with me."

Wraith Arrow stepped closer so that his personal shield overlapped Wolf. The howl of the horror reduced enough that they could hear each other shout.

"The runes on the horror! It's the same spell that the oni used on little dogs to make them bigger than a horse. It's why your blades aren't damaging it; the outside is a solid illusion created by magic. The other four small scorpions in camp can be this size instantly; all the oni need to do is trigger the spell."

Wraith Arrow nodded slowly as he grasped the implications. "Stormhorse said that you needed to kill the beast within the illusion, but that his bullets wouldn't pass straight through the outer layer. They were deflected from a killing blow within the illusion."

"The metal of the bullet would be influenced by the spell. A spell arrow would fly straight."

"If we could see the inner flesh," Wraith Arrow pointed out. "There's no guessing where the beast actually is inside that monstrosity."

The horror in front of them was larger than a building but the creature at its core was only the size of a horse. The sekasha would need to see the vulnerable heart protected within the illusion. Tinker had disrupted the constructs at the junkyard with the powerful magnet that she used to lift automobiles. How could he replicate that effect with his magic without making the scorpion more dangerous? Wait—when he had shot the dogs, the metal within the bullet disrupted the illusion momentarily even as the spell changed the bullet's path.

"Try shooting it," Wolf said.

Wraith Arrow nodded his understanding. He flashed instructions in blade talk. His people normally carried custom-made, low-metal assault rifles. The guns still had the possibility of warping the *sekasha*'s personal shield, so many of the older warriors refused to carry them in active combat. They preferred to rely on spell arrows. With the *laedin* deployed to the Stone Clan, it meant that only five of his people had rifles. While the rest stood ready with spell arrows, the five opened fire.

The bullets pinged off the glowing chitin.

Wraith Arrow signaled a cease-fire. "We need something bigger to punch through that shell."

Wolf needed a big piece of metal. Was there something he could use in the oni camp? He focused on the signatures from Cana Lily's large scry. There was a small knot of oni loading up a mortar launcher. The weapon was a tall tube of metal with an explosive dropped down into it. As the shell soared out, Wolf grabbed hold of the rocket-like round with his wind and jerked it toward him.

"Get ready!" he shouted although he knew that his people probably wouldn't hear him over the monster's din. He needed to trust that they would guess what he was doing.

Wraith Arrow must have recognized what spell Wolf cast. His First flashed "Ready arrows!" in blade talk. Those holding rifles swapped quickly to bows.

It was like trying to guide an invisible fish through a raging river. The wind didn't allow more than violent pushes and pulls. The mortar roared across the distance and slammed into the massive horror. For a moment, the illusion flickered, going transparent to reveal the phoenix scorpion inside like a small gleaming heart. A moment was all the *sekasha* needed. They released their taut bowstrings. Fifteen shafts of pure light leapt the distance and struck home. The massive form crumpled to the ground, the illusion spell continuing even after the heart was dead.

The sudden quiet was blissful.

"You said that there were four more?" Wraith Arrow asked as he shouldered his bow.

Wolf nodded as he focused again on Cana Lily's ground scry. Darkness and his people were killing everything inside the oni camp with force strikes and spell arrows. Darkness blocked the eastern gate out of the fort. To the north, columns of fire marked where Prince True Flame fought. With the cages holding the horrors in the west, most of the oni were choosing to flee south toward Sunder. Hir let them come in a massive wave and then cast the spell "liquefy." The oni foundered in the sudden pool of liquid mud. Hir followed with "condense" and the ground returned to solid, encasing the oni under the rock-hard surface.

The small phoenix scorpions were still in their cages. Wolf started a call-lightning, hoping to kill them before they could be enlarged. Even as he focused on them, someone worked to free them. Like most of the Skin Clan creations, the beasts were untamed monsters, meaning that they would kill even their owners if they came into range. The cages were stout and the oni were having trouble getting close to the already enraged beasts.

Wolf made their life harder by raining lightning down on their heads. The thick ironwood timbers of the magically reinforced cages, though, were protecting the scorpions. The horrors were unharmed even as their handlers were killed. Darkness retreated farther east, his shields flickering as he switched to one that would protect his people from Wolf's spells.

"Can't you see that I'm not doing damage?" Wolf growled at the distant *domana* that had no way of hearing him. "Hit them!"

Forest Moss dropped the shield he'd been holding for Sunder and cast liquefy under the cage furthest from Darkness. The trapped horror sunk into the earth. Once it was entombed, Forest Moss solidified the ground around it.

"Good!" Wolf reported to Wraith Arrow what the Stone Clan *domana* were doing.

"But will that kill them?" Wraith Arrow asked.

"It will keep the oni from enlarging them. The cages should hold; they're magically reinforced iron-wood." Wolf cast his shield, waiting to see how the fight within the fort resolved. He couldn't do much more without endangering Darkness's people.

Forest Moss carefully entombed two more cages while Darkness attempted to back out of the fort, away from the earth turning to mud. He was hampered by the flood of oni who had realized that the south was a death trap.

Wolf did flame strikes to clear the way for Darkness. Once the Stone Clan moved back, Forest Moss entombed the last cage.

Wolf paused in his attack to take stock of the battlefield. The oni seemed to be moving without plan, attacking whatever lay in front of them instead of acting as units. Were all the oni commanders dead? Or were there never commanders present? Considering the black-willow-infested swamp, the trench of poisoned stakes, and the caged horrors, the camp felt like a huge trap. Wolf couldn't have taken it alone. He suspected even the Harbingers would have found it difficult. True Flame would have been helpless against the scorpions.

The others might consider it an easy battle, but it could have been very different if they hadn't worked together. Wolf wouldn't have wanted to go into this fight with Earth Son or Cana Lily at his back. The Harbingers understood the need to put differences aside.

Did the oni not expect *domana* from three clans to move against them? Wolf would have been hard-pressed to win by himself. Queen Soulful Ember had been bracing for this battle since before Pittsburgh arrived on Elfhome. The speed at which Prince True Flame had arrived in force meant that his cousin had been standing ready for the call. He could have had his brother Blue Jay here if he'd been wise enough to ask.

Cana Lily cast a wide scry to the east. The oni reinforcements were coming.

There could be no doubt: this *was* a trap.

26: TRIGGER THE TRAP

➤━━◦○◦━━➤

Tristan had just finished up piecing together a solid fake identity when he noticed a hush falling over the camp. He had been only vaguely aware of the low murmur of voices as the troops worked around the cabin he occupied. But now the warriors had all gone silent. Tristan lifted his head and listened intently. The high whine of a speeding hoverbike was growing louder as it raced toward them.

"We're getting company!" Lucien called out in English. "One of the Eyes! Remember, I don't want them to know about your mission."

Tristan stuffed the iPad and all the papers back into the messenger bag. With his work hidden away, he pulled on his demon mask and went out to greet the incoming rider.

"I have what I need," Tristan said, adjusting his mask. He handed back Lucien's messenger bag. "Are you sure it's one of our little sisters?"

Lucien took the bag and handed it to one of his

trusted underlings. "No one else would ride at that speed."

True, while they weren't that far from Pittsburgh, they were in virgin forest. There were nothing more than deer trails through the thick forest bracken and fallen branches.

They had had five little sisters: Adele, Bethany, Chloe, Danni, and Felicie. Chloe was dead. Which of the four was coming? He hadn't seen any of them since they graduated from college. He hoped it was Bethany. She was his favorite. He was afraid, though, that something horrible had happened to sweet little Bethany.

A few years back, he'd been suddenly forbidden to even mention his younger sisters. He had thought it had been in reaction to his mother having dreams of stolen children. In hindsight, the nightmares had been triggered by the birth of the twins, but he had assumed that his mother's gift had uncovered the truth about the Eyes.

Since he'd arrived on Elfhome, he had caught guarded references to the girls—no, women, as they were no longer young. All except Bethany. If she'd ever been in Pittsburgh, all traces of her had been wiped out. He suspected now that the sudden silence on Earth hadn't been about his mother's dreams but something that his father had done. Something that his father didn't want to be known by his mother and perhaps the other Eyes, and maybe even Tristan himself.

What had their father done to Bethany?

He pushed the question out of his mind, focusing instead on the sound of the hoverbike. It was most

likely to be Danni, who worked closest to Lucien. She
had been the one who forced Lucien into transforming
Boo. She was also the one most likely to oppose any
plan of recapturing Lucien's lost love.

"Our baby sisters can't read minds," Lucien murmured even as the whine of the engine grew louder,
"but I've found it's best not to think of things you
don't want them to know about. Thoughts are the
precursor of actions. When you create a plan, it's as
if you've set up vibrations in the likely outcome to
your actions. The Eyes sense those vibrations, just
like sharks can detect the thrashing of a swimmer."

In other words, Tristan should clear his head of
any plans he had for tracking down Boo.

What was safe to think about? What possibly could
have happened to Bethany? Probably not.

The hoverbike roared through camp, ten feet up and
going close to a hundred miles per hour. It slammed into
an insane turn to spiral upward even as it braked hard.
The woman on the bike was wearing camo coveralls, a
green helmet, and an assault rifle strapped across her
back. Danni wouldn't be caught dead in camo. It was
Adele.

Once her forward momentum was at zero, Adele
floated back down to land beside Tristan.

"Oh, look at you!" She killed the hoverbike's engine.
"You're still so tiny! Have you grown at all since I
left New York?"

"I'm bigger." Tristan resisted the urge to stand up
straighter. Humans used to say it to him all the time.
He'd forgotten how annoying it was. At least now it
didn't make him cry because he knew that one day
he *would* eventually grow up.

She threw back her head and laughed. She sounded like Lucien when she laughed like that. She picked Tristan up, spun him around, and then gave his head a hard knuckle rub.

"Ow!" Tristan cried.

"You're hurting him," Lucien said. "Leave him be. You might be seen."

"I won't. You know that I know that I won't," Adele said.

Tristan glanced about and saw that she was right. They were screened on all sides by the cabins.

"What are you doing here?" Lucien said.

"*Pffft.*" She pulled off her helmet, revealing that she had buzzcut her hair to a military crop. Their father wouldn't be pleased; he had a thing about long hair. Her pale blond hair had started to gray already. Chloe's picture in the paper had looked so much like their mother that it hurt. Adele never had the same polished style; she looked like she could be a long-lost, chain-smoking biker aunt. "I need to talk to our glorious god-emperor father. It was easier to come here than to head out cross-country for a *mei* and hope to catch Heaven's Blessing."

During his thousands of years exiled on Earth, their father had used many false names. Adele had used his true name, the one he had been known by when he ruled all of Elfhome.

"He's coming here?" Lucien pointed at the ground at his feet littered with gnawed bones.

Adele posed dramatically, the back of her right hand pressed to her forehead, her eyes closed. "So I have foreseen!" She threw her hands up to spin in a circle. "Oh, my God! Sunshine! It feels so good to get out of that cave! I've been stuck there in the dark for forever!"

"Stuck?" Tristan asked. "Why were you stuck in a cave?"

"Because Heaven's Blessing wanted me to see what was happening on Earth! It was one of those tiny, tiny spyholes between worlds. I've been stuffed inside a small cave, waiting for some useful vision to hit me, and praying that a family of raccoons wouldn't show up wanting to den for the winter. Do you have any candy? I'm dying for chocolate."

"Who has never grown up?" Lucien rooted through his satchel to pull out a plastic bag filled with individually wrapped chocolate truffles. It surprised Tristan that Lucien had candy with him, considering how light they were traveling. Had his brother "seen" that Adele would show up? Or was the candy just a side product of Lucien's excessive sweet tooth? Lucien held out the bag but pulled it back just before Adele took any. "What did you see?"

"Oh, don't be like that." Adele pouted.

"Once they're gone, they're gone." Lucien rustled the bag. "We won't see chocolate from Earth until the war is won."

Adele snorted. "I know you've got an entire warehouse of food stocked up with things like that."

"For me and the people that make me happy," Lucien said.

"Fine." Adele promised to share information by reaching out and twiddling her fingers. "I might as well tell you. Heaven's Blessing won't give me a private audience, so my news will be common knowledge in about an hour."

Lucien dipped the bag forward and she grabbed a big handful of the truffles.

"You're his heir now," she continued, unwrapping the first truffle. "As much as the immortal god-emperor Heaven's Blessing needs a heir."

Lucien's eyes went wide and then he pulled his mask down over his face. "Yves is dead?"

Adele popped the truffle in her mouth. "Uh-huh."

"What happened to him?" Tristan asked.

"Hm?" Adele shrugged, eyes closed, focusing on the taste of the chocolate. "So good."

"Adele," Lucien said sternly. It seemed even more menacing when coming from behind his demonic-looking mask.

Adele spread her hands to indicate she had no idea, then unwrapped another truffle. "Sometimes the visions are crystal clear and sometimes they're all weird, dreamy things, like being naked at school or trying to take a final for a class you forgot that you signed up for. I can't make heads or tail of it—there were these giant birds and a talking dog and lots and lots of mice, but Yves definitely ended up under a ton of rocks. I think there was a cave-in. I'm not sure, but I think the tengu Nestlings were buried with him."

Tristan had always assumed that he would be glad if Yves died; the male had been cold and distant and often cruel to him. In his heart of hearts, though, he must have always loved his older half brother despite all that. It hurt to know Yves was dead.

Lucien stood silent, looking skyward as if gazing at something written there. After a minute, he murmured, "I see. Yves was supposed to be here to oversee this part. Father must have decided that I didn't have enough experience. He's not waiting at Shikaakwa like we planned."

"Or Fefe saw something go wrong," Adele said around a mouthful of chocolate.

Lucien turned sharply to her. "Like what? Have the rebels turned back from the trap?"

Adele snorted as she unwrapped her last truffle. "I've been tuned into a different wavelength for days. I only checked to see where Heaven's Blessing was going to be, not why. That would be a whole lot harder for me. It's always worst to be first. Heaven's Blessing had all the kinks ironed out by the time he got to tweaking Fefe. That's why she's with him and I've been stuck in a cave."

Adele popped the chocolate into her mouth.

"Please see what you can find out," Lucien said.

"Fine. I will." She pulled out the red ribbon of the *intanyai seyosa* caste and tied it as a blindfold over her eyes.

Their father's servants had tried to train the Eyes but there was much they didn't know or couldn't remember. Why a red ribbon? Was it just symbolic or was there a reason it needed to be red? None of the elves at the mansion had known. They left it to the Eyes to determine what worked best for them and the girls had adopted the caste's badge of power.

Adele liked to move her hands while "seeing" in graceful dance-like motions. It reminded Tristan of hula. She swayed in place, languidly moving her hands. She hummed softly to herself. He couldn't recognize the tune.

"The sun is setting." Adele traced the arc of a setting sun with her right hand, dipping down into the west. She elegantly raised her left hand. "The radiance is fading. The dawn will bring a new world. Heaven's Blessing stands poised to take back what was . . ."

Adele went still. Slowly she cocked her head.

"What is it?" Lucien said.

"The moon is waning. It's full of mice, nibbling away at the cheese?" Adele cocked her head the other way. "It's making the moon's orbit wonky and it might fall?"

"What's that supposed to mean?" Lucien said.

Adele tore off her blindfold and stuffed the red fabric back into her pocket. "It's the damn giant birds and talking dog and lots and lots of mice again. I don't understand. They were on Earth. How are they here too? They're running all over the place, ruining everything."

"Ruining everything?" Lucien echoed. "They going to stop us from using the device?"

"I don't . . . I don't know. It's all weird and wiggly. Most people have one or two paths of action that you can see but this is *thousands* of paths, all crisscrossing, moving so fast its blurry. I can't tell if the mice are supposed to represent one person I've never met or a group of people."

"If they were on Earth first, then they're probably human," Tristan said. "Maybe it's agents like the NSA pair or maybe it's a corporation."

"Danni sent a strike team to take out Midas," Lucien said. "If they are your mice, then they should not be a problem much longer."

This was news to Tristan. Who or what was Midas? He didn't want to ask and betray to Adele how little he knew about the current plans. He would need to ask Lucien privately, if the day allowed.

Adele took out the blindfold and ran the piece of

fabric through her fingers as if she were considering donning it again. "I shouldn't be seeing the mice if Danni has already taken steps to eliminate them. Their impact on our plans is still massive. Fefe must have seen our rodent infestation and warned Heaven's Blessing."

"Here they come," Lucien said.

Tristan pulled on his oni mask even as he scanned the forest around them. He could sense no movement. Both Adele and Lucien were gazing upward.

He wasn't sure how Lucien sensed their father's arrival. One moment the sky over them was gray with rain clouds. The next it was filled with a massive gossamer airship. The displaced air boomed loudly as it washed the briny scent of the gossamer down over them.

"What in the world?" Tristan gasped. "Did that gossamer just teleport?"

"It was my 'welcome home' present to Father. A bit of a flex to show him what I can do."

Tristan stared upward, stunned by the achievement. How in the world had Lucien managed that? When did he do it? The shimmering, nearly transparent gossamer seemed too large for being less than three decades old but it couldn't be older. Or could it? Had Lucien spell-worked an adult gossamer? The gondola was lavish imperial red with gleaming gold trim. There were black Elvish runes on the bow that spelled out "Heaven's Light," which was a play on Lucien's name.

What did Tristan have to offer their father? Nothing as impressive as this. His last major feat had been ferreting out the Chosen bloodline, but that had all been rendered moot. They were on the cusp of a new world order. He might desperately need Lucien's protection. He'd been growing hesitant about finding Boo. To keep Lucien's good will, though, Tristan might have to swallow the sense of wrong that he had gotten about the entire mess. For better or worse, the girl was now an important game piece in the war. If their father managed to find Haven and kill the rest of the Chosen bloodline, she would be the lynchpin to controlling the tengu Flock. She was young and had been meticulously sheltered in Lucien's care. She wouldn't be able to rule the Flock alone. Someone would take control of her; it might as well be Lucien. He, at least, loved her.

Mooring lines were cast down and made fast to anchors that Tristan hadn't noticed before. He drifted back. Now was not the time to catch his father's attention. The war had not gone well in the last two months. The news of Yves' death was going to hit hard.

I shouldn't be so terrified of the man that gave me life.

But his father wasn't a man. He was an ancient being that was ruthless and ambitious. He'd proved over and over again that he'd use his own flesh and blood to achieve his goals. How many of his children had he put in the grave? As his father's people had briefed Lucien on the incoming Harbingers, it became clear that he and his brother were not his father's first brood. There had been countless half brothers and half sisters born long ago. All the others had died in their father's service. Yves had been the only survivor, but now even he was gone.

It was clear now why Lucien had been careful to make himself so valuable to their father.

The metal elevator descended from the gondola.

Father had given up his human clothes, returning to his rich purple imperial robes. They were hand embroidered with red orchids. He wore a duster of red fairy silk with the shimmer of protective spells carefully painted in silver. His hair was no longer carefully contained in a discreet braid but flowed down his shoulders like gleaming white silk, a testament to his health and vitality. It had been something carefully beaten into Tristan after he had left his mother's care: hair was a badge of honor. He was to wear it as long as possible despite his covert missions.

It wasn't until Tristan came to Elfhome, and had been told their true history, that he realized why his father was so focused on long hair. His father had been born a sickly albino with extremely weak eyesight. If he had not been the firstborn child of a powerful female, he would have been cast aside, perhaps even drowned as an infant. Instead he'd been painstakingly spell-worked to be perfect in every way that magic could make him. It was said that a hundred thousand slaves had been blinded so that spells could be developed to allow him to see and, more importantly, he would not pass the weakness on to the royal bloodline. His father's eyes were no longer the light pink color that they had been at birth but a striking amber color flecked with vivid red. It was like looking into the heart of a bonfire.

Tens of thousands of years, though, had not erased his father's shame of being flawed at birth.

His father stepped off the elevator as if he already ruled the world. He swept his fiery gaze over Lucien and Tristan to focus on Adele. "Where is my son?"

He said it as if he had only one.

"Forgiveness." Adele bowed low. "Yves is dead. He was killed in a landslide while still on Earth."

His father took the blow with only a slight tightening of the muscles of his face. He lifted his right hand slightly.

Felicie ghosted forward from behind their father. She styled herself after Pure Radiance, dressed in a flowing gown of white fairy silk with a red ribbon tied over her eyes. She had even painted her fingernails a frosted white. Her white hair spilled down her back almost to her knees. She walked as if gliding on air. She looked decades younger than Adele instead of just being a few hours' difference in age. "This explains why Yves was absent from my visions. His death is not unexpected. It does not require us to change our plans."

"The Harbingers took the bait." Lucien spoke without removing his mask. "They are moving into position to attack the eastern camps. The Fire Clan accompanies them. As expected, none of the wood sprites are part of the rebel forces. Danni is orchestrating the collection of them."

Felicie waved lazily as if dismissing what Lucien said. "Something has stirred the changeling. Neither she nor her cousin is in place. Danni has tracked the cousin but the changeling will evade her—as she is wont to do. Our strike on Midas is also uncertain—someone is meddling in our efforts."

Tristan wished he knew who or what Midas was. It reminded him again of how little he'd been involved in the overall battle plan. Most of what he knew, he'd gleaned from careful observation.

"Mice," Adele whispered. "Most likely."

If anyone else heard her complaint, they ignored it.

"I can deploy my little brother to investigate," Lucien said. "He can go into the city without a second glance from anyone."

It made a good cover story to explain Tristan's absence as he searched for Boo.

Heaven's Blessing flicked his hand, allowing the venture.

Lucien nodded his acknowledgment, only a slight loosing of his hands to indicate his excitement.

Tristan was glad he had on the oni mask so that he didn't need to control his face. He wasn't sure what emotion he should have displayed. Excitement for Lucien? Eagerness for their father? Cool disinterest for the Eyes?

Lucien was updating their father. "Turtle Creek was no longer viable. The levels of magic here are suitable. The platform was not damaged by Malice or the rebels. We have made the needed preparations."

By saying "we" instead of "I," Lucien shared the credit with him despite the fact that Tristan hadn't done anything. It was a safe gift considering Lucien's spellcasting prowess.

"Let us proceed," Heaven's Blessing said.

Tristan had been working out a cover identity longer than he realized. While he'd been searching city records for a child that the Kryskills wouldn't know but could verify existed, Lucien and his most trusted people had taken the wooden covers off the massive white marble casting circle, and cleaned the stone until it gleamed. There was no need to check the power levels of the *fiutana;* the flow of magic was so strong that it was visible to the naked eye.

Lucien had traced out the complex transformation spell, most likely similar to the one he'd used to transform his beloved Boo from human to tengu. At its center were connection points that would interlock with the spell tracings on the *nactka's* shell.

Heaven's Blessing took off his duster and handed it to Felicie. He walked out onto the casting circle, his bootsteps loud on the stone. He said nothing but nodded at what he saw. "Put the *nactka* into place."

Lucien took the large egg-like *nactka* out of its bag and carried it to the center of the spell. He turned it slightly, eyeing the spell tracings, until he was sure it was perfectly aligned, and then set it into place. With the *nactka* in place, he added the blood taken from Jewel Tear while she had been drugged.

"Thousands of years I've worked and planned and waited for this day," their father said. "I had a palace grander than anything Earth has ever seen. An empire that stretched from the shores of the Great Western Ocean to the islands off the coast of the Far East Sea. The idiots burned it all to the ground and then squabbled over the cinders. We will take it back and rebuild to the grandeur that it once was. We start now."

Heaven's Blessing spoke the initiation word, activating the spell. The outer shell of the spell took form and rose up to rotate clockwise. A second and third shell shimmered into being as Heaven's Blessing triggered the limiters. They canted up to spin counterclockwise at 45- and 135-degree angles. The magic grew dense, a visible shimmer. The power spread inward, activating segment after segment, spiraling inward toward the *nactka*.

The last shell encircled the *nactka*, waiting for the final parameters.

Heaven's Blessing raised his hand and spoke: "*Nota. Kirat. Naerat. Dashavat.*"

With each parameter command, the interlock activated at a cardinal point on the *nactka*. After the last, it sat there pulsing with potential.

With a quiet, pleased smile, Heaven's Blessing spoke the last command.

The spell activated in a blinding flash and a blast of warm wind that sent the dead leaves swirling away. Tristan felt the power wash over him, backed by the full strength of the *fiutana*. The fine hairs on his arms rose.

"It is done," their father said. "The *domana* will fall and we will take the Westernlands. Once we have this bastion secure, we will take Winter Court."

27: THE TINKER DOMI COMPUTING AND RESEARCH CENTER

So much had happened since the start of summer, Tinker often lost track of all the little details. She couldn't remember what day exactly she rescued Windwolf except it had been during the June Shutdown. After accidently agreeing to be magically transformed into an elf, she'd been dragged off to Aum Renau by the Wyverns to meet with the queen. Said meeting lasted for days and days to become the most boring three weeks that Tinker had ever endured in her life. Windwolf's coastal palace was like living in the middle of the forest as some of the "rooms" were just groves of trees with a network of glass roofs suspended between their trunks. There had been no electricity. No computers. No internet. Paper was a rare commodity, treated like it was edged with real gold. Windwolf had a library but it contained mostly books that were over two hundred years old. The most scientifically minded of them was a copy of *Philosophiæ*

Naturalis Principia Mathematica by Sir Isaac Newton but it was written in Latin or something.

She'd been bored, bored, bored to the point that she had learned to ride a horse and use a bow and arrow. (Granted, the latter skill came in handy for killing Lord Tomtom but at the time she was simply out-of-her-skull bored.)

When Queen Soulful Ember finally—*finally*—gave her royal permission for Windwolf and Tinker to return to their interrupted life, they arrived during the July Shutdown. Pittsburgh was missing. It had gone to Earth, leaving Tinker behind. All that remained on Elfhome with her were the enclaves built along the northern arch of the Rim.

The enclaves proved to be just as primitive as Aum Renau.

A great many truths dawned on Tinker that day. One of which was that she had been utterly plucked out of the cycle of life as she knew it. Eternity loomed before her—huge and massive and boring as hell if she didn't have her normal level of technology. The other truth was that nothing in human civilization ever lasted more than a few hundred years. Even the Chinese imperial rule had been a series of various dynasties rising and falling. Sooner or later (and it proved to be sooner rather than later—by her own doing no less) she was going to be stuck on Elfhome with whatever happened to be there when the gate failed.

She'd freaked out.

The next morning she had commandeered a fleet of construction vehicles and began to create infrastructure. Almost as soon as she had started, though, she was kidnapped by the oni, never to return to the hilltop. She had managed to totally forget about it—which seemed inconceivable until one considered what the rest of her summer had been like.

That morning, they had cut down five acres of virgin ironwood forest. She had left the hilltop denuded except for massive stumps. (She had thought that they would need to use dynamite to blast out the rootballs, but the elves had said they had some kind of magic to excise the huge remains.) There had been detailed, ambitious, but often unrealistic plans tacked to a hastily erected bulletin board. (She wasn't thinking too sanely that day.) She was sure that the shanghaied humans from the EIA and the city would have fled shortly after she had left. Windwolf had told her that the work had continued after she disappeared, but she figured that was just his people. Yes, the landscaping would be beautiful but would there be any electricity?

Tinker doubted it.

Stormsong had promised, though, that the Tinker Domi Computer and Research Center had honest-to-God technology. More importantly, it had a casting circle. Tinker hadn't included one in her plans, so someone else must have decided to put it in. Windwolf? Tooloo? Being that Tinker couldn't think of any other place with computers and a casting circle—that she hadn't blown up or dismantled—she had decided to give it a try.

The construction site seemed like a totally different place. Someone had pushed farther into the virgin forest, clearing a full twenty acres of the snaking ridgeline until it lay windswept. The massive stumps had been removed, the hilltop leveled, and wild flowers sown. White drifts of yarrow covered the ground. Lobelia and phlox created islands of color. Tinker had designed wind turbines made out of Ford 150 trucks. She had barely finished one base tower before Lain pulled her down off it and talked sense into her. Someone had finished her work. A line of sixty-foot-tall wind turbines crowned the ridge, facing west, their long white sails turned against a sky filled with rain clouds. Her bare-bones tower had been modified to something more elven in design with a solid stone base and wood shingle sheathing. (This made her happy as the structures would be able to offer more defense during an attack—which was probably the point of the changes.) To the north and east, the ironwood forest stretched out as far as the eye could see as a sea of green. To the west, the white dome of the Observatory peeked out over the forest roof. To the south, the land dipped down to the river with tips of the skyscrapers barely visible. At one time, the Rim cut its arc clean through the area but time had pushed the forest into the city proper, diffusing the line.

The dirt road had been graveled to make it more passible. There had been a stout gate with royal marines standing guard. The marines had waved the Rolls-Royce through once they saw Pony at the wheel. A ten-foot-tall fence of rough-hewn ironwood lined the edge of the perimeter of the hilltop, protecting the compound from anything that might venture out of the virgin forest.

Tinker expected elves, perhaps some horses and maybe even *indi*. She hadn't expected the surprising number of EIA trucks and cars parked just inside the gate. Yes, there were more royal marines within the fence line, but the bulk of the people in sight were men.

"What the hell?" Tinker muttered. "What are all these humans doing here?"

"Wolf asked Maynard to assign someone to oversee

the technology side of the project," Stormsong explained. "Considering the progress made, the person must have been given command of an entire section of the EIA."

A tall EIA officer spotted the Rolls and crossed the compound to meet it. Tinker recognized him but it took her a minute to remember from where. He'd led the squad of EIA commandos who had helped rescue Oilcan's kids. Oh, good, he should be willing to cooperate if he'd followed her into the whelping pens. She hadn't bothered to catch names as she charged into the pens but she'd collected Captain Roger A. Josephson's name and phone number just in case she couldn't get hold of Maynard and needed backup.

The captain was a tall human, solid without being thick, with his reddish blond hair shaved on the sides in a military cut. "*Domi*, we didn't expect you to... well, I guess we never expect anything you do. How can we help?"

"You're in charge here?" Tinker said. "I thought you were some kind of combat commander."

"Yes, I am—and I am. My command are special operations forces. We're a combat unit that specializes in establishing infrastructure if it's been compromised by sabotage or nature. I'm actually new to Pittsburgh; we were deployed after the Viceroy was attacked. Maynard assigned me to the tech center in July. My unit was the only one close enough to respond when you needed help in the whelping pens."

"I was told that you have a casting circle here." Tinker scanned the compound. There were lots of buildings of all varieties, some still under construction. She was pleased that the idea of being "separate from Pittsburgh's infrastructure" seemed to continue after she left. There was a water tower and men were installing a large septic system to handle sewage.

"The casting circle is in the last tent on the right." Captain Josephson pointed at a large white tent of elf canvas. "A strong ley line crosses the area that we cleared, so I had one put in—"

"You did?" Tinker said in surprise.

"The Viceroy made it clear that if I were to discover any gaps in your plans, I should see they were filled. The casting circle is just one of several items that I thought were needed to complete the project. We haven't gotten around to building the permanent shelter as it needs to be constructed without nails."

"Good, good, good." Tinker pointed to the only thing that had an electrical panel on it. It was a small mobile office. "Computers? Printers? The type that can print spells?"

"Yes." Josephson trailed after Tinker as she started for the computers. "We're building a permanent building to house the equipment but it's not finished yet. We focused on finishing the wind turbines and securing the area."

"Oh! Oh my," Tinker whispered at the set up inside the mobile office. She wanted it all. The huge monitors. The sleek computers. The printers. The digital whiteboards. The climate control. All of it must have come straight from Earth with the rest of Josephson's command. "My cousin just sent me something that I need to print out."

Josephson gave her the password for the network. She connected and sent the spell to the printer.

"Do you need anything else?" Josephson asked.

"We might get company if the oni managed to track me." Tinker copied the list that she'd been making on her datapad. She emailed it to Josephson's contact information. "Here's a list of things and where your people can find them. Items at the top of the list are the most important. Anything you can collect will help."

His eyebrow rose at the list. "I'll get right on it."

Oilcan had given no explanation as to where he'd gotten the spell that he'd sent her. He merely wrote, "*Cast this spell as soon as possible, it will shield you from the magic bombs in Dufae's box.*"

Tinker had studied the photographs that Oilcan had sent her. They were disturbing on so many levels. The new spell that suggested a brilliance that matched hers. The crayon notes reminded Tinker that she'd been at her most dangerous when she thought she totally understood the world. The comprehension of what Tinker and Oilcan had accessible to them and what they didn't, though, suggested that one or both of the twins could match Tooloo in *knowing* unknowable things. It was as if after making her, the gods twisted the dials to eleven and let loose a flood.

Tinker printed out the spell, cued up other spells that she thought might be useful in the upcoming fight and headed to the casting circle. Shortly after Oilcan signaled her with Morse code, the *domana* in the east began to fight in earnest. Tinker could feel the call for magic to all three Spell Stones as small pings on her awareness. Tooloo said that the other players in the deadly poker game were about to use the Dufaes' bombs. Tinker hadn't completely believed her. Tooloo twisted the truth into pretzels. The twins, however, seemed to be confirming what Tooloo had said. The timing was terrifyingly logical: strike while the *domana* were preoccupied on the eastern front.

Tooloo said that Tinker had everything she needed, that she didn't need the unedited Codex, and that time was ticking down quickly. Tooloo must have known that the twins were going to crack the problem of the shield. Looking at the resulting spell, Tooloo had been right that Tinker wouldn't have been able to quickly come to this answer. She wasn't even sure how the twins had managed it.

What did Tooloo expect Tinker to do? Or more exactly, what did Tooloo want?

Pure Radiance had come personally to the Westernlands to find Tinker. The queen's oracle had said that the pivot was the person who had been marked with a Wind Clan *dau*. They thought at first it would be Sparrow, but Pure Radiance had pointed directly at Tinker as the person on whom the fate of the world would spin. Pure Radiance had gone on and on about open doors and pivots and closing the door tight.

Tinker thought that when she'd stranded Pittsburgh on Elfhome, closing the two gates open between Elfhome, Earth, and Onihida, her work was done. She was wrong.

Tooloo hadn't wanted Windwolf to mark Tinker. She didn't want Tinker to become an elf. Tooloo had tried to keep her hidden. Tinker getting kidnapped by the oni hadn't been in Tooloo's game plan. Tooloo suggested that was her daughter's plan all along: use Tinker as a "baited trap." Tooloo might not even have wanted the gate destroyed. But she'd taught Tinker—and probably her father and grandfather—magic. Tooloo had made sure Tinker had a copy of the Codex. Tooloo wanted her to do *something* with magic. Something related to the magical bomb that been locked in Dufae's chest. Tooloo obviously had waylaid the chest, followed Unbounded Brilliance from Elfhome, and then babysat all the little hidden wood sprites since the French Revolution.

Pure Radiance wanted the Skin Clan stopped. But what else? What did she want that required her to have her own mother bound hand and foot? Or perhaps the better question was what did Tooloo want that Pure Radiance was so against? Why were they fighting? Over what?

Tinker kept looping back to one basic fact: Tooloo lies. A lot.

Did it matter what Tooloo wanted? Did Tinker want to blindly buy into Tooloo's plan? Granted, Nathan had been a horrific lesson showing that Tinker didn't understand the world as well as Tooloo—but there was a difference between understanding the world and wishing it well.

Tooloo's own daughter had turned against her. Whatever Tooloo wanted, it had been drastic enough that she had only allied herself with a wood sprite still in his doubles. If "allied" was the right term for their teamwork. Unbounded Brilliance might have been an unwitting tool—just like Tinker was. Or possibly would be—if she didn't figure this out.

Assuming, of course, that Pure Radiance hadn't turned the Skin Clan against her mother for selfish reasons. Pure Radiance's own daughter, Stormsong, believed that the female was capable of infanticide to achieve her goals.

Maynard had told her once elves believed that the end justified the means. Pure Radiance could commit horrific acts and everyone would turn a blind eye because they were assuming that she was acting for the common good.

Who did Tinker help? The female who helped raise her but lied to her almost every day of her life? Or the queen's most trusted advisor? Or neither?

The only thing Tinker was sure of was she didn't want the Skin Clan to wipe out everyone that she loved. They had already tried to kill Windwolf. They'd enslaved her. They had kidnapped and threatened Pony. They'd killed a thousand royal marines as if they were nothing. They would kill Tinker's entire Hand.

Tinker wouldn't allow that. She had to stop them.

The Skin Clan had eleven *nactka*. Eleven chances to destroy what the elves had in Pittsburgh. Tinker could set the shield up to protect her and her Hand and whoever else was at the center—but what then? Whatever the spell did, Windwolf, Prince True Flame, Forest Moss, and the Harbingers were all going to fall under its influence, deep in the forest, surrounded by the enemy. Part of her wanted to rush out there and find Windwolf—but her gut was telling her that she didn't have time. She had very little time.

Even if the twins' spell protected her this time, the Skin Clan only needed to cast their spell a second time when she was least expecting it. If their plan worked—on their first or second or third try—then they could take the remaining *nactka* to the Easternlands and use them there.

Tinker was fairly sure that neither Pure Radiance nor Tooloo wanted that. Tooloo had protected the Dufaes for hundreds of years, so the twins' spell probably was part of her plan. Tooloo hadn't struggled for generations to create a temporary protection. Her plan required Tinker to do something clever. Something very wood-sprite-like.

Tooloo said that she had given Tinker everything she needed in her copy of the Dufae Codex. If Tinker didn't need the Codex to create a shield against the Skin Clan's spell, then what was she supposed to do what?

"Can you guys take over?" She handed the spell to Pony. "I need to figure something out."

"Certainly, *domi*," Pony said.

There was a moment as the warriors conferred as to who would stand guard while the rest worked at laying out the spell. Stormsong took charge of the tracing while Pony followed Tinker back to the mobile office.

Tinker thought better on whiteboards. She ported the spell onto the board and started to tease it apart. She tried not to hear Tooloo's voice in the back of her brain, saying that she was wasting time. The twins had done the heavy lifting. What could she figure out from their work? If Tooloo hadn't lied, then everything she did have in her copy of the Codex was all she needed. Her Codex had been heavily edited, supposedly to keep her safe from her own curiosity. While it had all the various shields written out, it didn't have the initialization spell to link her to the Stone Clan Spell Stones...

Tinker's breath caught in her chest as the thought connected to all the elements of the new shield spell.

The elves had nothing like computers. Dufae had never dealt with a software virus. He couldn't grasp what the Skin Clan spell did as a whole, but Tinker recognized an attempt to stop a virus. The spell identified the *domana* genetic key that allowed them to link with Spell Stones and rewrote it. Of course, none of the shield spells that Dufae knew would block that link. It would make no sense for the elves to create something that interfered with their most powerful weapon. An enclave's defensive barriers wouldn't hamper their *domana* from setting up a connection in the middle of battle. Nor would a *sekasha*'s shield spell, since they often overlapped with their *domana*. Dufae had been a double; he might have known a great deal of lore on the Spell Stone construction but he had been born long after the Rebellion and the Clan War ended. It was possible that the creators of the Spell Stones designed the initialization process in the way that they had because it was the one thing that couldn't be blocked.

Any *domana* not shielded by the twins' spell would lose their ability to call the Spell Stones. With one spell, the elves were about to lose their greatest weapons against the oni horde.

There was a muffled boom from the southwest.

"What was that?" Tinker glanced out the windows of the mobile office.

Fireworks burst across the river, somewhere over the Hill District—a bright bloom of color and then a deep boom.

"What idiot is setting off fireworks in a war zone?" she growled.

Even as a second fireworks display went off over the Hill District, another shot upward from Downtown. A sudden golden flower painted against the dark rain clouds. Then a third set over Mount Washington.

This wasn't one random jerk setting off fireworks. This was a signal. She had a very bad feeling about this. The first fireworks had been over Oakland.

"*Domi!*" Stormsong shouted from the casting circle.

Tinker felt it shiver down her back. She was out of time. She ran toward the casting circle. "Oh shit, this is it. Trigger it!"

Out in the northeast where Haven must lie, she felt a massive shield go up. The twins must have created a spell to encompass the entire village. A few moments later, one went up in the heart of McKees Rocks. It could only be Oilcan.

Tinker hit the edge of the casting circle and Stormsong triggered the spell.

Tinker had expected something in Oakland and as various shells of the shield spell rose around her, she felt the enclaves react, starting with Sacred Heart. The newly finished enclave defensive shield rose. The other enclaves triggered their powerful defenses, nearly identical to the one on Sacred Heart. The new shield, however, didn't go up in Oakland.

"Shit, shit, get the new spell up, Forge!"

Forge or Jewel Tear cast a Stone Clan scry, revealing a massive number of ground troops moving uphill from the river's edge.

"Oh, I'm sorry, Forge," she whispered as she realized that Oilcan hadn't gotten a copy of the spell to their grandfather.

There was a massive flare of power to the southeast near the Rim. The scale of it took her breath away. Almost instantly the outer shell of the shield flashed to a blinding light as it deflected the power of the incoming spell.

Tinker whimpered. What would it do to the people whom she loved? All the people who looked to her for protection? Would anything be left after the oni had crushed all the resistance?

Wen Spencer's Tinker:
A Heck of a Gal in a Whole Lot of Trouble

TINKER
978-1-4814-8347-6 • $16.00 US/$22.00 CAN

Move over, Buffy! Tinker not only kicks supernatural elvenbutt—she's a techie genius, too! Armed with an intelligence the size of a planet, steel-toed boots, and a junkyard dog attitude, Tinker is ready for anything—except her first kiss.

WOLF WHO RULES
978-1-4165-7381-4 • $7.99 US/$9.99 CAN

Tinker and her noble elven lover, Wolf Who Rules, find themselves besieged on all sides as Tinker strives to solve the mystery of a growing discontinuity that could shatter three worlds.

ELFHOME
978-1-4516-3912-4 • $7.99 US/$9.99 CAN

Tinker must root out and destroy an evil plot that involves the kidnapping and breeding of elf children.

WOOD SPRITES
978-1-4767-8078-8 • $7.99 US/$9.99 CAN

As war breaks out on the planet Elfhome and riots rock New York City, twin geniuses Louise and Jillian Mayer must use science and magic to save their baby brother and sisters.

PROJECT ELFHOME
978-1-4814-8290-5 • $7.99 US/$10.99 CAN